A BROKEN THRONE OF BRONZE

OF METALS AND CURSES: BOOK ONE

RENNA ASHLEY

A BROKEN THRONE OF BRONZE (OF METALS AND CURSES, BOOK 1)

Copyright © 2023 by Renna Ashley

Map Design by: Ryan Correa

All rights reserved.

To the little girl that dreamed—

Look at you now.

CONTENT WARNINGS

This book contains depictions of minor unwanted touching, descriptions of death, mention of birth trauma and infant loss, as well as sexual content and situations that is not suitable for readers under eighteen years of age.

Happy reading!

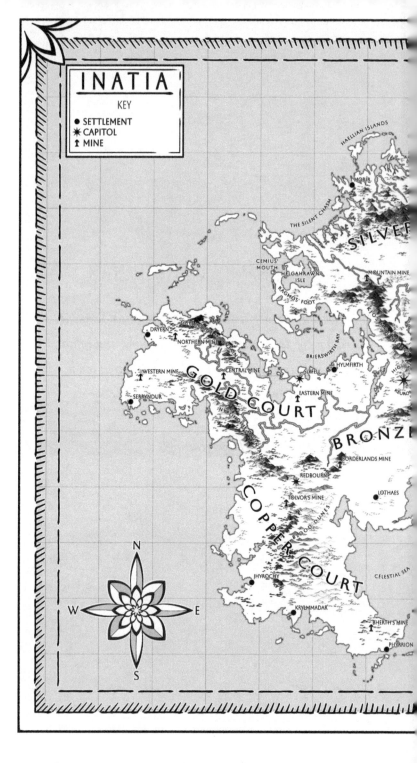

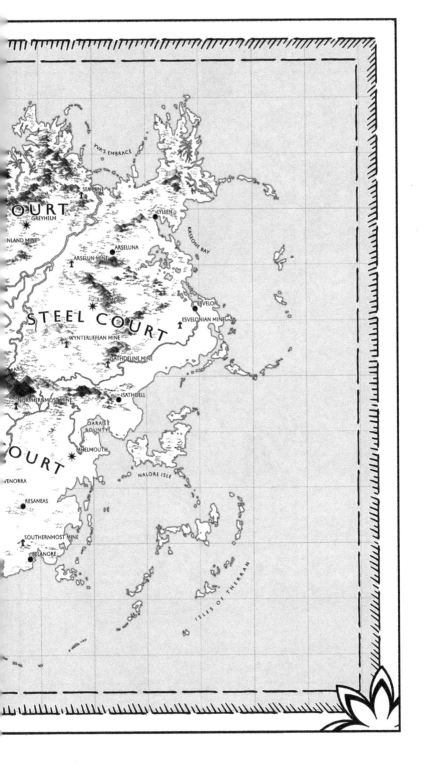

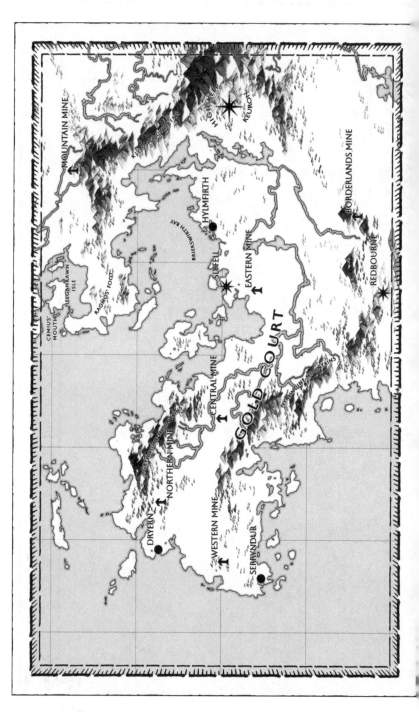

THE FIVE INATIAN
COURTS & NOBLE HOUSES

THE BRONZE COURT
HOUSE AVANOS (CURRENT RULING HOUSE)

VORR AVANOS
HIGH KING

VIRIDIAN AVANOS
CROWN PRINCE

BRONZE METAL: ELEMENTAL MANIPULATION

THE COPPER COURT
HOUSE TARRANTREE

TANYL TARRANTREE
HEAD OF HOUSE

MYRDIN TARRANTREE
HEIR-APPARENT

COPPER METAL: ALCHEMY

THE STEEL COURT
HOUSE WYNTERLIFF

KYLANTHA WYNTERLIFF
HEAD OF HOUSE

VESTELLA WYNTERLIFF
HEIR-APPARENT

STEEL METAL: TRANSMUTATION

THE SILVER COURT
HOUSE LARMANNE

ELDRED LARMANNE
HEAD OF HOUSE

ASHEROS LARMANNE
HEIR-APPARENT

SILVER METAL: CONJURING

THE GOLD COURT
HOUSE PELLEVERON

MAELYRRA PELLEVERON
HEAD OF HOUSE

NISROTH PELLEVERON
HEIR-APPARENT

GOLD METAL: SUMMONING

PROLOGUE

MANY YEARS AGO—KEURON, CAPITAL OF INATIA

N O ONE STOPS when both doors open.

Instead, the celebration continues, filling the large ballroom with music and chatter and drunken laughter. More wine gets poured into goblets. Waitstaff float through the sea of guests with delicacies on silver platters. Couples dance in the center while others stand around them, watching and talking and eating.

At the front of it all, sit the High King and Queen of all Inatia.

And the child cradled in the High Queen's arms.

Representatives from each of the five Noble Houses have traveled to Keuron for the occasion, all donning their finery. The Heads of Houses mingle with each other, discussing pleasure, wine, and business. The metal trade is abundant—the flow of magic and riches amongst the five Courts is plentiful. Casting glances at the royals upon their bronze thrones every so often, the guests whisper to one another.

"I heard she was barren," someone says. "That they'd been trying for decades to produce an heir, with no success."

"I did, too." Eyes dart away from the royals, as if they can hear every word. The guests know they can't, but it still feels strange to gossip while they're breathing the same air as the ones they speak of in hushed tones.

So instead, the onlookers toast to the royal family.

"To the birth of the crown prince!"

Smiling, the High King raises his goblet. Pride rolls from his shoulders. "To the birth of the crown prince."

"What are we to call him?" someone asks the queen.

The High Queen looks down at her son, warmth filling her gaze. "Viridian. You shall call him Crown Prince Viridian Avanos."

"A wonderful choice, Your Majesties." The guest bows. "May the gods smile down at you, and may the metals be pure."

"Thank you." The High Queen beams, still beholding the child she never thought she would have.

They should have looked when both doors opened.

Now, it is much too late.

The sorceress shoves her way through the crowd. She is powerful, and while she may look fae, she does not belong to any one of the five Noble Houses. No, anyone that beholds her knows she is not of this world. She is darkness made flesh. Her pointed ears slice through sheets of black hair, hanging down like curtains around her long, pale face. Like a beast hunting its prey, she stalks to the bronze thrones and stops, holding her head high.

Her eyes simmer with rage. Raw power radiates from her, an electric current buzzing through the stone floor.

"You," she sneers at the High King. "You have taken *everything* from me."

The High Queen holds the child closer, clutching him to her chest. But the High King only laughs.

"I don't even know who you are."

"Oh, but you will never forget me." The sorceress raises her hands over her head. "From this day forth, you shall carry my words. They will weigh down on you, just as my pain does to me."

By now, all of the guests have stopped to look. Silence

3

sweeps the ballroom. Wine goes un-poured. Waitstaff stand still and lower their silver platters. Couples no longer dance in the center. There is no gossiping, no talking, and no eating.

The ballroom has gone utterly still.

"Vorr," the High Queen asks, her voice laced with dread. "What is the meaning of this?"

"Nothing, my darling Azalinah, I assure you," the High King promises. "This female is simply deranged."

The sorceress's expression hardens.

As if the High King's dismissal of her threat is a very grave mistake.

"Hear me," she bellows, "all of you!" Her dark eyes scan the room, finding every face, every ounce of fear. Then she turns her cold eyes back to the High King, gazing deep into his very being.

"A cursed sickness shall poison everything the wrongdoer touches." As the sorceress speaks, a thickness takes hold of the air, ripe and thrumming with power. Dark, old magic. Older than even the kingdom itself.

Her eyes fall on the child. "But by the blessing of Theelia, the righteous heir and lost golden daughter will unite as one. For from the bonds of love will come the ultimate sacrifice. And only from that sacred gift, shall these wrongs be made right, and this curse be broken."

With the final word uttered, a flash of lightning strikes the High King's throne.

The bronze wails and splinters right down the middle.

Gasping, the High King falls to his knees. He places a palm to his chest, eyes wild, as if something is not right.

Perhaps it never will be again.

"You shall keep your broken throne of bronze," the sorceress tells him, anger seeping into these last and final words. Her quiet rage is so unholy, that even the gods turn away. "But I shall take pleasure in descending into hell while knowing your reign has been spoiled forever."

Thunder roars. Then her body goes limp and crumples to the ground.

One does not need to approach her to know that she is dead.

The crowd shrieks.

Then the High Queen turns to her husband, her beautiful face twisting in horror.

"What have you done?"

CHAPTER
ONE

I COME ALIVE when night falls.

Swinging my legs from the bed, I tiptoe across the small room, careful not to wake my sister, Acantha. Pulling my cloak from its hook on the wall between our beds, I drape it around my shoulders while making my way toward the window.

I push open the glass pane, careful to guard it against the wind. Over my shoulder, Acantha lays in her bed, still sound asleep.

I reach for the tree that sits right outside our window and firmly grasp the closest branch. Our house is not very tall, but falling from this distance would surely result in several broken bones. Pushing the thought from my mind, I pull myself over the windowsill and clasp the branch with my other hand. Like I've done so many times before, I pull myself up and swing my body, so my legs make contact with the tree. Lifting my feet from the trunk, I position them on lower branches. I wait a moment, so I'm sure they're sturdy, and then I start to climb down.

Once my feet touch the ground, I pull up my hood, looking back at the house one more time. The window is ajar, moving slightly in the wind. Even if Acantha wakes up, I'll be long gone.

I head for town, moving swiftly. The only place bustling with activity is the tavern, lit by candlelight. Ale-infused laughter slips through the cracks as I pass. I'm sure the inn's guests sleeping in the rooms above aren't pleased about the noise. That is, if they are in bed and not drinking themselves into a stupor with the others.

The night is clear, save for the occasional cloud or two that passes in front of the moon. It's picturesque, shining brightly over my head to light my path. If I had my sketchbook with me, I'd draw what I see.

I turn the corner, keeping close to the buildings, and duck into the stables as soon as I get the chance.

Moving further inside, I find what I've come for.

Loren lounges in a spot of hay, with his hands clasped behind his head. Moonlight washes over him, highlighting the planes of his bare chest. His dark eyes instantly find mine, deep with hunger. His light brown hair is tousled and unruly, curling slightly at the ends. He stands when he sees me.

"You came."

"Of course I did," I tell him, staring up at his handsome face. His lips part, eyes roaming down my body.

"Mmm, good." Loren grins, and it makes me weak in the knees. "I'd have been driven mad with longing if you hadn't come."

I touch his chest, slowly moving my hand up. Not once breaking eye contact. "And you think you would have been the only one?"

"No," Loren breathes. "Not at all."

I step closer. "Good."

He runs his hands up and down my body, sending tingles scattering across my waist. My clothing dulls the sensation, but it's still enough to awaken my desire. Pressing my palms to his chest, I do the same to him, dragging my hands down his torso in slow, lazy strokes. Even under the pads of my fingers, his skin is noticeably hot. All it does is make me want him to touch me everywhere.

He lets out a breath, mouth parted. I can feel his muscles loosen beneath me.

Loren moves his hand to my shoulder, poised to pull my dress down. He waits for a moment, but when I don't tell him to stop, he tugs it down, exposing my skin to the night.

I watch him, my breaths becoming quicker.

Loren pulls my dress down more, his hands tugging at both sleeves now.

The dress falls over my leather corset, and more of my skin is kissed by the cool air.

Loren's hands roam back up my torso, then cup my breasts over my corset. He dips his head down and kisses me, his lips soft and inviting. Then his tongue slips into my mouth, claiming it for his own. He breaks from the kiss, only to drag his mouth, his tongue, down my neck.

I shiver, my hands grabbing at his arms. I need his skin on mine. Now.

"Untie it," I say, my voice lacking its usual strength. "Please."

With a wicked look in his eyes that sends heat thrumming through my body, Loren obliges me. Still sucking at my neck, he makes quick work of my corset and lets it fall to the wooden floor. His hands cup my breasts again, this time lightly squeezing. Teasing. He traces burning circles around them, before brushing his thumbs back and forth across my nipples.

My eyes flutter, and I gasp.

The sound has Loren picking me up with a low growl escaping his throat. He lays me down onto the hay and kneels before me. He wraps his fingers around my legs, just above my ankles, and gradually moves them upward, pushing my skirts up as he does. With my skirts pooled around my hips, Loren drags his hands back down my thighs until they reach my knees. Then, he parts my legs until they're open wide.

My body tingles everywhere he touches my skin, burning, aching for more.

I have no doubt I'm gleaming with wetness.

Loren's eyes darken, drinking me in. His hands go lower, between my legs, and his fingers hover just above my most sensitive spot. He's barely touching me, but it's enough to make my hips buck upward. When his skin touches me there, I open my mouth, letting out a soft moan.

Loren looks at me like he wants to devour me.

"Tell me what you want, Cryssa." My name on his tongue sounds like a prayer. A plea. "Tell me how you want me to please you."

"Your mouth," I pant. "I want you to use your

11

mouth."

Loren's lips curve upward. "With pleasure."

He sinks lower, and I lift myself up onto my elbows to watch him.

His dark eyes never part from mine, even as he lowers his mouth to my sex. The sight of him with his head between my legs has me balling my fists, as if that could contain the sensations his tongue has rippling through me.

He licks me, slowly dragging his tongue upward. My back arches, and the motion rubs my tender mound against his tongue again.

My hands find Loren's head, grabbing fistfuls of those thick curls.

Slowly, he continues to torture me with his mouth.

"Loren," I pant. "More."

Loren doesn't fight me. He quickens his pace, sucking my sex and lapping his tongue at my wetness. While he does, he slips a finger inside me, drawing a moan from my lips. Then he pulls his finger out, before plunging two into me the next time.

Loren's fingers stroke me from the inside, while his mouth sets me ablaze.

My shallow breaths quicken, turning into fervent whimpers and moans.

Loren maintains his pace, fingers steadily coaxing me

to climax.

Shattering into what feels like a thousand pieces, I cry out, tightening my grip on Loren's hair. My hands slip from his head and rest on my stomach.

But he's not finished.

He moves on top of me, hips pinning me to the floor beneath him. Loren's mouth crashes into mine, and I can taste my sweetness that still lingers on his tongue.

His hands slip under me, palms pressed to my skin while they slide up my back. Holding me close, Loren's other hand finds its way back to my chest, kneading my now fully exposed breast.

I moan into his lips. If I hadn't already succumbed to him, I do now.

All I can think about are his hands, the subtle motion of his hips, his lips.

I don't even register the slight scraping sound the door makes when it opens until Loren abruptly breaks from our kiss, whipping his head around.

A male cough echoes. If it weren't for the horses' breathing, the stables would be utterly silent.

Loren shifts his body in front of me, blocking me from the stranger's view. I scramble to cover myself, haphazardly pulling my dress back up.

Once I'm covered, I peer over Loren's shoulder to see

who disturbed us.

A man that's much too beautiful to be human stands at the front of the stables, his tall, lean body partially in the doorway. His black hair falls in front of his face, but I can still make out sharp, amber eyes scrutinizing us in the low light. Seeing more of him, I realize he must be of noble birth—his fine clothes are of a much higher quality than anyone in this area of the city could afford. I'd have recognized him if he were a Pelleveron, of that, I'm certain—the Pelleverons have an undeniable arrogance and a perpetual look of displeasure playing at their mouths. Meaning, he can't hail from this part of the kingdom. He's from one of the other Courts, then. If he's here, in Slyfell, then he must seek to gain the favor of Lady Maelyrra Pelleveron—Head of House Pelleveron and all of the Gold Court—no doubt. The thought makes me wrinkle my nose in disgust.

Anyone that willingly associates with the Pelleverons is probably just as haughty as they are. Though, for noble fae, that's all too common.

"If I didn't know better, I'd assume you were trespassing." The nobleman's voice is rich and smooth, like that of a delicacy laced with poison.

Loren's response is curt. Unyielding. "Then we'll leave."

Taking my hand, he picks up my worn-out corset and helps me to my feet.

When he sees me, the nobleman's eyes widen ever so slightly. Drawn to him, I can't help but meet his gaze.

Warmth thrums in my chest, a strange, buzzing sensation gripping me. A burnt-orange light surrounds the nobleman, as if he were shining from the inside out. Judging by the look of surprise taking hold of his chiseled features, he feels the buzzing, too.

Loren turns to me, his face void of color.

"Cryssa," he whispers, voice heavy with dread.

Lifting my hands, I look down at my palms.

The same burnt-orange light is coming from within me.

My stomach constricts with nausea, horror clenching my abdomen.

Mouth agape, I look back at the nobleman. As the light surrounding him fades, mine does too. In perfect sync.

The muscles in his jaw flex. And the undeniable truth of what we just witnessed settles into both of us. The gods seldom interfere with our world, more content to watch from afar. And when they do, it is only when absolutely necessary. As the Goddess of Fate, a blessing from Theelia signals one of the two strongest forces that can alter one's

15

fate: lover or killer. Even for the fae, being blessed by Theelia is rare. For humans... it is almost unheard of.

The will of Theelia is clear, and one way or another, our destinies are inextricably intertwined.

"The Lady of Fate has spoken," the nobleman says, voice cold, his amber gaze still locked on me. He's composed himself, keeping his shock at bay. "The little fawn lost in the stables is mine."

No.

My breath is caught in my throat. I choke on it.

No, no, no. Not him. Not a noble fae.

It's not until Loren cups my elbow that I realize I'm shaking. He steps closer to me as he does, steadying me.

Breaking from Loren's grip, I bolt out of the stables.

I barrel through the backdoor, my hands riddled with fresh splinters. But I barely feel the pain. Clutching my corset to my chest, I run to the road.

I need to get far away.

The farther, the better. Maybe then, I can pretend this was all a dream.

A nightmare.

"Cryssa!" Loren calls.

The sounds of footsteps behind me get louder.

I push myself further, harder, until my legs burn.

"Cryssa, wait!"

Loren catches up to me, and his arms wrap around my waist, tackling me to the ground. He rolls me over. I squirm, but his hand to my chest keeps me in place.

"Cryssa, listen to me," Loren says, breathing heavily. "This doesn't mean anything."

"How can you say that?" I shoot out. The sight of Theelia bestowing her divine blessing around the nobleman and me will forever be burned into my memory. "You know what this means."

"Yes," Loren says, his voice calm. It should make me feel better—it *has* made me feel better countless times—but tonight, it doesn't. "All Theelia's blessing means is that your fate is bound to his—whoever he is."

"He's a *nobleman*, Loren! One of the fae!" I hiss. "I am no one. For a human girl like me, being bound to him can only mean one of two things—that he is my destiny, or he will be my undoing."

Either way, the course of my life will change forever.

No matter how desperately I wish to escape it.

Loren presses his lips together, staring me down. He knows what I say is true. Even he can't explain this away.

"Then run away with me." Desperation bleeds into Loren's voice. He takes both of my hands into his. "We can leave this place and never come back."

My heart is heavy.

"We can't," I say, hoping he'll see reason. "You know how possessive the fae are. There's no telling what he might do. And what about your mother? Your sister?" Since his father's death several winters ago, Loren has supported his family by working in the gold mines alongside my father. "They need you."

"And I need you, Cryssa." His gaze bears into mine, deep with pain. "I refuse to give up on our plans to marry."

"Where would we go?" I ask, though I already know the answer. "There is no place we can go where *he* won't find us."

Fae males' jealous nature is notorious throughout all of Inatia. I would never forgive myself if something happened to Loren because of me.

"I don't care where we go," Loren tells me. "I'd take you and run to the ends of the earth if it meant I could live out my days at your side."

"Please, Loren," I beg. "This is already hard enough. We must...We must stop seeing each other." My voice threatens to crack, tears welling in my eyes. "With my destiny bound to another man, a fae male at that, we both know how this will end."

"Cryssa, please, don't do this."

"There is no running from this. It will only hurt more if we allow our relationship to continue."

Loren furrows his brow, agony brimming in his expression. "You can't mean that."

I reach out, cupping his cheek. "You've been my best friend since we were children. For that, I will always, *always*, love you, Loren Grayweaver. But my fate is sealed. I—" I swallow the lump that's lodged in my throat. "I cannot bear to drag you down with me."

Twisting out of his grip, I stand and walk away.

The wind nips at my arms, and I fear I abandoned my cloak in the stables. But I do not turn back.

It kills me to leave Loren there. Kills me to break his heart.

I meant what I said to him. Out of all the people in my life, he's one of the few that knows me better than anyone. One of the few people that has stood by my side through it all.

It's because I love him that I must let him go.

CHAPTER TWO

WHEN MY FEET carry me back through my bedroom window, I wish I had never left home in the first place.

Normally, when I return after a night of bliss with Loren, I wish the night would never end. I often wish I could lay in his arms forever, even if it meant I would never see daylight again.

That is not how I feel tonight.

Tonight, I want morning to come quickly and wash away all that happened within the past few hours.

If only it could.

My worn leather corset falls from my hands, and I don't care to pick it up. Instead, I turn around and pull the window closed, blocking out the wind.

"Cryssa!" Acantha huffs, sitting up. "You'll break your neck sneaking out that gods-forsaken window."

"Never mind that," I tell her, stripping my dress from my body before replacing it with my nightgown.

"Well, do tell!" Her voice turns giddy. "What has Loren been up to this time? More romantic gestures? Has he asked Father for your hand yet?"

I approach my bed, wrapping my arms around my torso. Loren's romantic gestures are the farthest thing from my mind.

Acantha's brows knit together, suddenly ripe with concern. Even though she's newly nineteen, only a few months younger than me, she wears a motherly expression. "What is it?" She takes my hand, pulling me closer. "He hasn't done something to hurt you, has he?"

"No, no," I assure her. "It's nothing like that, I promise."

"Then what is it? You can confide in me, Cryssa."

"I know." I take a deep breath and put on a brave face. "Tomorrow. I'm too tired to talk tonight."

Acantha's hazel eyes search my expression, and by the looks of it, she doesn't like what she sees. But she nods and lets go of my hand, watching me while I climb into bed.

Under the covers, I turn onto my side and curl my legs toward my chest.

It takes me too long to fall asleep.

IT'S BEEN NEARLY a week since I've spoken to Loren. Nearly a week since Theelia's blessing made it known that the foreign nobleman and I were fated.

I've managed to go about my chores without running into either of them, but I can't shake the dread that lines my stomach, even now. The will of the gods isn't something to be ignored.

I pray the nobleman didn't get a good enough look at my face, that he won't be able to find me. After all, it's been a week, and he hasn't come to claim me.

Yet.

Balancing a basket of eggs from the market on my hip, I step past the threshold of our small house. Father sits at the table, chewing on a bite of bread and cheese. Acantha stands across the room from him, tending to the hearth. Not yet spring, the warmth has yet to come.

"Cryssa," Father says with a smile. He glances down at the basket. "That's quite a few eggs."

"A dozen," I tell him proudly, putting the basket onto the table. "It seems the farmer can be bargained with."

"If you're stubborn enough," Acantha calls, stifling a snort.

Putting my hands on my hips, I throw her a pretend scowl.

Father laughs, but then his expression darkens.

"What is it, Father?" I ask, pulling out a stool to sit with him.

"Manfred is sick," Father says, taking a breath. "The physician says he likely won't live another week."

"Oh, Father." Acantha leaves the hearth and drapes her arms around his neck. "That's awful."

The same, long expression adorns both of their faces, emphasized by their shared eyes and mouth. Acantha has always taken after our father—inheriting his chestnut brown hair and infectious smile. With my rusty auburn hair and fair complexion, I'm the one that stands out.

"How many have gotten sick this week alone?" I ask, leaning forward. Manfred is one of many miners who's succumbed to the mysterious sickness this winter. Even though spring is nearly upon us, the numbers of miners falling ill, and dying, has been steadily increasing.

"More than I can count," Father says, rubbing his forehead. "Those of us left will need to work double time to make up for our losses."

Fear takes hold of my stomach. "Is Loren all right?" Oh gods. Maybe that's why I haven't seen him.

"Loren is well," Father tells me. "Busy, is all. You have no need to worry, my darling."

My shoulders relax a little. But the worry I felt mere minutes ago morphs into frustration.

I stand, the force of my movement pushing the stool back with a screech. "You would think the Head of House would do something. After all, it's the hard work of the gold miners filling her coffers." Crossing my arms, I start to pace. My voice rises in volume, dripping with sarcasm. "But of course, how silly of me to expect the Pelleverons to care for the lives of the lowly humans living under them."

"Come now, Cryssa," Father's voice is calm. His expression soothes me in an instant. My anger dims but doesn't fade. And why should it? It's not as if the Pelleverons—or any noble fae, for that matter—act like humans aren't anything but a means to an end. "The Gold Court isn't the only one affected by the mining sickness."

"It's not?"

Father shakes his head. "We've heard rumors that it's happening in the Steel and Silver Courts as well."

I swallow, realizing the implications of this rumor, if true. Made up of five Courts, each territory in Inatia belongs to one of the five Noble Houses. And each noble house has a leader, the Head of House, that reigns over their court. The Gold Court, my home, is loyal to House Pelleveron. The Silver Court, House Larmanne; the Steel Court, House Wynterliff; the Copper Court, House Tarrantree; and the Bronze Court, House Avanos—the current ruling house of all Inatia.

Each of the five Courts produces the metal of its namesake. Each, a vital piece of Inatia's overall prosperity. Here, in the Gold Court, we're lucky we can afford what we can. In some other Courts, others aren't so lucky. If some or all of the Courts stopped producing metal...

I shudder to think about what would happen to the unlucky ones at the bottom of the hierarchy.

"I'm worried for you, Father." Acantha tightens her grip around him, lowering her head so it's parallel to his. "What if you fall ill?"

My father turns, pressing a kiss to her cheek. "I'll be all right." He reaches for my hand and squeezes it. "This sickness will die down come spring, girls. You'll see."

Still holding his hand, I nod like I believe him.

In reality, I'm not so sure.

But I don't have time to consider the matter.

Pounding sounds at our door. The thin wood rattles against the doorframe.

I move to answer it, but Father holds up his palm, mouth wary.

Blood pounds in my ears. I'm frozen, staring at the door.

Father stands and crosses the room. He opens the door and all the color drains from his cheeks.

Two armored guards wait outside. I don't need to see their pointed ears to know they're fae.

"Grorth Thurdred?"

"Yes." Father nods, eyes dropping to the swords sheathed at their hips. "Can I help you?"

"We're here for your daughter, Cryssa Thurdred."

My father shifts his weight, shielding me from view. "Has Cryssa done something wrong?"

"Not at all. She's been personally chosen by her fated to be his bride. With Theelia's blessing, the High King bids it."

If I'd eaten a heartier meal this morning, it would have wound up all over the floor. My stomach threatens to empty itself, and I force myself to swallow the growing lump in my throat.

He found me.

Acantha covers her mouth and grabs onto me with her free hand, wrapping an arm around my shoulders.

"Is Cryssa home?" the guard asks gruffly.

Father hesitates.

"If you're hiding her, we are authorized to use force as needed."

"I'm here!" I cry, rushing forward. "No one's hiding me."

The guard tilts his head back a little, still eyeing Father with suspicion. Then he turns to me. "You're to come with us."

My heart rams against my ribcage. I think of my beloved sketchbook upstairs, filled with drawings of home and the people I love. "May I have a moment to pack my things?"

"That won't be necessary," the other guard tells me, much kinder than his companion. "All you require will be provided at the castle."

I choke. "Castle?"

"Yes." The guard nods. "In Keuron."

My throat burns from holding back the tears welling in my eyes.

Keuron. They're taking me to Inatia's capital.

To marry some noble fae male I don't know.

I puff my chest, forcing myself to be brave, like Mother always was when things were uncertain. "Then may I have time to say goodbye?" I hope they'll at least give me that.

The gruff-sounding guard opens his mouth to speak, but the kind one cuts him off. "Very well. We'll allow it."

I throw my arms around Father and hold him close. He does the same, pressing me to his chest. Father sniffles, pulling away from me only to place a kiss onto my forehead. He extends his arm to Acantha. She crashes into us, tears flowing down her cheeks.

"Cryssa," Father says. The severity in his tone unnerves me. "Cryssa, there is something you must know. Something I have been meaning to tell you. You are—"

He doesn't have time to finish before the gruff guard interrupts him. "Time's up."

"Father," I say. "What is it?"

Ignoring me, the guard takes me by the arm and pulls me out of the house.

"Father!" I shout, twisting my body to keep him in view.

Father, with a sobbing Acantha on his arm, follows me outside. But they quickly get swallowed by the crowd gathering on the streets, and I lose sight of them. Loud voices close in around me, echoing off the cobblestone beneath my feet.

With both guards at my sides, gripping my arms, they lead me farther away from home.

Humans and lesser fae alike gather in the town

square. Shop doors stay open while more people pour out of them, wiping their hands clean of their work on their pants or skirts.

Some faces, I recognize.

Others, I don't.

But they all look at me.

The humans look horrified. The lesser fae, shocked.

None of them could have even fathomed something like this happening to a girl like me. A girl like their wives. A girl like their daughters. Their sisters. In the crowd, some people pull the women next to them closer, as if they have the same thought.

More guards stand in the center of the town square, surrounded by onlookers. Though the angry faces spread throughout the crowd tell me that the guards aren't just here to take me away.

Oh gods.

My chest constricts.

Loren.

Two guards restrain Loren, while a third clamps heavy, steel handcuffs around his wrists. Black and blue bruises mar his handsome face, his right eye swollen shut. Loren bucks against them, knocking his head back into one of the guard's noses. The guard in front of him lands a punch to Loren's jaw, but he doesn't stop fighting.

"Loren!" I cry out, finally letting the tears fall.

He whirls his head around, his good eye widening in shock when he sees me. "Cryssa!" His voice is a desperate, strangled cry. "Cryssa!"

The guards shove him into a prison wagon and chain his hands to the ceiling. They slam the door shut once he's inside and lock that, too.

"Make way!" a guard orders, and the crowd parts for the wagon. He hops up onto the seat and takes the horses' reins, urging them forward.

A coach moves ahead and stops, taking the prison wagon's place.

The guards at each of my sides move me forward, and I stumble.

I look at the crowd. Fear-stricken, Loren's mother, Catia Grayweaver, clutches a sobbing Jemetha, his younger sister. The girl clings to her mother's skirts, her eyes puffy and red from crying.

"What's happened?" I ask Loren's mother as we pass by her. "What are they doing with Loren?"

"He's been arrested," she tells me, voice breaking. "For trespassing and the contempt of a royal."

"A *royal*," I breathe.

The guards urge me ahead. They open the coach door for me, and I step inside. Without giving me time to react, they close it. A click sounds. Then, the coach shudders when they climb on. Dread lines my stomach and tightens its fist around my throat. I almost forget how to breathe.

Sitting in the ornate bronze coach, the gravity of my situation hits me all at once, like a tidal wave.

The stranger that interrupted Loren and me that night—the stranger whose fate is inextricably bound to mine—wasn't just any noble fae.

He was the Crown Prince Viridian Avanos.

CHAPTER THREE

THE RIDE TO KEURON is four or five days, at most.

I ride in the carriage alone. It seems that the Crown Prince can't be bothered to spend the days of travel with his betrothed. Though I can't say I'm unhappy about it. After everything he's done, I might have strangled him had I been forced to accompany him.

For the whole ride, and when we stop to make camp for the night, I try to see the prison wagon ahead of us. But it's no use—the coach and the horses that pull it obstruct my view.

It's only when we finally arrive in the city that I perk up in my seat. When we pass through the city gates, I uncross my arms and lean to look out the window.

Tall buildings reach for the skies. Multi-story homes with cobbled roofs line the streets. Colorful banners hang on lines of string that stretch overhead. Bustling shops filled with people, of many different backgrounds, fill the roads with chatter, mingling as if they're the greatest of friends. Smells of baked goods I don't recognize fill my nose. There are market stands outside of the shops, with vendors calling out to people that pass by.

One vendor, a lesser fae merchant, holds out a gold necklace and a paperweight made from *gohlrunn*—a weighted kind of gold alloy that Slyfell's artisans use for crafting expensive items—shouting out ridiculous prices. Sure, crafted pieces are more valuable than raw metal, but the gold seems to be worth more here than back home. The lack of men and women covered in dirt and dust makes me remember that there are no miners in Keuron. All the mining is done in the Courts, so any metal found here is imported. That explains the higher price.

My mouth parts in awe. Slyfell is by no means a small city. But the sheer number of people I see here in Keuron makes it seem so. Even though it wasn't my choice to come here, I can't help but feel drawn to the city's vibrant activity. Whereas Slyfell is relatively quiet and safe, Keuron is loud and new and exciting. It makes me wonder what else is out there, what the cities in the other Courts look like.

We ride through the city until we reach a wooden drawbridge. A moat separates the land across the bridge from the rest of the city. In the center of the man-made island sits a large castle—High Keep. The seat of power of all Inatia, home to the royal family. The Crown Prince.

And now, it's my home, too.

My gilded prison.

We wait a moment, and then chains lower the drawbridge.

Once it's secure, the horses pull the carriage over the bridge, and more of the castle comes into view. The stone bricks are worn with age but look well-maintained. There isn't much greenery, but what vegetation is there is finely trimmed into neat squares and rectangles. Two thin towers stand guard at either side of the bridge, where a steel gate stands between the castle and the outside world. Bronze colored banners, adorned with the circular crest of House Avanos, hang down from the towers and sway gently in the wind.

The gate rises as we approach, and the carriage passes under its teeth.

Panic grips my stomach when I realize I've lost sight of the prison wagon. I have no idea where Loren is now.

Or what fate awaits him.

But my own fate surges to the forefront of my mind. Unease skitters across the back of my neck, my stomach twisting into knots. Seeing what lies ahead, I mutter a prayer to Imone, Goddess of Mercy, for Loren. And for myself.

A line of guards stand at the castle's entrance.

And front and center, stands who I assume to be the High King, with the Crown Prince at his side.

High King Vorr smiles when the carriage slows to a stop. It's a polite smile, a decent attempt at warmth. He wears leather gloves, and his clasped hands rest by his waist. A regal, bronze crown sits atop his head of cropped black hair. To his right, wearing a similar crown made from the same metal, the Crown Prince Viridian doesn't even attempt to mask his displeasure.

The carriage trembles when the guards disembark.

I wait for them to come around to my door. The guard closest to the carriage opens the door and holds out his hand.

I don't take it and exit on my own. The guard doesn't say anything, merely shutting the carriage door after me. With nothing more to do, the guards position themselves around me, one on each side. As if they're waiting to see if I'll run.

The thought does cross my mind. But with the drawbridge likely up, I doubt I would make it far.

"Cryssa, is it?" the High King asks. Much to my surprise, his voice is warmer than his smile or his burnt-orange eyes. "Welcome to Keuron."

There's a tense silence, and then the High King turns to his son with a pointed look.

"Yes, welcome," Viridian echoes, as if he forgot why we were all here.

Out here, in broad daylight, I see more of him than I did that night in the stables. His fair skin seems to shimmer in the sunlight, his wispy, medium-length black hair combed away from his face. Still, tendrils of it fall in front of his eyes. Those amber eyes study me, with a tightness in his jaw that I can't read.

Part of me wants to stay quiet. To deny them the pleasure of my response.

But I also want to live long enough to free Loren and make our escape. And being rude to the High King and Crown Prince seems contradictory to that goal.

So, I force myself to bow, even though I would rather walk across hot coals. "Thank you, Your Majesty."

"If you'll excuse me, I have business to attend to.

Viridian," the High King says, gloved hands gesturing to me, "escort your betrothed to her chambers."

Viridian dips his head in response. "Very well."

Just as I expected, his voice is cold, monotone.

Pretentious noble fae prick.

With that, the High King and a slew of guards enter the castle. The remaining guards stand at attention, looking to Viridian for his command.

"Come," Viridian says, keeping his eyes away from me. He turns on his heels, using two fingers to motion for the guards to follow. The female guard closest to him nods, then signals to the rest, who move to form a unit around me—two in front of me, two behind, and one on each of my sides. Viridian leads us, with the female guard trailing him, and the guards surrounding me move as one.

I have no choice but to follow.

There is no turning back.

Lifting my skirts so I don't trip over them, I climb the small set of stairs and enter High Keep. A bitter laugh coats my tongue. I know so many girls back home that would kill to be in my position. Who would give anything to be hand-picked by the Crown Prince to be his bride. To come live here, in Keuron, and wear lavish gowns and attend balls.

And I would give anything to trade places with any

one of them.

Oh, how the Lady of Fate is cruel.

The stone walls swallow me as soon as I pass through the threshold, surrounding me with cool air. Perhaps everything—and everyone—here is cold. I long for the warmth of our hearth already.

Viridian leads us through a long hallway, lined with more of House Avanos's bronze banners. A bronze colored carpet runs the length of the hallway, with actual bronze metal lining the edges. Tall, stone arches make up the walls on either side, with large open spaces that let me see into the adjoining rooms. Through the arches, I see an array of decorative suits of armor—made from metals from each of the five Courts—standing neatly in a row along the far wall.

Viridian turns a corner, taking us up a flight of stairs. Above us, hangs a steel chandelier, its circular rows of lit candles giving off a warm glow. We reach the landing and continue beyond an intricately carved stone railing, decorated with twisting copper vines and roses, into a large open space. More carpet lies beneath my feet, and to the right, is a corridor adorned with glorious paintings unlike anything I've ever seen before—all depicting portraits of people I assume to be members of House Avanos. The sight of them makes me long for my sketchbook.

One of the guards nudges me with her elbow, and I quicken my pace to match Viridian's swift stride.

We enter another hallway, this one with a row of gold-rimmed windows. It's the brightest place in High Keep I've encountered so far, and I close my eyes to bask in the sunlight while we pass.

It's possible that I might not get the chance to do so again.

Turning left, into yet another corridor, I see this one is lined with heavy-looking wooden doors sitting on steel hinges. Approaching one, Viridian slows to a stop and waits for me with his hands behind his back. The female guard with him stands to his right, about a little less than a shoulder length behind him. Gray eyes focused, she stands tall, her blue-black hair seeming to reflect the stone surrounding us. She's young-looking, too—her tan face shows no sign of age. Then again, she could be older than she seems. The fae age slower than humans.

Still avoiding my eyes, Viridian turns his head to the female guard. I take note of the twin, steel short swords that hang sheathed at her hips. "This is Lady Lymseia Wynterliff, second-born daughter of Head of House Wynterliff, and Captain of the High King's Guard."

Lymseia bows her head. "It's an honor to meet you, Miss Thurdred."

I try to release the tension in my shoulders before responding. Though, I don't succeed. "The same to you, Lady Wynterliff."

"Lady Wynterliff will stay to assist you in getting settled in," Viridian tells me, sounding distant. "Should you need anything, call on her." After that, he starts down the hallway, and thankfully, the cluster of guards—except for Lymseia—leave with him.

Lymseia holds her hands out toward the door. "Shall we?"

I nod, taking a deep breath.

Lymseia opens the door for me and waits for me to pass. I do, and then she comes in after me, leaving the door open.

I pause, taking it all in.

A large, four-poster bed sits in the center of the room. Thick, bronze colored bedding hangs over a huge mattress. A collection of long, fluffy pillows is neatly arranged by the headboard. Matching bedside tables sit on either side of the bed, with silver candelabras placed atop them. An oval-shaped rug covers most of the stone floor, with bronze metal woven into the threads. There are two windows on the far wall, both clothed with heavy-looking cream drapes. On the opposite wall, closest to where I'm standing, is a mahogany wardrobe and a vanity table with

41

a mirror and padded chair.

Lymseia moves ahead and leads me to a doorway opposite the bed. "The washroom is right over here."

I follow her deeper into the room and peer through the open threshold.

A massive copper tub sits inside, with a stack of clean towels on a shelf beside it. There's another mirror in here, hanging in front of a small table with a washbowl set down on top.

"The main areas of the castle are free for you to explore," Lymseia tells me, leading me back to the room's center. Her tone shifts, becoming more authoritative, like a general laying down the law. "The Crown Prince's only request is that you stay inside High Keep. So don't get any ideas."

I press my lips together, hardening my expression. My mind translates the words.

I'm not allowed to leave the castle.

"If you ever need anything," Lymseia continues, her voice relaxing again as she looks at me, "just ask. The Crown Prince's first priority is your comfort."

I snort. "Of course it is."

Lymseia's expression softens. "I know you must feel alone here. Please, know that I'm here for you, whenever you need me."

I nod, but don't meet her eyes. It's hard to believe that she's here for me, when she's the one telling me that I'm a prisoner here. And when as the Captain of the High King's Guard, she'll be the one enforcing the Crown Prince's 'request.'

"Your ladies' maids will be arriving shortly to attend to you. They'll see to all your needs." Lymseia's voice warms. "You will be cared for here, Cryssa. On my honor, you have my word."

She lingers for a moment, searching my face. I give her nothing. Then, she bows her head and leaves, gently closing the door behind her.

I may have come here willingly to protect my family, but I won't be a prisoner. And I won't condemn myself to be shackled to this life by marrying the Crown Prince.

I need to escape.

My body goes utterly still. I wait a moment until I'm sure Lymseia's gone.

Then, I launch across the room to the window. If I can see how high I am, I can use the bedding to make a rope that I can then use to climb down. My fingers slide across the windowpane to open it.

I curse. The windows don't open.

So much for being *free*.

Looking around the room, my eyes land on the vanity

43

table. Perhaps there's something in the drawers that I can use to get out of here.

Swiftly, I cross the room and crouch before the vanity table. Pulling the drawers open, I rummage through them. There's a hairbrush, some powder puffs along with other beauty products I don't recognize, and loose hair pins.

The hair pins seem promising. There might come a time when I'll need to pick a lock, so I take a few and slip them into my hair.

Racking my brain, I try to think of something else. The window isn't a dead end yet. It can still be my way out, but I'll need to find something strong enough to break the glass. But breaking the window will surely draw attention, and I'll need to act quickly if I choose to escape that way.

I move to the wardrobe and open it. Finely made gowns hang within it, and I push them aside, searching for anything useful. My hands linger on the one piece of clothing I would have never expected to see here, of all places.

My cloak.

The gray wool looks out of place amidst all the silks and satins.

I reach out to touch it, rubbing the material between my thumb and forefinger.

Viridian must have brought it here. He and Loren

were the only others there that night, and I didn't see it in Loren's hand when he came running after me.

He noticed that I left it behind.

The thought stirs something in my stomach. But I promptly dismiss the feeling. Viridian may have thought to bring my cloak, but he is still the one holding me captive.

Footsteps sound in the hallway.

I quickly shut the wardrobe. The wood makes a banging noise when I do, and I wince. When the chamber door opens, I jerk back, putting some distance between myself and the wardrobe.

A cluster of servants enter, flocking to me. All of them are human.

My ladies' maids. Lymseia meant it when she told me they'd be arriving shortly.

I hold back a sigh. I'll have to continue planning my escape once they leave. Which I hope is soon.

With the ease of someone who's done this many times, the ladies maids usher me into the washroom and strip me of my clothes. They turn on a faucet, and once the tub is full, they herd me into the water.

Hot water meets my skin. I suck in a breath.

One of the ladies' maids places her hands on my shoulders, guiding them lower so my body is enveloped in the hot water. Then, there's tugging at my hair and scrubbing at my scalp. They stretch out my arms, rubbing soap and washcloths into my skin until it's raw. I'm embarrassed at how much grime comes out. At home, I've undressed in front of Acantha, and never once felt self-conscious during any of the times I've been naked in front of her.

But I do now.

Once they're satisfied with my cleanliness, the ladies' maids help me out of the tub and dry me off. Wrapping me in a silk dressing gown, they guide me out of the washroom and sit me down in front of the vanity table. In the mirror, I get a good look at myself.

My fair skin looks clearer, cleaned of all dirt and oil. My golden-brown eyes narrow while I study the reflections of the ladies' maids as they work. My auburn hair is already curling, pulled in several directions while two servants run combs through it. The ladies' maids that are not laboring to tame my hair leaf through the gowns in the wardrobe and pull one out, laying it flat on the bed.

The servants combing my hair set down the combs and run their fingers through my locks, weaving half of it into braids that they secure to my head. The rest of my hair hangs free down my back.

Pulling me to my feet, the ladies' maids steer me to the

other servants, who now hold up the gown, ready to dress me with it. They hold the garment out in front of them, and I step into it. Then the servants move behind me and button it up before fussing over my skirts.

When they're satisfied with the way my skirts fall, the ladies' maids step back to look at me. They exchange nods, and then bow to me again before seeing themselves out just as swiftly as they came.

It's then that I realize I didn't say a word to any of them.

Not even a "thank you." If he were here, Father would scold me for my rudeness. A knot twists in my chest.

Father.

He and Acantha must be worried sick about me, not knowing when I'll be home—if at all—or if I'm all right. The bite of their absence is an ache in my chest.

All the more reason for me to leave this gods-forsaken place.

With the room to myself again, I continue my search for anything I can use to aid my escape. I find pairs of heeled shoes sitting beneath the dresses in the wardrobe. While I could use them to shatter the window, I hoped to find something more substantial. Much to my disappointment, I don't find much else that can be of use.

47

Not long after my measly discovery, more human servants arrive. This time, they come with a cart of steaming food, covered by silver domes with curved handles on top. The aromas reach my nose before I answer the door, and it makes me realize how hungry I am.

After I open my chamber door, the servants roll the cart into my room. They bow and ask me if I need anything else.

I decline, and say "thank you" this time, not forgetting my manners. The servants stiffen when I do, as if they're not used to being thanked for their service.

They leave, and I'm alone again.

Part of me doesn't want to accept the meal. Or any sort of gift that can be traced back to Viridian. But I'm not a fool. I'll need my strength if I want to find Loren and run.

My stomach growls, as if to emphasize my need for the food.

Swallowing my pride, I drag the cart closer to the vanity table and sit on the chair. I remove the silver covers from the dishes, my mouth watering at the sight.

There's some kind of roasted poultry—duck or turkey, if I had to guess—with a fruity glaze, vegetables sauteed in butter and garlic, thinly sliced potatoes with copious amounts of aged cheese, and a thick slice of chocolate cake for dessert. To pair with the meal, there's a pitcher of a dark liquid with the tangy, aged scent of wine.

I don't touch the wine. It's not wise to impair my thinking while trapped in the wolves' den.

The flavors and textures melt in my mouth, and I eat slowly, savoring every bite. Guilt creeps into my chest, turning the experience sour. It feels wrong to be here, eating like this, when so many miners and their families struggle to make ends meet. Even more so now that the families of many miners mourn the loss of their loved ones, left with no one to care for them.

When I'm done, I leave my dirty plate and fork on the cart.

My hunger recedes, and I'm left to my own devices. What more can I do?

Homesickness and despair close in around me, all at once. I've been forcing myself to think of my escape and nothing else. But now, as night falls, all the emotions I've worked to ignore force their way in.

Fear. Sadness. Anger. Powerlessness.

Standing, I move to the bed and pull the covers back. Without undressing, I climb into it and bury myself under the expensive-looking blankets. I curl into the fetal position, with my arms raised so my hands are parallel to my head.

It's early, but fatigue settles into my bones. There's a hollowness in my chest.

This is the first time I've ever left home. The first time I've slept in a bedroom alone, without Acantha. It feels empty without her.

I squeeze my eyes shut, fighting the tears that gather there.

I stay like that until I eventually fall asleep, and don't feel anything at all.

CHAPTER FOUR

WHEN MORNING COMES, I want to believe that the past few days were nothing more than a dream. To hope that maybe, when I open my eyes, I'll be in my bed at home. That Father and Acantha will be downstairs, waiting for me to join them for breakfast.

I want to believe that. But the truth stops me.

Opening my eyes, I take a deep breath. I don't move from bed, wishing I could go back to sleep and escape my reality.

Yet, time and time again, the gods show me their cruelty.

There's a gentle knock at my door, and before I can respond, my ladies' maids enter my chamber. I notice the cart with my dirty dishes from dinner is gone.

The first one inside pauses when she sees me still in bed, her eyes wide. "Have we woken you, miss?"

Sitting up, I flash her a polite smile. "Not at all."

"Oh, good." She relaxes, the tension leaving her face. She looks to be about my age, but her demeanor makes her seem much older. Then she smiles warmly, holding out a hand to help me up. "Good morning. You slept well, I hope?"

"As well as I could have," I say with a snide tone, taking her hand. Standing, I brush my curls out of my face. "I'm Cryssa," I tell her.

The servant bows. "Tiffy, my lady."

"It's wonderful to meet you, Tiffy." And I mean it. I'll need allies if I want to survive here.

Tiffy smiles again and tilts her head toward the washroom. "Come, let's get you ready."

"Ready for what?" I ask, but her hands are already on my arms, maneuvering me there.

"For the day, of course. You can't very well stay in yesterday's clothes, can you?"

My cheeks warm. At home, I wore the same two dresses. Sometimes for multiple days in a row. Clothes weren't the priority. Not with mouths to feed.

I press my lips together.

I'm not at home anymore.

I'm at High Keep and I'm betrothed to the Crown Prince. Maybe now, appearances are a priority.

Not if I have anything to say about it.

I'm not staying here long enough to start caring about my appearance.

I nod to Tiffy, and that seems to satisfy her. The ladies' maids wash my face, style my hair, and dress me.

"Will you take breakfast in here, miss?" Tiffy asks.

"Yes," I shoot out. The Crown Prince may think he's my betrothed, but I have no intention of going through with the marriage. And no desire to spend time with him.

Tiffy bows her head, and then leads my ladies' maids out of my chamber.

Breakfast arrives not much longer after they leave, brought in on another rolling cart by more servants. Like they did with dinner last night, the servants leave me to my meal once they've asked if I need anything else. I decline and have my meal at the vanity table. So far, I've used it more for eating than for making myself look more appealing.

The breakfast assortment is just as tantalizing as last night's dinner. Freshly baked pastries make my mouth water, topped with ripe berries, and chopped chocolate. There's a fancy looking bowl cradling an egg-dish and a small plate of buttered toast. Instead of wine, there's a small pitcher of some kind of fruit juice.

I pour some juice into the glass and sip it in between bites of pastries and eggs. Once I'm finished, I leave my empty dishes on the cart. I assume the servants will come for it like they did last night.

Lymseia's words from yesterday ascend to the forefront of my mind.

"The main areas of the castle are free for you to explore."

And explore I shall.

If I want to free Loren and make our escape, I'll need to find him first.

Crossing the room, I rest my hand on the door handle and slowly push it open. I poke my head into the hallway.

The sounds of far-off footsteps and distinct chatter meet my ears, but there doesn't seem to be anyone around.

I leave my chamber, gently closing the door behind me.

Careful not to make too much noise, I start down the hallway toward the stairs that the guards led me up yesterday. I come into the bright corridor and make it halfway through before I pause.

Voices echo.

I press my body to the cold, stone wall, my palms flat to keep me steady. Cocking my head, I focus. The voices are coming from ahead of me, where I remember there's an open area at the top of the staircase. I inch closer, stopping until I'm just behind the archway that leads out of this hallway.

"She is your *betrothed*, Viridian," a sharp, feminine voice says. It's Lymseia. "You should go see her."

I hold my breath.

"You know I didn't want this," a deep voice replies. That one, I instantly recognize as the Crown Prince. "My father—even the gods, it would seem—is the one who wants this marriage. Not me."

Why would the High King force Viridian to marry me?

"It doesn't matter whether you want it or not," Lymseia says. "She's here because of you. For you. It's time you stopped being so pig-headed and started acting like an engaged male."

"Pig-headed?" he scoffs.

"Yes. Pig-headed."

I cover my mouth to stifle my laugh. I barely know Lymseia, but now, I can't help but respect her.

There's a tense silence. Then, Viridian lets out a long

55

sigh. "Fine."

"Fine?"

"Fine. I'll court her, if she wishes to be courted. But if she doesn't," he says, voice hardening, "I won't force her."

"I'll hold you to that."

"Very well." He doesn't sound pleased. If anything, it sounds like he despises the thought of courting me. Disappointment sinks in my chest, weighing me down like *gohlrunn*.

The knowledge that Viridian doesn't want to court me shouldn't upset me. It doesn't change my plan—to find Loren and run away together, somewhere far from here. Far from Viridian.

So why does it bother me?

Footsteps echo on stone, growing louder in volume, until I'm facing Viridian. His dark brows rise in surprise, just for a moment, before they furrow again.

"Good morning," he says gruffly. Embarrassment heats my cheeks. He must know I overheard him.

Scowling at him, I say nothing. His mouth tightens. Letting out a forceful breath, he brushes past me and storms down the hall.

I step forward, moving out from behind the corner. Lymseia's expression softens when she sees me, mouth curving downward with something that looks like pity. I don't like it.

I don't need her pity.

After all, Viridian and I don't want to marry each other.

"Don't mind him," she tells me. "He's a pleasure to be around once he gets his head out of his ass."

"Oh, I bet he's a delight," I say, my voice dripping with sarcasm.

Lymseia pretends to frown. "You may not believe me now. But just watch, you'll see."

Striding past her, I roll my eyes. The day I enjoy Viridian's company is a day that will surely never come.

"I wouldn't go that way if I were you," Lymseia calls after me.

I stop and turn my upper body to look at her. "Why not?"

"That hallway takes you to the East Tower," she says, gesturing behind me. "The High King's private quarters."

I glance back at the hallway in front of me. It's the one with all the beautiful portraits hanging. The ones that make me wish I could draw. Missing my sketchbook only emphasizes how alone I feel here. How out of place.

"Am I not allowed in there?"

Lymseia shakes her head. Her voice softens. "No one is. Not since the High Queen died."

"No one?"

"No one but the High King and his private security detail."

"Not even the Crown Prince?"

She gives me a look. "Not even His Highness."

Interesting.

I take a step toward her. Curiosity colors my words. "Aren't *you* allowed in there?"

"No," Lymseia says, like a parent trying to dissuade a child from doing something they shouldn't. "Not even me."

"But you're the Captain of the High King's Guard. Doesn't the High King's private security detail report to you?"

"They do," Lymseia says, leveling her tone. As if she were picking her words very carefully.

But her tone of voice tells me everything her words don't.

The High King's hiding something.

My mind itches to know what. To sneak into the East Tower and uncover all of the High King's secrets.

I open my mouth to ask another question, but I don't get the opportunity. A young-looking man rises to the top of the stairs. His crimson eyes catch my attention almost instantly, as do his pointed ears. If his eyes weren't obvious enough, his ears give away his fae heritage immediately. Staring intently, he cranes his neck to look down at the stack of papers in his hands, all while muttering to himself. His rich brown hair is disheveled, as if he couldn't be bothered to care about how others may see him.

"Ah, Myrdin." Lymseia plasters on a smile. "Just the male I wanted to see."

He doesn't seem to hear her, too focused on whatever it is on the parchment that's captured his attention. Slowly, he continues ahead. Lymseia holds out her arm, and Myrdin walks right into it, dropping some of his papers.

"Myrdin!" Lymseia demands.

"Huh?" Myrdin's eyes widen when he sees her. "What?"

"Myrdin," Lymseia says, using her hand on his arm to turn his body toward me. "This is Miss Cryssa Thurdred."

Recognition flashes in his eyes, and his mouth spreads into a genuine smile. "Miss Thurdred, it's wonderful to meet you."

I smile politely while arching a brow. "And you are?"

"This is Lord Myrdin Tarrantree," Lymseia cuts in, patting him on the shoulder. "Son of Head of House, Lord Tanyl and Lady Phaendarra Tarrantree—the Crown Prince's cousin."

He's from the Copper Court. That explains the color of his eyes.

I bow. "It's a pleasure to meet you, Lord Tarrantree."

"Lord Tarrantree is my father," he says, waving me off. "Please, call me Myrdin."

Lymseia looks at him expectantly. "Miss Thurdred is interested in exploring High Keep. Why don't you give her a tour?"

My brows stitch together. If I didn't know better, I would think Lymseia was trying to distract me. To pull me away from the East Tower.

And that only makes me more curious about what secrets lie there.

"A tour," Myrdin repeats, looking between Lymseia and me. "Of course, a tour."

Warily, I eye Lymseia. She's smiling, clearly satisfied with herself. If she thinks I'll give up this easily, then she's in for quite the rude awakening.

"Just a moment, then." Myrdin crouches to pick up his papers, organizing them on his knee. "Excellent." Then he stands, facing me. "What would you like to see first?"

"Whatever you think is best," I tell him. "I'm in your capable hands."

Myrdin blushes, running a hand through his hair. "Very well, then. Come with me, Miss Thurdred."

"Cryssa."

"Cryssa," he echoes, as if he were trying not to forget.

He holds out a hand, gesturing to the staircase. "This way."

Meeting my pace, Myrdin falls in line beside me as we descend the staircase.

"What are those?" I ask, my eyes falling to his stack of papers.

"Oh, just some council documents. Nothing exciting, I assure you."

"Council?"

"The High King's Council. My father and I serve as members, alongside the other Heads of Houses and heir-apparents."

That gets my attention. "The Crown Prince sits on this council, too, then?"

"Yes," Myrdin says.

"Interesting," I muse. This gives me an opportunity. Perhaps, Loren and I can make our escape while a council meeting is in session. If we play our cards right, we just might be able to slip out while all the important people are preoccupied.

I clench my teeth. Still, none of this will be of any use until I know where to find him.

We step off the last stair and enter the main hallway—

the one with all the arches. I can't help but crane my neck to look at them as we pass through.

The suits of armor visible through the archways catch my eye. I point. "Let's go in there."

"Of course," Myrdin says. He leads me through the nearest doorway and into the room.

Aside from the suits of armor, there are sizable, long banners—each bearing one of the five Noble House's emblems and colors—with lists of names at the bottom. The closest banner to me is that of House Pelleveron, from the Gold Court.

I step closer to it, mouth parted in awe at the craftsmanship. Like many of the woven pieces here, the banner has gold metal intertwined. Gently, I run my hand underneath the names. I don't recognize the given names, but they all have the same family name—Pelleveron.

The question already on my tongue, I glance over my shoulder to ask Myrdin.

"This is the hall of kings," Myrdin answers before I can form the words. "Each banner bears the names of the High Kings and Queens who reigned while each of the Noble Houses was in power."

Scanning the room, I realize the list of names underneath the Gold Court's banner is the longest.

"How long has House Avanos been on the throne?"

"Not long." Myrdin motions to the Bronze Court's banner. "High King Vorr is the first of his line. In fact," Myrdin says, excitement rising in his voice, "Head of House, Lady Maelyrra Pelleveron's aunt was the last in her line, before Vorr ascended to the throne."

"What happened?" I lean forward. "Why didn't the Pelleverons stay in power?"

"The last High Queen died without an heir," Myrdin explains. "When that happens, the Heads of Houses or heir-apparents who seek to be the next High King or Queen challenge each other for the throne in a rite called the Fyrelith."

My eyes widen. "They fight?"

Myrdin nods. "To the death."

I wince.

"It's a grisly scene, no doubt. Luckily for us," Myrdin continues, "the centuries-long life spans of noble fae make it rare for a monarch to die without a legitimate heir." He tilts his head to the door. "Shall we continue?"

Tearing my gaze from the Gold Court's banner, I nod and follow him out.

We continue down the hall, passing the staircase this time.

"So, the Crown Prince is your cousin?" I ask, glancing at him.

"Yes," Myrdin replies. His expression dims. "His mother was my father's sister."

My chest tightens. Having lost my own mother at a young age, I know the feeling of grief all too well. Perhaps that is one thing the Crown Prince and I have in common.

Finally, I say, "It seems the High King truly loved her."

Myrdin's expression brightens slightly. "He did." Then he scrunches his brows. "But what makes you say that?"

"Lymseia told me that no one's been allowed in the East Tower since she died."

Myrdin only meets me with a blank stare.

"He must still be in mourning," I say quickly, so he doesn't suspect anything.

"Ah, yes, mourning." Myrdin nods, turning his face from mine. "Of course."

I look away from him and face ahead. There is something very strange going on at High Keep.

Something the High King wants to keep hidden.

But it seems the High King doesn't trust anyone but his personal guard with his secret. Does Viridian know what his father hides in the shadows? Or has he been shut out, too?

Myrdin shows me everything. The great hall, the

courtyard—which, to my pleasant surprise, is much greener than the front gates—the armory, and the kitchens, if I ever find myself in need of something to eat late at night.

"The servants don't like it," Myrdin tells me. "But they won't stop you."

"What of the dungeons?" I know it's a slim chance that he'll answer, but I ask anyway. "Where are they?"

"I—" Myrdin swallows. "I'm not at liberty to tell you that."

I ball my hands into fists, digging my fingernails into my palms. Of course he's not.

I'll have to find Loren on my own.

I'm not leaving here without him. No matter how long it takes. It's my fault he's here.

At the end of the tour, Myrdin walks me back to my chambers. "I hope I didn't bore you too much."

"No," I assure him, over emphasizing my enthusiasm to hide my disappointment. "Not at all."

Myrdin flashes me a warm smile. Out of everyone here, I think I like him the most. He has this boyish charm about him that makes him seem like the younger brother I never had.

"I'll take my leave." He bows his head, clutching his stack of papers to his chest. "I bid you good evening."

Myrdin departs, busying himself with his council documents. Closing the door behind me, I cross the threshold into my chamber and rest my body against it, leaning my head back.

I've been here for a day, and I've made no progress in formulating an escape plan.

Squeezing my eyes shut, I fight the burning lump growing in the back of my throat. My chest constricts, stomach swimming with anguish.

Tears sting my eyes. This will be the second time I've cried in the span of a few days.

I swallow to keep them at bay.

This isn't me. I'm not the girl who cries at the hint of distress. No, I'm the girl who acts. The girl who fights back. The girl who does something to change her situation. That's the girl my father raised me to be.

If only Father was here. He'd know what to do.

Still, tears fall and run down my cheeks.

And I let them.

Staggering away from the door, I sink to my knees.

Even if I do manage to find Loren, I don't know what's become of him. He could be hurt. Bound and gagged. Maybe they've tortured him.

Or worse, he could be dead.

I banish the horde of unkind thoughts. I can't let

myself drown in them. If I do, there'll be no hope for either of us.

I sit in silence for a while, making no move to wipe away the tears or clean myself up.

There's a hard knock at my door. I wait a moment, and the knock sounds again, harder still, as if the person outside is rapidly growing impatient.

I have half a mind to ignore it, but the third knock has me up and on my feet. The idea of shouting profanities at whoever is so intent to disrupt my solitude becomes more appealing by the second.

Can't a girl cry in peace?

When I open it, the Crown Prince stands in the hall, chin raised. The profanities I'd been looking forward to spewing vanish, and my mouth feels like it's been latched shut. I swear I see the hard lines of his face soften ever so slightly, but it must be a trick of the light.

"Good evening." His voice is cordial but lacks true sincerity. Or at least, to me, it does. "Dine with me tonight."

I can tell that's not a request. The annoyance it stirs within me is enough to free my tongue from whatever stupor has frozen it. He brought me to High Keep against my will. He's the reason Loren has been arrested. And now he's here, asking—no, *commanding*—me to dine with him, as if none of that happened.

"Or what?" I say, my voice carrying the weight of my challenge. "I don't eat at all?"

"Yes." Viridian's icy tone is much lower than I'd like. His quiet temper is unsettling, but I would die before I let him see that.

"I'd rather starve than share your company." Does he honestly expect me to play nice with him, while Loren rots in a prison cell somewhere? "And if you think otherwise, then you're delusional."

"If that's how it's going to be, then fine." Viridian's eyes narrow, amber storms raging within them. "You can starve, for all I care."

My brows furrow, chest rising and falling with my angry breaths.

He spins on his heels, his back facing me now. With his hands behind him, one clasped firmly around his wrist, he looks at the guards.

"Stand guard. I want to know the moment she changes her mind."

"Trust me," I declare to his back, "I won't."

Viridian says nothing, but I see his shoulders tense. He storms down the hall, bronze robes swishing when he turns the corner.

I slam my chamber door shut.

A FEW HOURS later, there's a voice calling my name from the hall.

"Cryssa!" Lymseia raises her voice so I can hear her through the door. "Cryssa, I've brought you something to eat."

Wiping my face to make myself look at least a little more presentable, I move from the bed and answer the door.

Lymseia waits outside, holding a plate of food under a silver cover. Steam escapes from under it, telling me the food's hot. My stomach grumbles, and the smell already has my mouth watering.

"But my Lady..." The guard outside my room stumbles over his words, stepping forward. "The Crown Prince said—"

"I know what he said," Lymseia interjects, an air of authority rolling off her. "And I don't care. I'm giving the poor girl dinner, and if the Crown Prince has a problem with that, then he knows where to find me. Have I made myself clear?"

"Yes, my Lady," the guard says with a nod, moving back to his post.

"Very good." Seeming satisfied with herself, Lymseia turns to me with a smile, extending her arms toward me.

Warily, my eyes fall to the food. "Why are you helping me?"

It's not like I've done anything to earn her allegiance. Plus, she's fae. Noble fae, at that. What does she stand to gain?

Lymseia shifts her weight, as if to make herself appear more casual. "I don't know you, but I can already tell you're stubborn. You won't eat with him. Not tonight, at least."

"Why do you care about whether or not I eat tonight?"

I try to make it seem like it doesn't matter, but even as I say the words, the growling noises coming from my abdomen betray me.

"You're my future High Queen," she says, as if that's enough explanation. "Now take the gods-damned food. My arm's getting tired."

I take the plate, stomach rumbling again. "Thank you."

"It's no problem." Lymseia winks at me and hands over a set of silverware. "If these two give you any trouble," she says, jabbing her thumb at the guards behind her, "I'll set them straight for you."

I muster a laugh. "Noted."

"Very good." She glances down at the plate in my hands. "Enjoy."

"I will," I tell her, hoping my eyes convey my gratitude. And I mean it.

With that, she turns sharply, and leaves me to eat my dinner.

Maybe I do have a friend in this place, after all.

CHAPTER FIVE

I RISE EARLIER the next morning.

I'm already up and out of bed when Tiffy and the rest of my ladies' maids come in to dress me and style my hair for the day. When they're satisfied with how I look, they bow and trail from the room as quickly as they came.

As soon as they're gone, I loosen my corset and take a deep breath.

I don't know how noblewomen breathe with these cursed things tied so tightly.

Perhaps that's why noble fae females are so pretentious.

With a chuckle, I slip into the hall. Even though my bed chamber alone is the size of our entire first floor back home, I'll grow restless if I stay in here, confined to these four walls.

Instead of turning left outside my room—which leads toward the main stairwell—I turn right, itching to explore and discover what's waiting for me this way.

More wooden doors that look like mine line the hallway. More bedchambers, or sitting rooms, perhaps? I continue ahead until I reach a small circular area, lined by more stone archways.

A large library sits beyond the arches, with books filling shelves that stretch all the way up to the ceiling. I wander inside and crane my neck to look up. Exposed wooden beams cross above my head, below a grand cathedral ceiling. Tall windows, lined with gold, sit between the colossal shelves, filling the room with bright sunlight.

I move deeper inside.

Intricately carved mahogany tables and chairs are spread throughout the space. Silver candelabras sit atop them, some joined by stacks of leather-bound books.

"Ah, Miss Thurdred." Myrdin presses his lips together, flashing an embarrassed smile. "I mean, Cryssa. It's lovely to see you."

I offer him a polite smile in return. "Lord—Myrdin Tarrantree. It's a pleasure to see you as well."

Myrdin's not alone. Sitting with him is another fae male, with white-blond hair that looks like pure silk. His crystal-blue eyes find mine, a stark contrast to his sun-kissed complexion.

Myrdin extends his hand to his companion. "Cryssa, I would like you to meet Lord Asheros Larmanne. Son of Head of House, Lord Eldred and Lady Avourel Larmanne, and heir-apparent to the Silver Court."

Asheros dips his head. "I'm honored to make your acquaintance, Miss Thurdred. I am afraid I can't say I know much about you." His voice is smooth, but not like Viridian's. While Viridian's is deep and rich, Asheros's voice is lighter, with an airy quality to it.

I bow my head. "The same to you, Lord Larmanne."

"I'm sorry if I've disturbed you," I say, glancing back at Myrdin. "I was exploring."

"Not at all." Myrdin waves me off. "Asheros and I were merely discussing politics."

"Indeed," Asheros agrees. "We were due for a distraction."

I get the sense that they were debating, or arguing, rather than merely discussing. But I keep that to myself.

"Where are you from, Miss Thurdred?" he asks.

"Slyfell, my Lord."

"Ah, the Gold Court. I'm sure the summers there are a sight to behold."

"They are," I say, suddenly homesick. "The entire valley is lush with greenery and the wildflowers in full bloom."

I think of running through the meadows as a child with Acantha. We would play games while Father foraged for berries and mushrooms and filled baskets with richly colored flowers to proudly show him.

Now, the memory only makes my heart hurt.

Asheros laughs. "Whereas all you will find in the Silver Court is snow and rock."

"I've heard the fjords are beautiful," I say. "The Silent Chasm especially."

Asheros leans back in his chair. "Indeed, our cliffs and waters are beautiful. But few brave the cold winds to see them."

"If you're looking for a place to honeymoon," Myrdin cuts in, his voice rolling with pride, "I'd suggest the Copper Court."

I cross my arms with a smirk. "Is that so?"

Asheros's expression lights up at my challenge. He leans toward Myrdin. "Oh, I like her."

"The Blood Dunes are a sight to see," Myrdin

explains, ignoring Asheros's remark. "Crimson sands softer than anything you've ever felt before. Warm waters you'll want to dip your feet in, and the food…" He places a hand on his stomach. "Oh, the most wonderful cuisine you'll ever taste."

"He's only saying that because it's his home court." Asheros rolls his eyes.

"No," Myrdin counters, the thrill of the debate rising to his face. "I'm saying that because it's true. The use of spices in the Copper Court is truly exceptional."

Asheros just grins, amused.

Myrdin holds up his hands. "I've yet to be proven wrong."

I laugh. "I'll consider that when it's time to decide where we'll honeymoon." Though, I know that time will never come. I won't be marrying Viridian, and I certainly won't be honeymooning with him.

"The Crown Prince is a lucky male," Asheros says, looking me up and down. "You are a rare beauty."

"She is."

Myrdin and Asheros instantly rise to their feet. Their faces pale.

"Your Highness." Asheros bows, voice tight, as if he knows he's been caught doing something he shouldn't. "My apologies for being so forward."

"I'll accept your apologies." Viridian levels his tone, as if to keep himself in line. His cool stare lingers on Asheros before turning to me.

"I've been looking for you," he says, eyes locked with mine.

"Have you now?" I taunt.

"You weren't in your room."

"Am I not allowed to leave?" I uncross my arms and put my hands on my hips.

"I didn't say that," Viridian growls, amber eyes stormy.

"You certainly implied it," I snap.

"I have no recollection of doing such a thing."

I lean back, face hot with irritation. "I seem to recall it quite differently."

Viridian presses his mouth into a fine line and takes a deep breath. "Then perhaps I should choose my words more carefully next time."

"Perhaps you should."

He looks away from me, clenching his jaw.

"Will you join me for dinner this evening?"

I could say no and deny him in front of two other males. I'm sure that would absolutely infuriate him. Or wound his pride. But as much as I don't want to spend any more time with him, it would be beneficial to dine with good silverware. If I want to make my escape, I'll need some kind of easily concealed weapon.

So, I raise my chin and even out my expression.

"Yes," I tell him. I let toxic sweetness flow freely from my voice. "I'll be so lovely as to grace you with my presence this evening."

Viridian's jaw ticks, and for a moment, I think he'll say something rude back to me. But to my surprise, he doesn't. He reins in his temper.

"Very well," he grinds out. "I will see you tonight."

Myrdin and Asheros exchange an awkward glance.

Frustration still clear on his face, Viridian turns to them stiffly, as if suddenly remembering that they're still here. "My Lords."

Before I can say anything in return, he spins around on his heels and storms from the library.

Throwing up my hands, I let out a groan and do the same. Though I make sure to keep him out of my sight.

It's only once I'm back in my room that I let out my aggravation. Pacing about my room, I cross my arms.

"The *nerve* of the male!" I fume. There's no doubt in my mind that my cheeks have grown a deep shade of red. "Does he expect me to be a pretty face, merely existing to be at his beck and call?"

I let out a huff and sit on my bed. Then I lay back

with my arms outstretched.

I have no desire to dine with Viridian.

Crown Prince or not, he's an arrogant, possessive fae male like the rest of them. We're not even married, and he probably thinks he owns me.

My anger bubbles over at the thought.

"I am not going through with this marriage," I promise myself.

This dinner is my opportunity to arm myself.

And that is the only reason I'll be going.

HOURS LATER, my ladies' maids arrive.

"Come, come," Tiffy says, practically picking me up and dragging me to the washroom. "We must get you cleaned up."

"Cleaned up?" I ask, looking down at myself. "Didn't we do that this morning?"

"Well, yes," she says, without stopping. "But we must prepare you for dinner with the Crown Prince. You want to look your best to see your betrothed, don't you?"

I roll my eyes. "I couldn't care less."

Tiffy clicks her tongue and shoots me a disapproving look. "Nonsense."

"I mean it."

She merely puts her hands on her hips and stares me down the way a mother would a naughty child.

"Fine," I groan.

With a drawn-out sigh, I let her and the others scrub me until my skin is raw. Once I'm clean, they stuff me into a lacy evening gown. It's richly colored emerald, with gold metal sewn along the hemline. I look in the mirror while the ladies' maids style my hair, pinning most of it to my head while leaving elegant ringlets hanging down my back.

"There," Tiffy says when they finish tapping powder puffs to my face. "You look wonderful."

And I have to admit she's right. The emerald color makes a striking match to the vibrant auburn of my hair and my golden-brown eyes.

"Now you must get going," Tiffy says, ushering me out the door. "The Crown Prince is expecting you."

I take a deep breath, filling my lungs. Nerves jitter in my stomach, and I wonder if I'll be able to eat at all. Exhaling, I smooth my skirts.

I can do this, I tell myself. It's just dinner.

I'll find something I can use, take it, and leave. It's that simple.

I have to do this, I remind myself. *I'm Loren's only hope.*

81

Gathering my courage, I make for the great hall.

When I arrive, I find Viridian sitting at the long dining table alone. At the head of the table, he leans back in his chair, elbows resting on its arms. One of his hands drapes nonchalantly over the side, while the other cradles a silver goblet in a relaxed grip. Free of his bronze crown, his black hair hangs loose, as if he's been running his hands through it. His gaze is stormy, brows knit together like his mind is far from here.

Guards stand at attention around the room. The two closest to me are positioned on both sides of the entrance. I take a mental note of where they are. I'll have to be stealthy if I want to slip past them with a weapon of some kind.

Viridian takes a swig from his goblet when he sees me.

I approach the other end of the table, closest to the door, and sit. The table is empty, save for a bronze tablecloth, candelabras throwing off dim light, and silverware.

I eye the butter knife resting on the table before me. With a serrated edge, it's not much of a weapon, but it seems to be my best option.

He doesn't say anything to me, and instead signals to the servants waiting along the wall. "Bring the first course."

"Of course, Your Highness." The servants bow, and then slip into the adjoining room.

Viridian and I sit in silence until the servants return with trays of steaming bowls.

Simultaneously, they place the bowls in front of Viridian and me.

"Thank you," I say, offering the servant a small smile.

He blushes, eyes lingering on me for a moment before backing away.

Viridian clears his throat. He glowers at the servant, tightening his hand around the armrest until his knuckles go white.

Is that...jealousy?

It couldn't be. Other than what I look like, he doesn't know anything about me. And he said it himself when I overheard him with Lymseia. He doesn't want this betrothal. He has no claim on me. No right to be jealous.

I wait for Viridian to pick up his spoon before doing the same. Then I dip it into my still hot bowl of what seems to be a pale broth with chopped vegetables and a leafy garnish.

Still keeping a close eye on each other, we both lift our spoons to our mouths and blow on them before swallowing.

"So," Viridian says, finally breaking the silence. "How

83

has your stay been?"

I snort, making no effort to hide my scorn. "Delightful."

Viridian's jaw tightens. "Unpleasant, it would seem."

"Don't tell me that surprises you."

"Then perhaps, if it's so awful," he says roughly, in an attempt to be cordial, "you should tell me what would make your time here more bearable."

I have half a mind to demand that he tell me where the dungeons are, and to let me go, while I'm at it. But I know how that conversation will go, so I don't waste my energy.

I settle for something else. Something he can do for me. "A sketchbook."

Viridian arches a dark brow. As if he expected something more. "A sketchbook?"

"Yes." My tone shifts, becoming defensive. "Is that too *common* for you?"

He doesn't take the bait.

"No." He considers the thought while sipping another spoonful of soup. "I'll have a sketchbook brought for you."

"How gracious of you," I say, my voice sickeningly sweet.

Viridian's cheek twitches.

My eyes fall to my soup. We sit there, in tense silence, until we finish our bowls. It's as if neither of us know what to say to each other, yet we're forced to suffer in each other's company. It brings me some joy to know he's not enjoying this any more than I am.

The servants bring out the main course—baked fish with warm, buttery potatoes seasoned with aromatic herbs, and freshly baked artisan bread loaves.

My tastebuds buzz with the rich flavors, but I harden my expression, so Viridian doesn't know how much it pleases me. And it seems to be working—every time I catch his gaze, he's scowling.

Viridian holds out his goblet, and the servants fill it with more wine. They move to do the same for me.

"No," Viridian orders, voice blunt, like a dulled sword. "No wine for her."

"Why not?" I challenge, defiance brewing within me. Who does he think he is? "You're not my keeper," I snarl. "You don't get to make decisions for me."

To my dismay, I don't get a rise out of him. He simply says, "It's for your own good."

I roll my eyes with a huff. The arrogance of the male, thinking *he* knows what's best for *me*.

"As if you care," I mutter, loud enough for him to hear.

Viridian ignores me, but his hands curl around his fork and knife. I can't help but notice the way it makes the muscles in his forearms flex.

A blush rises to my cheeks. I hate that he has this effect on me.

Guilt grips my stomach. How would Loren feel if he could see me now? Blushing in the presence of the enemy?

I know there's still one more course, but I've suddenly lost what was left of my appetite.

"Am I excused?" I keep my eyes trained ahead of me, though I don't look at Viridian.

His eyes flick up to me. "Yes."

I press my hands to the table as I stand, sliding the butter knife toward me. Slowly, I wrap my fingers around it, and tuck it to my body. I bow, clutching my skirt to obscure the knife.

Then I turn around and make for the door.

My skirts swish with my movement, further concealing the silver in my grasp. I slow my strides, so I don't give myself away, and briefly make eye contact with the closest guards.

They merely dip their heads in return, just short of a bow. Completely normal, the way they would to a guest.

I'm only a few paces from the exit.

So close now.

"Stop."

I freeze. My heartbeat accelerates, but I breathe, forcing myself to calm down.

I hear the chair slide across the floor behind me. Footsteps follow.

Viridian grabs my arm and spins me around. In a whirl, I collide with his hard, muscled body, my palm to his chest the only thing between us. My other hand has the butter knife to his throat.

The guards quickly draw their swords.

No doubt aware of the cool metal pressed to his jugular, Viridian's eyes glint with amusement.

"Do you really think I would be so much of a fool as to let you leave with that?"

I play innocent. "It's just a dull butter knife."

His face is inches away from mine now. "We both know how much damage you could do with that, Little Fawn."

His pet name for me has me wrinkling my nose. Who is he to call me "little" and compare me to a weak, feeble creature? Still, I don't acknowledge it, merely to deny him the pleasure of a response.

Instead, I tighten my grasp around the butter knife. "You don't know me."

"Perhaps you're not so hard to read."

His hand clasps around mine and squeezes, hard enough that I'm forced to let go. The butter knife falls to the floor with a clang.

But Viridian doesn't release his iron-grip on my hand.

"If you ever try to cross me again," he hisses, amber eyes ablaze, "I will personally see to it that your lover pays the price. Understand?"

I clench my jaw, hardening my expression. Anger swirls in my chest, and I don't care if it shows.

"Coward. I *hate* you." Venom laces each of my syllables.

But Viridian doesn't even flinch. "Do you understand me, Little Fawn?"

Curling my lip, I say nothing, and my silence makes my disdain for him all the more clear. My nostrils flare with the force of my loathing, barely able to keep myself from screaming in his face.

"I said, do you understand me?" His face hardens even more than I thought possible, amber eyes looking as if they could slice right through my flesh. "I won't ask again."

It takes everything in me not to continue fighting, but I can't risk pushing him too far. If I step out of line again, he'll hurt Loren to punish me. I can't let that happen.

"Yes," I spit. "I understand."

"Good." He releases me and backs away. The guards relax, lowering their weapons.

Gesturing to me, he tells them, "See to it she makes it back to her quarters without any more trouble."

The two closest guards take me by the arms. I tug and wriggle against them, but their hold on me is too strong.

"Oh, and one more thing," Viridian says, the spite in his voice more than palpable.

"What?" I croak, looking back at him over my shoulder.

"Since you can't be trusted not to mishandle your silverware, you'll be dining with me from now on. Every night."

Anger sets my cheeks on fire.

"Fine." I don't need to see myself to know that my eyes shoot poison his way.

"Good." Viridian glowers back at me. His tone matches mine.

When the guards pull me away, I let him have the last word.

Because I vow to be so insufferable, that he regrets his decision to spend any more time with me.

CHAPTER
SIX

A FEW DAYS LATER, a wooden box sits outside my chamber door. The past few nights Viridian and I have dined together have been tensely silent, as though neither of us knows what to say to each other. Well, I can think of multiple things—only, anything I have to say to him right now would most likely end in an argument. Perhaps he feels the same.

I pick up the box and bring it into my room. Sitting on the bed, I place it on my lap and open it. Inside, I see an array of art supplies—a collection of drawing pencils, charcoal sticks, a small cloth to wipe my hands with after smudging the charcoal, and a large sketchbook lying in the center.

Speechless, I close the box and pull it closer to my torso. Even after that stunt I pulled with the butter knife, Viridian still brought me the sketchbook I asked for. And so much more.

My chest fills with warmth. Though I immediately furrow my brows.

The sketchbook doesn't undo everything he's done. How could it?

I almost consider not using it, solely because it's a gift from the male I despise. The male holding me here against my will. Forcing me into a life I will never want.

But I take the sketchbook and the charcoal sticks out. Spite isn't a good enough reason to let them go to waste.

At least, that's what I tell myself.

I make my way from my chambers and find myself outside in the courtyard. A circular hallway lines the area, with open arches that lead back into the castle. The plant-growth here is well-kept and tamed. Nothing like the wildflowers that grow in the meadow behind our house in the summertime. Every year since we were children, Acantha and I would spend hours laying in the grass. We would make flower crowns and stare up at the clouds, while pointing out what we see in them.

The sun shines overhead, its warmth dampening the chill of the wind. The weather here isn't much different from home. Like Keuron, spring will be coming to the Gold Court soon. I think of Acantha and Father. Of my basket for collecting wildflowers that will stay empty.

Don't think like that, I scold myself. *I'll be home come spring.*

Can I ever go home? If I make it out of High Keep, they'll come looking for me. If not to drag me back and force me to marry the Crown Prince, then certainly to arrest me for treason.

There's no way the royals would let me run away with no repercussions.

If I want to be free, I'll have to leave Inatia. For good.

There's a chance I'll never see Acantha or Father again.

The threat of tears sting at my eyes. Taking a breath, I walk closer to the center of the courtyard and kneel on the grass. Then I open the sketchbook, putting the charcoal sticks down in a pile on my lap. They leave black smudges on my dress when I move, but I've never been one to care much for my clothes.

Picking up one of the charcoal sticks, I lower my hand to the page and let it wander.

My mind drifts, my thoughts fading into the

background as I draw. That's one of the things I've always loved about drawing—no matter how much is on my mind, no matter the emotions I feel, everything vanishes the moment shapes start to take form on the paper.

It almost feels as if I am no longer in control as I draw. Like some unseen force guides my hand into swirls and lines and edges. I can lose myself in it. And when I emerge on the other side, I see something on the paper that didn't exist before.

When I stop, I hold out the sketchbook to look at my drawing.

It's Acantha, lying in a summer meadow with her face turned to the viewer. A poorly made flower crown slips a little too far down her forehead. She's beaming, with her eyes crinkled in the corners like they are when she's very happy. It's a scene taken directly from my memory—an image of her I've seen enough times to memorize nearly every detail.

Closing my eyes, I press the drawing to my chest and hold it near my heart.

Gods, I miss her.

The sound of many footsteps echoes on the stone behind me. Standing, I turn around, holding the sketchbook even tighter, desperately clinging to whatever piece of my sister I have left.

In the castle, the High King walks, flocked by his personal guard. Two noble fae are with him—one male and one female. They're dressed in similar attire and carry an air of grace and power.

The female leans toward the High King as she walks. I immediately notice a resemblance to Lymseia—sharing the same blue-black hair and gray eyes. Her pointed face is drawn with concern, dark brows knitted together.

"Your Majesty, the mines... They aren't producing metal like they have in years past. I fear there is a decline."

"A decline?" the High King asks. Worry pinches his voice.

"A severe decline," the female—Lymseia's mother, I realize—says. "And there aren't enough miners left to mine what metal is there. If we cannot find a solution, I fear we will be unable to produce enough steel to keep ourselves afloat."

I hold my breath as I listen in.

The High King's jaw tenses. "And what of the Silver Court?" he asks the male.

"The same, Your Majesty."

The male must be Asheros's father—Head of House Larmanne. Though, unlike Lymseia and her mother, Asheros and his father look nothing alike. While Asheros has white-blond hair the color of snow and ice-blue eyes, his father's hair is dark brown, and eyes such a light shade of silver, that they almost look white.

Those eyes fall to his feet. "It's as if there is something draining the land of metal."

I knew of the mining sickness sweeping our lands, but...

The metals are disappearing?

"Thank you for your concerns, Lady Kylantha and Lord Eldred," the High King says. "I shall discuss this issue with the council when we meet next."

Lady Kylantha and Lord Eldred give their praises to the High King. They continue speaking, but the farther away they go, the less I'm able to hear.

Fear grips my stomach.

What will become of Acantha and Father if the gold mines run dry?

What if they already have?

I feel utterly powerless. If I were home, maybe I could help. I could *do* something. As long as I'm trapped here, there is nothing I can do to save my family from ruin.

I can't stay.

Whatever I'm going to do, I must do it soon.

VIRIDIAN IS QUIET at dinner tonight. Again.

The main course for tonight's meal is roasted duck served on a bed of fresh greens. The meal is wonderful, no doubt, but I can't stop thinking about what I heard earlier. I think of the metals being drained from the land and wonder what will become of all the human families who depend on them.

Fear grips my stomach.

What will become of Father and Acantha if the gold runs dry?

"Has the duck offended you?"

"What?" I look up, torn from my thoughts.

"You seem very intent on cutting it into a thousand little pieces," Viridian says, briefly looking at me. Something flicks across his face, though it's too brief for me to make out what it is. "Has the duck done something to offend you?"

"No." I rest my fork.

Viridian's eyes meet mine, and he holds my gaze. The tight expression he wears softens.

"What is it?"

I cock my head. My voice comes out hard. Cold, even. "What is what?"

"What's wrong?" His tone matches his expression, even after I spat venom his way. The softness shocks me. I struggle to make sense of it.

"Nothing," I tell him, picking up my fork again. The bitterness doesn't fade from my tone. "There's nothing wrong."

Viridian doesn't look away. The tightness returns to his mouth, as if he doesn't believe me. But even if that's true, he doesn't press me for more.

"Thank you," I say awkwardly, changing the subject. "For the drawing supplies."

I feel like he's won this battle, and I'm returning with my tail between my legs. I hate being indebted to him, even for something as minor as a sketchbook. How is it that even when he's done something kind, I despise him for it? For the way it makes me feel?

"Of course." His voice is subdued, as if he doesn't know how to respond.

Then the tense silence I'm becoming all too familiar with falls over us. And my mind can't help but run in more circles.

"Why were you there that night, in the stables?" I ask. There's a sting of accusation in my voice, as if he were somehow at fault for Theelia making her will be known.

"I don't know, really," Viridian admits. His candor surprises me. I would have thought that he'd refuse to answer. "I was in the Gold Court for political reasons."

"Political reasons?"

"Yes," he replies. "As you may know, relations between the Gold and Bronze Courts have been... strained, since the last Pelleveron queen's death."

"Ah," I muse in understanding. "The Lady Maelyrra isn't one to let go of old grudges, is she?" Even with what little knowledge I have of her, that wouldn't surprise me at all.

"No." Viridian lets out a long, tired sigh. "She isn't." He continues, averting his gaze, "When I'm overcome with worry or stress, I ride. Sometimes I do it when I can't sleep." He pauses, looking up at me now.

My eyes lock with his, and I can practically feel my hardened stare melting as he speaks.

"I don't know what it was that night—fate, destiny, or noise, perhaps. I couldn't sleep, no matter how much I tossed and turned. I was staying at an inn not far from the stables—I preferred that to staying at the Pelleveron manor—and went to prepare my horse."

I finish the thought for him. "When you found us."

"When I found you."

Something about his words, the way he says them, strikes a chord inside me. So much so that I almost forget who he is, what he's done.

Almost.

Then I remember that he's holding me captive here. That he's keeping Loren prisoner. And the bite of my hatred returns to me.

I've been here too long. For too long, I have been dining and lounging and waiting. Living lavishly, while Loren suffers. While Acantha and Father worry for me at home. It's time. I can't wait any longer.

Swallowing, I narrow my eyes. My mind is made up.

Loren and I are leaving.

Tonight.

CHAPTER
SEVEN

I WAIT UNTIL AFTER nightfall, when the moon is high in the sky and the castle has gone deathly silent.

Launching myself out of bed, I make for the wardrobe and pull out a riding dress and boots. Quickly, I step into it and secure it to my body. I nearly stab myself sticking the hair pins into my braid much faster than I should have, but I don't have any time to spare.

Once my boots are on, I drape my wool cloak over my shoulders. I remember to take a candelabra with me from my bedside before stepping into the dark hallway. The dim light of the candles lights my path without drawing too much attention.

Good.

I'm still not sure where the dungeons are, but my common sense tells me they're somewhere below us. So, that's where I go.

I make my way down the main staircase and turn right when I get to the bottom. Sidestepping into a narrow opening in the wall meant for archers, I press my body flat to the stone and wait for the guards on patrol to pass by before advancing.

As I move through the corridor, I peek behind the doors. Some are locked. It's hard to see in the dark, but the closer I get to the kitchens, more and more of the ones I can open seem to be storage closets or pantries.

I continue farther down the hall until I reach the end. There's a heavy-looking door to my right, with a large steel handle.

Holding up the candelabra to get a better look, I reach out to open it. As I expected, one tug on the handle tells me it's locked.

Plucking the hair pin from my head, I slip it into the lock, grateful that I thought to bring it. The motion brings me back to a time when Loren and I were children, and we snuck into the nearby bakery to steal some sweets. We made it out of the bakery without being caught, thank the gods, but Father was there waiting for me when I returned home, my little arms full of pastries. I remember how angry he was, at first. But like always, Father couldn't stay upset with me for long.

Narrowing my eyes, I renew my focus. The days of stealing sweets are long gone. And if I get caught, the stakes are so much higher now. I could be imprisoned, like Loren is at the moment. Or, if the Crown Prince grows tired of my defiance, I could be killed.

Imagining that it's a dagger in Viridian's chest, I drive the hair pin deeper, until I face some resistance from the lock's mechanism. Then, keeping a firm grip on it, I turn it counterclockwise.

A click sounds.

On high alert, I glance over my shoulder to make sure there's no one around. The guards on patrol seem to have passed this area of the castle, but I don't want to stay here for long, in case they circle back this way. Placing my palms on the door, I push it open, careful not to make much noise. A set of long, stone stairs waits before me, descending into gods know what.

Sucking in a breath, I creep down the steps. I find myself in a long hallway, lined with thick, reinforced steel bars. The ones closest to me are empty, and my feet carry me forward. As I do, I desperately search for Loren, anxious to find him.

I hear him before I see him.

"Cryssa?" He whispers, loud enough for me to hear. The dungeons are so quiet that any sound seems much louder than it should be.

"Loren," I breathe, breaking into a light jog. When I reach Loren's cell, I wrap my fingers around the bars. Clutching them so hard, my knuckles go white.

"Cryssa," Loren says again, cupping my cheek through a gap in the steel. "You're here."

"I'm here." I nod and my lower lip quivers without my permission.

Viridian's threat from dinner, the night I held the butter knife to his throat, rises to the forefront of my mind.

"If you ever try to cross me again, I will personally see to it that your lover pays the price."

I remember how angry he was. How his eyes blazed.

"Has he hurt you?" I ask Loren, frantically scanning him for injuries. "The Crown Prince?"

"No," he assures me, brushing his thumb back and forth against my cheek. "I haven't seen him since that first day."

I sigh in relief, and the tension in my shoulders

lessens.

"We have to go," I tell him. Dropping to my knees, I inspect the metal bars, looking for the lock.

"We can't." Loren's words hang over me, heavy with the sting of defeat.

"What do you mean, we can't?" I look up at him, eyes wide. "We can't stay here."

"Believe me, I know—I don't want to stay here. I..." His voice slows. "I want a quiet life with you, in Slyfell. Maybe a farm, children, I don't know."

I drop my gaze from his.

A quiet life in Slyfell. A safe life. The life I always thought I would have.

"You don't... You don't want more than that?" I ask. I know this isn't the time to have this conversation, but I can't seem to stop the question from leaving my lips.

Loren crouches, so he's at my level. "What more is there to want?"

"I don't know," I murmur, shaking my head a little. "*Something.*"

There's so much out there—so much to see, so much to do. The whole world waits at our fingertips. There has to be something else.

Something more.

Right?

105

But Loren only chuckles softly, looking at me as if I've said something adorable. I don't like it.

"The cell," I say, my voice grainy as I direct his attention back to the steel that cages him. Anything to make him stop looking at me like that—like wanting more out of life is so unfathomable. "We need to open this door."

"We can't, Cryssa. There's no lock."

"No lock?" My words come out fast and garbled. "How can there not be—"

"Magic," Loren cuts in. "It's magically secured." His expression lifts slightly, as if he's remembering the bakery incident, too. "There's no lock for you to pick this time. Trust me, I wish there were."

"Then we'll find another way out," I say, rising to my feet. "We'll think of something, we can—"

Loren's entire body goes rigid. He holds up his palm, and the motion silences me immediately.

Cocking his head, he flicks his eyes toward the dungeons' entrance and then back to me. Clearing my mind, I strain to listen.

Voices.

There are voices coming from the top of the staircase leading down here.

"You need to leave," Loren tells me, his words firm. "Now."

"Like hell I'm leaving you." He's here because of me. The thought of leaving him here alone has guilt twisting in my stomach.

"Yes, you are," he says, more forcefully this time. "If you get caught down here, Cryssa... Fated or not, I can't let myself think of what *he'll* do to you."

The Crown Prince.

My nostrils flare, brows pinched together. Even when he's not here, he infuriates me.

"That gods-damned bastard." I hate him for putting us in this situation.

"You can give him hell later," Loren says, as if he can read my mind.

I open my mouth to protest.

"Please, Cryssa," he begs. *"Go."*

I stare at him for a moment, unblinking.

"Fine," I grind out at last. "But I'm coming back for you, and you can't stop me."

Loren flashes me that toothy grin. "Of course not."

I reach through the bars to give his upper arm a squeeze before backing away. Once he's no longer in my line of sight, I quicken my pace, staying close to the stone walls.

Lowering my body, I climb the stairs. My thighs burn, begging for release, but I don't rise to my full height until I'm back upstairs.

Poking my head out, my eyes sweep the surrounding area.

Whoever was here a moment ago is gone. But I know they can't be far.

Tiptoeing back into the main floor of the castle, I push the door closed behind me. Hair pin in hand, I quickly turn around to lock it, so there's no evidence of me being here.

"Where do you think you're going?" a deep voice says behind me.

Panic rises in my chest. I whirl around.

Viridian stands before me. His pants hang low on his waist, and his thin, white shirt does little to hide his muscular frame. The top of his shirt is untied, revealing the smooth planes of his chest. His shaggy black hair is mussed with sleep, falling in front of his calculating amber eyes.

"How long have you been standing there?" I snap, forcing myself to take my eyes off his physique.

Fear claws at my throat. Does he know I was in the dungeons?

"Long enough." Viridian's gaze narrows. The way he

says it makes me think that he wants me to believe that he's been trailing me for longer than he actually has. "I asked you a question, Little Fawn. Where do you think you're going?"

"To the kitchens," I lie, leveling my expression. If there's a chance that he doesn't know what I've been up to, then I can't slip up now. "I'm feeling a bit hungry."

"You're hungry? At this hour?"

"Yes. I'm hungry."

"You passed the kitchens."

"Did I?" I ask. "How silly of me."

Unconvinced, Viridian takes the candelabra from me.

"You may be a good liar," he says and steps closer, cornering me until my back is pressed to the wall. His chest is like an impenetrable barrier before me, keeping me pinned here, under his intense stare. "But I'm not fool enough to fall for it."

My body betrays me. Heat rises to my cheeks and gathers in my core. I exhale, forcing myself to breathe through the sensation.

He tilts his head down, close enough that I can feel his warm breath on my neck. It sends chills dancing down my skin, and I can't help but shudder.

"I know what you were attempting."

"Do you now?" I stick out my chin in defiance. His

words only confirm my suspicions—he thinks he caught me *before* I made it into the dungeons.

Relief loosens some of the panic constricting my lungs. But only some.

"Yes. It doesn't take much to put the pieces together." His eyes burn like hot coals. Still, the way they're focused on me makes me want to buck my hips against his.

"Arrogant male. You think much too highly of yourself, Your *Highness*."

That gets a rise out of him. "Oh, really? We're going to play this game, then, aren't we?"

"Game?" I sneer, wrinkling my nose. I lean my head back against the wall, eager to put some distance between us, though I'm unsuccessful. "Unlike you, I'm not here to play games."

"You just can't admit defeat, can you?" He lets out a laugh, and it's a raw, bitter sound. It's warm on my face. "This is the second time I've caught you red-handed. You wouldn't be sneaking around in a cloak if you just wanted *something to eat*." He bares his teeth. "I told you, Little Fawn. You're not so hard to read."

That lights a spark in my stomach. My anger simmers and bubbles over, overpowering the hint of desire I feel.

"Fuck you." I touch my palms to his chest and shove him.

Hard.

Viridian's eyes flare, though he doesn't say anything. He doesn't have to. I can see the way he looks at me—with that familiar, self-righteous, noble fae disgust.

Even though he's doing nothing but stand there, watching me, the mere sight of him only makes my blood boil even more.

"What is it now?" I blurt out, gritting my teeth.

Those amber eyes go cold, though they still burn like embers. "You're a fool if you think I'm going to just walk away after catching you trying to escape."

"Don't even *think* about following me back to my room," I demand, not caring to undercut the harshness of my tone. "I can get there perfectly fine on my own."

To my surprise, he listens.

"Fine." Holding up his hands in surrender, he backs away from me.

Despite the triumph I feel having won this battle, part of me is disappointed that he doesn't protest.

What the hell is wrong with me?

Still, he watches me closely, as if I were a wild animal. Tendrils of his hair fall in front of his eyes. "It's in your best interest that you don't get into any more trouble tonight."

The way he says it is so icy, I can practically feel the chill on my skin. It only makes my face hotter, my skin

111

heated by my rage.

But that does little to stifle my craving to grab him by the collar and taste those soft lips.

"Gods-*damn* you," I curse.

I hate him. I'm furious with him. I shouldn't be so attracted to this male.

Frustrated with him, and with myself, I storm to my chambers and slam the door.

CHAPTER EIGHT

I STRUGGLE TO FALL asleep that night. And the next. And the night after that.

The fourth night, as I lie in bed, I know I probably won't sleep yet again. My mind runs in circles, refusing to cease. I press my eyes closed, snuggling my head into the pillow. Though even when I try to focus on my breathing, all I can do is replay my conversation with Loren over and over again in my mind. Torturing myself with it, like I have every night since.

"You don't... You don't want more than that?"

"What more is there to want?"

Moving into an upright position, my brows knit together. The blankets fall from my chest.

"What more is there to want?" I echo, struggling to believe that he really said that. Loren, the carefree, outgoing man that he is, content to live a simple, quiet life in the same city we were born. The same city where our parents were born, where our grandparents—and gods above, even our great-grandparents—lived and died. The city we know like the back of our hands.

"What more is there to want?" I shake my head now, lips drawn back. So much more. I'll be damned if I spend the next sixty years of my life in the same corner of the world. In the same gods-damned neighborhood.

I'd always thought that he and I would want the same things. That we'd both want to travel, to explore the world. To see as much as we possibly could, before our time in this realm came to an end.

But now... Now, I'm not so sure.

Maybe—

I pause.

Maybe Loren isn't who I thought he was. Maybe, I let myself fall for an idea of him. One I so desperately wanted to be real.

Inhaling deeply through my nose, I take a long, full breath, thinking back to the day we met. My father was much younger, back then. It had been long enough after Mother's death that he'd finally opened himself up again. And with only two young daughters to talk to at home, he'd begun seeking adult connections. Friends. I remember he'd come home one night with a charming, smiling man I didn't know—Reth Grayweaver, Loren's father. Beside him was a scraggly boy with the same bright expression. The same toothy grin. Acantha had run to my father instantly, peering at the strangers from behind his legs. I had stormed right up to them, demanding to know who they were and why they were in our house. Reth had only laughed and urged Loren forward to introduce himself. From that day on, Father and Reth became great friends. Because of that, we saw more of him.

And Loren.

I touch my fingers to my mouth. When we were children, it was so easy. We'd sit on the floor of our house while our fathers talked about work. We'd come up with imaginary friends and play games. We were content to have someone to play with. We didn't need more than that.

I wish things could always be that simple.

Scooting back against the headboard, I pull my knees to my chest.

Looking back now, the human districts in Slyfell are so tight-knit, that I probably would have met him regardless. We were neighbors, and our fathers worked closely together in the mines. Why wouldn't we have become friends? But if things had been different, if there were more children Acantha's and my age, would we still have been *best* friends? If not for our fathers' friendship, would I have sought him out?

Something in my heart tells me that I wouldn't have.

My abdomen constricts, winding my stomach.

Soon after Jemetha was born, Reth died in a mining accident. One day, the underground ceiling collapsed, killing all who were caught beneath it. Father would have been there, too, if not for me coming down with a fever the night before.

Our families only got closer in the wake of Reth's absence. Father knew all too well what it was like to be on your own, raising young children while grieving the loss of your spouse. Because of that, he helped Catia were he could. And whenever he stopped by the Grayweavers' house, he brought Acantha and I with him.

I press my lips together, tensing the muscles in my jaw.

What would have happened if Reth hadn't died? Would Loren and I have spent so much time together? Would we have gotten so close?

Tilting my head down, I wrap my arms around my

knees.

Maybe—

I don't want to finish the thought. But I can't stop myself.

Maybe our families were the only thing that ever kept us together. The only thing that let us get so close.

After all, what do we truly have in common? Loren enjoys social gatherings and mingling with others. I would much rather be alone in the summer meadows, drawing to my heart's content. Loren's the type to have many friends, the kind of man that every girl can't help but fall for. Me, on the other hand, I've always thought of myself as an acquired taste. That I need time to warm up to someone, before trusting them with the things about myself that I'd rather keep tucked away.

As children, we would get into mischief. That, I remember with a small smile, was fun. Exciting. But as we grew older, the fun dimmed. Spending time with Loren shifted. No longer getting into harmless trouble, no longer going on adventures. Spending time with Loren became night-time visits to the stables, of being physically intimate with each other, instead of connecting—of truly *seeing* each other for who we are as individuals—on a deeper level.

There's no doubt in my mind that I love Loren. He's

been there for me through it all. We grew up together. He is, and always will be, my childhood best friend.

But maybe, that's all he is. My best friend. Someone that knows me as well as Father and Acantha. He may be an important part of my past, but maybe, that's all he'll ever be.

My past. Not my future.

I swallow the lump in my throat. That thought feels like a betrayal.

Because I know Loren loves me. He wants a future with me.

But the future he wants, and the future I want are not the same. And they never will be.

Tears gather in my eyes, a new, burning lump forming where air should be. I let out a breath. But my breathing only quickens and I gasp for air at the onset of my tears.

I scramble from my bed, so forcefully that I nearly trip. I wish that I had fallen asleep. That I didn't have this realization.

I wish I never went to the stables that fateful night. That I never saw Loren or Viridian. That Theelia never bestowed her blessing on us, and I could go back to the way things were before.

I'm out the door and into the hall when my movements slow.

But would that have made me happy? Would I have been satisfied with the way things were before?

The sinking feeling in my stomach tells me that this would have happened anyway, regardless of whether I was brought to High Keep. Though, our current circumstances only seem to exacerbate this disconnect between Loren and me.

Maybe it's better this way, I reason with myself. *Maybe this spares us both from more pain.*

I don't know if I believe that.

Needing to move, I weave through the halls. Too caught up in the guilt eating away at me, I don't pay attention to my surroundings.

Until I find myself outside.

Glancing over my shoulder, I stare at the castle behind me. High Keep looms overhead, making me feel so much smaller than I already do. Now that I'm out here, in the fresh night air, I finally let my tears fall.

My feet carry me forward while my shoulders shake.

I curse Theelia, for making her will be known.

I curse my mother, for dying and setting all of these events into motion.

And I curse myself, for not realizing how incompatible Loren and I are sooner.

"Can't sleep?"

Wiping my tears with the back of my wrist, I spin around.

Sweat gleaming at his brow, Viridian stands before me, loosely holding onto a horse's reins. A midnight stallion waits next to him, releasing a gentle huff from its nostrils.

"No," I say, my eyes flicking between him and the horse. "And you?"

"No." He sighs, a long expression wearing down his face.

I press my lips together, looking away.

Viridian dips his chin slightly, understanding crossing his features. I expect him to say something, but he doesn't. Instead, he continues ahead, lightly tugging the horse's reins. The creature responds, trotting alongside him.

He passes me, and I turn around to watch him. The sweat on his back makes his white shirt slick against his skin—revealing a clear outline of his back. Illuminated by the moonlight, his broad shoulder blades flex with his slight movements. And his ass...

Biting my lip, I avert my gaze.

Viridian pauses, looking back at me over his shoulder. "Are you coming?"

"Uh—sure."

I jog to catch up, and then we head for the stables.

Viridian is quiet. I am, too. Only, instead of feeling the need to fill the silence, like I would with Loren, I feel calm. Relaxed. There's no pressure for me to say something. No awkwardness in the silence.

It's... Refreshing.

Viridian leads the horse to the stables and into the nearest open stall. The horse obediently stays put, merely shaking its mane. Viridian crosses the stables and removes a brush from a hook on the wall, and then returns to the horse.

Craning his neck down, he places the brush on the horse's coat and begins to brush it in long, smooth strokes. It's not long before he falls into a rhythm, and he moves with such ease that I can't help but think he's done this before. Many, many times.

I cock my head, the corner of my mouth tugged upward, into a questioning look.

"You groom your own horse?"

"Yes," Viridian glances at me, amusement playing at those delicious-looking lips. "I'm sure you find that shocking."

As much as I don't want him to be right, I can't say otherwise. I didn't expect that from him.

"I thought such a menial task would be beneath you."

121

He pauses, turning his face to look at me. "So because I'm the Crown Prince, I can't enjoy 'menial tasks?' Now whose the one making assumptions based on one's birth?"

"I didn't—" I stammer. "I didn't mean—"

"Relax, Little Fawn." Viridian grins at me, and sure enough, I do find the tension in my shoulders fading. "I'm only poking fun."

Still, I turn my face and cross my arms.

We're quiet for a moment.

"It soothes me," Viridian says at last. "Grooming the horse. It's one of the rare moments I have to myself. You'd be surprised at how difficult it is to slip away."

"Oh." My expression softens. I'd never thought of it like that before.

"Yes." He lets out a long, tired sigh.

I step forward, holding out my hand. "May I?"

Viridian's mouth brightens. "Of course."

I stroke the horse's dark coat. "What's his name?"

"Nightfoot," Viridian tells me, eyes on the horse. He raises his fingers to the horse's muzzle. The creature tips its head forward in response.

"Nightfoot," I repeat, still moving my hand back and forth. "He seems to like you."

"He does," Viridian smiles.

"And you seem to like him, too."

"I do." He turns those amber eyes onto me now, meeting my gaze.

I hold his stare for a moment, before looking away. A blush rises to my cheeks.

Viridian does the same, pressing his lips together. He adjusts his grip on the brush before returning it to its spot on the wall.

I back away from Nightfoot, giving Viridian room to close the stall door and secure the latch.

"You should try to get some sleep," he says softly.

I nod. "You, too."

He looks at me again. "I will."

My mouth suddenly dry, I swallow.

Viridian's eyes linger on me as he steps back toward the door into the castle. Opening it, he gestures to the threshold, motioning for me to go ahead. I duck into the castle, and he follows me inside.

I can feel his body behind me. It sends waves of heightened sensation trickling along my back. Just for a moment, I close my eyes and imagine what it would feel like to have him behind me, with his chest pressed to my back. His hips against my ass.

The subtle echo of the door closing bounces off the castle walls. It's enough to snap me out of my stupor. Brushing my hair behind my ears, I quickly start down the hall.

Keeping my pace, I climb the stairs, highly aware of Viridian trailing behind me the entire time. It's only once I'm back in my bedchamber that I let out a deep breath.

After talking to Loren, I can't help but question where my allegiances lie.

Viridian is still an arrogant, cruel noble fae male. Like all the other noble fae.

And Loren...

We may not be compatible romantically, but I still love him. Don't I? Guilt fills my chest again. Regardless of our romantic relationship, or lack thereof, it's still my fault he's here.

Because of that, I have to break him out of that cell. No matter what it takes.

We may not have a future together, like I once believed, but he's still my best friend. And now, he's suffering, all because of me.

I owe him his freedom.

After we escape, we can figure things out between us.

We'll deal with that when the time comes, I think as I climb back into bed.

Clearing my mind, I focus on the sound of my breaths. And before I know it, I slip into unconsciousness.

CHAPTER NINE

D ESPITE NOT GETTING much sleep the night before, I feel energized come morning. Contrary to what I would have thought, talking to Viridian last night made it easier for me to fall asleep.

Even Tiffy notices the shift in my mood.

"Good morning, Miss." She flashes me a cheery smile. "You look rested this morning. You slept well, I assume?"

"I did," I reply. My voice is lighter than it has been.

"I'm glad to hear it," Tiffy says, and I can tell that she means it.

I follow her into the washroom, and as usual, a hot bath is already waiting for me. I sink into it, letting out a relaxed breath when I do. I can already feel the water working out the knots in my shoulders and upper back, loosening the tension that's gathered there for however long it's been since I arrived. Spending all my time in the castle, it's easy to lose count how many days it's been since I left home.

The thought makes my heart heavy. Even though I'm feeling better this morning—a phenomenon that I still can't seem to wrap my mind around—thoughts of home always come over me like a storm cloud.

Though, Father wouldn't want me to be sad the entire time I'm here. No, he would want me to look for the good in every situation.

And in every person.

Even Viridian.

I brush away the thought. I'm not ready to let my guard down around him yet. Or let myself even consider the thought of getting close to him. Like my mother before me, it takes me a while to let go of grudges. From what Father's told me of her, she was stubborn, too. And even though she forgave those who wronged her, she never forgot.

A small smile clings to my lips.

Tiffy and two of my other ladies' maids finish bathing me, and then help me to my feet. Using a towel, one dries my body, while the other does the same to my hair. Tiffy gives them a satisfied nod, before entering my bedchamber to lay out today's ensemble.

Wearing only my dressing robe, I emerge from the washroom. My eyes immediately land on my bed, at the garment that Tiffy's laid out there.

The day dress is a pale green, the color of wild sage. It reminds me of the sage that grows in the meadows back home in the spring and fall.

Following my line of sight, Tiffy gestures to the dress. "Since you're in a better mood today, I thought you might like to wear something in a brighter color."

"It's perfect," I tell her warmly.

"Wonderful!" she exclaims.

She and my other ladies' maids remove my dressing robe, and then help me step into the dress. Once it's secured to my body, Tiffy weaves my hair into a simple braid.

"There," she says, draping the braid over my shoulder. "All done."

I open my mouth to thank her, when my chamber door bursts open. The entire room goes still.

Viridian stands in the arched doorway, a deathly calm

falling over him. It's more than clear that the Viridian I talked to last night, in the stables, is nowhere to be found. No, this is the face of the Crown Prince, dealing with a pest.

I swallow.

The sight of him—of that quiet rage—nearly chills me to the bone. It doesn't take me long to piece together why he's here, looking like he's about to unleash hell on earth.

He knows.

I don't know how, but he knows that I saw Loren, four nights ago. I knew it was only a matter of time before he found out, but I hadn't anticipated that it would be so soon.

How could he have found out?

Then, cursing under my breath, I realize my mistake. Irritation directed toward my own carelessness rushes to the surface.

The door to the dungeons.

I wasn't able to lock it before Viridian found me.

His eyes stay fixed on me, even when he addresses the servants that stand on either side of us with their mouths clamped shut.

"Leave us. *Now.*"

Tiffy shoots me a concerned look, as if she doesn't

128

want to leave me alone with him. But my ladies' maids do as they're told and drop into hurried bows before scurrying from the room. Leaving me alone with a very, very angry fae male.

Raising my chin, I level my expression and meet his glare head on.

"You weren't just attempting to escape that night." His voice is lower than I expected. Every word is isolated, as if he's restraining himself. That scares me more than it would if he were shouting at me. "You made it into the dungeons. Didn't you?"

A statement, not a question. A condemnation.

I only look back at him, no doubt mirroring the expression he now wears.

My silence only seems to stoke the flames. "Answer me."

"Why? You already know," I retort. Anger fuels me, making my face hot. "So why make me say it? To bask in my humiliation?"

"Nothing is ever easy with you, is it?" he snaps, his voice elevating in volume. At his sides, he balls his hands into fists.

"What did you expect?" I raise my voice to match his. "That you'd keep me trapped in here and I would just lie down and take it? *Fuck* you, Viridian." I use his first name, and I don't care if I'm crossing a line.

He draws his lips back, baring his teeth. "I would choose your next words very carefully, if I were you."

"Well, you're not me. You and I are *nothing* alike." Ignoring his warning, I take a step forward, sharpening my words so they fly at him like iron-tipped arrows. "You took everything from me—my life, my family, my lover—and you think I'm just going to be some docile little creature that does as she's told?"

"That *lover* of yours is still mine to do with as I please," Viridian seethes.

"As if you would let me forget that." Bitterness drips from my words.

"It appears that you need some motivation to stay in line."

"You *arrogant,* pompous, entitled fae bastard!" The force of my fury is so strong that I'm shaking. "If I'm so difficult to manage, then why don't you send me home and pick someone else to be your bride?"

The way his jaw ticks tells me that I've hit a nerve.

"Send me away," I continue, daring to press him further. "Then neither of us has to suffer the other's presence anymore."

Viridian only glowers at me, clenching his jaw. He lowers his face to mine, until our noses nearly touch. "If only it was that easy to be rid of you."

That catches me off guard. He's the Crown Prince of all Inatia. What in the gods-damned world could make it difficult for him to send me away?

I falter. Even though it's only for a moment, it gives Viridian enough time to cross the room and stop with his hand on the door.

He pauses, still standing with his back to me. When he speaks, he doesn't even look my way.

"Your doors are to be locked after sunset."

"*What?*" My voice goes shrill. "You're locking me in here at night?"

Viridian says nothing. But his silence is answer enough.

"You can't do this!"

"*I* am the Crown Prince!" Viridian yells, turning around to face me now. His eyes are wild. I think I've finally pushed him past the point of no return. "And you are a commoner. I can do as I please."

Then, he strides into the hall without another word. As if he can't get away from me fast enough.

The door closes behind him just as quickly, sealing my fate with the single click of a lock.

I run to the vanity table and yank open the drawer.

All the hair pins are gone.

"Argh!"

Running to the door, I fling myself at it.

"Viridian!" I shout. "You noble fae prick! Unlock this door!"

Though I know it's no use, I pound my fists into the wood over, and over, and over, while letting out wordless screams. Ramming my hands into the door, I howl until my throat feels raw, and my voice ragged.

I scream for Loren.

I scream for Father. For Acantha.

I scream for myself. Because I'm locked in the wolves' den, forced to live among them for the rest of my inconsequential, mortal life.

And, because I'll be forced to marry the worst one of all.

CHAPTER
TEN

D ESPITE HAVING DINNER with him every
night, I haven't spoken to Viridian in weeks. Since
he confronted me after I found Loren in the dungeon.

I haven't left my room much, either. Not like he gave
me much of a choice. True to his word, one of the guards
posted outside my bedchamber locks the door every night,
right after sunset. Though even if I could, I wouldn't dare
to be caught sneaking around again.

Caught by him.

Maybe it's my wounded pride.

Or maybe I'm losing hope that I can free Loren and escape this gods-forsaken place at all.

I sit at my vanity table, bent over a drawing. This one is of Father. He sits on the floor in front of the hearth in our house, the way he does in the winter after a long, cold day in the gold mines. There's dirt on his nose and in his hair, but his eyes are warm and alight with joy. I could stare at it for hours.

But the knock at my door pulls me away, and I rise to answer it.

"Good morning," Viridian says awkwardly, running a hand through his hair. He wears an untucked, loose-fitting white shirt, the V-neck collar showing off part of his chiseled collarbones. His black pants hang low on his hips, and it takes more strength than I'd like to admit not to look.

"Good morning." I force myself to look up at his face. Though, even still, I'm tempted to stare. His strong jawline, aquiline nose, high cheekbones...

Then I remember my anger. My loathing. The locks on my chamber door, for gods' sake.

Enough of that.

"You..." Viridian's voice trails off, amber gaze fixed to my lips. "You have charcoal on your face."

I laugh, though it's a humorless sound. "Typical."

I pull my sleeve down to hold it in place before moving my arm up to rub away the charcoal.

"Let me," Viridian says softly. He touches his thumb to his tongue and reaches for my face. As he does, he watches me and moves slowly, as if he expects me to turn away.

But I don't.

This male stole me from my home, from my family, and is holding me captive.

Why don't I turn away?

Looking down at me, staring into my eyes, Viridian brushes his thumb back and forth across my cheek to wipe away the black smudges.

When he's done, his hand lingers on my face for a moment. His touch sends electricity rippling through my skin. I feel captivated by him, drawn to his proximity. Then he pulls away, his eyes still locked with mine. It makes me wonder if he feels it, too.

"There," he says at last. "It's gone now."

"Thank you," I tell him. He's close enough that I can feel the warmth of his body. I could reach out and touch him, if I wanted to. Could run my hands along his lean, muscled abdomen. Could bring my hand lower, beneath the waistband of his pants.

You are in love with another man, I remind myself.

Though, I'm not even sure of that anymore.

Still, I shouldn't be having these thoughts about someone other than Loren while he's imprisoned. Especially not about someone I despise. The one responsible for everything Loren and I have had to endure.

"You're welcome." Viridian's deep voice rumbles in his throat. He lowers his hands, though his fingers curl out, as if to take mine.

"Is there something you need?" I ask. The hardness returns to my voice.

"Something I need?" he echoes, looking lost.

"Yes. You came to see me, didn't you?"

"Oh. Yes." He nods, like he suddenly remembers. "It seems that we weren't—we didn't get off on the right foot." He swallows, glancing away from me. "I'd like to start again."

"Start again?" I hold back a snort. To truly start again, he'd need to take me home to Slyfell. But that will never happen.

"Yes," he says earnestly. "I'd like to court you, if you'll allow it."

"Court me?" This time, I do let out a snort. "Are you serious?"

"Perfectly serious," he echoes, tightening his mouth.

"Why now?" I ask. Doing little to hide my suspicion,

I narrow my eyes.

"My father, he—" Viridian pauses. His forehead creases with focus, as if he's working to collect his thoughts. "Neither of us asked for this betrothal, yet here we are. I believe—I *hope*—there's still time for us to be friends. Because I would rather marry a friend, than some human woman that barely knows me, and hates me anyway."

I lean back and cross my arms. He looks at me with such hope, that it almost feels too cruel to crush it.

"If I agree to this," I say, raising my chin, "then I want the locks off my door."

He sighs, as if he knew this was coming. "Very well," he says at last. "No more locks."

I stare at him for a moment, mulling over his proposal. Though, despite how much I'd rather not spend time with him, I know it would be foolish of me to reject it.

"Fine," I sigh, cursing myself for agreeing to this. "I'll allow you to court me. But I can't promise that I won't still hate you once we get to know each other."

"I wouldn't dream of it."

Then, Viridian flashes me a smile. It lights something in my chest—a spark that catches and sends heat flooding through me.

I extinguish it with a single thought.

No. Not him.

Aggravation has me grinding my teeth. Why does he affect me like this?

"Walk with me," Viridian says abruptly. He clears his throat. "Erm—will you walk with me?"

He watches me intently, practically pinning me in place with the intensity of his stare.

"Yes." I look over my shoulder at my sketchbook. I'll come back to it later.

He holds out his arm for me to take, but I don't. Receiving the message, he lowers his arm and falls in step beside me.

Viridian and I walk downstairs. I expect him to lead me to the courtyard, but he doesn't. We walk through the castle and turn past the kitchens, avoiding the area where he caught me poking around. He stops and opens a door for me, waiting until I'm through.

When we pass the stables, he leans his head back to soak up the sun. Inhaling, his expression relaxes.

"I've always felt more at home out here," he says, looking over at me as we walk. "The castle walls..." His voice trails off.

"They suffocate you." I know how that feels.

"Yes." Viridian nods, amber eyes narrowing. "I know

what you must think of me."

"And what do you think I think of you, Your Highness?" I arch a brow.

Viridian trains his stare ahead. "That I'm some pig-headed, cruel, arrogant male. You said so yourself. And I'm sure the list goes on."

It's my turn to look away now.

"As much as I want to assure you that I am none of those things, I know words alone will not be enough."

"Then how do you plan to woo me?" I ask. My voice is lighter than it has been for days—laced with an almost humorous quality.

Viridian's mouth perks up. "Only with the grandest of romantic gestures, of course."

I can't help but grin. "I'd expect nothing less from the Crown Prince."

His expression loses some of its light. It makes me feel as if I've said something wrong.

"What is it?" I ask. I shouldn't care about offending him. After all, I've already said worse things to him without so much of a second thought.

"Nothing." He flashes me a polite smile, but it doesn't reach his eyes.

"I know that's not true." My voice gets harder now. "Have I offended you?"

"No," he says quickly, straightening his posture. "My feelings aren't so easily hurt, I assure you."

"Fine." If he doesn't want to tell me, then so be it.

We walk in silence for a moment. It hangs heavy between us.

Then, Viridian exhales. "It's—well, everyone seems to expect so much of me. As they should, I am the Crown Prince, after all."

I lift my gaze and can't help but look at him while he speaks. His expression is genuine, as if he's beginning to lower his mask.

"But they only see me as the heir to the throne. No one, not even my father, sees me as simply Viridian." He slows, and it even affects his stride. "My mother, she was the only one who saw me like that. Just Viridian."

"What happened to her?" I ask. I know that the High Queen died some time ago, but I don't know the cause.

"I was very young. I was going to have a sibling, so I'm told. She—" he swallows. Pain gathers in his expression, tightening his features. "She didn't survive. Neither did the child."

I press my lips together, unsure of what to say.

"I understand that feeling," I tell him at last. "When my sister, Acantha, was born, I lost my mother. One life for another, I suppose."

140

Viridian turns to me, his stare bearing into mine. His eyes widen slightly, like he didn't expect me to share in his grief. Like no one had ever looked past his bloodline, his position, and seen him for who he is.

"I'm sure you love your sister very much."

"I do." I offer a small smile. "I miss her dearly."

Viridian goes quiet again.

I turn my face away and look to the castle grounds instead. There are more flower beds and clusters of thick rose bushes out here than there are in the courtyard. At the edge, farther off in the distance, a line of dense forest envelops High Keep.

Viridian's stone-faced demeanor returns. "I've been meaning to tell you that there's to be a ball hosted in our honor."

"Is there?" My stomach already pools with dread.

"Yes. To celebrate our engagement."

"Ah. I see."

"You don't seem enthused."

"I'm not one for dancing. Nor lacy gowns." Loren was the only thing that made the festivals in Slyfell of any enjoyment. He'd grab my hand with that boyish grin on his face and pull me all the way to the town square with a tankard of ale in his other hand.

But Loren won't be with me at the ball.

No, he'll be locked away in that cell, trapped in the dark behind unforgiving steel bars. And I'll be in a room full of noble fae who think I'm beneath them.

How exciting, I think dryly.

"If it's any consolation," Viridian says, silencing my thoughts, "I won't be enjoying myself either. I'll only attend to maintain appearances."

"Appearances," I mutter. "To hell with appearances."

"I know you don't want this," he says. "You've made that quite clear. It's not my choice, either."

"Oh, really?" I taunt, recalling what the guards told me the day they arrived at our door to take me away. "Supposedly I was hand-picked to be your bride. Hand-picked by *you*."

There's more venom in my voice than I intended. Viridian flinches.

"The gods are to blame for our arrangement." His icy tone matches mine. "Not me."

"You're the Crown Prince. No one can force *you* to do anything."

"Is that so?" That sets his eyes ablaze. "Let me tell you something, Little Fawn. Even I bow to the High King. You'd do well to remember that."

I glower at him, silently fuming. He's the only male in the realm who can get under my skin this way. This quickly.

"For someone who supposedly doesn't want me to hate him," I say, refusing to let him have the last word, "you're doing a poor job of changing that."

Viridian's voice goes cold and quiet. "There will be a tutor to instruct you. It seems that you have much to learn about conducting yourself like a lady. Now, if you'll excuse me." He brushes past me, and stalks back toward the castle, shoulders wound tight.

My feet seem fixed to the ground. I shake my head with frustration, balling my hands into fists.

"Argh!" I groan.

Guilt lines my stomach. I let my temper get the better of me.

And for the first time since I arrived, I feel like I ruined something.

So be it.

Viridian and I will never marry. So why do I care if I've ruined things between us?

I HAVE MY first lesson with the tutor this afternoon. I pass Viridian on the way to the ballroom, but he pretends not to see me.

Coward.

I tell myself that it's better this way. Better to be truthful with him, than let him believe there may be a future for us.

But that thought doesn't sit right with me.

I keep mulling over how he looked at me earlier. How he flinched when I lashed out at him.

And it makes me wonder if anyone has ever treated him right.

If anyone has shown him love. Genuine, unconditional love.

What am I saying?

What do I care if Viridian's been given love or affection? Since when did I care about him at all?

I don't.

I don't care about him. I hate him.

When I arrive, the tutor is already there, waiting. She's fae, that's for sure. Her pointed ears emerge through silky black hair that's wound into a tight bun at the base of her head, hunter-green eyes studying me the moment I cross the threshold. Her dark, violet dress is fitted to her too slim figure, and the high neckline makes her seem taller than she already is. She holds her hands in front of her, calm and collected. The way a lady should be.

Not brash and unruly like me.

"Good afternoon, Miss Thurdred." The tutor's voice is lower than I expect. Rigid, with a dry quality to it. She must be older than she appears. "I am Nefine Hrudarrk. I have heard that you are quite the force to be reckoned with."

I scowl at the female. "I assume you're here to break my spirit."

But my remark doesn't rouse her. "No," Nefine says simply. "I am here to teach you proper etiquette. You will need to be headstrong if you are to demand respect from the noble fae that will one day bow at your feet."

My body goes still at her words.

It hadn't occurred to me that I could become High Queen.

If I did marry Viridian, someday I would.

If being the operative word.

Do I even want to be High Queen? If I do, maybe I could bridge the gap between humans and fae. I could show the realm that we are strong. That we may be mortal, but we are a worthy equal.

"Well," Nefine says, demanding my attention, "since your engagement ball is quickly approaching, we shall begin with ballroom dancing."

I groan. As if I need to be reminded.

"There will be none of that here," she scolds.

"Appearances are key to one's reputation. And at court, your reputation is your sharpest sword. Now," she directs, raising the crown of her head, "stand tall, with your shoulders back."

I do.

"Very good," Nefine muses, taking on a strict, but motherly tone. She steps toward me, holding up her hands. "I shall be your dance partner for today."

She doesn't give me a chance to respond before continuing her instruction. "Take my hand. You will follow your partner's lead—my lead, for our purposes."

I take her outstretched hand, and she puts her free hand on my waist, keeping a substantial amount of space between us.

She starts to dance, taking small steps back and then to the sides. I do my best to follow, and my movements are stiff.

"Relax," Nefine urges. "Release the tension in your body. Let the music flow through you."

I sigh. Closing my eyes, I take a breath and try to do what she says.

"Better," Nefine says approvingly.

"Who will come to the ball?" I ask while we dance.

"The Heads of Houses, their consorts, and the heir-apparents," Nefine answers. "Fae who hold positions at

146

any of the five Courts will also attend with their Head of House."

Nerves gather in my stomach.

Crowds never bothered me before. When Loren and I would go to festivals in Slyfell with food, music, and dancing, we'd always be just one in a sea of many. They're always full of people standing wherever they can find room in the square. I've only ever been but one face in a crowd.

Never the one standing before them.

"Your entrance will be announced," Nefine explains. "Then you will proceed into the ballroom. You will be expected to dance with the Crown Prince, and when your dance ends, the two of you will greet the High King. Once you have done so, you will mingle with the crowd at the Crown Prince's side."

I nod. Though, I don't plan to be at Viridian's side the entire night. As if I would ever willingly do that.

I stumble.

Nefine hisses. "Do not anticipate. Respond to your partner's movements instead."

I grumble an apology.

"Again," she commands. "From the top."

We start over. This time, my movements are less stiff, and I wait for her to move before I step. Nefine gives me a satisfactory nod.

"Will the High King dance?" I ask.

"No. His Majesty is not one for social events, I am afraid," Nefine tells me. Her mouth stretches thin, brows stitching together. "He has not been since—" she clears her throat "—for a very long time."

"Why?" I lean forward. Something in her voice tells me that there's more to the story than she wants me to believe.

Nefine adjusts her posture. "Nothing you need to concern yourself with. Let us go again, shall we?"

We practice the dance routine again, but I can't stop thinking about what she told me.

What happened that made High King Vorr wary of social events?

And what does it have to do with the secrets hidden within the East Tower?

"You must carry yourself as a lady does," Nefine chides me, demanding my full attention. "Chin up, back straight. You must glide across the floor as if you were balancing a tome on your head."

I nod, taking a breath.

We continue to practice until my feet whine in protest.

Nefine must notice, because she releases me and steps

back. "That is enough for tonight. We shall meet daily until the ball."

I hold back a groan. How am I supposed to piece together the mystery of High Keep if I'm to attend these lessons every evening?

"Do not give me that look." Nefine straightens her shoulders. "Time is of the essence, my dear. You must be ready for your first appearance as the Crown Prince's betrothed."

I wrap my arms around myself, pretending to listen.

"He has not been since—for a very long time."

There's something Nefine isn't telling me. Even Lymseia dodged my questions when I first arrived.

There's something no one will talk about.

Something the High King doesn't want to be discussed.

If I'm going to stay here, I need answers. I need to unravel the truth.

And I know exactly where to start.

The East Tower.

CHAPTER ELEVEN

AFTER BREAKFAST the next morning, I make my way up to the second floor. I dart into the hallway, opposite the entrance to the East Tower, and press my body to the wall. I slow my breathing, urging my beating heart to slow.

Feet shuffle on stone, echoing through the open space.

Leaning forward, I crane my neck just enough to see the High King and his personal guard emerge from the East Tower. The five guards are stoic, arranged around him to form a protective barrier. The High King descends the main staircase, the guards moving in perfect time around him.

This is my opportunity.

My chance to see what lurks in the East Tower.

I wait a moment until I'm sure the High King won't be returning any time soon. Then, I move from the hall and carefully approach the entrance. When I reach it, I hesitate.

Adrenaline courses through me and nerves dance in my stomach. If I get caught, I could be arrested. Or worse, executed for treason.

But I find myself frozen in place.

I have to do this.

I have to know.

So, I take a deep breath and trudge forward. As I move farther into the hall, I can't tear my eyes from the many paintings that hang on each side. Framed canvases of many shapes and sizes don the walls, and a thick bronze colored carpet runs under my feet.

But the deeper I get, something awful fills my nose.

Rot.

Cracks form in the walls, getting deeper and more ragged the farther I go. Paintings hang crooked on rusted nails. Rocky debris litters the floor. Big holes fill the carpet, as if moths have eaten away at it.

A sickly murk muddles the air. I raise my hand to my mouth to keep myself from choking on the rancid odor.

What's wrong with this place?

When I reach the end of the corridor, I enter a rounded area, with the mouth of a spiral staircase.

Curiosity begs me forward. Moving carefully, I walk to the steps and climb up them. As I do, darkness falls around me, even though there are windows on either side of the tower.

The stone bricks making up the walls have deteriorated, crumbling into dust in some areas. A few stairs are crushed, and some are missing all together.

Dodging the gaps, I reach the top of the staircase.

It's a bedchamber.

There are no paintings here. No banners or drapes. Not even a chair or sitting area. The only cloth I can see is draped over a huge four-poster bed with splintered posts. There's barely any light, but there aren't any candles or candelabras to illuminate the room.

The long table opposite the bed draws my attention. It's the only other piece of furniture, save for the bed. It looks as if it's barely kept together—many nails are hammered into the strangest of places. On top of it, rests a collection of black leather gloves. They're laid out neatly. Each pair is identical in every way.

The gloves look familiar. It only takes me a moment to recall why.

The High King wore a pair of these exact gloves when I arrived. In fact, he's worn them every single time I've seen him.

I stagger back, my chest rising and falling with each of my breaths.

This is *his* bedchamber.

And these are *his* gloves.

Whatever secret the High King is hiding, the state of his private chambers makes one thing certain.

It's so much worse than I could have ever imagined.

My heart rate accelerates, and my breathing quickens until I feel almost lightheaded.

Picking up my skirts, I flee from the chamber, down the stairs, and run the length of the hallway. The beautiful paintings that once captivated me pass in a blur.

I slow my pace to a fast stride when I reach the open area at the top of the main staircase. But I don't stop to catch my breath. I continue at my adjusted speed, eager to put more distance between myself and the East Tower.

"You there!" a voice shouts.

I stop and turn around. A guard approaches me, his expression pinched.

"Yes?" I ask, feigning innocence.

"What were you doing in the East Tower?" he demands.

I gasp, placing the daintiest hand I can muster on my chest. "You'd dare assume that I would defy the High King's command?"

"Well, if you weren't in the East Tower," the guard says, his voice dripping with disbelief, "then why were you coming from that direction?"

"I was looking for my betrothed," I snap. "You know, His Highness, the Crown Prince?"

The guard arches a brow. "You were looking for His Highness?"

"Yes." I cross my arms, sticking out my chin. "He was supposed to join me for a walk on the grounds. Though, now, since he's late, I can't say I'll accompany him."

The guard sneers at me. "You think you can lie to me, human?"

"Fine, don't believe me." I throw up my hands in surrender. "Throw me in the dungeons, for all I care. Go ahead and invoke His Highness's wrath. I dare you."

"That won't be necessary," a deep voice commands.

The guard and I turn simultaneously. Viridian stands before us, holding his hands behind his back. The picture of regality.

He looks at me first, meeting my eyes. Interest sparks

155

in his expression, a questioning look flashing in his gaze. Then he turns to the guard, his face hardening to stone almost instantly.

"When my betrothed speaks to you, she is to be believed." Viridian's voice turns icy. "Is that clear?"

The guard swallows nervously and bows his head. "Yes, Your Highness. My mistake."

"Your mistake indeed," Viridian echoes. "One that is not to be repeated." He waves his hand. "Return to your post."

The guard bows again, and then leaves swiftly.

"I apologize for my tardiness, Miss Thurdred," Viridian says, loudly enough for any other nearby guards or servants to hear. "I had business to attend to."

I play along, thanking him with my eyes. "Very well. Perhaps I'll allow you to walk me to my room to make up for it."

"I'd like that." Viridian smiles, and it's hard for me to decipher whether it's genuine or simply part of the act. Unclasping his hands, he gestures for me to go ahead.

I do. Viridian falls into step beside me.

Once the guards are out of earshot, he peers over at me.

"Care to explain to me what it was you were doing?" he whispers.

"Nothing."

His lips curve upward, but it's not a smile. "Oh, really? Nothing at all?"

"Yes."

Viridian presses his lips together. "You will be the death of me, won't you, Little Fawn?"

"Don't assume you'll be so lucky," I counter.

This time, he grins. "My mistake."

We stop when we reach my room.

"Thank you," I tell him. This is the second time I've had to thank him. It feels like defeat. Like surrender. What would Loren say if he saw me conspiring with the enemy?

Viridian pauses, surprise raising his brows. "You're welcome."

I expect him to leave, but he doesn't.

"What are you doing?" I ask bluntly. "You can go now."

"Don't flatter yourself." Without looking away from me, he steps backward and reaches for the knob of the door next to mine. He says simply, "I'm not staying for you. I'm going to my room."

Before I can respond, he opens the door and steps inside.

Now, it's my turn to stand in the hallway looking like a fool.

I stare after him, the realization ringing in my head. As if things could get any worse.

Viridian's bedchamber shares a wall with mine.

"Of course it does," I huff dryly. The gods would be that cruel, wouldn't they?

Stepping into my room, I shut the door with a groan. Even though I'm back in my own chamber, the sight and smell of the East Tower lingers. I can't stop seeing the decay that's taken root there. The sickly sight of the High King's quarters. The filth that he returns to night after night.

So many questions run through my mind.

What caused the decay in the East Tower?

Why does the High King have so many pairs of black gloves?

And what does all of this have to do with my betrothal?

I thought investigating the East Tower would give me answers. But all it's done is leave me with more dead ends. More unanswered questions.

I know one thing.

If I want to survive here, I need to find out what's wrong with the East Tower.

Before whatever evil lurks there swallows me whole.

CHAPTER
TWELVE

T HE DAY I'VE BEEN dreading has finally arrived.
Come evening, my ladies' maids swarm my
bedchamber, with Tiffy leading the charge. Cradling a
gown in her arms, she approaches and holds it out for me
to see.

"His Highness had it made for this evening," Tiffy
tells me, beaming. "Isn't it lovely, Miss?"

My mouth parts while my eyes drink in the fabric. It's
a brilliant royal blue that seems to shimmer in the light. An
intricate twist of swirling vines and roses decorate the skirt
and bodice. I reach out to touch it, expecting some kind of

lace detailing. But I find it's not lace—it's spun gold metal woven into the gown. The skirt is full, with a layer of taffeta to thank for its shape, and the sleeves reach just past my elbows, hemmed with more gold.

I shudder when I think of how much this dress must cost.

"Viridian..." I murmur. "He commissioned this? For me?"

Tiffy nods. "He did."

As much as I hate to admit it, the dress is gorgeous. Allora, the Goddess of Peace and Beauty, herself would envy its beauty.

"Come," Tiffy says once she's laid the gown on my bed. "Let's get you ready."

She leads me to the washroom and into a tub of hot water. Much like they did my first night at High Keep, my ladies' maids scrub my skin and scalp until I'm free of any dirt or oil. Then Tiffy leads me back into my bedchamber and sits me at my vanity table. She and one other servant braid my hair and twist it around my head in an intricate style. When they finish, I barely recognize myself in the mirror.

Who is this girl I see before me?

She looks like a lady. If it weren't for my rounded ears, I would look fae.

I look away, curling my fingers.

I am not a lady. Am I?

Rising to my feet, I turn and hold out my arms. The servants tighten my corset, and then guide me while I step into my gown.

"You are a vision," Tiffy says, admiring her handiwork. "You will be the talk of the evening—I just know it!"

I nod and force a smile.

I feel as though there's an egg lodged in my throat. Perhaps I should tell them I'm feeling ill and can't go.

The knock at my chamber door tells me it's too late for that.

"Ah," Tiffy exclaims. "That'll be your escort, Miss."

My heart catches in my throat.

But when the door opens, it's not Viridian standing outside.

It's Lymseia.

Disappointment sinks in my stomach.

"Hello, Miss Thurdred." She bows her head. "I'll be your escort for tonight."

"Thank you," I say, my mouth suddenly dry, like I've swallowed sand.

Lymseia holds out her arm and I take it.

We walk through the halls and descend the main

staircase. Sweat gathers on my palms. I fight the urge to wipe them on my gown.

My nerves threaten to overtake me, but Nefine's teaching runs through my mind.

"Appearances are key to one's reputation."

I force myself to breathe.

I hone my energy, channeling it into what I hope is the picture of grace.

"Your reputation is your sharpest sword."

Then I will come armed.

We stop before the double doors.

Lymseia looks at me, her expression kind. "Are you ready?"

I take a deep breath. Once I go through these doors, there's no going back.

"I'm ready."

Lymseia nods and gestures to the guards standing before us. They open the doors.

Just inside the ballroom stands a man in fine clothes. His rounded ears tell me he's human.

Lymseia leaves my side and whispers to him. She steps back, falling in place next to me.

The steward clears his throat. "Miss Cryssa Thurdred, promised bride to His Highness, the Crown Prince."

The ballroom falls silent. Everyone's looking at me.

My heart thrums in my chest, beating against my ribcage. The muscles in my throat constrict, making it harder to breathe.

At some point, Lymseia breaks from me and stands next to the steward. I descend the stairs into the ballroom. The crowd parts for me, like I'm someone important.

To them, I am someone important.

I'm the Crown Prince's betrothed.

But once I escape, I'll go back to being Cryssa, the miner's daughter. I won't be someone important. And I won't be married to an arrogant fae male.

Viridian waits for me in the center of the ballroom with his hands clasped behind his back. Alone. The guests have distanced themselves from him, forming a large circle. Behind him, at the far end of the room, sits the High King on his bronze throne. Watching closely, like an instructor evaluating a pupil.

I force myself to move forward. When I approach, he holds out a hand for me.

Ever the gentleman, I think bitterly. I take it, and he pulls me closer until I'm nearly pressed to his chest. I stiffen, and he clenches his jaw.

Viridian's stare heats my cheeks. "You look stunning tonight."

I scowl, wishing his approval didn't please me. Wishing I wasn't here, dancing with him, while wearing the dress he commissioned for me. But we dance, and I follow his lead, relying on Nefine's lessons. I try to pull back, to put more distance between us, but Viridian's hand is firm on my back. Holding me in place.

"Would you do me the honor of at least pretending to enjoy my company?" he asks, looking past me.

Trying not to call attention to myself, I follow his line of sight. People peer at us over their goblets, glancing our way between sips.

"Why should I?" I hiss. He's given me no reason to.

"Stealing you from your family, tucking you away in the castle all this time..." Viridian's voice softens. For the first time since I've arrived, he looks at me. As if he's staring into my soul, his amber gaze smoldering with an intensity I haven't seen before. "I know that in your eyes, I am the villain."

He pauses and swallows. Then he spins me around, his hand on my waist securing me to him after my twirl.

Some of the guests watch us through shrouded eyes, others with curiosity. Some even look my way with envy written all over their faces.

Viridian's voice brings my focus back to him. "But this marriage is so much more than you know. Like you, I didn't want this. But you and I have no choice. There are forces greater than either of us that are beyond my control."

"The gods?" I ask, my voice harsh. "I haven't forgotten Theelia's blessing." How could I, when it ruined my life?

Viridian stays silent, leveling his expression. Maintaining decorum, as a crown prince should. To any onlookers, we're simply a couple dancing.

Those in the crowd watching us finally look away, distracted by waitstaff serving small delicacies and more wine.

I start, "Your Highness—"

"Viridian," he interjects, eyes locking with mine. "Please. Call me Viridian."

"Fine," I grumble. "Viridian. If I am to be your bride, then you should be honest with me. Why am I here?"

"To marry me," he says, evading my question while we dance.

"That's not what I asked, and you know it."

"You're right," he concedes, turning his face from mine again.

"Then tell me."

He twirls me again, the music humming in my ears much louder than it should be.

"*Viridian.*"

"Has anyone told you how stubborn you are?"

Simmering, I glower at him.

"You forget, Little Fawn, that this is all a game." With Virdian's hand on my waist, we glide across the floor. "We must play our cards right. I will answer your questions. All in due time."

He flashes me a polite smile, but it does little to hide the tension that still gathers in his jaw. Though it's not anger—that much I can tell.

It's much closer to fear or worry.

Concern pangs in my chest. For a moment, I forget my hatred for the male before me.

Instead, I almost want to wrap my arms around him. To hold him close.

He takes an abrupt step back. I do the same, banishing the thought from my mind.

What's wrong with me?

A momentary lapse of judgment is all. And it won't happen again.

I'll make sure of it.

Viridian bows to me, and then I curtsy before him. I know what Nefine would say if she were here. I should stay at Viridian's side tonight.

That is what people will expect of me.

But I don't care.

I wait for him to leave the dance floor, and when he does, I march into the sea of guests.

Waitstaff circulate with goblets of wine. As one passes me, I grab a goblet and immediately bring it to my lips.

Maybe the drink will wash this night from my memory. All I know is that I need to get away from Viridian.

I take several, greedy gulps, draining my goblet. Placing the empty goblet onto the tray carried by another servant, I take a deep breath.

I only make it a few steps closer to the exit before the dark liquid muddles my thoughts.

That's strange. Normally, wine doesn't hit me this quickly.

My head feels heavy, and I feel myself following in the direction it leads, swaying like I'm standing on a ship. A thick fog takes hold of my mind, and I find myself acting on pure instinct—however little of it remains.

I stumble my way through the throng of partygoers and into the hallway just outside the ballroom. My legs wobble, and the ceiling seems to elevate.

People I don't recognize—servants, I think—flock to me.

"Miss! Are you alright?"

I must really look unwell—two faces loom before mine, their mouths tight with concern. Though, they look awfully similar. Brothers, perhaps?

"Miss, can you hear me? Miss?"

Two hands wave in front of my face. Or perhaps it's the same hand? I can't tell.

"What is the meaning of this?"

The servants merge when he drops into a bow. "Your Highness."

Viridian's—at least I think it's his—angry voice sounds dulled, even though he's not far from me. "I told you that she wasn't to be served the wine, did I not?"

The servant gushes his apologies, though I can't make out the words. Perhaps I'm not paying attention. I'm *not* paying attention, am I? Or is it the wine?

"Viridian, please," I swat at him. "I'm a grown woman. I can have wine if I so choose."

He frowns. "Not this wine, Little Fawn."

"Don't be ridiculous. All wine is good wine."

"Not this one," Viridian repeats, firmer this time. "Not for you."

I only scowl at him. "You're no fun."

"It's *fae* wine," Viridian grumbles. Pinching the bridge of his nose, he sighs. "Gods above. How much did you drink?"

"A whole goblet." I giggle like a child who knows she's done wrong.

He curses under his breath.

"Come now." Viridian scoops me up and cradles me to his chest. "Let's bring you upstairs, shall we?"

"You're not my keeper," I slur. "I can take care of myself."

"And you're not yourself. You need to come upstairs."

"Upstairs?" I whine. "But I'm not tired."

"You will be in a moment."

"I won't," I protest.

He ignores me and starts down the hall.

My skin is hot, little fires spreading everywhere his fingers touch. Even through my thick gown. The fabric is too hot against my skin, and more than anything, I want it off. And I know I shouldn't, but all I can think about are his hands on my body.

All the naughty places I would rather have them instead.

I must have said that out loud, because Viridian's pupils dilate.

"The wine has gotten to your head," he says, his voice rough and gravelly.

Now it's my turn to frown. "You don't want me?"

"Oh, believe me, Little Fawn," he growls, voice rumbling in his chest. "I want you. Desperately. But when I have you for the first time, it'll be when you accept me as your mate."

"Mate?" I ask. Perhaps the wine really is getting to my head.

"Yes." Possessiveness laces his words. "Mate."

Before I know it, we reach the top of the main staircase, and round the corner to my bedchamber.

Shifting my weight slightly, Viridian opens my chamber door and brings me inside. He kicks the door shut behind him and moves farther into the room. Lowering me onto my bed, his hand slips up my back to set me down gently.

"Stay there," he commands, turning to the wardrobe.

My limbs seem to sink into the mattress, heavy like *gohlrunn*. I do as he says.

Viridian pulls something from the wardrobe and then faces me.

Slowly, he takes my hands and pulls me up into a sitting position. He kneels on the bed behind me and undoes my corset, pulling it off. Then, he helps me out of my sleeves, and pulls the gown off, past my feet.

I know I should feel something. Embarrassment, desire, *something*. Instead, my mind is foggy, wiped clear of any coherent thought.

But maybe he's right. Maybe I am tired.

Though I'll never admit it.

Viridian pulls my nightgown over my head, adjusting it until my arms are through the sleeves and the skirt covers my body.

"Lie down," he says, grabbing the edge of my blankets.

I fall back into the pillows. My eyelids droop, weighed down by drowsiness.

"I'm only doing this for me, not you," I say. My voice is dulled by the fatigue pulling at the edges of my vision.

Viridian rolls his eyes with a soft chuckle. "I wouldn't dare assume otherwise."

He tugs the blankets over me and tucks them under my chin. My eyes close. I feel him linger, his face inches from mine.

I think he might kiss me.

I think I want him to.

But he doesn't. His fingers graze my cheek, and he brushes my hair out of my face. Then he pulls away, the closeness of him replaced by a cool breeze.

The mattress groans when he stands. I just barely hear my chamber door open and close before sleep overtakes me.

CHAPTER THIRTEEN

M Y HEAD KILLS.

I roll over when the morning light cuts through my window. It stings my eyes, jabbing my skull.

My ladies' maids flow into my room. I groan.

"Good morning," Tiffy chirps. Her expression tightens when she sees me. "Oh, Miss... You—shall we leave you?"

Yes, I want to say.

"We can tell His Highness that you're unwell today," Tiffy continues when I don't respond.

"No," I grumble, mustering the energy to sit up. If I stay in bed all day, Viridian will know that he was right about the wine. The thought of denying him that pleasure is enough to motivate me. "That won't be necessary."

Tiffy eyes me up and down. "Are you sure? You look dreadful, Miss."

I press my lips together to stop myself from saying something rude. "Could you help me look less dreadful?"

"I'll do my best," she says, giving me another once-over.

I exhale. Perhaps I should have stayed in bed today.

Tiffy washes my face, braids my hair, and dresses me. When she finishes, she steps back.

"Much better," she assures me. Her words are much too cheery and over-emphasized, that I know she's only trying to make me feel better.

"Oh gods," I mumble, wiping my face with both hands. "Still that bad?"

She winces. "Um, well, yes. But don't worry," she adds quickly, "with a day's rest, you'll be good as new!"

"Yes," I say, purposefully avoiding the mirror. "You're right."

Perhaps a day's rest and a little help from the gods themselves, I think dryly. My abdomen lurches. I feel as awful as I look.

Tiffy bows, and then she and the other ladies' maids exit.

I emerge not too long after them and make my way to the kitchens in search of something to eat. Toast should do nicely for my uneasy stomach.

When I get there, the kitchens are bustling with servants. Lymseia is here, too, spreading some kind of fruit jam onto a slice of bread.

"Miss Thurdred." She bows her head. "How are you this morning?"

"All right," I tell her.

"I bet." She smirks. "The wine will do that."

I sigh, pinching the bridge of my nose. "You heard about that?"

"I did." Lymseia laughs. "Don't worry. Viridian only told me to keep an eye on you. No embarrassing details, I swear." She motions to the bread and jam. "Want some?"

"Yes, please," I say.

Lymseia cuts a slice and adds a generous helping of jam before handing it to me.

I take it. "Thank you." Sinking my teeth into it, I find the bread is still warm from the oven.

"That pairs quite nicely with Lydia's herbal tea blend," she says, gesturing to one of the women behind her. "It's the only cure for wine-induced headaches."

My lips curve into a half-smile. "Speaking from experience, are we?"

"Oh, yes." Lymseia nods, emphasizing the motion. She leans forward, eyes glinting with mischief. "I'd say it's a mistake I've only made once, but that would be a lie."

I snort, throwing my head back. "I'm shocked to hear this from the Captain of the High King's Guard," I say, feigning surprise.

Lymseia holds up both of her palms. "It does come as quite a shock, doesn't it?"

We laugh and both take another bite of bread.

"How did you become Captain of the High King's Guard?" I ask, and my tone shifts, becoming more serious. "You're a Lady."

"Well, as the second-born, I had more freedom to forge my own path," she says. "As heir-apparents, Myrdin and Viridian's courses have been charted since birth. For Myrdin, to one day become Head of House. And for His Highness, to become High King."

Her words strike a chord within me. I've always thought of the noble fae as pretentious, that they couldn't want for anything. That they led easy lives, free of restrictions.

I'd never considered that such luxury could also come with chains.

Lymseia glances at me before taking another bite of bread. She swallows. "My older sister, Vestella, shares that burden. So, when I came of age, I chose to train as a warrior. My predecessor took me on as her apprentice. When she retired, the High King appointed me as her successor at her recommendation."

My voice softens. "What happened to her?"

"You need not worry. She's not dead," she says, waving me off. "She simply decided she'd served the crown long enough."

"Oh," I say, adopting a more light-hearted tone.

Amused, Lymseia raises her brows. "Did you think we served until we died?"

"No," I lie. Embarrassment heats my cheeks, and I rub the back of my neck. "Not at all."

Lymseia chuckles. "We're not barbarians, Miss Thurdred."

"Of course not," I shoot out. "I didn't mean to—"

"It's all right." Lymseia pats my arm. "Truly." She shoves the last of her bread and jam into her mouth, in a way that strikes me as very unladylike, and sets the used butter knife on top of a pile of dirty dishes.

"I must be off." She turns back to me and points to my bread. "Enjoy."

BY DINNERTIME, I feel much better. Surprisingly, my headache is nearly gone, with only faint traces of pain left. The thought of food is appealing now, and my stomach grumbles like it should at this time of day.

I arrive at the great hall, and as per usual, Viridian waits for me alone.

"Why doesn't His Majesty dine with us?" I ask, peering at him.

Viridian's movements slow. "He prefers to dine alone, in his chamber."

Raising a hand to my mouth, I think back to what I saw in the East Tower. How could High King Vorr dine in such filth every night? The thought alone is enough to have my stomach threatening to empty itself.

"Has he always done that?" I force myself to banish the image from my mind and continue eating.

"Ever since my mother's death."

His words hang between us.

His Majesty started dining alone after the High Queen's death. That must also be when he stopped attending balls.

If that's true, then both must share a common cause.

Perhaps the High Queen's death is to blame. Before I saw the East Tower, that would have been enough to explain the High King's withdrawal from society. But now, something tells me more than just the High Queen's death alone is at the heart of it. What turned the High King into a recluse? And what role does the decayed condition of the East Tower play in all this?

"I'm sorry," I tell Viridian at last. "That sounds lonely."

"It was." He looks at me, meeting my eyes. The corners of his mouth perk up. "Though, I'm not so lonely now."

The way he looks at me rustles the butterflies in my stomach.

My gaze drops to my food, and I move it around with my fork.

Neither one of us speaks for a moment. I feel as though I should say something, but no words come to mind.

"Tell me what's on your mind," Viridian finally says.

I push away my finished plate. My voice constricts, taut with accusation. "There's something you're not telling me."

He leans back in his chair, dark brows knitted together. Though, something tells me he expected this.

"Not here. Walk with me." Viridian rises to his feet, motioning his head to the door.

I stand, falling in step at his side.

We walk out of the great hall and down the corridor until we reach one of High Keep's smaller libraries. When we arrive, a human servant dusts the shelves.

She averts her gaze when I look at her. Like she would with one of the noble fae.

I'm not married to Viridian, yet the servants still treat me as if I were. I'm not fae, but to them, it seems like I'm not fully human either.

The thought leaves a sour taste on my tongue.

Viridian's voice is reserved. "Leave us."

The maid retracts her feather duster from the bookshelves and bows before making her exit.

"You told me you'd answer my questions." I cross my arms, staring Viridian down once we're alone. "Now answer them."

"What is it you'd like to have answered?"

"Why am I here, Viridian?"

"You are here to marry me. On that, I was forthcoming." He pauses, touching the tips of his fingers to his chin. "What I still cannot seem to understand is why my father is so intent on this marriage, seeing as you're not fae of noble blood."

I scowl and lift the crown of my head. "Yes, I can't imagine why you'd ever want a common, *human* bride."

Viridian's gaze meets mine. He lowers his hand from his face. "That's not—I only meant—"

My tone goes cold. "I know what you meant."

He pauses, looking away from me. Those amber eyes flare. The way he stares at the floor makes me think that he'd burn a hole through the stone, if that were possible.

"I know that you think I'm just like the rest of them." He purses his lips, furrowing his brow. "And I know you won't believe me when I tell you that I'm not."

"Of course I don't," I shoot out. Everything he's done comes crashing into me all at once—that night in the stables, the guards at my childhood home, seeing Loren in that cell, the locks on my chamber door. "From what I've seen, you *are* just like them."

He just stares at me for a moment. Hurt flashes across his face, as if what I've said wounds him, somehow. He opens his mouth as if to say something, but closes it and tenses his jaw instead, the muscles flexing.

"The Heads of House all know something," Viridian continues, ignoring my remark. "Something they refuse to acknowledge." He shakes his head while he speaks, as if he can't wrap his mind around it. "I've consulted the royal historian, skimmed the recorded texts, but whatever it is, it's been well concealed."

His words pique my curiosity, and I tell myself that's the only reason my resentment subsides.

"The East Tower..." I murmur. Whatever secrets Viridian is looking for, they must be there.

"The East Tower?" Viridian echoes. "You've been to the East Tower?" His eyes widen, as if he's putting the pieces together. "Your run in with the guard... You *were* in the East Tower, weren't you?"

"Yes," I say, thinking back to what I saw there. "You haven't?"

I know that no one but the High King and his personal guards are allowed in there, but seeing as Vorr is his father, I would've thought that he'd broken the rules once or twice. That his curiosity would have gotten the better of him, like mine did.

"No," he says, like he's never even considered it. "It's forbidden."

I swallow. "Viridian, it's—"

He doesn't let me finish.

"Show me."

CHAPTER
FOURTEEN

"WHAT ABOUT the High King?" I ask, quickening my pace to match Viridian's stride. "Won't he catch us? Or the guards?"

"No," Viridian tells me, looking straight ahead. "My father's not here. Nor are his guards."

"What? What do you mean he's not here?" I shake my head, struggling to understand. "Our engagement ball was only last night."

"I'm well aware," he growls. "It appears that my father slipped away from the castle grounds after he'd done his kingly duties as host."

"He left after greeting the guests? Why?"

"I would love to know." His voice is barely above a simmer.

"But—"

"He won't lie to me anymore." Viridian looks at me now, amber eyes blazing like fire. "I won't let him."

"Viridian..." My voice trails off. We approach the entrance to the East Tower. Turning my face from his, I slow to a stop. "You won't want to see this."

"That is all the more reason for me to see it." Even though I can't see him, I can feel the intensity of his gaze heating my cheeks. "And I don't want to do this alone." His voice softens, and I can't help but face him now. "Please, Cryssa."

I swallow. My name sounds like a plea on his lips.

No one has ever said my name like that before. This is the first time Viridian has ever said it.

To him, I've only been Miss Thurdred. Or Little Fawn.

"Please, Cryssa."

I think of my own father. If I were in Viridian's place, I would want to know. I would want the truth.

I hear his voice in my head again.

"Please, Cryssa."

How can I deny him this?

"All right." I nod. "Brace yourself."

Viridian nods and faces forward. I enter first, leading him down the hall. Every fiber in my body urges me to quicken my pace, to pass through this horrible place as quickly as possible. But I don't. I move slowly, glancing over my shoulder from time to time to watch Viridian.

His eyes roam the walls, the floor, the moth-eaten carpet. His face twists, dark brows furrowed. He reaches out to run his fingers along a large crack in the wall, but brings it to his nose once the rot sets in.

Viridian's shoulders tense, but he doesn't say anything.

I continue onward, until I reach the spiral staircase at the base of the tower.

I pause. "The worst of it is up here."

"Very well." Viridian takes a deep breath, clenching his jaw. He motions his hands forward, as if to say, *"Onward."*

We ascend the stairs, just as slowly as our trek through the hall. I step aside once we reach the top. I stay back, but Viridian moves deeper into the chamber. He crosses his arms, mouth tight, like he's holding his breath. I turn away.

Viridian's footsteps take him farther from me. I look his way and find him inspecting the array of leather gloves on the table.

"How..." he murmurs, shaking his head with disbelief. "There is magic here. Dark magic."

"How do you know?" I step forward.

"I can sense it."

"Sense it?"

"It's buzzing in the air all around us." He furrows his brow, as if he can't wrap his mind around my confusion. "You can't feel it?"

"No," I say.

I'm not like you, I want to add. *I'm not fae.*

It's times like these that I'm painfully aware of that fact. I know very little of magic, but I know most fae, especially noble fae, are attuned to magic and can channel it. Humans, on the other hand... It's rare for humans to harness magic of any kind.

"Oh." He averts his eyes.

Is he looking down on me? On my feeble humanness? Does he feel as though he's said something wrong? When it comes to him, I can't tell. He masks his emotions well, to the point that it makes him difficult to read.

"Well, there is," he adds, arms tense at his sides.

Dark magic? Here? I press my lips together. I didn't expect this. How could I have expected this?

"Who would have—"

"I don't know." Viridian's words are clipped. His eyes linger on me for a moment longer than I'd like. Is that an accusation I see in them?

"I'm not to blame for this," I shoot out. My defenses come up, sharp like steel. Since I'm human, he must know I can't use magic. Still, he doesn't trust me, and I sure as hell don't trust him. Because of that, I can't help but think he's suspicious of me. Like I am somehow to blame. Perhaps I was wrong to help him.

"Cryssa, I—I know." Seeming worn out, he takes a breath and closes his eyes. After a moment, he opens them, and I can see the unspoken apology in his expression.

I unclench my jaw, but my walls don't come down. Not all the way. I can't keep letting my guard down around him.

"You won't find answers here." I cross my arms.

Viridian sighs and wipes his face. "I'm quite aware."

Neither one of us speaks for a moment.

"And we're not going to find answers standing here," I say bluntly.

He pinches the bridge of his nose. "Then what would you suggest?"

"We won't find answers *here*," I say, "but commoners talk. If there are any answers, they'll be outside the castle walls."

Viridian's eyes fall to the floor. He purses his lips as if he were mulling over the thought.

Then, he looks up at me. "How do I know that this isn't all part of some plan to escape?"

"You don't," I tell him. "But you know I'm right."

He presses his mouth into a fine line and levels his gaze. If the royal historian and records were a dead end, then he has no other leads. I *am* right, and he despises it.

"Fine," he grumbles. "We leave tonight."

"What of the guards?" I protest. "We have to tell someone."

His lip curls, venom spilling from his mouth. "If the High King can slither away unannounced, then so can we."

"What about appearances?" I cock my head. "People will talk when they find out we're gone."

Viridian's voice loses its edge and is much lighter now. Calmer. More calculated. "Myrdin and Lymseia will tell them that I've taken you on a romantic getaway."

"Oh, will they now?" I lean back, amused. "And where is it they'll tell everyone we've gone?"

"That depends. Where would you like to go, Little Fawn?"

"I've heard the food in the Copper Court is to die for and that the fjords of the Silver Court are beautiful."

"Hmm," Viridian says, stroking his chin. "Visiting both would be quite the trip. Pick one, for now. Whichever one we don't get to this time, will be our next hypothetical destination."

The choice between delicious food and beautiful views is an easy one.

"Copper."

Viridian smirks. "Then that's where they'll think we are."

I almost feel the urge to smile.

We're not really going to the Copper Court, I remind myself. *And we won't be going on any future trips together.*

I still plan to escape. I will find Loren and set him free. After that, I'm not so sure what I'll do. But I won't be here.

My mouth tightens.

The thought doesn't ring true like it used to.

"Come," Viridian says, motioning for me to follow.

"Wait," I say. "There are some things you should know first."

He stops and turns around to face me.

"A mining sickness is sweeping the land," I tell him. "Miners are dying, and the metals are disappearing."

"What?" Viridian steps forward. "How did you learn

189

this?"

"I heard about the sickness before I left home. Miners my father works with—well, used to work with—were falling ill and dying every day." I wrap my arms around myself. Worry for my father and Acantha tightens my chest. Not knowing how they are—if they're well, or if they're safe—eats me up inside.

He reaches for me, cupping my elbow. "I'm sorry. I didn't know."

"How could you?" I ask. My voice sounds empty, but not bitter.

"I should have made it a priority to find out." Viridian's resolve takes hold on his face.

My eyes find his, and he holds my gaze. I believe him.

"As for the metals disappearing," I continue, looking away, "I overheard the High King speaking with some Heads of House."

Viridian's eyes widen. "This should have been discussed with the council."

"The High King said he would discuss it with the council," I say, recalling what I heard. "Did he not?"

"No." Viridian's anger returns to his expression. "He did not."

"Do you... Do you think it's all connected to the dark magic?" I ask.

"I don't know." Viridian seems to sink deeper into himself. "It's entirely possible."

My heart rises to my throat. If they are all connected, that means whatever dark magic has its hold over the High King is the same dark magic that's killing miners. The same dark magic that puts our livelihood at risk. That threatens my father's life.

Now, there is so much more at stake.

And I'm just as desperate for the truth as Viridian.

He must know it, because he gestures for me to follow him again. "Come. Let's see Myrdin and Lymseia."

"YOU WERE IN the East Tower?" Lymseia's eyebrows rise. "You know it's forbidden. Mischief, rule-breaking... I thought I might see this from you," she says, pointing a finger at me, "but not from *you*, Viridian Avanos."

"Lymseia!" Myrdin gasps. "You cannot speak like that to—"

"I don't care who he is," Lymseia snaps, jabbing a finger into Viridian's chest. "*He* disobeyed the High King."

Myrdin opens his mouth.

"Enough," Viridian bellows, power rippling from

him. "I went into the East Tower. That's the end of it."

Lymseia clamps her mouth shut, annoyance brewing in her eyes and clear on her face.

"I take it that's part of the reason you called us here," Myrdin says, keeping his voice even.

"Yes. Cryssa and I are leaving High Keep," Viridian says, like it's non-negotiable. "Tonight."

"What?" Lymseia's voice cracks like a whip.

"It won't be for long," Viridian explains, holding up his palms. "A day or two at most."

"Why?" Lymseia crosses her arms, her upper body rigid. "You owe us that."

Viridian leans his head back and takes a deep breath. "There's dark magic in the East Tower."

"Dark magic?" All the irritation leaves Lymseia's voice. Her face pales.

Myrdin touches his fingertips to his temple.

"Yes," I interject. "Whatever it is, we think it's infecting the land, too."

"An unknown sickness is killing miners," Viridian continues, "and if that wasn't already bad enough, the mines are drained of metal."

"How could the council not know of this?" Myrdin's brows knit together.

"Because my father didn't tell the council," Viridian

says, voice hardening. "He's hiding something. And I fear whatever it is will be our ruin."

"You're leaving to find answers." Understanding crosses Lymseia's face, relaxing her mouth. "Where will you go?"

"Into the city," Viridian says. "Cryssa believes we may learn something from the people's gossip."

"You'll be very exposed out in the city." Lymseia's steel gaze flicks to me and then back to Viridian. "Are you sure she can be trusted not to run?"

I tighten my mouth. Her distrust doesn't surprise me. Nor does it offend me. She has every right to be suspicious of my loyalty. We're not friends.

Yet.

Yet?

No. There is no "yet." I won't be here long enough for that. I'll help Viridian get his answers, and then I'm leaving.

That's still my plan.

Isn't it?

"Yes." Viridian's voice is firm. "I trust her."

My lips part in surprise. I look at him with my brows raised.

He doesn't look at me, still focused on Lymseia.

"What do you need from us?" Myrdin asks, eyeing

her.

"People at court will talk once they realize we're gone," Viridian says. "We need you to answer their questions. Tell them I've surprised Cryssa with a romantic getaway to the Copper Court."

"Where in the Copper Court?" Myrdin asks.

"Not Redbourne," Viridian reasons. "If word gets out, Uncle will know we weren't there."

"My thoughts exactly," Myrdin agrees. "You can't go to Redbourne and not visit my father."

"Why not?" I ask.

Myrdin turns to me. "It would be rude not to visit the Head of House when visiting his home city."

Lymseia wrinkles her nose. "Etiquette."

I laugh.

"We'll say you're north of the city," Myrdin says. "Near the border, somewhere quiet."

"Excellent," Viridian muses. His attention shifts. "Lymseia?"

"Yes," she groans. "We'll tell anyone asking where you are that you're out frolicking on a romantic getaway north of Redbourne. All right?"

"Very well." Viridian nods, looking as if he were far from here.

Myrdin places a hand on Viridian's shoulder. "Find

out what's happening. We'll be here when you need us."

"Will do." Viridian dips his head. "Thank you. Both of you."

"You can thank me by staying out of trouble," Lymseia says, putting her hands on her hips.

Viridian only grins, rolling his eyes.

CHAPTER FIFTEEN

MEET VIRIDIAN in the royal stables. He wears a dark cloak with the hood pulled up over his head.

Lifting the hood of my own cloak over my head, I suppress the memories it raises. I don't want to think about the stables back home in Slyfell. Or how far I've fallen.

He rests his hand on a midnight stallion, holding the reins. It only takes me a moment to remember the horse's name—Nightfoot. Seeing him again for the first time in weeks, I remember how beautiful Nightfoot is, but I keep that to myself.

When Viridian sees me, he steps forward, hand outstretched.

I approach slowly, looking at it. "Which horse will I take?"

He pats Nightfoot's ebony coat. "This one."

"What about you?"

"I'll also ride this one."

I swallow. "I can ride alone."

"Can you?" Viridian arches a brow. "You know how to ride?"

I simmer, turning my face.

"That's what I thought," he says. Is that triumph I hear? Perhaps I'm imagining it. Either way, it makes my face hot with anger. "We'll ride together."

I move to mount the horse, ignoring his outstretched hand.

I secure my foot in the stirrup and attempt to swing my leg over the horse. My dress limits my movement, my skirts bunching. I try to lift my leg again, but all I end up doing is fighting with the fabric.

Strong hands grip my rear and lift me up onto the saddle. Once I'm up, I swing my leg over the horse. My skirts gather around my knees, but I don't care if it's unladylike.

Viridian gets up behind me and sits so his chest is

pressed to my back.

"I didn't need help." I scowl, even though he can't see my face.

"You could have fooled me," he says, sarcasm coloring his tone.

"I had it under control."

"Your pride will recover, I'm sure."

I clutch the saddle and deny him the pleasure of a response. But Viridian only chuckles and urges Nightfoot forward, applying slight pressure with his legs as he does.

"What is so amusing?" I ask, letting my aggravation show.

"You."

"What about me?"

Viridian only laughs. "I fear you'll bite my head off if I tell you the truth."

"Tell me," I demand, quickly losing my patience.

"You're rather cute when you're angry with me." He laughs and holds up his hands in surrender. The horse continues to trot. "Please, I beg of you, spare my life!"

I turn around and lightly punch his arm. "It's not funny."

"I find it amusing."

"Of course you do."

"I do."

"Must you always have the last word?" I ask with a roll of my eyes.

"I must."

"Why?"

"Because it vexes you," Viridian quips. I can hear the smile in his voice.

"Because it vexes me?" I echo. "Why must you vex me, Viridian?"

"Because it amuses me."

"Ah, I see we've come full circle now." The last of my annoyance melts away. Now I'm smiling, too.

"Indeed, we have."

My smile widens. Viridian grips the reins, tightening his arms around me. With my irritation subsiding, I'm hyper aware of his body next to mine. His muscled chest to my back, his thighs gripping my rear, arms around my waist, hands within reach of my breasts...

I cough, grateful that he can't see the blush rising to my cheeks.

Viridian shifts in the saddle, and the motion moves his manhood closer to my rear. I arch my back a little in response, subtly pushing myself against him.

He lets out a shallow breath on my neck.

"What are you doing, Little Fawn?"

"Nothing," I say.

"Oh," he says, voice low and gravelly, "we both know it's not nothing."

I swallow. His voice sends electricity rippling down my skin. Warmth spreads through me, hardening my nipples to attention.

Curse this male.

How can his voice alone be enough to arouse me?

He leans forward, tilting his mouth down to my neck. "Are you teasing me, Little Fawn?"

My lips part for my breath. My words lack their usual bravado. "Me? Tease you? Never."

Viridian chuckles, a low and seductive sound. "Mmm, I think you are."

I lick my lips. The warmth of his body and the way it makes me feel has me at a loss for words. His closeness is addicting. All I can think about is him.

How much more of him I want.

"What makes you say that?" I ask at last.

"Well, let's see," he drawls, bucking his hips against me. "Your perfect ass against my erection, perhaps."

I gasp. His hardness presses into my rear. Our clothes are the only thing stopping him from slipping into my wetness.

"Perhaps," I muse, trying to keep my voice even.

"I thought so." I can hear the wicked smirk in his

voice, though I don't dare look back.

"How do I know you're not the one teasing me?" I ask, scooching my hips back more.

A growl catches in Viridian's throat. The sound sends heat trickling down my neck. I shudder.

"Teasing you?" His voice sounds strained.

"Yes," I breathe. "Teasing me with your rubbing."

"Mmm," he purrs. "That would imply that I'm the one with all the power." He touches his lips to my neck. "And we both know that's not true. Don't we, Little Fawn?"

I can't deny that.

We approach the castle gates. Viridian clears his throat and waves to the guards up in the tower. I look down at my hands to hide my flushed cheeks. A moment later, the gate screeches as it rises. Wood creaks when the drawbridge sinks to its lowered position.

We pass under the gate and cross the drawbridge. Nightfoot's hooves clack on cobblestone as we advance further into the city.

I try not to think of how close Viridian is while we ride through the city. To suppress the desire thrumming in my core.

Though, the task proves to be more difficult than I'd like. All the things he whispered in my ear just moments ago still run through my mind.

So, I study the city instead.

Keuron is much different than Slyfell. At home, I'd gotten used to wooden and cobblestone houses with thatched roofs lining gravel roads. Here, I'm surrounded by multistory buildings made from stone bricks and marble, topped with richly colored clay roof tiles. Shops and artisan workshops make up the bottom floor, and I assume living spaces sit above them. Cobblestone streets run between the buildings, connecting every part of the city. It's only sunset, but glowing oil lamps sit at every street corner, giving off warm light.

Even the human districts here are wealthier than the ones back home. It only reminds me of how much we have to lose if the mines run dry.

"Where to?" Viridian asks.

"Let's find a stable," I say. "Did you bring coins?"

"Yes." Viridian taps his pocket.

"Don't do that," I scold him.

"What?"

"Don't tap your pocket. That'll only tell thieves where your valuables are."

"Oh." His voice goes soft. "Thank you."

"Of course," I say. It feels strange to be on the same side. I brush away the thought.

Our alliance is only temporary.

We ride down the main road until we see a sign marking a stable. Viridian tugs on the reins, and Nightfoot slows to a stop.

He puts a hand on the flap of the saddle and swings his leg over Nightfoot to dismount. Then, he turns to face me, holding out his hand.

"Take it, Cryssa."

I look at him for a moment. Letting out a breath, I put my hand in his. Viridian's amber gaze locks with mine when he helps me down.

With my feet on solid ground, I look away and smooth my skirts.

"How often have you gone into the city?" I ask. I don't feel the need to adjust my cloak—no one here knows who I am. They have no reason to.

At least, not yet.

"Like this?" Viridian asks, shoulders raised. "Never."

"What?" I can't help but gawk. "You've never left High Keep? Ever?"

"Yes." His cheeks redden, and he turns away from me.

"But the castle is—"

"I'm aware." His response is curt. I must have hit a nerve.

I lead us into the stable office and approach the

counter. Viridian follows, mouth pressed into a fine line.

Behind the counter, an older man leans against the wall. When he notices us, he corrects his posture.

"Hello," he says gruffly. "What can I do for ya?"

"How much for one horse?" I ask.

"How long would ya need?"

"Until tomorrow evening."

The man names his price. Viridian slips a hand into his pocket and hands over the coins.

Pulling open a coin drawer, the man drops the coins in before closing it again. He calls for a boy, who runs from a door behind him.

"We'll take care of yer horse."

At that, the boy moves to the front door and opens it for us. I go first, then Viridian. The boy trails after us and takes Nightfoot's reins before leading him into the stable.

"All right," I mutter to myself.

Now what?

"I'm following you," Viridian tells me, pulling his hood down farther to cover his face.

"People always gossip in taverns," I say. "Let's eat and then look for an inn to sleep in for the night."

Viridian just nods.

"Now to find a tavern," I murmur, turning. In Slyfell, we have more taverns in the center of the city, near the market. I assume that will be the case here, too.

I look around before deciding which direction to go. Viridian stays close by my side.

People carrying empty baskets pass us on the other side of the road. Women tugging on children's hands, men, and others. After looking both ways, we cross the street to follow them.

Up ahead, there's a large opening between the buildings.

That must be the center of the city.

Viridian's eyes widen in wonder, and he leans his head back to take in more of our surroundings. His steps slow, and he cranes his neck to look up at how high some of the buildings stretch. People move around him on either side, advancing farther into the bustle of the city square.

"Come on," I say.

I take his hand and pull him forward as I walk. He adjusts his pace to match mine, but his focus is still elsewhere. Market stalls packed with goods fill the square. The sounds of wagon wheels rolling on stone and loud voices fill my ears, and the aroma of freshly baked bread graces my nostrils. Street vendors call out prices on each of our sides, holding out their wares as we pass. We saunter by a stall with fresh produce, one with leather goods, and another with fine jewelry. I wave my hand at all of them, so they know we aren't interested in buying anything. That's not why we're here, after all.

I look back over my shoulder. The childlike awe on Viridian's face captivates me. The stone-faced expression I'm used to is nowhere to be found. Even though he's away from High Keep, experiencing the human districts for the first time, he's not reserved, or stiff, the way I thought he would be. For once, it seems like he's completely at ease. Completely himself.

I can't look away.

Viridian's eyes meet mine. He smiles, and it's a wide, toothy grin, lit up like the brightest of stars.

I avert my gaze, a blush rising to my cheeks. Looking forward again, I tighten my hand around Viridian's, leading us through the crowd. We weave through bodies until we reach the road that runs perpendicular to the square. Small shops line the road, and there are some people that linger outside, but it's much less crowded here.

Glancing up at the buildings, I find what I've been looking for.

"In here." I tug his hand and step through an open doorway.

CHAPTER
SIXTEEN

A WARM GLOW from the hearth illuminates the tavern. Some men sit at the bar, where the barkeep fills their tankards. Others sit spread out across the wooden tables, talking over a hot meal.

I step forward but stop when I don't feel Viridian behind me.

Turning to him, I see him standing in the doorway. His smile is gone, replaced by stitched brows and a tight mouth.

"What is it?" I ask, lowering my voice. "Is something wrong?"

"Nothing, it's—" he pauses. "I don't know how to go about this."

"Don't worry," I tell him, waving my hand. "I'll do the talking. I know how humans gossip."

"Well, that, too, but that's not what I meant."

I cock my head. "Then what did you mean?"

"Do we..." he gestures at the tables. "Do we simply walk in and sit down?"

My eyes close briefly when my lips perk up. All my life, I've thought the noble fae were free from fear or uncertainty. That they were so sure of everything. But here he is, the Crown Prince of all Inatia, a fae belonging to one of the five Noble Houses, unsure of himself when entering a tavern.

Perhaps humans and fae aren't so different after all.

"Yes," I say, taking Viridian's hand. "Come with me."

He nods, his rich amber eyes staring back at me. His expression relaxes, though his brows still knit together.

I pull him deeper into the tavern and sit at one of the empty tables near the center.

"I'll be right there," a woman calls, carrying a tray of tankards to a nearby table.

I smile back at her with a wave. Viridian stiffens, watching her as she goes.

"It's all right." I put my hand on his arm. "There

aren't any rules here. No etiquette to keep track of."

At my touch, the tension in his body melts away. His eyes find mine again, and it feels like we're the only ones in the tavern. As if everything else has faded away.

"Hello," the woman says when she approaches our table, wiping her hands on her dirty apron. "What can I get for you two?"

"Two ales and hot meals, please," I tell her.

"Can do." The woman nods. "I'll be back with those shortly."

I smile again before she leaves. Viridian is silent, expression wary.

"Relax," I tell him. "No one here knows who you are."

That seems to ease him a bit.

"Give me your coin purse," I say, holding out my hand.

"Why?" The tension returns to Viridian's jaw. A flicker of distrust.

"I'm not going to take the money and run," I explain. Part of me flinches at his lack of faith in me, but I understand it. If I were in his place, that thought would cross my mind, too. "Contrary to what you might think, information isn't free."

He holds my stare for a moment, before producing

the coin purse from his pocket and placing it in my palm.

"Wait here." I stand, gesturing over my shoulder. "I'll talk to the barkeep."

He nods.

I weave through the tables until I reach the bar. Those men are still there. Now that I'm closer, I see there are two of them, both knee-deep in their ale. The barkeep stands with his arms crossed but lowers them when he sees me.

"What can I get for ya?" he asks.

"Nothing at the moment," I reply, leaning on the bar with my hands clasped. "I just want to talk."

"All right," the barkeep says. His body language tells me that he's used to this.

"My friend's not one for gossip." I keep my voice light, taking out a couple coins. "Got anything good?"

The barkeep's eyes fall to the silver in my hand. "Depends on what gossip interests you."

"Something about the nobles?" I press the coins to the counter. "The High King?"

The barkeep snorts and takes the coins, dropping them into the pocket of his apron. "You're one of those."

"You can't blame a lady for her tastes." I slide my elbows forward. "So, you have something for me?"

"Yes." The barkeep nods, adjusting the towel on his shoulder. "I might."

Withdrawing another coin, I wave my hand toward myself. "Do tell."

The barkeep moves closer to me. "The High King just threw his first ball in years, a night or two ago."

Viridian's and my engagement ball.

"Oh?" I arch a brow, acting like this is new information. "How long ago was the last ball he hosted?"

"A long, long time ago." The barkeep lowers his voice. "Before the High Queen died."

"How long ago did the High Queen die?" Vorr has ruled alone for as long as I can remember.

I give him another coin.

"One hundred years, at least." The barkeep strokes his chin, adding the silver piece to his pocket. "Maybe more."

My eyes widen.

That means...

Viridian is at least one hundred years old.

Fae lifespans.

I knew the fae lived for ages, practically immortal unless they were killed, but knowing how old Viridian is lets me see it in a whole new light.

I ask, "Why's it been so long?"

The barkeep shrugs. "No one knows. The nobles don't talk about it. We only have theories."

"Theories?" I furrow my brows. "What kind of theories?"

He waits. Then I sigh, handing over another silver coin.

"They're all pure speculation. Some say the High King was jealous of the male guests spending too much time with the High Queen and vowed to keep her all to himself. Others think it's a political statement."

"What do you think?" I ask.

"I don't know, and I don't care. What the nobles do and don't do is none of my business."

One of the men at the bar raises his tankard. "Another!"

The barkeep dips his head to me. "That's all I've got."

"Thanks," I say, offering him a polite smile. I tie Viridian's coin purse shut and clutch it tightly with my fist.

I lift my weight from the counter and turn to leave.

"You're a pretty one, aren't you?" a voice slurs. There's a hard grip on my arm.

"Let me go." My voice sharpens.

"Easy there, sweetheart," the drunk man says between sips. "I'm only trying to compliment you."

"Well, I don't want your compliments." I wriggle against his grasp. For a drunk, it's iron tight.

214

"She's feisty, too," another adds, leering at me. "They're fun when they've got some fire in 'em."

"I said, let go of me," I repeat, firmer this time.

The drunk man doesn't release me. He would if he knew what was good for him.

Instead, he laughs.

"We could have some fun with this one," he snickers to his companion.

"Oh, I reckon we'd go for hours." The other smiles, revealing a row of crooked teeth. "Wouldn't we, sweetheart?"

My mouth twists in disgust. I raise my free hand, balling it into a fist.

"Release her." The command rumbles behind me.

The men's drunken laughter goes silent.

"Who do you think you are?" The one holding my arm stands on wobbly legs.

"It doesn't matter who I am," Viridian says, his voice deathly calm. "You're going to let her go. Now."

"You listen here—"

The man's words get cut off by Viridian's hand around his throat. Squeezing.

The drunk man's eyes bulge. He lets me go and plucks at Viridian's hold on him with both hands, to no avail. Face reddening, he pants and gasps for air.

"That's enough!" The barkeep slams his fist onto the counter. "Cut it out or take it outside!"

Viridian gives the man's neck one last squeeze before letting him go. Rage simmers in his expression, but he doesn't say another word.

"Come on." I tug at Viridian's sleeve. Sneering, I say, "It's not worth it."

Reluctantly, he follows me back to our table. Still simmering, his eyes are locked on the drunk men at the bar when we sit.

"Here you are." Our waitress arrives with a tray. She places steaming bowls of stew in front of us, then two ales.

As soon as the tankards are set on the table, the waitress leaves as quickly as she came, beckoned by another patron.

I pick up my spoon and dip it into my stew. It looks to be a simple beef broth with vegetables and some meat.

"Are you all right?" Viridian asks, voice laced with concern.

"I am." I look up at him and return his coin purse. "Thanks to you."

His eyes meet mine, and he holds my gaze. I don't know how long we stare at each other, but I can't seem to tear my focus away from him. It's as if he's the flame, and I am the moth drawn to it.

"It was worth it, you know."

"What?"

"Back at the counter." Viridian's resolve is clear on his face. "You said it's not worth it, but to me, defending you always will be."

"Oh." Warmth blossoms in my chest. I don't know what to say.

"So," he says, changing the subject. "What did the barkeep tell you?"

I brush my hair behind my ear, finally breaking from his stare. "Something about the last ball your fa—" I catch myself just in time to look around to make sure no one overhears us— "the High King hosted."

Viridian cocks his head, raising a dark brow.

"Supposedly, it's been over one hundred years since the last royal ball."

He goes quiet. "Before my mother died."

"Yes," I say. "Something happened there. Something the High King doesn't want anyone to know." When he doesn't say anything, I continue, furrowing my brow. "The royal historians, the nobles... They're hiding something. I know it."

I don't know why, or how, but I'm sure of it.

"Right," Viridian murmurs. "Then we look into the last ball hosted at High Keep."

I nod. "That's our only lead."

"There must be some record of it at the castle," he continues, picking up his spoon. "If there is, we'll find it."

I swallow, directing my attention to my food. Lifting the tankard to my lips, I take a swig of ale.

"Ahh," I breathe. "That's good."

"Is it?" Viridian eyes his tankard with suspicion.

I gesture to his ale with my own in hand. "Try it and see for yourself."

He puts his spoon back down and picks up his tankard. He sniffs it first, still seeming wary of it. Then, he takes a sip. Grimacing, he swallows and sets the tankard down, placing a hand on his chest.

"Is this the first time you've tried ale?" I ask, stifling a laugh.

He wipes his mouth. "It's that obvious, isn't it?"

"Yes." This time I don't hold back my laughter.

Viridian's own laughter blends with mine, a rich and full sound. I can't help but grin.

I cast my eyes down at my stew while we eat, glancing at him every so often. We finish our meals—and I finish both my ale and his—before pushing our emptied bowls to the end of the table.

"Give me your coin purse again," I say, holding out my palm.

This time, he retrieves it from his pocket without question and places it in my hand. I count his gold pieces, taking just enough to cover our bill, and place them on the table next to our pile of dirty dishes. When I'm done, I hand the coin purse back to him.

Then I stand and brush off my skirts. Viridian rises after me, following my lead.

Night has fallen when we emerge from the tavern. The oil lamps at the street corners shine in the darkness, their faint glow enough to light our path.

"Let's find an inn to stay the night," I say. "It's better to ride back in the morning."

"And that will help our ruse," Viridian adds.

"Of course," I murmur. "Our ruse." That we're in the Copper Court on some romantic getaway. I'd nearly forgotten about it. I already dread having to play along with that lie once we return to High Keep.

"Yes." Viridian's voice sounds constricted.

Begging for a distraction, I look elsewhere. A wooden sign hanging across the street blows in the wind, catching my attention. It's exactly what I was hoping to find.

Thank Yoldor.

It seems the God of Good Fortune is on our side.

"There," I say, pointing to the sign. "An inn."

Without waiting for his response, I march ahead and

go inside. There's an older woman sitting behind a counter when we enter, leafing through a stack of parchment with a quill in hand.

"Hello," she says. "A room for the happy couple?"

"Yes, but we're not a couple," I say quickly. "Perhaps two rooms?"

She winces. "I'm sorry—we only have one room left."

I start, "Then we'll go else—"

"We'll take it," Viridian interjects.

"Wonderful!" The innkeeper stands and removes a set of keys from a hook on the wall to her left. She hands them to Viridian, and in return, he gives her a few gold coins.

I glower at him.

"What?" he asks, clearly unaware of what he's gotten us into.

"You'll see," I grumble and cross my arms. It's too late now.

We follow the innkeeper upstairs, to our room. Viridian unlocks the door and steps inside.

"Ah." Realization sets into his expression, mouth curved downward.

I step in after him and look around. The room is cozy—much too cozy for my liking. A full-sized bed adorned with woolen blankets sits in the center of the room, with rickety wooden bedside tables on either side. A similar-looking wardrobe leans against the far wall—quite literally *leans*—and a small cheval mirror stands in the far corner. On the floor is a faded knit rug.

"Yes," I say, drawing out the word. "There's only one bed."

"You take the bed," Viridian says decisively. As if sleeping next to me is the last thing he'd ever do. Am I so horrible that he can't stand to be close to me?

"No, you take the bed," I counter. I know it shouldn't bother me, but his desire to stay as far away from me as possible bruises my ego. "Unlike you, I'll be perfectly fine on the floor."

"That's a lie," he retorts, "and you know it. You're taking the bed, and that's final."

"Ugh," I groan. "You arrogant male. Already making decisions for me?"

"Arrogant?" Viridian echoes, voice raising in volume. "Excuse me for having manners, unlike you."

"Ah yes, the uncivilized human," I drawl, throwing my hands up. My voice goes shrill. "I'm aware."

"That's—that's not—"

"I don't care." My words are tired and lack their usual strength.

Viridian is silent for a moment. So am I.

221

"I only want you to be comfortable, Cryssa," he says at last. "After everything I've done to you... It only seems fair."

That softens my brutish exterior. "I appreciate that." I swallow the lump in my throat. "But it's your first time away from High Keep, and I—I want you to be comfortable, too."

He steps closer to me. Intrigue plays at his lips. "Is that so?"

"Yes," I say, avoiding his gaze. I can feel his stare, hot on my cheeks. "Why don't we share?"

"Share?" he prompts. The pitch of his voice curves up at the end, as if he knows what I'm trying to say, yet still asks the question anyway.

"The bed," I stammer, in some attempt to seem more confident than I actually am. "We can share. I'll stay on my side, and you'll stay on yours. It'll only be for tonight."

I expect him to fight me, to stand his ground and insist that he sleep on the floor.

But he doesn't.

"Very well," he agrees. "We'll share the bed."

"Then it's settled," I say. Jitters consume my stomach, as if summoned from thin air.

Turning my back to him, I remove my cloak and hang it on one of the hooks by the door. At my side, Viridian does the same.

I linger by the hook, while he moves to the bed. The wood creaks under his weight.

When I turn around, my breath catches in my throat.

Viridian lays with his hands behind his head. His shirt is untucked, the thin, white fabric doing little to hide his chiseled physique. His leather pants hang sinfully low on his hips. Even though his shaggy black hair has fallen over his eyes, I can still feel his white-hot stare on my body.

He averts his gaze once he notices me looking.

How can he be so effortlessly beautiful?

Forcing myself to regulate my breathing, I cross the distance to the bed and sit. The cheap mattress gives way under me when I do. I fiddle with the blankets, purely to give my hands something to do, and then blow out the candle at my bedside. My eyes adjust to the darkness, and we lay there, in silence, for what feels like ages.

"I'm sorry," I say suddenly, turning my head to him. "For earlier. I shouldn't have lashed out at you."

Understanding washes over his face. "It's all right. I understand."

"You do?"

"Yes," Viridian says slowly. "Our society teaches us things about those who differ from us. Things that might not necessarily be true. It's difficult to unlearn all the awful things you've been taught to believe. For me, things about humans. For you, things about noble fae."

He takes my hand. "So, thank you, Cryssa Thurdred. For showing me all the things that I've been too blind to see."

I part my lips. But all I can do is stare.

While I came at him with sharpened daggers, he met each of my attacks with grace. With compassion.

With humanity.

Maybe Viridian is someone I can see myself spending the rest of my life with.

I blink, driving the thought from my mind.

No.

I can't forget why I'm here.

For Father and Acantha. For Loren. I still have a life outside of High Keep.

Don't I?

Now, I'm not so sure.

"Goodnight, Cryssa." Viridian's voice snaps me back to reality.

"Goodnight," I murmur as he turns onto his side so his back faces me. I do the same, slipping an arm under my pillow to cradle my head. After pulling the covers up to my chin, I close my eyes.

Relaxing my body, I imagine my limbs sinking deeper

into the mattress.

I should be drifting off into oblivion. Instead, I'm hyper aware of the male lying next to me. Of his breaths. His movements—or rather, lack thereof.

The even pacing of his breath tells me he's asleep. I should be, too.

I press my eyes shut and try to block him out.

But it's only when I let go, when I stop resisting, that I start to feel myself fall.

And as fate would have it, the sound of Viridian's soft breathing lulls me into unconsciousness.

CHAPTER
SEVENTEEN

S UNLIGHT FILLS the compact room when I wake.
I nestle into my pillow, wanting to go back to sleep.

I'm so comfortable.

Maybe these beds are of a higher quality than I
thought. My hands are parallel with my face, clutching
fabric. Then I realize. It's not a pillow I'm resting on.

It's Viridian's chest.

Instantly letting go of his shirt, I lurch upright into a
sitting position. Viridian lays on his back, chest rising and
falling with sleep. His arm still lingers around me, hand

dangerously close to where my lower back was just a moment ago.

How long did I sleep in his arms?

I brush my hair off my face in some effort to make myself look presentable.

Viridian stirs, eyelids fluttering as he adjusts to the light.

"Morning," he says, voice low from having just woken up.

"Morning," I reply, lowering my hands.

He merely looks at me, not bothering to move his arm. Then, he smirks. "So much for keeping to our sides."

I don't have to see myself to know that my cheeks turn a deep red.

"It was probably your fault." Humor fills my voice. I poke his shoulder.

"Is it now?" Viridian challenges, voice light with amusement.

"Yes," I say, letting the grin rise to my cheeks.

"I beg to differ." He sits up, leaning forward so that his face is inches away from mine. "It was *my* side you woke up on, was it not?"

"All part of your ruse." My words slow. Heat trickles over my face.

"My ruse."

"Yes."

I swallow. Abruptly, I stand and back away from the bed.

"We should gather our things."

"Yes." He tilts his head and presses his lips together.

I approach the door and pull my cloak from the hook, wrapping it around myself. Viridian crosses the room and does the same, adjusting his hood so it covers more of his face.

"Are you ready?" he asks.

"Yes." I nod.

Even though I only want to stay here with him, away from the castle, away from our designated roles, for just a bit longer.

THE RIDE BACK to High Keep is shorter than I thought it would be.

I expected to feel resistant upon our return. That I would feel the same as I did when I first arrived. Hesitant and unwilling to enter.

But I don't.

Instead, I feel oddly relieved. As if I am returning to a place I've come to know.

229

There's a pang in my chest. Have I truly been here that long?

We disembark, and Viridian returns Nightfoot to the stable. Following him inside, we remove our hoods.

Servants bow and greet us as we pass through the main corridor.

Viridian dips his head, acknowledging all of them with a polite smile. I offer a small wave.

Then, he takes my hand.

My eyes widen, and it takes nearly all of my effort not to stare at his hand clasped around mine. Butterflies swirl in my stomach, yet all I want is for them to be chained in iron.

I can feel the servants eyes on us as we pass and I know they see our hands together. I move to pull my hand away, but Viridian tightens his grip.

"Play along," he whispers, his mouth by my ear.

Ah yes. The ruse of the happy couple. Our cover story for our little excursion in Keuron.

I frown at him. He turns his face from mine, beaming.

I do the same, plastering a smile on my face. Dread lines my stomach.

It isn't as difficult to pretend as it should be. Viridian must be a better actor than I am.

"You there," he beckons to the closest servant. "Find Lord Tarrantree and Lady Wynterliff. Tell them to meet us in the first-floor library."

"Of course, Your Highness." The servant bows.

Still holding my hand, Viridian and I move further down the corridor, past the staircase, and toward the first floor-library.

Without warning, he hooks his arm around my waist and pulls me to him. But this time, there is no butter knife between us.

I slam into him, with only my palms to his chest to catch myself.

The intensity of his amber stare steals the breath from my lungs. He parts his lips, filling my head with unholy thoughts.

Thoughts of his mouth on my neck. His tongue on my collarbones.

My breasts.

Is this all part of the ruse?

If so, then he truly is far more convincing than I could ever be.

He smirks, eyes falling to my lips, and then back up to mine.

"Tell me, Little Fawn. Are your thoughts as impure as mine?"

"No," I lie, though my voice is a shell of what it should be.

Viridian clicks his tongue, a dark haze coloring his expression. "I don't believe you."

"Well, you should."

"Mmm, is that so? Why should I believe your words when your eyes are saying something else?"

"And what are my eyes saying?" I ask coyly.

He lowers his face to mine, until our mouths are merely inches apart. "That you crave my touch as badly as I crave yours."

I suck in a breath.

"Is that true, Little Fawn? Do you want me to touch you?"

I can't deny it. Not anymore.

"Yes." Disgust courses through me. I shouldn't do this with him, but I can't seem to stop myself. Why do I want him so desperately?

"Good." He grins, and I hate myself for encouraging him.

I turn my face, but his hand on my cheek stops me. My eyes are drawn to his, and I can't look away.

Molten amber pours from him and into me, melting my core.

Viridian presses his face to my neck and inhales

232

deeply. "You smell divine."

If it's true that fae males can smell arousal, then there's no way I can hide from him.

"If you want me to please you, then you need only say the word." His words only confirm my suspicions.

"There could be others around," I tell him. He seems to have forgotten that. Or maybe he wants them to see. To think we're smitten with each other after our "romantic" time away.

"I don't care." His voice is hoarse, as if he's holding himself back.

Part of me wishes he wouldn't. That he means every word he says.

He moves his leg in between mine and raises his knee to apply pressure to my sex.

I gasp.

Viridian groans in my ear. The sound sends an electric current trickling across my skin.

"Tell me how that feels, Little Fawn."

"So good," I breathe. I'm so aroused now that even the faintest touch to my erogenous zones will be enough to send pleasure flowing through my body.

"That was quick," Viridian remarks, no doubt sensing it.

I blush. My body has never responded like this to a

man. Not even Loren.

Oh gods.

Loren.

In all this time gallivanting around Keuron with his captor, I've forgotten all about him.

Viridian touches his lips to my neck. I let out a breath.

He drags his lips down to my shoulder, then back up again. I grab his arm and squeeze it, so I don't make a noise.

"If only we were alone," Viridian purrs. "Then you wouldn't have to be so quiet."

"Gods," I grind out. Since when was he so seductive?

"The gods are not looking, Little Fawn. There is only me and my mercy."

I bite my lip.

A cough behind us tells me that we have an audience. Footsteps scurry in the other direction.

My heart leaps into my throat.

"Myrdin and Lymseia will be waiting for us," I say, my voice stiffening. "We should stop this."

His hands loosen their grip, but don't leave my body. "Yes," he murmurs, seeming to remember himself.

I slip from his touch, starting down the corridor. Viridian's steps quicken behind me, and he falls in line beside me, keeping his distance.

I peer at him from the corner of my eye. His eyes have narrowed and are fixed ahead. Tensing his arms, he keeps them stiff, rigid at his sides.

Something in him has shifted.

What changed?

I almost think to ask, but the words don't form on my tongue.

My stomach sinks. Perhaps he's merely dropping the act now that there are no servants around to watch us. Somehow, that thought makes me feel so much worse.

When we arrive, Myrdin and Lymseia are already waiting for us. Myrdin sits at the small desk, while Lymseia paces about the room.

"You've returned," Lymseia says when she sees us.

"Yes." Viridian nods. "Thank you for meeting us."

"Of course, cousin." Myrdin's brows furrow. "Your faces tell me you weren't as successful as you would have liked."

"No," Viridian says while glancing at me. "But we did learn something."

"Do tell." Lymseia puts her hands on her hips.

"The talk of the town is of our engagement ball," I say. "And how it's the first ball to be hosted by the crown in a century."

"The people seem to think that something happened

at the last ball." Viridian's voice slows. "Something that turned my father into a recluse."

"You mean..." Myrdin pauses. "Something that happened before your mother died?"

"Yes," Viridian says.

"What do the people think happened at this ball to make the High King wary of the world?" Lymseia asks, crossing her arms.

"Nothing conclusive," Viridian answers.

"Ah." She leans her head back. "Very helpful."

"It's given us a starting point," I say, my defenses rising. "We're not finished."

"Cryssa is right," Viridian says. His support eases my rough exterior. "We must continue searching for the answers."

"Have you given this some thought?" Lymseia asks slowly, as if she were treading with caution. "If your father truly wants these secrets to stay buried, and he finds out that we've been poking around his dirty laundry, we could be arrested for treason."

"Or worse, hanged," Myrdin adds darkly.

My stomach clenches at the thought.

"I have," Viridian says, firm in his resolve. "I won't let any more miners die. My father might choose to do nothing, but that doesn't mean I will. Human families need the metals to survive. They are the backbone of our kingdom." He turns to me, and his eyes instantly find mine. "Without them, we are nothing."

I open my mouth slightly, lips curving into the hint of a smile. His words resonate, striking a chord within me.

Spoken by the future High King of all Inatia. Spoken like a true king, who cares for and protects all of his people. Not only those closest to him.

Viridian's gaze lingers on me for a moment, before turning his face back to Myrdin and Lymseia. "I understand if you don't want to be part of this."

"If you're doing this, then so are we." Lymseia bows her head. "I would follow you into the fires of hell."

"As would I." Myrdin copies her motion.

Viridian places a hand on Myrdin's shoulder, glancing between him and Lymseia. "Thank you."

"Of course," Myrdin says. "For Inatia."

"For Inatia," Lymseia echoes.

"For Inatia." Viridian's words are solid, like the earth.

"For Inatia," I say. For Father and Acantha. For every human family who has lost someone to the mining sickness or risks losing their livelihood if the earth is fully drained of metal.

Viridian looks at me and nods, setting his jaw.

"Well then," Lymseia says, puffing her chest. "Where shall we begin?"

CHAPTER EIGHTEEN

IT'S BEEN DAYS, and the High King still hasn't returned. No one knows where he's gone or how long he'll be away.

Not even Viridian.

He's simmered every night at dinner, scowling into his meal as if it's the reason his father vanished without a word.

He does the same now.

"Viridian," I say. "What is it?"

Though, I already know the answer.

"He's left me to deal with the council," Viridian seethes. Raw power ripples through the room. "The Heads of House all look to me for answers, yet I have none. *He* left me none."

"I know."

While the High King's absence angers him, it only leaves me puzzled. I can't help but think that his father's sudden departure has something to do with the answers we're chasing—the common cause of the East Tower's rot, the mining sickness, and the draining of the mines.

The look on his face tells me that Viridian knows it, too.

He presses his lips into a fine line, hands gripping his fork and knife. "Leave us," he orders, without looking at the guards or servants who wait in a line against the wall.

Silently, they do as he commands. They exit, leaving just the two of us. Alone.

"Have you learned anything?" he finally asks me.

In the time since we've returned, we've been snooping around the castle where we can. For Lymseia and me, talking to servants and trying to listen in on conversations where we can. For him and Myrdin, searching the libraries when they have free time. Though, something tells me that Viridian's been much too busy with the council to do much else.

"No." I wish I had. "Have you?"

"No." A pause. "Myrdin and Lymseia haven't either."

I look down at my half-eaten plate. "We will find something."

We have to.

He sighs. "You're right. I know that."

"But?"

"But I can't help but wonder if there even is anything to be found."

"You and I both know that isn't true," I say. "Not after what we've seen."

The vision of the East Tower flashes in Viridian's expression. "I know." Using a napkin, he wipes his mouth. "What should we do?"

"What we've been doing," I say, turning my attention back to my dinner. "We keep pressing for answers and looking where we can. Something will turn up."

I say the words with confidence that I don't have.

Because the truth is, I'm just as lost as Viridian. But I don't have any other choice but to keep looking.

Please, if you're listening, I pray, to any god that will listen, *guide us.*

Viridian searches my face. "Then that's what we'll do."

MY SLEEP ISN'T kind to me that night.

Images flash before me.

I see my father. Acantha.

Loren.

People are wailing around me. Their grief is so strong, so palpable, that I feel as if I'm drowning in their sea of sorrow.

Slowly, I turn. I cover my mouth in horror.

All around me are holes. Pickaxes strewn about. Some whole, some broken. They're all scattered between the graves.

The grisly headstones span as far as I can see. There are no houses, no farmland, no windmills.

Only graves.

Miners' graves. One by one, claimed by the sickness. Until there were none left.

When I turn back around, Father, Acantha, and Loren are gone.

"Father!" I cry until my voice runs ragged. "Acantha! Where are you?"

I start to run through the graves, reading each one with desperation. Praying I'll find them. Praying they're not in the ground.

"Father! Acantha! Loren!"

"Cryssa!"

"Father!" I shout. "Father, where are you?"

But my father's cry grows faint. "Cryssa!"

"Father!"

I force myself to go faster, pushing myself through the burning in my thighs. I trip. Lifting myself up onto my elbows, I spit the dirt from my mouth.

"Cryssa!" My father's voice is nearly gone.

I move to stand.

And then...

Darkness.

"Hello?" I call out, whirling around. Ebony nothingness surrounds me.

A figure steps out from the shadows.

"Who are you?" I ask. "Step back."

But the figure keeps walking. I move away from it, though no matter how fast I am, it always closes the gap between us.

I freeze. Though, it's not of my own accord. It's as if my feet cling to the earth, even though there is nothing below me.

The figure stands, eerily still.

"Who are you?" I ask again.

The figure's blank face morphs into a masculine one.

243

Pale and angular, with high cheekbones.

I know that face.

Viridian.

Only, the amber of his eyes has been drained, leaving them colorless. Shadows swirl over his face.

"I am Death," Viridian says. But it's not his voice—no, this voice is darker, but not evil. Colder, but not cruel. "And I have come with a warning."

Death?

I shake my head. "This can't be. This is—this can't be."

"Beware, lost golden daughter," Viridian—no, *Death*—says. "Old and ancient magic surrounds you. It is cunning and it is vengeful. When the time comes, you must choose."

"Choose?" I echo. My head swirls.

"Choose life, without love, in a cursed land." Death pauses. "Or choose death in the name of love, and sacred sacrifice."

Choose between life and death?

Cursed land?

Sacred sacrifice?

"What does that mean?" I ask.

But Death is silent.

"What does that mean?" My words become more

frantic. "Am I going to die?"

Death steps back into the shadows.

"Wait!" I cry, running after him. "Wait!"

But he's already gone.

"Cryssa!" Someone calls my name. They sound like they're far from here.

I whirl around, but there's no one there. My breathing quickens, catching in my throat.

I squeeze my eyes shut.

Then I wake up.

"Cryssa," Viridian says gently, with both his hands on my shoulders. "Wake up, Cryssa."

I turn my face to look at him. His brows are stitched together, jaw tight with worry. Then his warm, amber eyes find mine, and all the tension bleeds from his face.

He cups my face, brushing his thumb back and forth against my chin. "You're all right. You're safe."

With his other hand, he wipes my eyes.

Have I been crying?

My impaired nostrils would suggest that I have.

The image of Death flashes in my mind. I shudder and tear my eyes from him.

"Come here," Viridian says, with a newfound tenderness. Gently, he pulls me to his chest and wraps me in his arms.

I close my eyes and breathe in through my nose and out through my mouth.

"Nightmare?" Viridian asks. I can feel the faint rumble in his chest when he speaks.

"Yes."

"Do you want to talk about it?"

When I don't say anything, he speaks again.

"Ah—erm." He pauses, as if unsure how to proceed. More quickly this time, as if jumbled by nerves or awkwardness, he says, "You don't have to, if you'd rather not."

"I think I'd rather not," I say. I don't want to think about my nightmare any longer tonight. Because that's all it is. A nightmare. Nothing more.

"But—" Stopping himself, he closes his eyes and exhales. "As you wish."

Viridian shifts his weight and moves to stand.

The words leave my lips before I can process what I'm saying. "Stay with me tonight. Please."

He turns, tilting his head down to look at me. I think he might say something, but he doesn't. He only nods and lays next to me.

I lift the covers so he can swing his legs underneath them. Then he lays on his back, with an arm extended to me. He doesn't quite reach me, but the gesture positions him in a way that makes him seem open to my touch.

I move my body closer to his and rest my head on his chest. Viridian's arms circle me, with one of his hands stroking my hair.

"Sleep well, Cryssa," he says softly.

I'm asleep before I can respond.

CHAPTER
NINETEEN

VIRIDIAN IS GONE when I wake.

An emptiness permeates me, and I reach my hand out across the mattress where he would have been if he'd stayed. The emptiness is replaced by an ache.

I wish he had stayed.

I sit up and wipe my face, brushing my hair back.

I know it was likely nothing but a figment of my imagination, but I can't help replaying my dream in my head again. Could it be a coincidence that my dream came after praying to the gods for guidance? Was it really Nemos, the God of Death, who spoke to me last night?

Why not Theelia? After all, it's her fault that I'm in this mess. Her fault that I'd been taken from my home and brought to High Keep to begin with.

I stand and cross the room to my vanity table. I sit and look at myself in the mirror.

I expected to see dark circles under my eyes, but I don't. Though, I don't see the old Cryssa staring back at me, either.

I'm not the same girl that was brought to High Keep.

When my chamber door opens, I look away from the mirror.

Tiffy comes in. "Good morning, Miss."

I smile. "Good morning, Tiffy."

I stand and follow her into the washroom, where she and two of my other ladies' maids wash me. I've come to know our routine, and I glide through the motions as if I were dancing.

Perhaps I'm more like a lady than I used to be.

That thought would have distressed the old Cryssa. But now, it brings me a sense of triumph.

Tiffy guides me back to my vanity table to comb my hair.

"Tiffy," I start, glancing at her reflection in the mirror. I know it may be a longshot, but I have to try. "Do you know anything about the last ball hosted by the crown?"

The Heads of House may be tight-lipped, but perhaps the servants still gossip about what happened here one hundred years ago.

"You mean, before your engagement ball?"

"Yes," I say.

"Not much, I'm afraid." Tiffy cocks her head and purses her lips. "But I have heard rumors."

That sparks my interest. "Rumors?"

"Yes." She nods slowly. "My great-grandmother worked as a housekeeper here, at the castle, when the late High Queen was still alive. She told us stories she'd heard from her time in service to the crown."

Adrenaline thrums through me. "Do you remember them?"

"Yes," Tiffy says, pausing briefly as she braids my hair. Her eyes move in the mirror, to the other ladies' maids behind us. They tidy up my bedchamber, and then disappear into the washroom.

"What you share with me stays in this room," I promise, hoping that will ease her fear. "I won't tell anyone what you've told me. Your position here is safe. You have my word."

And I mean it. I'll share what I've learned with Viridian, but I'll keep Tiffy anonymous. I'd never forgive myself if something happened to her because of me.

That seems to loosen her tongue. "It's only servants' gossip, mind you, but..." she hesitates. "Well, people used to say that there was...an unwanted visitor at the last ball. Someone the High King feared."

"Someone he feared?" The High King is one of the most—if not the most—powerful individuals in all of Inatia, politically speaking. And it is common knowledge that the noble fae possess potent magical power, even if no human has ever seen them wield it. Who could be formidable enough to make the High King, a powerful noble fae, fear them? "Did they know who?"

Tiffy shakes her head. "No, Miss. The servants who were there were too afraid to speak of her."

"Her?" I ask.

"Yes," Tiffy says. "All I know is that they described her as a walking storm. They say wherever she went, thunder followed."

"And she brought that thunder to the High King's doorstep," I murmur.

"Yes." Tiffy finishes my braid and drapes it over my shoulder.

"Thank you," I tell her earnestly. "Your story is safe with me."

And Viridian. He has to know.

"Thank you, Miss." Tiffy bows her head.

"Of course." I smile.

The other two ladies' maids emerge from the washroom. I stand, and then they help me into my gown.

All three curtsy before me, while Tiffy and I share a knowing look. They rise and leave my chamber.

But Tiffy's words run wild through my mind.

I need to find Viridian.

If we can learn the identity of this stranger, this woman that even the High King fears, then maybe, we can discover what's at the heart of the dark magic poisoning our land from the inside out.

Swiftly, I exit my chamber, skirts swishing behind me while I round the corner. I'm so focused that I nearly topple into Myrdin.

"Oh, I'm—" I stammer, touching my fingers to my forehead. "I'm sorry, Myrdin, I almost crashed into you."

"No need," Myrdin assures me. "I should have been paying more attention to where I was going." His brows scrunch together. "Something troubles you."

"I'm looking for Viridian," I say. "Do you know where he is?"

"He's locked in a room with the High King's advisers," he says. The tone of his voice tells me he's not at all envious of Viridian's situation.

"I see," I muse. "All of whom are harassing him with questions he can't answer."

"Precisely," Myrdin sighs, pinching the bridge of his nose. Each breath seems to be laced with frustration toward his uncle—who, I often forget, is the High King.

"Have they been targeting you, too?" I ask.

"Unfortunately," he groans. "Though, not nearly as severely as they do to Viridian. I am only Vorr's nephew, after all."

My own aggravation brews. Vorr simply up and left, leaving the burden of running the kingdom to Viridian. And to some extent, Myrdin. Without any warning.

Unless the High King is careless, only something grave would have drawn him away so quickly.

Something connected to the stranger from the ball.

"Where are they?" I ask Myrdin, bringing our focus back to Viridian and his father's advisers.

"The council chamber," he answers. "Across from the first-floor library."

I give him my thanks before taking off down the hall.

I glide down the staircase and round the corner, keeping up my pace until I reach the council chamber. The door is shut, and a mix of masculine and feminine voices sound through the wood.

Crossing my arms, I pace in the hallway.

I lose track of how long I trek back and forth before the door opens.

I pause. A slew of well-dressed fae trail out, and I stay in place, waiting for Viridian.

He emerges last, with a worn look hanging at the edge of his features. But his eyes brighten when he sees me.

"Cryssa. It's—it's good to see you."

"Viridian, I have news."

"News?" He raises his brows. Then, he glances both ways before retreating back into the council chamber. "Come, quickly."

I duck into the room after him, and he closes the door behind me. There's a long table in the center, with chairs positioned all around it. Bookcases filled with stacks of parchment line the back wall between leatherbound volumes.

"What have you learned?" he asks, pulling out two of the chairs.

I sit across from him. I trust him not to expose Tiffy, but still choose to keep her anonymous, just in case. "There was a stranger at the last ball. Someone that the servants were afraid to speak of."

Viridian's gaze finds mine. I hold his stare.

"Someone it's rumored that your father feared, too."

He presses his mouth into a fine line, a pensive look

clouding his eyes. "So, this stranger is the key."

"Yes," I say. "I know it's been helpful thus far, but I don't think we'll learn anymore from gossip."

"Neither do I," Viridian agrees, rising to his feet. "Now, we need to look for a paper trail."

"But how?" I ask. "If your father truly wanted to bury any trace of what happened, he would've had the evidence destroyed."

"That's true," Viridian admits. "But it's nearly impossible to destroy everything. Something must have survived."

I consider his words. "Perhaps."

"I know it, Cryssa." He says it with such strength that it's hard not to be swayed. "And we will find whatever scrap of evidence is left. In fact," he says, moving toward the bookshelves. "I've been meaning to look through the council records."

"The council records?" I arch a brow.

"Yes," he says, looking back at me over his shoulders. "Balls are costly, are they not? The council holds all the records from the royal treasury here, in this chamber."

My eyes widen. I fall into place beside him. "If we can find those, maybe we can find something else. Another lead."

Viridian nods, looking at me. He gestures to the

shelves in front of us. "Shall we?"

"Of course," I say, not wanting to waste another minute.

A smile tugs at his lips, and he turns to the far-right side of the shelves. I do the same, to the far left. I pull out a few leatherbound volumes—detailing supply inventories, servants' wages, even monetary aid dispersed through the five Courts—at a time and bring them to the table, where I leaf through them, scanning the pages. Across from me, Viridian does the same. Every so often, I feel the heat of his stare on my cheeks. Seeming to have a mind of their own, my eyes dart up from the pages to look at him, and then back down, just missing his gaze. Our eyes are like ships passing in the night. It rustles the butterflies in my stomach, and for the first time in years, I feel like a much younger girl again.

"Anything?" he asks, breaking the silence.

"Not yet," I say, while turning another page. "So far, from what I can tell, all I've found are supply inventories."

He huffs. "As have I."

"We'll keep looking," I tell him. "If there is something here, we'll find it."

"Of course." Then he furrows his brow, focused on the stack of parchment in his hands.

I stand, clutching a small stack of heavy volumes, and

return them to the shelf. When I slide the last one back into its place, a piece of parchment slides out from behind it.

Pulling it out just enough to fit my hand through, I reach behind the volume and grab the loose parchment. With my attention fixed on it, I sit back down.

The parchment is small—much smaller than the size of the pages in the volumes or stacks of loose papers.

Upon further inspection, I see elegant calligraphy in the center, with neat, hand-written notes in the margins. The ink has bled through the parchment, making the margin notes illegible. But even though it takes me a while to decipher it, the calligraphy is readable.

It's then that I realize what I'm holding.

"Viridian..." My eyes widen. "I found something."

He looks up from the volume he's reading and stands. He makes his way around the table and stands by me, looking over my shoulder at the piece of parchment in my hands.

I read the calligraphy aloud. "The High King and Queen cordially invite you to High Keep to celebrate the birth..."

Viridian's mouth opens slightly. His face hardens to stone.

"...of the Crown Prince," I finish.

He backs away, with a hand pressed to his mouth.

The last ball hosted by the crown.

"You were there," I murmur, connecting the dots. "You were there when it happened. Whatever it was."

Viridian says nothing, his expression unreadable.

"What is it?" I ask, voice laced with concern.

"Do you..." he stumbles over his words. "Do you think it's my fault?"

"What?"

"That ball was for me," he says, avoiding my gaze. "Do you think I'm to blame for whatever happened there?"

"No," I shoot out. "Of course not. Viridian, you were an infant."

Why would he blame himself?

He nods, though I can tell he doesn't believe me.

"Look at me," I say softly. Closing the gap between us, I gently cup both of his cheeks. "You are *not* responsible for what happened that day. Or the aftermath."

His eyes find mine, deep amber brimming with pain. My chest aches when I see it.

"Please," I say. "Don't blame yourself for things you have no control over."

He searches my expression, and then takes a long

breath. "Thank you."

"For what? I've done nothing."

"You have, Cryssa." His voice is tender. "More than you know."

I hold his stare, knowing my eyes are telling him everything words can't say. An overwhelming desire warms my chest.

And this time, I give in.

Lifting myself up onto my toes, I move my hand to the back of Viridian's neck and bring his face down to mine. I touch my lips to his.

Our mouths lightly brush, at first.

But then, he reaches for my face, holding it between both hands. He deepens the kiss, sliding his hands back, so his fingers stretch behind my ears. Entangling them in my hair, he pulls me closer, lips claiming mine with need.

Fire burns everywhere he touches, and my insides become liquid flame.

His lips part from mine for a moment before his mouth finds me again. Sensation thrums through my body. My hands reach for his chest, grabbing fistfuls of his shirt and tugging him closer. It's as if I've been underwater all this time, holding my breath, and now, I'm breathing air for the first time.

I let out a small gasp.

Viridian breaks from me and takes a step back with his hands at his sides.

I watch him, breathless.

"I... I have to go," he says, catching his breath. It feels good seeing that our kiss has the same effect on him as it does on me. "More meetings to attend."

"That's unfortunate," I say.

"It is unfortunate." Viridian practically growls, looking at me through hungry eyes. "Will I see you tonight?"

"Yes," I tell him.

"Wonderful," he breathes, seeming as if this is the only place he wants to be. "Then I will see you tonight."

With a bow of his head, he leaves me alone in the council chamber.

I close my eyes and touch a hand to my lips.

CHAPTER TWENTY

A LL DAY, I look forward to dinner.
To seeing Viridian again.

Girlish excitement jumbles my thoughts, and tonight, I actually care about how I look. More than I'd like to admit.

I sit at my vanity table while Tiffy styles my hair.

She glances at my reflection in the mirror and then looks back down at her hands, chuckling.

"What?" I ask, arching a brow.

"Pardon my bluntness, Miss," Tiffy starts. "But I'm not used to seeing you be so cheerful. You're like a whole new person."

"Ah." My cheeks flush red. "I'm not either."

"It's a good thing, I'm sure," Tiffy adds, twisting some of my hair around her finger before pinning it to my head. She pauses and lowers her face so it's next to mine in the mirror. "And I'm sure His Highness is just as excited to see you."

"Oh?" I downplay my reaction. But my heart thrums in my ribcage. "What makes you say that?"

"You two have been absolutely smitten with each other since you returned from your romantic getaway together," Tiffy gushes. "Have you noticed the way he looks at you?"

"No," I say, keeping my head still so as not to ruin my hair. "How does he look at me?"

"Like he would do anything you asked," Tiffy swoons. "I would simply melt if a man looked at me the way His Highness looks at you, Miss."

"Oh," I murmur, more to myself than her.

I hadn't noticed *that*.

"Mmhmm." Tiffy nods, emphasizing the sound.

My stomach does a flip. What Tiffy's told me colors my view of Viridian, making him seem different, somehow.

As if there is something between us that wasn't there

before.

He's the same Viridian you know, I remind myself.

But is he? I hated the Viridian I once knew. The arrogant fae prince that ripped me from my home. The one that I thought was forcing me into a life I never wanted.

Now...

Now, he's the compassionate future king. The one that cares for his kingdom and *all* of his people.

And maybe, even me.

I'm not so sure I hate him anymore.

Oh gods.

The thought settles my nerves but doesn't dim the electric excitement I feel coursing through me.

When she finishes my hair, Tiffy helps me into my gown. It's a deep violet, rich in color like that of fae wine. The bodice sits perfectly at my waist, and the A-line of the skirt emphasizes my hips, giving me an hourglass figure.

One of the other ladies' maids hands Tiffy a box. She takes it and opens the lid.

"And now, for the finishing touch," Tiffy says. I try to get a better look in the mirror while she removes something from the box and drapes it around my neck.

I suck in a breath.

Hanging from a delicate gold chain is a beautiful rose.

It's made from a mix of gold and bronze metal strands that have been twisted and intertwined to form the rosebud.

"It's from His Highness," Tiffy tells me, with a knowing look on her face.

I touch my fingers to the rose. Warmth spreads through my chest.

I stand. Gently turning me around so my back faces the larger mirror, Tiffy hands me a handheld one to hold in front of my face. When I do, I get a full view of the back of my head. Tiffy has truly outdone herself—multiple smaller braids join into one large braid that wraps around my head, giving the illusion of a crown, framed by small circular twists of hair pinned underneath.

"Thank you," I tell her earnestly.

"You're welcome." Tiffy bows her head. "Enjoy dinner with his Highness."

I smile, and heat rushes to my cheeks. "I will."

Tiffy and the other two ladies' maids wait for me to leave my chamber first. They follow me out and close the door behind them.

Careful of my skirts, I glide through the corridor and down the main staircase. When I turn the corner toward the great hall, my heart leaps into my throat.

Dinner with Viridian is nothing unusual. It's our daily routine.

But after our kiss in the council chamber earlier, this dinner feels *different*. It feels new and wonderful and exhilarating. As if I were a bird, soaring across the skies with the wind blowing between my feathers.

Pausing, I approach the double doors that lead into the great hall. I close my eyes for a moment and take a deep breath before pushing them open.

I see Viridian instantly.

Sitting in his usual spot, he's replaced his usual attire with a fine, high-collared jacket the color of bronze, with sleeves lined with bronze metal. He wears it buttoned up, save for the top two buttons. His pants are made of the same material and metal lining, and his loose black hair has been combed back away from his face.

I drag my eyes up to his face, only to see his amber stare roaming my body.

His focus slowly trails up my figure, pausing at my waist, and then my breasts, before making its way up to my gaze.

I relish the feeling of his hungry stare on me. It only makes me want him closer.

He stands and crosses the length of the table to reach me. Then, he takes my hand and raises it to his mouth, pressing his lips to it.

"You look..." his voice trails off. "Absolutely

stunning."

"And you…" I drink him in again, not bothering to hide my approval. "You clean up well."

"I'm glad you approve."

Still looking at me, he licks his lips. He glances at the table, as if he were just remembering why we were here.

He strides to my chair and pulls it out for me. "My lady."

Cheeks warm, I sit. "Thank you."

"Of course." Viridian lingers for a moment, before taking his seat across the table from me.

As if on cue, the servants arrive with the first course and place it before us. It's a clear broth, with sliced mushrooms and topped with a delicate herb garnish.

Viridian waits for me to pick up his spoon, mirroring my movements.

I taste my soup, all while holding his gaze.

"So…" I clear my throat. Nerves tighten the muscles around my vocal cords.

"So…?" he echoes, the tone of his voice raised in question.

"That kiss was…" My eyes flick down to my soup, and I bite my lip.

"Amazing," Viridian finishes, as if he were breathless.

"Yes. Amazing." I repeat, looking back up at him. No

one has ever made me feel the way Viridian did with just one kiss. No one.

Kissing him felt so...

So *right*.

As if he were the only one that I was ever designed to kiss.

I know my thoughts sound silly. And that to anyone else, it would seem like I'm acting like a naïve teenage girl. Maybe I am.

But right now, I don't care.

I *don't* care.

"I'm glad." Viridian's mouth breaks into a wide grin, and I can't help but beam at him. This male I once despised. This male that I know I *should* still despise.

I can't find the energy to loathe him.

Not anymore.

We finish our first course, then the next. It goes by all too fast. I don't want this night to end.

Something tells me that Viridian doesn't either.

He rises from his seat and moves toward me purposefully. "Dance with me," he breathes.

"Here? But we don't have music," I say, standing.

"Who says we need music?" He stares at me intently, holding out his hand.

I take it, and he tugs me closer until I'm pressed to his

chest. He rests his other hand on the small of my back, holding me close.

He sways his hips to an imaginary beat. Still holding his hand, I interlock my fingers with his and follow his lead.

I don't know how long we dance like that, gazing into each other's eyes. We don't say much, but we don't need to. Our bodies, our eyes, and our faces tell each other anything and everything we want to say.

Even though no words are spoken, I feel as though I understand him better than I ever have. Perhaps even better than I'll ever understand anyone else.

The realization settles into my bones. Though, I don't fight it. This time, I embrace it. I welcome it with open arms.

There is nowhere else I would rather be at this moment.

With this male.

Viridian steps back and spins me. My mouth parts, the hint of a smile tugging at my cheeks, and I finish the twirl in his arms. He leans forward, tilting his head down into the crook of my neck. Breathing me in. Then his lips brush against my skin, sending shivers trembling through my body.

He pulls away, his eyes still fixed on the soft skin

there.

"Come." He motions his head toward the double doors. "It's late."

I nod. Fatigue weighs down my limbs, and I know I should sleep. But sleeping means that tonight ends.

I don't want tonight to end.

But when Viridian holds out his arm, I take it. He escorts me upstairs to my bedchamber.

"Goodnight, Little Fawn," he says, his voice a soft caress.

"Goodnight," I murmur, my own, a whisper of longing.

Back in my chamber, I peel off my dress and change into my nightgown. Slowly, I take my hair down. Unpinning my updo, my auburn locks start to tumble freely over my shoulders.

I glance at the wall while I work. Knowing his room shares a wall with mine, I wonder how Viridian feels to lie so close to me, yet so far, at the same time. Does he wish he were in my bed, holding me, the way I do? Is he looking at the wall that separates us, thinking the same things?

Moving to my bed, I sit, still removing the braids from my hair. When I'm finished, I lay back onto my pillow and rest my hands on my abdomen.

Closing my eyes, I imagine Viridian's lips on my neck.

CHAPTER
TWENTY-ONE

A BRIGHT HAZE distorts my vision.

I'm back in Slyfell, at the stables I'd snuck out to so many times. Someone is kissing me, his hands roaming up and down my body, driving me wild with the faintest touch. My body throbs with need. I throw my head back, my mouth forming an "O" shape. All I see is a head of dark hair while my lover moves his mouth down to my neck. Licking and sucking, he lightly nips at my skin with his teeth.

My breath quickens. He keeps going, moving his lips down to my collarbone, and then to my shoulders. I can barely contain my moans, my breath escaping from my parted lips.

My lover's arms slide down my back. His hands find my thighs, grabbing my rear when he picks me up. Instinctually, I wrap my legs around his waist as his mouth finds mine. His tongue claims my mine for his own, and I melt against him.

He presses me against the wall, pinning me in place with his hips. One of his hands stays under me to support my weight, while the other grabs my throat. Lightly squeezing.

Molten desire thrums through my core, heating me from the inside out until I'm hot to the touch.

"Please," I beg, panting. "I need you. I need you *right now.*"

My lover makes quick work of his pants, and enters my needy, needy sex with one rough thrust. I gasp, digging my fingernails into his back.

He pulls his length out of me almost completely before thrusting up into me again. White-hot pleasure sends shivers through my body with every deep, hard thrust.

As I near my climax, I can feel myself start to tremble with anticipation. Pleasure builds and builds and builds until it feels like I'm about to burst into a million pieces.

My lover slows his thrusts, drawing out the sensation until I almost can't take it anymore.

"Please," I manage to say between moans, "please, let me finish."

But he doesn't quicken his pace. Instead, he draws his head back, and his burning gaze locks with mine.

Amber eyes stare back at me.

It's Viridian.

Viridian is the one touching me like this.

My mind struggles to make sense of it all. How he's the one here with me, and not Loren.

But I can't concentrate. The only thing I can do is moan.

Somehow, the heat of Viridian's amber stare on me while I'm utterly exposed, bare in the throes of pleasure, heightens the sensation I feel. Without breaking eye contact, he quickens his thrusts, the full length of him entering me over and over and over.

Splintering, I cry out and grab both of his arms.

Viridian works himself through my climax, finally removing his length from my wetness.

He secures his hand behind my head and moves to kiss me.

And then I wake up.

I open my eyes and stare at the drapes above me. I

raise my arm to my forehead and rest it there while I catch my breath.

A dream.

It was all a dream.

I know now that none of it was real, but my body...

Lust courses through my veins. My nipples harden under my nightgown, poking through the thin fabric. I feel my tender mound throbbing at the apex of my thighs.

I run my hand up to my neck and gently touch my fingers to it.

My other hand grazes my chest. Then I slip my hands under the neckline of my nightgown and cup my breasts, inhaling deeply.

Closing my eyes, I open my mouth. I lightly squeeze my breasts and then I let go, turning my attention to my aching nipples. I swirl my fingers in circular motions around them, before flicking my thumbs back and forth across my nipples. I bring one of my hands lower, to my abdomen, while the other continues lightly pinching and rubbing my nipple.

The sensation sends pleasure tingling through me, soaking me with need. While keeping one hand on my breast, I move my other hand lower, until it rests just above my sex.

I kick off the covers and spread my legs wide.

The air meets my tender skin, intensifying the throbbing ache I feel gathering between my thighs.

I drag my fingers across my sex, letting my hands explore my inner thighs until I can barely take it. Then I press my fingers to my tender mound and slowly move them in circular motions.

A breathy moan slips from my mouth.

While I rub myself, I knead my breast with my free hand. Arching my back, I bite my lip to stifle my moans.

The door bursts open. Instinctually, I clamp my legs shut, my hand still caught between them.

Viridian barrels into my room, haggard and disheveled. His wispy black hair is tousled and unkempt, and his shirt untucked, like he rushed out of bed.

"How did you—"

"You think I can't hear your whimpers, Little Fawn? That I can't smell your arousal?"

I push my skirt down to cover myself.

"No." He pushes the door closed behind him, still lingering by the entry.

"No?"

"No. Lift your skirt."

Slowly, I do as he says, stopping when the hem of my skirt is just above my knees.

Viridian's voice is low, husky. Hungry. "More."

His gaze leaves burning traces on my skin. I pull my skirt up further, until it's bunched around my hips.

"Good," he says, lowering himself into the padded chair directly across from me. "Now spread your legs."

With heat dancing across my cheeks, I part my legs and open them until they're about a shoulder-width apart.

"Wider," Viridian growls.

I slide my ankles farther apart, fully exposing myself.

Gripping the armrest, Viridian's eyes darken, taking in the sight of me spread out before him. "Pull down your nightgown."

I drag my hands up my body and hook my fingers under the neckline of my nightgown. It falls past my waist when I pull it down. I'm fully naked now, save for the nightgown circling my hips.

My mind knows it's wrong to lay myself bare before him. But I'm too weak to fight the overwhelming sensation in my body that tells me I want this.

More than anything, I want this.

So, I run my hand along my chest, fingers grazing the base of my neck.

"That's it, Little Fawn. Touch your chest. Squeeze your breasts."

Cupping my breasts in my hands, I squeeze them. An airy breath escapes my lips. Losing myself in the feeling, I run my fingers around my nipples, and I feel them harden to attention even more. As if they weren't already hard enough.

"Those needy, needy nipples," Viridian says gruffly. "Play with them."

Flicking my thumbs across my nipples, I moan, arching my back. After playing with them for a little, I move one of my hands to touch myself.

"Not yet," Viridian orders, rubbing himself through his pants. "You'll touch yourself when I tell you."

Biting my lip, I groan, pinching and pulling at my nipples.

"Please," I whine. "Let me touch."

Viridian smirks, and he licks his lips. He watches me squirm on the bed, my body thrumming with anticipation. My skin is hot, and I feel like I'm filled to the brim with a torturously sweet sensation. The ache between my legs grows even stronger.

My breath quickens.

"Viridian," I whimper.

He only watches me, that starved expression working at his jaw.

"Viridian." My voice is desperate. Needy. "Please. Please."

His stare locks with mine. "Now you can touch

yourself."

My right hand releases my breast and moves back down between my legs. I can feel Viridian's burning gaze follow it all the way down.

Dipping my fingers into my wetness, I rub the soft mound at the apex of my thighs, moving my fingers in circular motions. My other hand squeezes my breast, thumb brushing back and forth across my nipple at the same time.

I tilt my head back in pleasure, eyelids drooping.

"Eyes on me," Viridian commands, his voice rough. "I want to see it in your eyes when you come for me. Understand?"

I nod.

"Do you understand, Little Fawn?"

"Yes," I pant.

"Yes, what?"

"Yes, Your Highness."

Viridian cocks his head. "There'll be none of that in here. In here, you'll call me sir. Understand?"

"Yes, *sir*."

Viridian's pupils dilate, his hand gripping the bulge in his pants. "There's a good girl."

I keep working my fingers, applying pressure to my most sensitive spot. It feels so good that I have to fight the urge to press my thighs together.

"Don't you dare close those legs," Viridian rasps, leaning back in his chair. He's still stroking himself through his pants, and the sight of it heightens the white-hot pleasure coursing through me.

I moan, and Viridian's breaths get heavier. My eyes lock with his, and I don't have the strength to look away.

Nor do I want to.

I moan again, but this time I bite my lip to keep the noise down.

"Louder, Little Fawn."

Too close to the edge to form words, I nod, opening my mouth slightly. My moans come faster now, louder. Viridian's motions across his hardness quicken, his strokes in time with my moans. The sensation between my legs builds, and builds, and builds, until I nearly can't take it.

I cry out when I come undone, utter bliss wracking through my body.

Chest heaving, I take deep breaths, still reeling from my climax.

Viridian stands, flexing his hands before balling them into fists. Then he makes for the door without another word, his mouth tense as if he's restraining himself.

CHAPTER TWENTY-TWO

'M STILL REPLAYING last night's events in my mind when I wake.

It's only when Tiffy and my ladies' maids arrive to prepare me for the day that I finally empty my mind of what Viridian and I did last night. Though, despite my trying, I can't fully clear my focus.

After I eat my breakfast, Tiffy sits me down at my vanity table to style my hair. She starts combing my auburn waves and flashes me a knowing grin.

"So," she gushes, wiggling her brows. "How did it go with His Highness?"

"Wonderful," I tell her, doing nothing to fight the hint of the smile that pulls at my lips.

"I knew it! You are positively radiant this morning, Miss," she purrs. "The Crown Prince is quite the lucky male."

I hold my hands in my lap and look down at them.

Maybe...

I dare to let myself finish the thought.

Maybe there is a future for Viridian and me.

One I hadn't allowed myself to consider before.

"In fact," Tiffy continues, her expression animated, "he's already asked to see you today."

I perk up. "He has?"

"Yes." Tiffy nods. "He's asked you to meet him by the main staircase once you're dressed."

That rustles the butterflies in my stomach. I let them spread their wings. "Then I'd better get dressed."

Tiffy helps me up and into my day gown, fussing over me like a mother hen until she's sure I look my best. Even though my outfit and hair today are nothing special.

When I leave my bedchamber, I can see that Viridian's already waiting for me in the open space between the main staircase and the East Tower's entrance.

"Cryssa," he breathes. "You're here."

"You asked to see me?" I say, looking at him

284

expectantly.

"Yes. Walk with me?" Viridian asks. He's practically bouncing on his heels, giddy as if he were a child on the eve of the winter solstice. It makes me wonder if he has something planned for us.

So, I nod, falling in step beside him as we continue down the hall past both of our bedchambers.

"Why did you leave last night? After I..." I let my voice trail off.

"Because," he says, looking at me now, "if I hadn't, any self-control I had left would have disintegrated."

"What's wrong with that?" I ask. Insecurities flood my mind. Have I misread his signals? Does he not want me the way I want him?

"There's nothing wrong with it," he assures me, voice firm. "But when I have you for the first time, Little Fawn, there's no going back. I want you to want it, entirely. Because once I get my hands on you, I will see to it that no other man ever touches you again."

When he has me.

He says that as if he knows it will happen, one day.

"Oh," I murmur. The insecurities that once clouded my mind float away, replaced by impure fantasies. Of all the ways he will coax bliss from me, all the places on my body he will shower with tenderness and affection.

Not *if*, but *when*.

Just thinking about it makes heat spread through my body. If Viridian can barely touch me, the way he does now, and still give me such pleasure, then I can only imagine how amazing it will be when he finally touches me.

I want him to touch me. To mark me as his.

His eyes darken, and I know he must want that, too.

But then he swallows. "Come," he says, the child-like glee returning to his demeanor. "There's something I'd like to show you."

"Oh?" I arch a brow. "What is it?"

Viridian smirks, as if he expected me to ask that question. "It's a surprise."

"I don't like surprises."

The first time someone surprised me, I was twelve. The morning of my birthday, Father told me that he'd planned a surprise for that evening. It ended up being a small get-together that I loved, but I'll never forget the anticipation. The constant wondering and uncertainty. I like to be prepared, to be ready for everything that comes my way—Father taught me that. For humans, it's safer that way. But I can't prepare myself if I don't know what's to come.

"Trust me, you'll like this one," Viridian says,

confidence bolstering his words.

"All right," I surrender, and a playful undertone seeps through my demeanor.

"Close your eyes." He grins. I love seeing him smile— the way his face lights up, free from the stony expression I'd come to know when I first arrived.

The cogs in my mind whirl, and I have so many questions waiting on the tip of my tongue. But I don't give voice to them, and I do as he asks.

He takes my hand, intertwining his fingers with mine.

My heart flutters, light in my chest. As much as I want to open them, I keep my eyes closed.

I follow him some distance, and the cool air that meets my skin tells me we've stayed in the castle the entire time.

What could he have to show me in the castle?

We go a bit farther, and then Viridian stops. The sound of wood scraping stone and creaking of hinges tells me that he's opened a door.

"All right," he murmurs, without letting go of my hand. "Now you can open your eyes."

I do, and I raise a hand to my mouth.

In the room before us, there's a mid-sized table made from richly colored wood. Its legs are ornately carved, with flowing swirls and curves to the wood—not the straight, plain ones I'm used to. There are shelves lining the walls, filled with leather-bound sketchbooks of varying sizes, and pencils, charcoals, and colored wax sticks for drawing. On the far wall, directly in front of us, there are several large, gold-rimmed windows that stretch as high as the ceiling. Sunlight shines through them, leaving the whole room awash with its rays.

"Your studio had to be on this side of the castle." Viridian says, noticing me looking at the windows. "So that you'll have all the natural light in here."

"It's beautiful," I say, in awe.

"I didn't know how you preferred to draw," he starts, gesturing to our surroundings. "I thought an easel might be an awkward angle for drawing, but I still included some anyway, in case you'd like to use one."

I follow his line of sight and see two easels sitting on the floor in the corner. They're not as large as a painter's easel, small enough that I could pick them up and set them on the table.

I've never had an easel.

At home, I never let myself dream that I might have one. For fear of living with the disappointment.

I have an easel.

A whole studio for my drawing.

"And the table," he adds, rushing to it while pulling me along. "The artists I consulted believed it to be a nice height for drawing. The wood is fine mahogany, smoothed so that you'll have a flat surface to draw on. If you don't use the easels, that is."

I approach the table and run my fingers along its surface. Viridian's put so much thought into every single detail—from the windows, the easels, the height of the table.

It must have taken him some time to organize this. To turn this space into something I'd like.

And to think that he did all of this, just for me.

"Do you like it?" he asks, looking as if he were hanging onto every slight shift in my expression. "We can make any changes you want."

"Viridian, it's..." I shake my head a little, unable to contain my emotion. My gratitude. The overwhelming feeling of joy I feel in knowing he did all of this to make me happy. "It's perfect. I love it."

He visibly relaxes, mouth parted into a broad smile. "That's all I ever hoped for."

"Thank you," I tell him, wrapping my arms around him. "This is... More than anyone has ever done for me."

"Of course." He tightens his arms around me and presses his mouth to the top of my head. "You deserve all of this, and more, Cryssa. So much more."

I close my eyes and breathe in his scent for a moment before pulling away. His amber eyes find mine, holding my gaze. Warmth blooms in my chest, making me feel lighter than air.

The gentle knock at the door has both of our heads turning.

"Enter," Viridian calls, his princely mask slipping into place. It's strange watching him shift from just Viridian to the Crown Prince.

I don't know if I'll ever get used to it.

"Your Highness—" the servant pauses, eyes flicking to me.

"What is it?" Viridian asks, leveling his expression.

"The prisoner, he..."

Viridian casts his eyes to the floor. Annoyance bleeds through his tone. "Go on."

"He's injured another one of the guards. And he won't stop fighting until you let him see her," the servant finishes, looking at me.

"When?" Viridian's voice is gravelly, as if someone has a knife to his throat. Though, he doesn't sound surprised.

Has this happened before?

The servant swallows. "Now."

CHAPTER TWENTY-THREE

M Y HEART CONSTRICTS and my throat tightens. If not for my body's natural instincts, I would have forgotten how to breathe.

Oh gods.

Loren.

I've forgotten all about him. Again.

An all too familiar guilt seeps through my chest, replacing the lightness I felt mere seconds ago with *gohlrunn*. I'd been so caught up in my own head the past few days, that I may have actually fallen for the illusion I so desperately wanted to believe.

That Viridian and I could be together. That we could be happy together.

The man I swore to save is still a prisoner. The man I once loved, above all else. And while he's been suffering in a tiny prison cell, afraid and alone, I've been dancing, and dining, and kissing the fae male that's responsible for all of it.

My cheeks sting.

I've been betraying him.

All this time. Every moment I've spent enjoying Viridian's company has been no better than a knife in Loren's back.

I press my palm to my chest in an effort to even my breath.

"Take me to him," I say to the servant.

"Cryssa—" Viridian starts.

"*Now.*"

The servant looks to Viridian.

Nostrils flaring, he takes a deep breath and balls his hands into fists. His voice is weak, barely above a whisper. "Do as she commands."

The servant bows his head, and then motions for me to follow. "Come with me."

THE DESCENT INTO the dungeons lasts longer than I'd like.

Viridian's eyes burn holes into my back the entire time, and he stays about a foot away from me. As if he can't bear to be any closer.

How could we have fallen so far, in such little time?

We pass several cells before the servant stops. I don't look into them as we pass, in fear of what—or who—I'll see inside.

But there is nothing that could have prepared me for this.

I follow the servant. And turn to the prisoner inside.

Loren stands with his back to me. He presses his forearm to the wall and leans forward, resting his forehead on it.

I take deep breaths. Though, my breathing grows more ragged with each one.

Viridian reaches for my hand, as if on instinct. His hand is warm on mine. It feels nice. Comforting, even.

But I can't bring myself to hold his hand in return.

No doubt sensing my stiffness, Viridian lets go of my hand, returning his own to his side.

I don't want him to let go of my hand.

But my mind is too focused on the man in front of me, too consumed by the guilt, and the discomfort that tears me in two, that I don't say anything. I don't say anything at all.

The servant clears his throat. He looks at me, before opening his mouth.

"She's here, as you requested."

Loren's shoulders rise, and he whirls around. The threat of violence that permeates his demeanor loosens. His face is dirty, and his light brown hair is longer than it was the last time I saw him, curls wild and unruly. My focus falls to his collarbones, at the black and blue bruises poking out from underneath his tattered shirt. Immediately, his green eyes land on me. Relief and love pool in them, and the way he looks at me makes me feel worse than I already do.

So much worse.

Because I know I'm not looking at him the same way.

My heart is torn in two. Half lies in the cell with Loren, and the other...

The other half is sworn to the male that's holding him behind bars.

"Cryssa," Loren breathes, like all he's ever wanted is to see me again. He looks past me, at Viridian, and his eyes shoot daggers his way. "Are you all right? I've been so worried since—" He swallows, as if to catch himself before he says too much.

My throat feels as if someone has their hand wrapped around it.

"Cryssa?" Loren asks, swiftly crossing his cell to the bars. "Talk to me."

"Yes," I choke out. Closing my eyes, I slow my breaths. "I'm fine."

"Fine?" Loren's voice sharpens. "You don't look *fine*." Then he openly glares at Viridian. "What have you done to her?"

"I assure you," Viridian begins, his voice cold. "I have done nothing but care for her."

Loren laughs, and it's a bitter sound. "As if I'd believe that."

Viridian's jaw ticks.

"It's true," I say, finding my voice. "I want for nothing."

Viridian's face hardens to stone, and more than anything, I want to take it back and say something better instead. Something that will chip away at the stone, until I get my Viridian back. Just Viridian, the real Viridian. Not the Crown Prince.

"That's a lie," Loren says, voice softening. "And you know it."

He's right. That is a lie.

"You want your freedom," Loren continues. "You want to go home. With *me*." The last sentence is a jab, practically aimed at Viridian's throat.

I turn my face from the cell.

Of course I want my freedom. How could I not? But now, even that is so much more complicated than it once was.

"You wanted to see me?" I ask.

"Of course I did," Loren says. "I've thought of you every day, for all these weeks. Wondering where you are, if you're all right. What's happening to you." A pause. "I've been worried sick about you, Cryssa."

I can hear the sincerity in his voice. To any other woman, the emotion in Loren's voice would have them swooning. But not me.

Not anymore.

I would ask myself why I don't feel as I once did.

But I already know the answer to that question.

I glance at Viridian before I respond.

"Oh."

"That's it? Oh?" Loren echoes, voice tightening.

I know what he wants me to say. That I've been thinking of him just as much. That I've been worried sick about him, yearning for the day I can see him again.

But I can't tell him that.

He knows me too well. He would know it's a lie.

So, I don't lie.

"Did he..." My eyes find his bruises again. I can't bear to think that Viridian... That he might be responsible for them. "Are those...?"

Loren looks down at his chest, and then back up at me. "I had a scuffle with the guards." He says it so casually, as if it's a common occurrence. "Nothing to worry about, I promise."

Has he tried to fight his way out? Has he tried to escape, desperate to find me, when I didn't come back for him, like I said I would?

"I'm so sorry." I sink to my knees and grip the prison bars. Tears prick at my eyes. "This is all my fault."

"No," Loren says, in an attempt to soothe me. He lowers himself to my level, reaching out to cup my face through the bars. "None of this is your fault."

Sobs slip through my defenses. "It *is* my fault," I repeat.

"Don't blame yourself for this, Cryssa." He takes my hand and places it over his heart. "I'm all right. Everything is going to be all right," he says, as if he genuinely believes it. "I promise."

But everything isn't all right.

How can I tell him I'm not the same Cryssa he once knew?

That my feelings for him have changed?

The girl I was when I first arrived at High Keep comes rushing back to me. The human girl, who felt out of place amongst the noble fae. The girl who wanted nothing more to leave this place and never come back.

The girl Loren loves.

Though, no matter how much I may want it, that girl is gone. She's never coming back.

I don't know who I am anymore.

I can feel Viridian's gaze on me. But I don't dare look back. I don't want him to see me like this.

To see me tearing apart at the seams.

And I know it's terrible, that I am terrible for wanting this, but...

I want nothing more than to be back upstairs in my studio with Viridian. To be back in that moment, before *this* happened.

Because now that it has, now that I've seen Loren again, I know things between Viridian and I will never be the same.

CHAPTER
TWENTY-FOUR

I SHUT MYSELF in my room for days. No one but Tiffy comes in, and she's the only one that comes out.

I eat. I sleep. I draw.

I've drawn so much that every free space in my bedchamber is filled with pages from my sketchbook.

All the drawings are the same.

High cheekbones, loose black hair, that serious expression...

My bedchamber is filled with images of Viridian.

I should be thinking of Loren. Part of me will always

love him, deep down. But my mind only forms one image. One face.

And my hands, as if controlled by some outside force, sketch it onto paper.

Though no matter how much I wish it could be otherwise, Viridian and I come from different worlds. We belong to different walks of life.

There is no future for us. No way around the inevitable heartbreak.

Even if we do marry.

Loren's mere presence has made that abundantly clear. Seeing him in that prison cell again resurfaced everything I'd first thought about Viridian when I arrived.

That noble fae and humans are too different. That I could never move past what Viridian's done. That in his gilded world, he could ever understand mine.

I sit at my vanity table, bent over another half-finished sketch.

Pushing my sketchbook away, I look at myself in the mirror. My auburn waves hang loose in a tangled mess. There are dark circles under my eyes, which don't surprise me. I haven't slept well—plagued by more dreams of Death and bodies in shallow graves.

Not that I know what the dreams mean.

But the words spoken by Death are the same each

time.

"When the time comes, you must choose. Choose life, without love, in a cursed land. Or choose death in the name of love and sacred sacrifice."

Choose love? I let out a bitter laugh. What love do I have left?

If we ever leave this place, I know Loren will welcome me back with open arms. But now, I'm not so sure that I will ever love him the way I once did.

And Viridian...

He hasn't made any attempt to see me. Hasn't sent any messages. Hasn't asked me to dine with him.

Nothing.

Perhaps he's turned his back on me. Perhaps he remembers why he didn't want me. Why would he marry a human, when there are so many eligible noble fae females who would make for a much better partner than me? And someday, a much better High Queen?

I hold my face in my hands, uncomfortably digging my elbows into my vanity table.

A gentle knock sounds at my door.

"Tiffy?" I ask, lifting my head. "Is that you?"

"No," Lymseia says, opening the door slightly so I can see her. "May I come in?"

I wipe my face and straighten my back. "Yes."

Lymseia slips into the room. She dons her usual fighting leathers, her blue-black hair pulled into a long braid that falls down her back. It's strange to see her without her steel short swords hanging from her hips.

"Hey."

"Hey," I reply weakly.

Lymseia sits across from me, on the edge of my bed. "I was going to ask if you were all right, but honestly, you look terrible."

I manage to chuckle. But even that sounds like a shell of what it should be. "Thank you for reminding me."

Lymseia's mouth perks up. "Don't mention it."

I hold my hands in my lap and look down at them. "I doubt you're here to tell me I look terrible."

"No." Her tone softens. "We're worried about you, Cryssa. Viridian is worried about you."

"Then why isn't he here?" I ask, looking up at her. My voice sharpens like knives, but I can feel tears welling in my eyes. "Why hasn't he reached out?" A more gut-wrenching thought pops into my mind. "Does he... Does he not want to see me anymore?"

To see him so cold again...

It was as if all the progress we'd made was for nothing.

"I can't speak for him," Lymseia starts, "but I think he's afraid."

"Afraid?" I echo. My mouth curls. "Afraid of what?"

Lymseia just looks at me for a moment before answering. "Of rejection."

I inhale and rub my forehead.

"But I'm not here to talk about him. Myrdin's taking care of that." She scoots forward and takes both of my hands. "I'm here for *you*, as your friend. How are you, really?"

"I feel terrible," I admit. Whatever was keeping me from falling apart crumbles. The floodgates are open, and I have no way to close them. Nor do I want to. "I'm so torn. Torn between my old life and my new one. Between what I should want and what I do want."

"What you 'should' want?" Lymseia cocks her head.

"Yes," I tell her. "I know I should want to be with Loren, to go home, to go back to being the old Cryssa. The girl that bartered for eggs at the market. The girl that did chores, the girl that wasn't afraid to get her hands dirty. The girl that didn't know how to dance."

My words hang between us.

"First, enough of this 'should' business," Lymseia says and breaks the silence, waving me off. "When you use that word, you're telling yourself that you've failed. You 'should' this, you 'should' that." She shakes her head a little as she speaks. "All you're doing is beating yourself down for what you're not."

My chest tightens, deep with guilt and resistance.

But at its core, fear.

"And second, whether you like it or not, you have changed," Lymseia continues, her tone warm, though firm. "But change is all right, Cryssa. Everyone changes and evolves as we go through life. It's all right to be someone new. But make no mistake—the 'old' Cryssa is still in there," she says, pointing a finger to my chest. "You haven't lost her, because she is you. Only, you're so much stronger now than you were before. You've learned to love unconditionally. To overcome your differences. To open up your mind to all the good you'd never let yourself imagine before."

She smiles. "And I think that's a very good thing. Something that will make you the High Queen you were always meant to be."

I consider her words for what feels like ages. Digesting them.

"You're right," I tell her at last.

Though, some part of me is still afraid to let go. Afraid to lower my shields.

Afraid that I'll bare my heart, only for it to be broken.

I remember something my father told me when I was young. I'd gotten stung by a bee while out picking wildflowers with Acantha one summer. After that, I was afraid to return to the meadow, even though it was my favorite place in the whole world. I remember wanting to stay at home while she and Father went, afraid the tiny creatures would hurt me again.

"Bravery doesn't mean the absence of fear, my darling," Father had said. *"Bravery is when you still choose to continue anyway, even though you're afraid."*

I take a deep breath.

I'll be brave, Father.

I won't let my fear hold me back.

VIRIDIAN IS IN THE main library, pulling books from the shelves, when I come in.

He doesn't turn around immediately, instead taking a breath before setting his books down on a nearby table. Slowly, he turns to face me.

Dark circles hang under his eyes, and his expression looks worn. His shoulders slump with fatigue, and the luster in his eyes is dim.

I close the distance between us, steadily approaching him.

"Hello," I say softly.

Viridian's tone matches mine. "Hello."

"I'm sorry," I tell him. "For disappearing like that."

"You don't have to apologize for that, Cryssa," he tells me solemnly.

"I just—I heard you were worried about me."

"I'll always worry about you."

I find his eyes. "I pushed you away."

"I know." He holds my gaze.

I search his expression. There's something else there, something he doesn't say.

"What is it?" I ask.

"Nothing," he tells me, his voice monotone. "I'm glad that you're all right."

"There's something else," I insist. "Tell me."

"No, there isn't." Viridian turns from me and picks up his books.

"Viridian," I protest. "You can talk to me."

"I'm fine, Cryssa." He clutches the books to his chest. "Really."

But I don't believe him.

Then he walks away from me, books in hand, and leaves.

He *leaves.*

I know there's something wrong. Something he's not telling me.

He's retreated behind his walls again. He's shutting me out.

I press my lips into a fine line and wrap my arms around myself. Still staring in the direction he went, there is only one question running through my mind.

Why is he running away?

CHAPTER
TWENTY-FIVE

F OR THE NEXT few days, Viridian avoids me. He doesn't even come to dinner.

I make it my mission to speak to him, but somehow, he continues to evade me.

Frustrated, I march through the halls, aiming for my bedchamber. I reach the top of the stairs, when Lymseia comes in my direction.

"Cryssa," she says, her expression tight.

"What is it?" Concern prickles the skin on my arms.

"The High King has returned. He wants to see you and Viridian in the throne room at once."

My stomach falls. Anxiety wraps its cold fist around my insides.

"Then I'll head there at once," I tell her, my mouth dry.

She nods. "I'll escort you."

Something in her eyes tells me she doesn't have much of a choice in the matter.

We're silent as we descend the staircase and turn the corner toward the throne room. I see Viridian first, standing some distance away from the cracked bronze throne, where Vorr sits.

The High King leans back, hands gripping the arms of the throne so tightly that if not for his gloves, I'm sure his knuckles would go white.

The tension between the two fae males is palpable, as though I could slice through it with a dagger.

Lymseia's feet stay planted outside the set of double doors when I enter.

I approach, stopping when I'm in line with Viridian, and bow.

"Your Majesty." I rise from my curtsy. "I'm glad to see that you've returned."

Vorr forces a polite smile. "Thank you, Miss Thurdred." His eyes move to Viridian. "If only my son shared your sentiment."

Deathly quiet, Viridian's voice comes out as a low snarl. "Where were you?"

"That is none of your concern." Vorr's words are curt.

"No?" Viridian cocks his head. Rage bubbles just beneath the surface, brimming in his expression. "Then why were your advisors left in the dark with me? You left with no warning."

"Do not question me." Vorr's voice goes cold.

Viridian tilts his head back, clenching his jaw.

"Everything I do, I do for this kingdom," Vorr continues, looking anywhere but at his son. "I shall do as I see fit."

He pauses, and silence falls over us.

"The two of you will be married in a fortnight." His words are those of the High King. Not of a father.

"What?" Viridian's voice is sharp, like the crack of a whip.

My head snaps toward him. I furrow my brows in an effort to contain my emotions.

"Father," Viridian protests, "you cannot return and simply—"

"I am the High King." Vorr stands, anger sharpening his tone. "My word is law. You *will* do as I command."

Viridian seethes, his amber eyes burning like hot

311

coals. His entire body goes rigid, hands curled into fists by his sides. He doesn't look at me—his anger seems to only be directed at his father.

Then why does he object to our marriage? Out of spite, or because...

My chest constricts.

Maybe he doesn't want to be tied to me forever.

Vorr is silent for a moment, and then sits back down. "You are dismissed. Both of you."

Viridian bows quickly before storming out of the throne room.

I curtsy, and then rush out into the hallway after him.

"Viridian!" I call, but he doesn't seem to hear me. "Viridian, stop. *Please*."

He freezes in his tracks, still facing forward. I catch up with him, and stand before him, looking up at his face.

Tempests rage in his eyes, yet I dare to reach out to him anyway. Gently, I place a hand on his arm.

"Look at me," I beg.

And he does. His expression softens when his eyes find mine, though I can still see that his walls are up, shielding what's inside.

"Talk to me," I say.

"Cryssa, please." Viridian sighs and presses a hand to his mouth. "Not now."

"Fine," I surrender. "But at least let me join you for dinner. I—I miss you."

For a moment, I see past his barriers. I see him—*my* Viridian.

"Very well," he says with a slight nod. "I will see you at dinner."

TIFFY IS QUIET when she does my hair tonight.

I am, too. It's not because I don't want to speak to her. It's because there's a numbness I feel, invading my bones. Emotions swirling in my mind, trapping me in my own skin.

It almost makes me yearn for the simplicity of life in Slyfell. The depth and range of emotions I've felt here, at High Keep, compares to nothing I've felt at home. Not even the death of my mother—after all, I was much too young at the time to truly understand it.

When Tiffy finishes, I stand, smoothing out my skirts. "Thank you, Tiffy."

"Of course, Miss." Tiffy bows her head, and then she and my other ladies' maids leave.

I wait in the comforts of my bedchamber for a moment.

Unfamiliar nerves jumble in my abdomen.

Am I doing the right thing?

Am I a fool for trying? Should I let Viridian go, and let the distance between us grow?

No.

The thought of letting him drift away makes my body go rigid. I don't want to let him go.

I have to try. I have to be brave.

No matter what it takes.

Taking a deep breath, I hold my head high and make for the great hall.

When I arrive, I take my seat across from Viridian. He tilts his head down, loose black hair falling in front of his eyes. Shielding them.

He doesn't say anything. No greeting, no acknowledgment.

Nothing.

Anger sparks in my chest, but I suppress it. If I give in to my anger, I'll only push him away more.

That's the opposite of what I want.

So, I say nothing, only speaking to thank the servants when they arrive with the first course. And then the second.

"Have I done something wrong?" I ask at last, breaking the silence. I move my food around my plate with

314

my fork. "If I have, then I'm sorry."

"No," Viridian says, his eyes cast down at some spot on the table. "You've done nothing wrong, Cryssa."

"Then what is it?" I ask. "And don't tell me it's nothing. I know that's not true."

"I—" he pauses, and swallows. "This isn't what you want."

"This?"

"Us. This betrothal. This *life.*" He practically spits out the last word.

I tighten my mouth.

I can only shake my head. "That's not true."

"Isn't it?" His voice increases in volume. "Then look me in the eyes and tell me that you do."

"Viridian, I..."

"You can't," he says, looking as if he tasted something sour. He looks away from me, avoiding my gaze.

"Viridian," I repeat, my voice firm. "This is about Loren, isn't it."

He hardens his expression, gripping his fork and knife.

"Isn't it?" I press.

"Yes," he shoots out. "It is."

I lean forward. "Why?"

"Because you *love* him!" His words rush from his

315

mouth, as if he's exploding on the inside. "You love him," he repeats, though this time, his words are barely above a whisper. "Don't you?"

My heart aches in my chest.

I was afraid of this.

The two halves of my heart are colliding. Crashing into one another.

"Viridian." My voice is faint.

"Tell me you don't love him." He looks at me with the face of defeat, and his voice trembles. It *trembles*.

I look away.

Because I can't give him the answer he wants.

I do love Loren. Part of me always will.

But I...

I'm falling for him, too.

"That's what I thought," Viridian continues bitterly, picking up his goblet of wine.

My stomach sinks.

I want to tell him otherwise, but my mouth feels as if it's been locked shut.

"So no, you haven't done anything wrong." He takes a greedy swig of wine, tipping his head back.

"Regardless," I say, finding the words, "we are to be married. I want to be friends again. Please, try. That's all I ask."

He takes another sip of wine, swishing it around in his mouth. He swallows, and then looks at me, eyes narrowed. "Fine. I'll carry on as usual. As if nothing's happened."

Tears prick at my eyes. This isn't what I wanted. How can I make him see that? How can I pierce the veil he's pulled between us?

I know it's unlike me, but I don't hide the sadness in my eyes. Part of me wants to say something. Anything, if not to let this conversation end like this.

But I have nothing more to say.

No energy to fight.

Viridian stands, and his chair scrapes across the floor when he does. Without another word, he slips from the great hall, leaving his dinner half-finished.

And me, all alone.

CHAPTER
TWENTY-SIX

A S MUCH AS I hate it, Viridian and I fall back into
our old habits. While we still dine together every
night, he's retreated behind his princely mask, cold like the
stone walls he's built between us.

Part of me wonders if this—*us*—is even worth
fighting for.

What happened to the Viridian I'd come to know? Is
he even there anymore? Or was he never real to begin with?

I spend more of my days in my studio. Though, being
there reminds me of how things used to be. Servants
interrupt my peace there with wedding preparations. With

endless questions about the ceremony, the flowers, the music.

I merely smile and nod.

Now, I sit in my studio, at the table. I have an easel before me, and I hold a pencil to the parchment it holds in place.

I trace an all too familiar outline of a face.

This time, I draw Viridian the way he used to look at me. Amber eyes bright, the hint of a smile tugging at his soft lips. An easy, relaxed expression at his jaw.

Leaning back, my eyes follow the outline of my sketch.

I barely have time to react when a flaming arrow flies through the window. It lands behind me, and the flames quickly spread across the floor. Dangerously close to the wooden doorway. The flames start to lick their way up the threshold.

If I don't act quickly, they'll block my way out.

I glance toward the windows. Like the others in the castle, they're adorned with thick, bronze colored drapes.

If I can pull one down...

Then I might be able to put out the fire before it grows.

Picking up my skirts, I rush to the closest window and grasp fistfuls of the curtains. Throwing my whole body into the motion, I tug on it.

"Come on," I mutter, trying again. "Please, Imone," I pray, begging the Goddess of Mercy to take pity on me.

I pull, leaning back as I do.

The curtain rod holding it in place whines and snaps. It gives way, and I fall, landing hard on my back. The metal rod clangs on the stone floor.

I drag the curtain toward the door and throw it over the flames. Then, I back away, waving smoke from my face.

Not even a moment later, the door swings open so violently, it crashes against the wall. Viridian darts inside. Immediately, his hands find my shoulders, and he scans me for injuries. Worry widens his eyes and drains his face of color.

"Are you all right?" he asks, voice jumbled in a panicked frenzy. "Cryssa, are you hurt?"

"No," I assure him. "I'm fine. The arrow missed me."

"Thank the gods." He closes his eyes in relief and pulls me to his chest, wrapping me in his arms.

I close mine, too, and take deep breaths while I rest my head against him.

Viridian's mouth curls.

"Who did this?" Holding me even tighter now, his head snaps toward the servant that came with him.

"Human miners. There's at least fifty of them

gathered outside, on strike, Your Highness," the servant says. "They're demanding an audience with the High King."

"Human miners?" I ask, pulling back a little.

"It's the mining sickness," Viridian tells me, his voice softening. "The death toll..." he turns his face from mine, as if he can't look me in the eyes. "It's increased. Dramatically."

My stomach drops.

Father. Acantha.

Since we visited Loren in the dungeon, I've been so focused on Viridian that I completely forgot about the world outside. About the mining sickness and the mines draining of metals.

I can only imagine how much worse it's gotten in all that time.

"Come," Viridian says, taking my hand. "My father must hear of this, if he hasn't already."

I nod. We move swiftly through the halls and down the main staircase until we reach the council chamber.

The door is closed when we arrive, and the muffled voices behind it tell me that the council is in session. A guard stands in front of the room, blocking our access.

"Let me in," Viridian says, his voice low with warning.

"Your Highness, the council is—"

"Must I repeat myself?" He takes a step closer and lets go of my hand. Power thrums through the air. "*Let me pass.*"

The guard's eyes widen. He swallows and steps aside.

Viridian looks back at me over his shoulder and reaches for me, intertwining his fingers with mine. Now that we're closer, I can begin to make out what they're saying on the other side of the door.

"Your Majesty, we must act," a male urges.

"They are refusing to work," a feminine voice adds. "There are *riots* in the square—"

Still holding my hand, Viridian pushes the door open and steps into the council chamber.

Silence falls over the room, and all heads turn to look at us. Seated at the head of the table, the High King glowers at his son.

"What is the meaning of this?" He bellows, rising to his feet.

"Fifty human miners are gathered outside our walls," Viridian seethes, his quiet rage settled into his voice. He pulls me closer. "A flaming arrow nearly killed my betrothed."

For a moment, Vorr's façade falls, and fear—true fear—flashes in his expression. Then he tightens his mouth, his hard demeanor restored.

The others at the table—the five Heads of House from each of the Courts, I assume—exchange nervous glances. The female bearing a close resemblance to Lymseia, her mother, Lady Kylantha, clears her throat.

"The Steel Court will not sit idly by while our people die." She stands. "Your Majesty, if I may be excused."

Vorr tightens his mouth. "You may, Lady Wynterliff."

"Thank you, Your Majesty." Head of House Wynterliff bows her head to Vorr, and then to Viridian when she passes us.

"What do the miners demand?" a male with rich brown hair asks Viridian.

"An audience with the High King," Viridian responds, staring down at his father.

The male nods and turns to Vorr. "Perhaps it would be wise to consider making a statement."

"And do what? Tell them the crown has no answers?" Vorr's voice sharpens. "You know that would only sow more panic, Tanyl."

Lord Tanyl Tarrantree—Myrdin's father, I realize—keeps his expression calm. "The people's fears may be eased if they know the crown hears their cries. Show them that the crown stands with them."

I recognize Head of House, Lady Maelyrra

Pelleveron, by the scowl on her face.

"Tensions have yet to reach the Gold Court," she says, raising the crown of her head. "Perhaps we should leave it to the affected Courts to manage their own issues."

Viridian's brows furrow, and he clenches his jaw. "That's—"

I place a hand on his arm. He closes his mouth and takes a breath.

"With all due respect, Lady Maelyrra," I say, addressing her, "the tensions will come to the Gold Court soon, if it's true they haven't already. We've already lost so many miners—so many good, hardworking miners—to the sickness. It won't be long before what's happening in the other Courts comes to your doorstep. Make no mistake, this is a kingdom-wide issue."

"And why should I take your word?" she sneers at me. I hear what she leaves unsaid. *You're a human.* "You are no one of importance."

Viridian tenses at my side. But before he can come to my defense, I glance at him, as if to say, *"Leave it to me."*

"You're right," I tell her, straightening my posture. "I am no one of importance. But I am a citizen of your Court. And I have seen the sickness firsthand. My lived experience gives me a better understanding of this issue." I pause, letting my words sink in. "Better than anyone else in this room."

Tanyl tilts his head back, his mouth curved into an approving smile. "Spoken like the future High Queen."

The other Heads of House, save for Maelyrra, share Tanyl's expression. To my side, I can feel Viridian watching me in awe.

Vorr's jaw ticks. His brows stitch together, creased with worry. With fear.

But his fear isn't the look of someone that's been left in the dark.

No, his fear has a knowing edge to it. As if he knows more than he's letting on. More than what he's telling the council.

And it terrifies him.

I think of what I saw in the East Tower. I remember the commoner's gossip in Keuron, what Tiffy told me about the stranger, the invitation Viridian and I found.

Whatever is happening, whatever dark magic is causing all of this, I know one thing.

The High King is at the center of it all.

"That is enough for today." Vorr's tone hardens. He stands. "This meeting is adjourned."

"What?" Viridian asks. "What of the humans outside?"

"What of them?" Vorr's face goes flat, burnt-orange

eyes empty.

"You really won't see them?" Viridian says, resigned, as if he already knows the answer.

Vorr says nothing and brushes past Viridian when he leaves.

The Heads of House rise from their seats, and some linger, talking amongst themselves.

Tanyl approaches Viridian, placing a hand on his shoulder. "I will speak to him."

Viridian exhales, pinching the bridge of his nose. "If anyone can speak some sense into him, it'll be you, Uncle. Though I doubt it's even possible."

Tanyl laughs, though the sound seems forced. "Try not to worry. Use this time to prepare for your wedding."

Viridian's face falls, and he presses his mouth into a fine line. "I will."

To me, Tanyl says, "You spoke well today."

"Thank you, Lord Tarrantree." I curtsy.

He hesitates for a moment, and then continues into the hall.

Slowly, I move from the council chamber and begin to pace. Worries and visions of the worst cloud my mind.

Father.

Maelyrra insisted the tensions haven't reached the Gold Court yet. But if it's true that the mining sickness's death toll has increased...

Father could have fallen ill.

Or worse.

He could have already succumbed to it. And then, Acantha would have no one.

My breathing quickens. Anxiety grips my stomach.

"Cryssa," Viridian says softly, approaching me. "What is it?"

"My father. I have to—" I pause, collecting my thoughts. "I have to know if he's all right."

Understanding crosses his face. "Of course. You must write to him."

"But I can't—I don't—"

"You don't what?" Viridian steps closer to me, tenderness filling his movements.

"I don't know how to write letters," I admit. Shame heats my cheeks. "I never learned."

He cocks his head. "But you can read?"

"Yes," I stammer. At home, I'd picked up enough to read shop signs, simple descriptions of things, and know the basics of what they were saying. Reading is one thing, but writing... "I know enough to get by."

Not enough to write a letter.

He seems to understand what I leave unsaid.

"Oh, Cryssa." He takes my chin between his thumb

and forefinger, tilting my face up to his. There's no judgment in his voice—only compassion and understanding, even though his background is so different from mine. "I'll be your scribe. Tell me what you want to say, and I'll write the letter for you."

"Thank you." I look up at him, into his eyes.

"Of course." Viridian holds my stare. For the first time in days, maybe even weeks, he doesn't look away. "Anything for you."

That familiar warmth swells in my chest. I don't want it to go away again.

"Come," Viridian says, holding out his arm for me. "We'll write the letter in the library."

CHAPTER
TWENTY-SEVEN

I N THE LIBRARY, Viridian retrieves a piece of parchment, a quill, and ink.

"Sit," he says, gesturing to one of the tables.

I do, and he pulls out the chair next to mine. Now that he's seated, he dips the quill in ink and hovers it over the parchment.

I open my mouth to speak but close it not even a moment later. Where do I begin? So much has happened since I left home. So much has changed.

I've changed.

"Speak to me," he says, looking my way, "as if you were speaking to your father."

I glance up in thought. "Hello, Father. It's me, Cryssa."

Viridian touches the quill to the parchment. It makes scratching sounds as he drags it across, using it to draw round, swooping shapes. When he's finished, he looks up at me.

I continue. "I have thought of you and Acantha every day, and I know you must be worried about me. I'm all right. I miss you both so, so much." I pause, briefly closing my eyes. "I hope you are well."

I wait for Viridian to write it down, and then go on. "I've heard more miners have fallen ill. Father, I pray that you are not one of them. How are things at home? Are Catia and Jemetha well? I love you. From, Cryssa."

Viridian copies my words down onto the parchment. Once he's done, his brows stitch together and he returns the quill to the ink.

"Who are Catia and Jemetha?" he asks.

I hesitate. "Loren's mother and sister."

"Ah," he leans back in his chair, crossing his arms. "I see."

We're both silent for a moment.

"Father can only read a little," I say, anxious to change

332

the subject. "How will he know what I've said?"

"I'll instruct the messenger delivering it to read it aloud to him," he answers, sounding as if he were worlds away.

I nod. But the silence returns. No matter how much I wish it wouldn't.

"You miss it, don't you." Viridian says quietly, staring down at the table. It's a statement. Not a question. "Home."

"Yes," I murmur, looking away from him. Dread lines my stomach. I know where this is going.

"Have you thought about returning?"

"Yes." I admit. It feels pointless to deny it. "I've thought about it."

He goes quiet, chewing on his bottom lip.

"And you—" he stops, as if he doesn't want to say what comes next. But he does anyway. "You miss being with him."

I instantly know he's referring to Loren.

This again?

"Viridian, please." How many times will we go over this?

"It's all right, Cryssa." He sounds defeated. "I can handle the truth. You don't need to spare me."

I press my lips together.

I do miss Loren. But not like that. Not the way he thinks.

So, why don't I tell him that? It's as if there's some part of me that's still holding on, that's still afraid to jump into the unknown.

"Your silence is answer enough." Viridian stands. "I won't get in the way of your happiness."

"Viridian," I protest.

But he's not listening. His back is to me, and he's walking to the door.

"I'll have your message delivered." Then he steps into the hall. And moves farther away from me.

I stand, my chair scraping across the floor when I do. When I reach the hallway, Lymseia places a hand on my shoulder.

"Give him time," she tells me.

"But—"

"It's not your fault, but he's hurting." She sighs.

"I know he is." And it tears me apart inside.

She gives my shoulder a light squeeze. "There's nothing you can do but let him work through it on his own. He's too stuck in his own head to see anything but what he's convinced himself to be true."

The rational part of my mind knows she's right. Still, I yearn to hold him. To make his hurt disappear.

But I nod. Though my eyes stay fixed in the place where I last saw Viridian.

I DEBATE WHETHER or not to see Viridian for hours. Trying to give him time, as Lymseia said, I fill my afternoon with mindless activities. Walking the grounds. Visiting Nightfoot in the stables. Drawing.

But nothing is able to pull my mind from how he looked at me in the library.

Not anger. Not denial. Gods above, not even sadness.

Pure and utter defeat.

Hopelessness.

And I realize I can't wait any longer. I have to see him.

I march through the halls. I go to the first-floor library, the grounds, and then the kitchens, to see if he's there.

Lastly, I climb the main staircase and turn the corner, not stopping until I've reached his bedchamber. It would be my luck that I've been searching all over the castle, when he's been right next to me the entire time.

When I reach the door, I raise my fist to knock. But I pause.

There are voices coming from behind the door.

And I know it's wrong, but I can't seem to stop myself from pressing my ear to it. From slowing my breathing.

"I have to break off the engagement." The voice is a low rumble. Viridian's. "Before my father forces my hand."

"Enough of this nonsense, cousin," another says with a sigh. Myrdin. He sounds tired. How long have they been discussing this? "You want to marry her, do you not?"

"Yes. Yes, I do. More than you know." Viridian hesitates. "But the gods were wrong. We are not fated."

"What do you mean? How could you possibly—"

"She is in love with someone else!" Viridian says harshly. I shudder, and it's not even directed at me.

No, I want to shout. I want to barge in and tell him that he's wrong, that I'm not in love with anyone else. Not anymore. But I find myself frozen, my feet fixed to the floor.

"Who is he?" Myrdin asks quietly. There's a knowing edge to his voice.

"The prisoner."

"The one—"

"Yes."

There's silence for a moment. And then Myrdin breaks it. "I see."

Someone releases a long exhale.

"I want to hurt him." Viridian's voice is barely above a whisper. "I want to beat him until my jealousy has had its fill of violence."

"Viridian," Myrdin warns.

"But I won't. Because she cares for him. And I—" Viridian stops abruptly. "I care about her. More than I know I should."

"There is nothing wrong with caring for your betrothed, cousin."

"Oh, but I care for her too much, you see. I would worship her, if she'd allow it. I would fall to my knees at her feet and if she commanded that I burn the whole realm to the ground for her, I would. And then I would follow her into hell, gladly."

A heavy silence follows.

"You know what this means," Myrdin says at last. "Have you told her?"

"No. Only once, when she was too drunk to remember." A pause. "How can I?"

"You must tell her, Viridian. She has a right to know."

"She doesn't want this. She doesn't want *me*." The last phrase is so full of anguish that I lean forward, holding my hand over my heart.

I stagger away from the door.

He thinks I don't want him.

He still thinks I want to leave.

After how much we've grown, after how close we were, he still sees me the way he did before. As the untrusting human, who could never love him. Who could never rule proudly at his side.

Stepping farther back, I turn and start down the hallway.

I need to get away. To go somewhere else. Anywhere but here.

My bedchamber is too close. Especially knowing that he's on the other side. And with his fae hearing, he'll know I'm there, too.

My feet carry me downstairs and through the double doors that lead to the stables. I don't stop, continuing until I reach the grounds. When I'm finally out in the open, I pick up my skirts and break into a run.

Viridian's words replay in my mind. Over, and over, and over.

"She doesn't want this. She doesn't want me."

Oh, but I do. I *do* want him. Too much.

But part of me is still afraid and wants to return to my old life. The one that had Loren.

It's as if they both represent one image of what could be. Loren, my common life in the Gold Court. The one without adventure.

And Viridian...

A life that's entirely new.

I push myself faster, my thighs burning.

Frustration courses through me, powering my legs. Why can't I tell Viridian how I feel? Why can't I answer any of his questions? If I could, it would free us both from this torment.

But if I did, what would I say? Would I tell him the truth, that I care for them both? That somehow, my heart belongs to both him and to Loren, at the same time?

No.

That wouldn't do any good. He wouldn't believe me. He'd think I was sparing his feelings. That it was merely a gross exaggeration to make some fragile peace between us.

I pause when I reach the tree line. But then I advance, even though my skirts get caught on the brambles.

I don't care. I need to move.

To *think.*

Viridian and I will be wed, regardless. There's nothing I can do to change that.

I'm not as resistant to it as I once was. Now, I can see a life with Viridian. A good life.

But I can also see a life with Loren, should both of us ever make it out of here. A quiet life. The life I'd always imagined for myself. But not the life that would set my soul free.

With Loren, I'd never leave Slyfell. I'd only ever see my little corner of the world. I'd only have control over my immediate circumstances, with no real power to effect change.

But with Viridian...

I'd see the world. Probably visit each of the five Courts. With Viridian, I would have a chance to do something that matters. I would have a chance to better the lives of countless humans, all over the kingdom. Despite my mortality shackling me, I'd feel so *alive*.

And I would do it with a male that I respect. A male that I enjoy talking to. A male whose companionship is enough to put a smile on my face.

A male that I can be myself with. My true self. Without having to put on a show.

Someone I can just *exist* with.

Before Viridian, I didn't know that was even possible.

Now, I can't imagine life without it.

How far am I willing to go to keep him?

I come to a stop.

How far am I willing to go to keep him? How much am I willing to sacrifice?

The truth is, even I can't answer that question.

I have no idea how far I would go. How much I would give.

Death's words fill the corners of my mind.

"When the time comes, you must choose. Choose life, without love, in a cursed land. Or choose death in the name of love, and sacred sacrifice."

Chills trickle down my spine.

I have a sickening feeling that I won't have long before I have to make that choice.

Before I realize just how far I would go for love.

CHAPTER TWENTY-EIGHT

T HE RED HUES of sunset bleed into the sky when I return to the castle. It's only when Tiffy's eyes go wide at the sight of me that I realize how long I've been gone.

"There you are!" she squeals, taking my arm. "I've been looking all over for you!" She looks down at my arms, and then my skirts. "What on the gods' green earth happened to you? You look like you've gone wild!"

"What time is it?" I ask, ignoring her remark.

"Nearly time for dinner." Her voice is rushed, and I swear it elevates several octaves. Pressing her hands to my upper back, she ushers me upstairs and into my bedchamber. "We have no time, no time at all, to get you ready."

"It's all right, Tiffy," I tell her. "Don't rush. I'll explain to His Highness that I simply lost track of time."

That doesn't seem to satisfy her, but she just takes a breath and busies herself with removing my tattered gown. I notice she's alone tonight. Following our routine, I head to the washroom, where the tub is already filled with water.

I step into it. My muscles constrict.

It's my own fault the water's cold.

I don't complain, but I can tell that Tiffy notices my reaction. She doesn't say anything, instead scrubbing my skin clean.

"You've scratched yourself," she mutters. "Shall I tend to them?"

I shake my head. "I'm fine, they're just minor scratches."

Tiffy meets my eyes for a moment, arching a brow.

"Really, Tiffy," I say, lightening my voice.

"Oh, all right." She smiles a little, moving her head back and forth slightly. She playfully nudges my shoulder. "What am I going to do with you?"

I shrug and make the best doe-eyed face I can muster.

Tiffy laughs with a roll of her eyes. "Enough of you," she teases.

I can't help but smirk. Then I remember what I overheard Viridian tell Myrdin.

And my stomach twists into knots.

How can I ignore it? How can I face him, and say nothing, knowing what I do?

Tiffy dresses me quickly and styles my hair into a simple knot. Once she finishes, I thank her and make my way to the great hall.

Viridian has already begun the first course when I arrive. He sits with his elbows resting on the table, head bent over his plate.

The door echoes when it closes behind me.

"You're here," Viridian says softly, looking up at me with a hint of surprise. As if he didn't think I would come.

"I'm here," I repeat, frozen in place.

"I'll have someone bring out your first course," he tells me, looking down at his own.

"That's not necessary," I say, taking my seat. "I'll just start with the second."

Viridian only nods.

I chew on my bottom lip. I had so many words a few hours ago. Where have they gone?

Viridian finishes his first course, and the servants

bring out the next. It's a meat pie of some kind tonight—meat stewed with vegetables and gravy, baked in a flaky, delectable crust.

I take my time eating it.

"You've been quiet tonight," Viridian remarks. Leaning forward, he looks at me, as if I were a puzzle he's trying to put together. "Something troubles you."

He's right. So, I finally tell him what's on my mind. The elephant in the room I can no longer ignore.

"You're jealous of Loren."

Viridian shuts his eyes and pinches the bridge of his nose. "You weren't supposed to hear that."

"But I did."

Viridian says nothing. He picks up his fork but doesn't use it.

"Did you... Did you mean what you said? About caring for me?"

Viridian's gaze locks with mine, and for the first time in a long while, he lets his barriers fall. "Every word, Little Fawn. I meant every word."

Warmth blooms in my chest. Relief skitters through my body, and I almost feel dizzy. As if I were drunk on the feeling.

I haven't lost him yet.

Viridian is quiet, amber eyes studying me instead. Is

he happy with what he sees in my expression? He's gone stone-faced, making him nearly impossible to read. I don't want those barriers up again so soon.

Before I realize what's happening, I utter the words I've been keeping locked away.

The words I've finally found the courage to say.

"I don't love Loren anymore." My voice is faint. "Not like that."

Deep down, I know I'll always love him. But now, I'm falling for another.

And soon, my heart will belong to him. Fully.

Viridian's stone-faced expression falls. The corner of his mouth perks up, a slight smile pulling at his lips. It delights me to see it. "Is that so?"

"Yes," I say solemnly, meeting his gaze. I even my breathing, fighting the nerves that threaten to close my mouth. "Let Loren go, Viridian. Please. You have no reason to keep him here anymore."

Viridian's smile falls, and he turns his face from mine. As if he's scolding himself for daring to hope I'd forgotten all about Loren. He's silent for a moment. Have I said something wrong?

"If that is what you wish," he says, breaking the silence.

"It is."

He hesitates and presses his mouth into a fine line. His whole upper body stiffens.

"Then it will be done." Viridian beckons to the nearest guard, resigned. "Release the prisoner at once. See to it that he's long gone before I change my mind."

"Right away, Your Highness." The guard bows her head, and then exits.

"Thank you," I tell him.

Viridian just nods, eyes falling to his plate. He doesn't say another word.

We finish our meals in silence.

I WAKE TO a hurried knock at my chamber door.

Suddenly alert, I sit up in bed, straining my ears to listen. My heart rate accelerates, beating fast. Swinging my legs from under the covers, I rise to my feet.

Who would want to see me at this hour?

The knocking sounds again. This time, it's accompanied by a voice.

"Cryssa! Cryssa, are you there?"

My eyes widen, and I fly to the door. When I open it, I cover my mouth.

"What are you doing here?" I ask, my shoulders

suddenly tense. My voice is harsher than I intend. "Have you lost your gods-damned mind?"

Loren flashes a smile at me. One that would have made my knees weak before coming to High Keep.

But that was then. And only then.

"I had to find you," he says. "I couldn't leave this wretched place without you."

"You must go," I tell him, my voice laced with urgency. "Viridian—he'll kill you if he finds you here."

"So, he won't find me," Loren says, as if it were that easy.

"I'm—look at me." I gesture to myself. "I'm not even dressed."

Loren doesn't miss a beat. "Then dress quickly."

I hesitate. Something tucked away in the corner of my mind is still screaming at me to run, to go with Loren and leave this place right now, appearances be damned. But my feet seem fixed to the floor, and I can't find the strength to move.

Because the rest of me doesn't want to.

"Cryssa," Loren says, brows stitching together. "What is it?"

"You can't stay."

"And neither can you." Loren frowns.

Blood thuds in my ears. My palms grow sweaty with

panic.

"Loren," I grind out. "Stop fighting me. You have to go *now*. Before Viridian—"

"Before I *what*, Cryssa?"

I turn to his deep rumble, my eyes wide. I've never heard him say my name like that before. So bitter and wounded, as if I've slapped him.

Guilt swirls in my stomach. I instantly wish I hadn't said anything at all, that he hadn't found me with Loren in nothing but my nightgown.

Gods above.

This looks bad. This looks very, *very* bad.

"Before you get angry," I say, forcing myself to look at him.

Viridian's expression hardens, the angles of his face growing sharp, like knives. His amber eyes fume, but he doesn't look at Loren. He only stares at me, his gaze locked with mine.

I press my lips together, fighting the tears that gather in my eyes.

"Viridian—"

"You." He says to Loren, not once breaking eye contact with me. "If you want to live, I'd suggest you leave. Now."

Loren balls his hands into fists, his face red with

anger. But he does. With one last glance at me, he takes off, running down the hall.

"Please," I beg. "This isn't what it looks like."

"Isn't it?" Viridian asks, his voice ripe with the sting of betrayal. "I thought we were past this, but..." He recoils, mouth curled with disgust. "You still see me as some horrible monster."

"No." I shake my head. "No, I don't."

But he steps back, turning his face from mine. "I dared to let myself think..." his voice trails off, tortured agony gripping his handsome features. "Perhaps I have been a fool, after all." His voice goes lower, heavy like a death sentence. "You will never, ever love me."

"No!" I cry. My heart aches, like it's breaking. It *is* breaking. "No, that's not true."

Viridian says nothing. And somehow, him saying nothing is so much worse.

Then he turns, facing his back to me.

"Viridian," I plead.

But he ignores me and walks away.

"Viridian!" I start after him.

Still no response.

"Viridian!"

I sink to my knees. In the middle of the corridor. Tilting my head down, I hold my face in my hands. Instead of bringing him closer, I've only pushed him farther away.

Somewhere far beyond my reach.

Oh, gods.

What have I done?

CHAPTER
TWENTY-NINE

WHAT LITTLE routine I'd had left is gone.

Viridian doesn't dine with me anymore. Still, I go to the great hall, and I wait for him. Hoping I'll see him sitting at the end of the table. Hoping he'll be waiting for me with that smile I adore. The smile I miss, so desperately. I would do anything, if it means I get to see that smile again.

But he doesn't come. And I eat my dinner alone.

Day, after day, after day.

Though no matter how much I wish to escape it, wedding preparations corner me at every turn. Cakes to try. Styles to choose from. Invitations to approve. As if that wasn't enough, servants pepper me with questions about the wedding.

Where would you like the ceremony to be held?
Which flowers would you like?
Shall we place them here or there?

I don't know how to tell them that I don't care about any of it. That none of it matters.

The few times I leave my chamber, the halls are bustling with preparations. The finest drapes adorn the walls, and I swear every ounce of metal in the castle shines.

Even as the day grows nearer, the numbness that's befallen me doesn't show any sign of letting go. I know I should feel something. Anticipation, excitement, nerves. Some flicker of emotion that tells me that I'm a bride to be.

But there's nothing.

Every feeling I would have had leading up to this day was silenced the last time Viridian spoke to me. The day I sentenced us to a lifetime of unhappiness.

"You will never, ever love me."

I've failed to show him otherwise. To prove to him that I could love him.

That maybe, I already do.

The knock at the door does little to pull me from my thoughts. When I don't answer, the door opens slightly.

Tiffy pokes her head in, wearing a long face when she sees me.

I'm sitting on the floor, supporting my back against the footboard of my bed. I balance a sketchbook on my lap, lightly pressing a charcoal stick to the page. I think of the colored wax that sits abandoned in my studio. Lately, I've opted for black-and-white instead.

"Miss," Tiffy says, gently, as if not to startle me. "It's time for your fitting."

"Fitting?" I ask, briefly looking up at her.

"For your wedding gown," she answers.

"Ah." I nod slowly. That is today, I remember.

"Shall I tell them to come back another time?" I hate the pity I hear in her voice.

"No," I tell her, standing. I place my sketchbook and charcoal stick onto my bed, careful to place the charcoal on the page and not my bedding. "I'm ready."

Tiffy eyes me like she doesn't believe me. I avoid looking at her.

"Onward." I gesture to the door.

Tiffy just presses her lips together, in what seems like an effort not to frown. She leads me out of my chamber, through the halls until we reach a sitting room.

Inside, there are three women—whom I assume to be seamstresses—fussing over a gown they've laid out on a divan. The women's rounded ears tell me they're human.

Some time ago, it would have been nice to be in the company of humans.

Some time ago, it would have helped me feel less alone.

But now, nothing can soothe the bite of loneliness. There is only one person whose company I care to share. Only, that person doesn't want to see me.

Tears sting my eyes, and I shut them to keep the waterworks at bay.

When I open them again, I catch Tiffy staring at me before she diverts her attention elsewhere. I force a smile and look at the seamstresses. Though, I don't reach their eyes.

"Good afternoon, Miss," the one closest to me says with a curtsy. Her graying hair tells me she's the oldest of the three, and the air of authority surrounding her tells me she's the one in charge. She sweeps her hand toward a round wooden platform. "If you could step up here, please."

I nod, and pick up my skirts to step forward, onto the platform.

Tiffy moves forward to untie my corset. Once it's loosened, she pulls my dress down and helps me step out of it. Then the seamstresses guide me into the gown they brought—my wedding dress, I realize—and pull it up until the sleeves reach my shoulders. They fasten the bodice around me and fluff out the skirt.

Tiffy moves a cheval mirror, placing it in front of me, but I turn my face away.

The seamstresses mutter amongst themselves, sticking pins into the skirt and in some places along my waist. One holds some fabric in place while the other two make adjustments, armed with sewing needles and small spools of delicate, white thread.

I feel as if I am merely a doll, standing in place. My mind is clear of thoughts, and I can't seem to summon any. If one of the seamstresses were to prick me with a needle, I doubt I would feel it.

I don't feel anything.

Not a single thing.

"Miss?" one of the seamstresses asks.

"Yes?" I reply, raising my brows. "Did you say something?"

"I asked if you like it, Miss?" The seamstress smooths my skirt. "Is there anything you'd like to have changed?"

Forcing myself to look in the mirror, I can't help but stare at my reflection. Now, I understand why Tiffy keeps looking at me the way she does—with that concerned look. My auburn hair hangs limp around my face. Dark circles gather under my eyes, and they're puffy from the lack of sleep. My golden-brown irises look dull, as if they've lost their shine. Lightly, I touch my fingers to my cheeks. My skin seems washed-out, as if I've neglected to care for myself.

How could I have let this happen?

The question is twofold. It pertains to my physical appearance, yes, but also the circumstances that led me here.

How *could* I have let this happen?

Why wasn't I willing to do what it took to show Viridian that I do care for him? That I *can* love him? That being apart from him feels as though my heart has been ripped from my chest?

"Miss?" Tiffy steps forward, her mouth tight with worry.

I snap out of my stupor and focus my attention on the dress. It's a beautiful ivory color, decorated with romantic lace detailing. It has long, lace sleeves that come down past my wrists, about half-way down my hands, and a flowing skirt with a sizable train. The sweeping neckline is also intricately detailed, with the same luminescent silver metal that's been spun into the small, flowery detailing at the skirt's hemline.

"It's..." My voice trails off. The never-ending

numbness eating at me takes away my ability to form an opinion. "It's beautiful."

And it is beautiful. Truly.

The seamstresses exchange glances. Though, I can't tell what kind.

"Well," Tiffy interjects, sparing me, "if Miss Thurdred thinks of anything she'd like altered, we will inform you immediately."

That seems to appease the seamstresses.

"Wonderful," the lead seamstress says. With that, she and Tiffy help me out of my wedding dress, and back into my day gown.

Tiffy escorts me back to my chamber and lingers in the threshold.

"Is there anything I can do for you, Miss?" she asks, pressing her hands to her abdomen.

I shake my head. "I'm all right."

Tiffy's expression seems to fall, sinking further into pity that I don't want to see. She swallows. "Very well, then. Do let me know if there's anything I can do." She reaches out and places her hand on my arm. "Anything at all."

I take a breath and meet her eyes, mustering the strength to offer her something akin to a smile. "I will. Thank you, Tiffy."

She just nods. Stepping back slowly, she gently closes my chamber door.

I move to my bed and let myself fall onto the mattress. Careful not to kick my sketchbook where I left it on the end of my bed earlier, I turn onto my side, and pull the covers over myself.

And even though it's not yet dark outside, and I haven't eaten dinner, I close my eyes.

It's not long before sleep pulls me under.

CHAPTER THIRTY

WHEN THE DREADED day comes, I wake before the sun.

I lay there, with my eyes closed, for hours. It's only when Tiffy and a slew of ladies' maids—much more than usual—arrive that I finally find the energy to rise.

Though, I wish I did not awaken. I wish I could sleep through this entire day, pretending like it's any other.

But I can't.

The guilt and despair that grips my chest is so strong, it's as if my rib cage will snap under the pressure. I lift my gaze from the floor.

Tiffy cradles a white dress in her arms.

My heart thunders in my chest.

Today is my wedding day.

Today, I'll be wed to a male that wants nothing to do with me.

I clench my jaw and grind my teeth. It's all I can do to keep the air flowing through my lungs. I take a series of deep breaths, preparing myself for what I know will be the longest day of my life.

Inhale.

Exhale.

Inhale.

Exhale.

Inhale.

Exhale.

It's all too easy to feel sorry for myself. But I have no one else to blame. Though, I wish I could blame someone else. I wish I could be angry at Viridian. That I could curse his name and all he stands for.

But I can't find it in myself to blame him for our situation.

I'm the one that ruined this day for us.

We both knew this day would come. Whether or not we wanted it to.

Still, neither of us could have known this is where we

would stand when it came time to say, "I do."

Tiffy lays the dress flat on my bed and lightly guides me into the washroom. I hold out my arms, and my ladies' maids remove my nightgown. I step into the full tub, the hot water kissing my skin.

It's the most sensation I've felt in days.

I sink lower into the tub until the water reaches my chin. I tilt my head back, so my hair is submerged. Tiffy gently pulls me up, so my scalp is above water, and begins to massage soap into my hair. While she does this, two of my other ladies' maids scrub my arms, and two rub stones into the soles of my feet.

They finish and help me out of the tub. Once my hair is dry, Tiffy wraps me in a dressing robe and sits me down at my vanity table to style my hair.

I've sat here so many times before.

But I've never felt like this. As if I were in a waking nightmare, mindlessly going through the motions. I wish this really was a nightmare. Because if it were, then I could wake up. And none of it would be real.

"What would you like today, Miss?" Tiffy asks, running her fingers through my hair.

I shrug. "Whatever you think is best."

Tiffy's shoulders rise and fall with a single, deep breath. She just nods and presses her lips together. She waits a moment before separating my hair into sections. I watch her as she braids, twists, and pins hair to my head. Before I know it, delicate braids swirl and curve around my head.

Tiffy helps me to my feet, placing a small handheld mirror in my hand so I can see my reflection. The braids twist around each other and intertwine into an intricate style, while the rest of my hair hangs down my back in loose waves.

"It's beautiful, Tiffy," I tell her. "Thank you."

"Of course." She dips her head. "Come," she says softly, leading me to my bed. "Let's get you dressed."

Tiffy and my ladies' maids help me into my wedding gown. They tighten the bodice, fastening it around my waist. The adjustments the seamstresses made hug my curves in all the right places, emphasizing my figure. Then, one of my ladies' maids places a small tiara upon my head and a lovely chiffon veil over my face.

They smooth out my train so that it elegantly flows behind me. Then Tiffy nods, giving me a look of approval. The other ladies' maids back away, clasping their hands.

"Are you ready?" Tiffy asks, meeting my eyes.

I take a deep breath, filling my lungs.

No, I want to say. *I don't think I'll ever be ready for this.*

But I flash her a small smile. "Yes. I'm ready."

Tiffy takes my arm and walks with me out of my bedchamber, and down the main staircase. We move through the halls and out onto the castle grounds.

There are rows of chairs, neatly arranged between long lines of flower arrangements, already filled with people. Other than Lymseia and Myrdin, I don't see any familiar faces. A long, bronze carpet has been rolled out between them, leading to a beautiful archway filled with red roses.

Beneath the archway, is Viridian.

My heart constricts at the sight of him.

He stands with his hands behind his back, holding his head high. He wears a fine, white brocade jacket with bronze-metal detailing, and matching pants. His clothes have been tailored perfectly to his body, highlighting his lean, muscled physique. His black hair has been combed back, but there's still a tendril of it that hangs in front of his eyes. His gaze narrows before him, mouth pressed into a fine line.

When we approach the end of the aisle, Tiffy moves away from my side, and takes her place behind me.

The musicians waiting on the outskirts of the gathering lift their instruments when they see me. They begin to play. A light, happy piece.

It does little to lessen the weight on my shoulders.

The people gathered here straighten in their seats and turn toward the aisle.

Viridian's tired eyes find mine.

I'm frozen in place. It takes everything I have to not turn around and run away. To not let my feet carry me all the way back to my bedchamber and lock myself inside.

At the front, sitting in the first row by Viridian, the High King's brows tighten.

Tiffy coughs behind me.

Swallowing, I move forward.

People flash smiles at me as I pass. When I approach Lymseia, she offers me a low-spirited look. As if to say, "*I know how difficult this is for you.*"

I look away and continue.

Reaching the archway, I come to a stop across from Viridian. Now, I can't avoid his expression.

I wish he was angry with me. Gods, I even wish he hated me. That he couldn't stand the sight of me.

Anything would be better than the lack of emotion I now see wearing down Viridian's handsome features. The empty expression that I know I share.

We're surrounded by people, but it feels as if we're alone. We stand only an arm's length from each other, yet it feels as if we're worlds away.

Behind me, Tiffy adjusts my veil and my train. She bows to Viridian, and then she retreats down the aisle, until she's out of sight.

My chest aches. I wish she'd stay.

I cast my eyes down at my hands. I know if I meet Viridian's eyes, I won't be able to maintain my composure.

The priestess of Ohesis stands before Viridian and me. I've never been to a temple of Ohesis, the God of Marriage and Family, but even I can tell the blush colored robes she now wears are ceremonial.

"Good afternoon to all that gather here on this beautiful day," the priestess begins, gesturing to the crowd on both sides. "It is with great pleasure that we meet here today, for the union of our Crown Prince, and his betrothed."

I don't look at the priestess while she speaks. I'm drawn to Viridian, and I can't look away. Even though it only brings me pain.

He hardens his expression, mouth tight. He looks anywhere but my direction.

"We ask that Ohesis bless this male and this female," the priestess continues, "as they both unite under his divine grace as husband and wife. Until both partners reach Death's embrace, they shall remain as one."

Viridian's expression darkens.

And a horrible truth falls over me.

There is no hope for us. We will never be happy together.

Arms outstretched with her palms facing up, the priestess smiles at us. "You may now take hands, to symbolize your partnership and commitment to one another."

Viridian hesitates. He takes a breath, and then takes my hands, recoiling as if the mere touch of my skin burns.

Looking over his shoulder, I see the High King furrow his brow. His burnt-orange eyes flare, and the muscles in his jaw tick with dissatisfaction. But I see through his mask. Underneath, I see what he tries to hide.

Fear.

There is something Vorr fears. Something that drives this marriage. And it is not love.

That, Viridian's demeanor makes painfully obvious.

I force myself to breathe.

Inhale.

Exhale.

The priestess continues leading the ceremony. My stomach twists into knots. She speaks of marriage, family, and the union of two souls.

But all I can think of is the darkness clawing at my chest. The guilt, and the knife it wields, carving me up inside.

I press my lips together, tightening my expression to hold back tears. If Acantha were here, she would know exactly what to say. With one embrace from my father, I would feel better. Stronger.

But Father and Acantha are not here.

I am alone, apart from my kind. Standing before a sea of noble fae that will never understand me or where I come from.

And Viridian...

The one person that I thought could bridge the gap can't even look me in the eyes.

That is what hurts the most.

We started as strangers. But somehow, we grew to be friends. More than friends.

Now, I've lost him forever. And it's all my fault.

Because I couldn't let go. Because I couldn't take a leap of faith.

Because I was afraid.

When I first arrived, I thought he was an arrogant, territorial fae male that only wanted to possess me. That he and I would never care for each other. That we would never overcome our differences.

If only I'd known, then, how wrong I was.

Then maybe, things between Viridian and I would be

different now.

I brush away the thought. No good can come from dwelling on the past.

"Cryssa Thurdred," the priestess says, her attention landing on me. "With Ohesis's blessing, do you accept His Highness, the Crown Prince Viridian Avanos, future High King of all Inatia, to be your wedded husband, from this day to your last?"

Feeling the High King's icy stare on me, I swallow the lump in my throat.

"Yes." I nod. Then I utter those fateful words. The words that swing down upon me like an executioner's blade. "I do."

The priestess looks at Viridian next. "And do you, Your Highness, Crown Prince Viridian Avanos, future High King of all Inatia, with Ohesis's blessing, accept Cryssa Thurdred to be your wedded wife, from this day to your last?"

Viridian hangs his head forward, briefly closing his eyes. I wish I could wipe away the heavy expression that I see there and ease his pain.

But I am only human, and I can't undo what I've done.

"Yes," he says at last. Still, he avoids my gaze, even as he says the words that will bind us until death. "I do."

The priestess raises her hands. "Then by the grace of Ohesis, we pray that this union pleases him, and all of the gods. And with his divine blessing, this union is sanctified."

Viridian turns to face the crowd. I do the same.

The audience claps. Instantly, I pick out Myrdin and Lymseia among the sea of faces. They don similar, disheartened expressions, their movements slow and labored.

Viridian takes my hand, though the motion is rigid and forced. Then, we walk down the aisle together, into the castle, and lead the crowd to the ballroom. There, we greet the guests. And when we've spoken to everyone, we take to the floor for our first dance.

It brings me back to the first time we danced here, in this ballroom.

He held me close then. Now, there is an uncomfortable distance between us, and we dance in silence.

What I would give, to rebuild what I've broken.

The dance ends, and Viridian releases me, taking a step back.

"Viridian..." I start.

But he doesn't listen. He turns his back to me and walks away.

My feet are frozen in place. All I can seem to do is look after him.

I find the strength to move, with half a mind to drown my sorrows in fae wine. Only now, there will be no Viridian to look out for me when I do.

So, I don't pick up a goblet when waitstaff pass me with a tray full of them.

"Cryssa!" Lymseia calls when she spots me. She advances, quickly closing the gap between us.

"What is it?" I ask. Chills trickle down my arms. I instantly know something's not right. "What's wrong?"

Her eyes flick behind me, to someone standing at my back. Then she levels her gaze. "It's your father."

My heart falls.

The way she says the words tells me that something terrible will follow. When she does, it's much worse than I could have ever imagined.

"He's fallen ill." Sorrow fills her expression. "It's the mining sickness."

CHAPTER THIRTY-ONE

P ANIC SEIZES ME, and it steals all the breath from my lungs.

Father is ill.

The mining sickness has finally caught him.

No.

My chest constricts.

Not Father.

How could the gods be so cruel?

"You must go to him," Viridian says quietly from behind me.

"What?" I whirl around to face him, my voice equally low.

"You must go to him," he repeats. His body has gone so still, that if not for the rise and fall of his breath, one might mistake him for a statue.

"But—"

"Go, Cryssa." His tone is firm. Cold, as it once was. "Your family needs you."

And I need you, I think. Though, I dare not say it aloud.

"What about the High King?" I ask, my head swimming. "He won't let me leave."

"My father has nothing to say on the matter," Viridian tells me. To Lymseia, he says, "Bring her now. Take my horse. It's the fastest we have."

Lymseia bows her head, body alert. Ready for anything. "Come," she says, pulling me with her. "We must leave, now."

I nod, letting her drag me forward. We make our way through the throng of guests blocking our path, quickening our pace once we reach the corridor. Lymseia breaks into a run, and I pick up my skirts to match her pace. We don't stop until we reach the stables.

Effortlessly, Lymseia hoists herself up onto Nightfoot's back, tugging me up after her.

Once I'm steady, she flicks the reins, and we take off into the night.

THE RIDE TO Slyfell isn't what I thought it would be. It's ridden with panic, my fear growing as we near our destination. We ride through the nights, only stopping to let Nightfoot drink and rest. I barely eat during the four-day journey.

When we reach Slyfell, Lymseia and I ride through the city, passing familiar buildings and places I once knew.

We don't stop until we reach my family's small cottage in the human districts.

It feels strange to be back here. I'm not the girl I was when I left home. I'm not the Cryssa that used to live here.

So, I hesitate when I approach the door.

Lymseia stands some distance behind me, patting the horse. When I reach for the door handle, she re-mounts Nightfoot and takes the reins.

"You're not staying?" I ask.

She shakes her head, eyes sad. "My place is in Keuron."

The true meaning of her words falls over me. It weighs me down like *gohlrunn*.

Viridian doesn't expect me to return.

When he told me to go home, he was saying goodbye.

I cover my mouth, eyes wide with the realization.

"Go," Lymseia urges me. "See your father. I know this is not goodbye for us, Cryssa Thurdred."

I nod. "Thank you. I will see you again."

She offers me a weak smirk. "I'm counting on it." Then, with a jerk of the horse's reins, she rides off.

Taking a deep breath, I push open the door.

Acantha sits at our small dining table, a dim fire cracking in the hearth behind her. She rests her elbows on the table, holding her face in her hands.

I move to her immediately, touching my hands to her upper back and shoulder. "Acantha," I breathe.

She snaps her head toward mine. Her cheeks are a bright red, stained with salty streaks left behind by her tears.

"Cryssa," she sobs at the sight of me. "Please tell me that's really you."

"It's really me." I throw my arms around her, holding her tight.

"We sent the message to you not knowing if you'd ever receive it," she whimpers, taking short breaths. "But we had to try to tell you."

"I know," I coo, rubbing my hand back and forth

across her back. "How... How is he?"

"He's stable, for now." Acantha pulls away, wiping her eyes with the back of her hand. "He's been asking for you." Her bottom lip trembles. "I didn't know how to tell him you were... That you weren't..."

"Shh." I pull her close again, lightly stroking her hair. "I'm here now. I'm here."

I push whatever emotions I had coming in here aside. Right now, she and Father are all that matters.

Viridian was right. They need me.

And I'm not going to falter.

"I'm going to go see Father now," I tell Acantha, stepping away. "But I'll be right back."

She hiccups, but manages to nod.

I cross the compact room to the stairs and climb them. Then I turn left, and step into Father's room.

Carefully, I open the door and cross the threshold. My father lays in bed, propped up with several pillows. Knit blankets cover his chest, and his head leans to the side, eyes closed. Though labored, his breath rises and falls evenly, which comes as a good sign.

Still, I can't help but wonder how long it will be before his condition deteriorates.

But I know it will be soon.

I swallow.

Father stirs, opening his eyes. He widens them when he sees me and rubs his forehead.

"Cryssa, my darling," Father says, moving to sit up. "Is that you or have I started hallucinating?"

"Rest, Father." I sit at the edge of his bed and hold out my palm to urge him back down. "It's really me. You're not hallucinating."

"How?" Father's brows stitch together, glancing down at my dress. "Is that... How did you escape?"

"It's a wedding dress," I tell him, my voice tightening. "And I didn't escape." My voice softens. "He let me go."

Understanding flashes in Father's expression, softened by a tender look.

"When I heard the news, I had to come see you," I continue before he can ask me more questions. "How are you feeling?"

Father coughs. It's an airy, grating sound. "I'm well enough, for now."

I press my lips together.

"Truly, my darling," he takes my hand and squeezes it. "You need not worry."

"How can I not worry," I start, looking away, "when no one has fallen ill with this sickness and survived?"

"There are a few who have." To everyone else, Father sounds sure of himself. Confident, even. But I know him.

The slight waver of pitch I hear in his voice tells me that he's lying.

I say nothing and opt for slightly shaking my head instead.

Determination surges in my gut.

I can save my father.

I can save all the miners. I can stop the draining of the mines.

I can cleanse the kingdom.

Death's voice fills my mind.

"When the time comes, you must choose. Choose life, without love, in a cursed land. Or choose death in the name of love, and sacred sacrifice."

And something tells me that I'm the only one who can.

"Cryssa..." Father's voice trails off. He takes both of my hands and looks me in the eyes. "If I don't survive this, there is something you should know."

"Father, whatever it is, it won't change how I see you," I say, firm in my resolve. "You're going to live through this. You don't have to tell me anything."

"Please, Cryssa," my father begs, and I go still. "You must know this, all the same."

I lean back a little, brows raised.

Father's gaze flicks down to his hands, and then back

up to my eyes. "Your mother and I…" he pauses and takes a breath. "We aren't your birth parents."

My brows knit together and my stomach twists into knots.

"What?"

"When you were a baby, your mother worked in the service of Lady Helenia Pelleveron."

"The younger sister of Lady Maelyrra?"

"Yes." Father nods. "At the time, Lady Helenia was unwed."

The sickening sensation in my stomach tells me exactly where this is going.

"Helenia had a lover," Father continues. "A human. The relationship was short-lived." Then he looks at me. "You are what came of that relationship."

I force myself to breathe.

"Maelyrra was furious when she found out." He says slowly, "She wouldn't allow Helenia to keep you."

"Of course not." Anger bubbles inside me. "You know how the Pelleverons are with humans."

"I know." Father's voice is low. "When that happened, Nira brought you home. And you've been with us ever since."

Silence sits between us.

The truth of what Father tells me sinks into my

bones.

I'm not—

I'm not fully human.

I'm demi-fae.

"And Acantha?" I ask at last, feeling like a shell of myself.

"She's ours," Father murmurs. "Nira was already pregnant with her when you were born."

I turn my face away.

"Make no mistake," Father says, tightening his hands around mine. I'm compelled to look at him when he does. "It might not be my blood running through your veins, but I am your father. Nira was your mother. You are *ours*." He reaches out to cup my face. "And you always will be."

I nod, tightening my mouth to rein in my raging emotions.

"I should let you rest." I gather my skirts to stand.

Father watches me through sad eyes. "I love you, Cryssa. More than anything."

"I love you, too." I give Father's hand a squeeze. "This doesn't change that. I just..." Swallowing, I find my words. "I just need time."

Father smiles weakly. "I understand."

I bend down and press a kiss to his cheek. Father closes his eyes, and I slip from the room.

Downstairs, Acantha stands by the hearth, stirring a pot that hangs over the fire.

"Stew will be ready in a moment," she says, glancing over her shoulder.

Food.

My stomach rumbles with hunger. It's been nearly two days since I've eaten.

"Wonderful." I hesitate and look down at my wedding dress, dirty and tattered from the journey here. "Is there..."

"Your other dress is still in your closet," Acantha tells me. Her stirring motions slow.

"Thank you," I say. Then I head upstairs to my room.

I step into the hall slowly, careful not to disturb Father. Opening the door, I peek inside. Emotions I can't seem to place grip me from the inside while my eyes roam the space. Taking it all in.

Everything is exactly how I left it.

Acantha's and my twin beds sit in the center of the room, separated by a small, wooden nightstand. My old sketchbook sits on my bed, which has been neatly made— likely thanks to Acantha. The only thing missing is my cloak, which I know still hangs inside of my wardrobe back at High Keep.

I move farther into the compact room and approach

the rickety wardrobe. I run my fingers along the worn wood before opening the door.

Acantha's spare dress hangs on the far-right side. Mine waits to the far-left.

I pull it from the wardrobe and raise it to my nose. Breathing in, a familiar scent washes over me, even though I can tell it's been washed in the time I've been gone.

Slowly, I cross the room and approach the window. Wrapping my arms around myself, still holding my dress, I stare through the glass. I look at the tree just outside. The one I used to climb down to go see Loren at night.

Some of its branches are cracked, still bare from the cold season. I yearn to open the window. To reach out and touch it.

But I don't.

This time, I stay inside, remembering all that's happened since the last time I snuck out. This time, I leave the window closed.

Returning to my bed, I set down my clean dress before freeing myself from my wedding gown's tight bodice. Contorting myself to reach the fastenings behind me, I find myself missing Tiffy. Her smile, the ease with which she gets me in and out of gowns. Her soft, motherly nature, despite being so young.

I wonder what she would say if she were here.

Eventually, I loosen the bodice enough to pull it down past my hips. I step out of it and into my old, familiar dress. Once I'm clothed, I pick up my ruined wedding gown and fold it, placing it on the floor of the wardrobe when I'm done.

Taking a deep breath, I leave my bedroom.

When I reach the first floor, I see Acantha has moved from the hearth to the table. She sets out three wooden bowls—one for her, one for Father, and one for me.

She fills one and sets it aside before spooning hot stew into the next two bowls. Then, she places wooden spoons into all three.

"I'll go bring this to Father," she tells me, her tone still muted.

Sitting, I nod.

When she returns, she takes the seat next to mine and pulls her bowl closer. I do the same and lift my spoon, gently blowing away the steam.

She smiles at me, though I can tell it's weak. "I'm glad you're home."

I return her expression. "Me, too. I've missed you."

Acantha's mouth wobbles. "I've missed you, too. So much."

"I know." It kills me, knowing I'll have to leave her again so soon.

But I can't stay. Even though I wish I could.

Now that I'm back here, it's all the more obvious that my heart is back at High Keep.

With Viridian.

I take a bite of stew, chewing slowly.

I have to go back to Keuron to save my father. Whatever dark magic is poisoning him, the way to undo it is there. I don't know how I know, but I do.

But I also have to go back for myself.

For my heart.

Acantha casts her eyes down, into her stew. "I understand if you can't stay."

That pulls my head up.

She meets my gaze, love and understanding shining in her expression. "We always knew you would never settle down here, Cryssa."

"Are you sure?" I ask her. Guilt creeps into my chest. "What about Father?"

"I'll look after him." Acantha nods, emphasizing her words. She places her palm over my forearm. "Go. Live your life. We'll be all right."

I nod. Tears gather in my eyes.

Acantha pulls me into an embrace.

Glancing down at my bowl, she points a finger at it. "You'd better finish that first."

385

I laugh, and then I do. Once my bowl's empty, I run up to see Father. He cradles his own bowl of stew in his hands, leaning forward as he eats.

"I have to go," I tell him, a sense of urgency permeating my words. I hug him and press my eyes shut for a moment before pulling away. "I'm going to help you, Father. You will be all right. I promise."

Father arches a brow my way, opening his mouth as if to speak.

"There's no time," I tell him, already moving to the door. "I'll explain everything when I see you again."

If I'm going to make things right with Viridian, and stop whatever dark magic is poisoning my father, then I need to leave.

Now.

CHAPTER
THIRTY-TWO

I EMERGE FROM my childhood home and into the night. The action is oddly familiar, yet foreign at the same time. But this time, I leave home with a newfound purpose.

Rough hands that don't seem familiar hook around my waist and drag me forward, until I'm pressed against a body. Lips find my own, and my body recoils.

Instinctually, I bite down, a copper tang coloring my tongue.

I shove.

Hard.

"Damn it, Cryssa!" a masculine voice curses. "It's me!"

My eyes come into focus, and I see the man that stands before me.

Wide-eyed, Loren raises his fingers to his lip, staring at the bright red that now stains them. "Have you lost your gods-damned mind?"

"*You*," I snarl, holding myself back so I won't be tempted to throttle him. "What are you doing here?" I ask, lowering my voice. "Haven't you done enough?"

He's the reason Viridian thinks I don't want him.

It would be all too easy to blame him for everything. But I know I'm the one that's really at fault. Purpose surges through me, the force of it giving me more than enough strength to do what I have to.

I'm returning to Keuron to repair what's been broken.

And I won't let Loren hold me back. Not anymore.

It's time to let him go.

"I'm here for you," Loren says, as if that should have been obvious. "Aren't you happy to see me?"

When I don't say anything, he continues.

"My feelings for you haven't changed, Cryssa." He takes a step toward me. "I'm sorry I left you in Keuron with *him*."

The way he refers to Viridian boils my blood.

"Don't be sorry," I snap. "He's good to me. More than you could ever know."

"Good to you?" Loren leans back incredulously. "He imprisoned me *for weeks*. Maybe longer. He held you captive. He took you away from us—from your family."

"I know." My voice goes quiet.

How could I forget?

"Have you forgotten what Theelia's blessing means?" he seethes, while jabbing a finger at me. "That male could be your undoing. Do you even realize that he could be the reason you di—" He stumbles and covers his mouth, as if he can't bear to say the word. "Does that mean nothing to you?"

I turn my face away from his.

"Cryssa."

I say nothing, silently fuming. It's as if Viridian's quiet rage has somehow passed onto me.

"*Cryssa*." He gapes at me in horror. "What the hell happened to you?"

"What are you talking about?"

"The Cryssa I know would never have defended one of *them*."

He doesn't know that I am one of them. But I don't have enough time to tell him that.

I clench my jaw. "You know nothing."

"I don't need to know anything," he spits. "I've seen more than enough."

I spin around on my heels, poised to march in the opposite direction.

Loren grabs my arm, hard enough to bruise. When I look back at him, his eyes plead with me. "Don't go back to him."

"Let me go." Each syllable is sharper than steel.

"Don't go back to him," he repeats, still holding onto me. "Please."

I wrench my arm from his grip. "You can't stop me."

"Then at least tell me why." Loren's face twists with pain. "Why have you chosen him over me?"

Why is it that I find myself in this exact situation again, with a different man? Only this time, I don't feel conflicted. Even though it's hard for me, my inability to give him the answer he wants doesn't tear me apart.

If anything, it feels *right*.

"You and I—we're not compatible, Loren. We have vastly different ideas of what we want our lives to look like."

"That can't be it," he says, shaking his head. "We could work through that. We could find common gro—"

"No, Loren." I say, my voice firm, like stone. My gut

tells me that I should have done this a long time ago. "I won't settle. Not anymore."

"Settle?" His eyebrows shoot up, as if I've slapped him. "You'd have to *settle* to be happy with me, but not him? The noble fae that was so horrible to you? Even if you don't want to marry me, why go back to him?"

Tightening my mouth, I harden my expression.

"Don't tell me you..." Loren falls silent. His eyes widen with realization. "You... Oh gods. You *love* him, don't you?"

I want to reply, but I can't seem to summon the words. My silence is confirmation.

He's right.

I have changed.

Loren just stares at me, an awful concoction of hurt, anger, and rejection burning on his face. Heat stings my cheeks and tears prick at my eyes.

I never wanted to hurt him. But I meant what I told him that fateful day.

Meeting Viridian changed the course of my life forever.

He's my destiny, my future, and my solace, all wrapped up into one.

My mate.

I pause, like the whole world has frozen around me.

Viridian is my mate. And I love him.

I *love* him.

I can't believe it took me this long to realize. Looking back now, I see that Viridian made it perfectly obvious, even though he never blatantly spelled it out for me.

Now, I am even more sure that I have to get back to Keuron.

To Viridian.

"Loren, I—"

"Don't." The word is a soft blow of defeat.

My face is hot with something akin to shame, but I respect him enough not to push him. More roughly than I intended, I brush past Loren. Despite what he said, I expect him to argue with me, to beg me to reconsider. To say something, anything.

But he doesn't. And I don't look back.

Maybe I should. Maybe I should try to make things right between us. But I know if I do that, it'll only leave me feeling more torn than I already do. I can't give Loren what he wants. Not anymore.

So, I leave him there. *He'll get over me,* I tell myself. He'll move on.

And I will, too.

Firm in my resolve, I head for the stables. Only, this time, I'm not going there to meet anyone. Or to sneak around under the cover of darkness.

No, this time, I have a new purpose.

I'm going to steal a horse.

CHAPTER THIRTY-THREE

A S I APPROACH the stables, I slow my pace and keep my body close to the buildings that line the street.

Across the way, the tavern emits a dim glow. The sound of drunken laughter that spills from cracks in the door, on the other hand, is anything but faint.

I roll my eyes.

It's like I never left.

Renewing my focus, I narrow my eyes ahead. The stables are dark, save for the one lantern that always hangs outside. There's no light coming from the stable office next door.

Good. That means there's no one here to stop me.

Crouching, I creep forward and sneak in through the back, the way I used to when I would meet Loren here. Horses stand in their stalls. Most are filled, except for two or three that aren't occupied.

Scanning the walls, I find a spare saddle that one of the stable boys must have left laying around. Carefully, I pick it up and approach the closest stall. The horse expels air through its muzzle when I do.

I hold out my palm to keep the creature still, and to my surprise, it does.

Nerves thrum through me, my blood buzzing with adrenaline. I silently pray to any god that will listen, begging that no one hears me. Or sees me walk out of here with a horse.

I unlatch the stall door and step inside. Then, I raise the saddle and set it onto the horse's back. After fumbling with it for some time, I manage to secure it in place. Tugging gently, I lead the horse out of its stall and onto the street.

Poking my head out before the rest of me, I walk back up the street, the way I came, slowly pulling the horse along.

As soon as I'm able, I turn left, bringing us out of sight, should anyone in the stable office wake up. I'd be a fool to think I have much time before someone finds out one of the horses is missing.

So, I have to ride. I have to leave. Now.

But I freeze. I've never ridden a horse on my own before.

Panic grips my throat.

There's no time, I tell myself. *It's now or never.*

Taking a deep breath, I think back to when Viridian and I rode into Keuron from High Keep. It feels like it was only yesterday since we were laughing and talking with such ease.

"What is so amusing?" I had asked him. I remember how annoyed I was that he'd been entertained by my frustration.

"You," he'd replied. Like I was the only person in the world that mattered.

I recall the feel of his chest to my back and let it linger. Holding onto the memory of how close to me he'd been.

How close we can be again.

"All right, Cryssa," I say, in some effort to motivate myself. "If Viridian can do it, then so can you."

I think back to that moment and try to picture in my mind how Viridian helped me up. I had my foot in the stirrup, and then he lifted me higher until I was able to swing my leg over.

Now, I put my foot in the stirrup, and move to pull myself up. Like I did then, I find myself stuck there, my skirts bunched between my legs, holding me in place.

I let out a frustrated exhale, my cheeks hot.

Lifting my skirts so they're out of my way, I lower myself again and launch my body upward.

This time, I'm able to reach the horse's back. I lean forward, arms trembling as I hold myself there long enough to swing my leg over. With my legs on either side of the horse, I fall into place on the saddle.

"Whew," I breathe, and wipe away the sweat gathering on my brow with the back of my wrist.

But I'm not out of the woods yet. I may have successfully mounted the horse, but I still don't know how to ride.

Again, I think back to how Viridian used his legs to apply light pressure when we rode.

Partly to vex me, I know, I think with the hint of a smile playing at my lips. The memory of his thighs around my rear raises a blush to my cheeks.

But maybe, there's another reason he did that. Maybe, using your legs to apply light pressure is proper horse-riding technique.

I have nothing else to go off. It's worth a try.

Tightening my calves around the horse's abdomen, I take the reins and give them a gentle flick. The horse lets out a whinny and shakes its head.

I flick the reins again, harder this time.

Then, the horse moves. I use my legs to urge it forward again, and to my shock and relief, it starts trotting ahead. Commotion echoes in the distance.

I quicken our pace.

As if aware of my growing anxiety, the horse responds, moving from a trot to a gallop. I ride down the streets, jerking the reins to weave left and right to confuse anyone that might be on our trail.

Soon, I emerge from the cluster of buildings and onto empty meadows and farmland. I keep my focus trained ahead, even as I ride farther away from the city.

Farther away from the home I've always known.

When I arrived, I was just Cryssa. But when I leave, I'm someone else.

I leave as Cryssa Thurdred Pelleveron Avanos: demi-fae, mate and wife of the Crown Prince. Future High Queen of all Inatia.

Once I'm far enough away, I glance back over my shoulder.

I watch the city of Slyfell become smaller and smaller.

Then I turn around and face what lies ahead. Gripping the reins, my destination sits at the forefront of my mind.

And I picture Viridian's face.

I RIDE through the night and into the afternoon.

At some point, I start struggling less and gain more control of the horse. Leaning my head back, I look at the sky, relieved that the horse I unknowingly chose was easy to handle. For all I knew, I could have ended up with one as stubborn as I am. If that had been the case, I surely would have gotten caught and been hauled off to the city jail to rot.

But I didn't. And now I'm one step closer to Viridian.

That's what matters.

Tugging at the reins, the horse—who, in my tired ramblings, I've decided to call Storm because of his gray coat—slows. We approach a small farming town, called Hylmfirth, that marks the half-way point between Slyfell and Keuron. In the distance, I see a linear, wooden structure, with a wide mouth that delves into the earth.

A mine.

Uneasy, I dismount and guide Storm into the town. Every fiber in my body urges me to get back on and ride as far away from this place as I can. Still, I press on. Both of us need food and water if we're to make it to Keuron.

Though, there's an apprehension that I can't shake. *Something isn't right here.*

I want to dismiss my anxiety, to think that I'm just tired. That I need to sleep, and when I wake, I'll be able to think straight.

But I only take one step into the town when a chill trickles down my spine, only confirming my discomfort. The air is heavy with a foul stench, and I wince when it reaches my nose. Even Storm shakes his head, as if in some feeble attempt to dispel the odor.

Resisting the all too familiar sensation, my lungs constrict, tight in my chest.

I've encountered this kind of reek before.

In the East Tower.

That means...

The dark magic affecting High Keep is here, too.

If it's spread this far, I realize, wondering how I wasn't able to put the pieces together before, *then it's not just any dark magic.*

It's a curse.

My eyes widen, and I clench my jaw, my upper body

suddenly rigid. The East Tower's decay, the mining sickness, the mines draining of metals, all of it...

It's all because of a curse that's swallowing the kingdom. Piece by piece.

My stomach clenches with waves of nausea.

I have to tell Viridian.

He has to know how far the curse reaches. How much worse it is than we thought.

And if we don't find a way to break it soon...

How much more damage it will cause.

Highly aware of my surroundings, I move deeper into Hylmfirth. My skin crawls, and I'm itching to leave as soon as I can. As I draw nearer to the center of town, I see there are people sitting with their backs pressed to the buildings, lining the street.

Men, women, children...

I don't have to know these people to know who they are.

They're the families of miners, left with nothing when the mines emptied. They're people who have lost their livelihoods and their loved ones.

They've lost everything.

All of them wear ragged clothing, their faces gaunt and scraggly from what I can only assume is starvation. Their rounded ears poke through limp hair, while some don't have hair long enough to cover them.

Humans.

Starving, dying, desperate humans.

Some mutter prayers to gods who have seemingly abandoned them, while others stare ahead, unmoving. My heart sinks when I pass a woman rocking an infant to sleep. The child wails, its cries of distress piercing my ears.

The woman reaches out and grasps my skirt.

I pause, tightly gripping Storm's reins.

"Please, Miss," the woman begs, sobs racking her chest. The child in her arms howls even louder. "Please, help us. Help us."

"I'm sorry," I say, pulling back against her hold on me. "I don't have any coins." I wish I did. Acantha was only able to give me enough money to pay for a day's worth of supplies.

But the woman doesn't seem to hear me. Her cries only grow in strength, more forceful now. "Please, please, please!" she shrieks, her body shaking violently. Though, it doesn't seem like she's talking to me anymore.

I stumble backward and wrench my skirt from her grip. The woman doesn't seem to notice, too wrapped up in her mania to process. Taking advantage of the opportunity, I urge Storm to move us forward.

To my horror, others seem to share the woman's

hysteria. Others cry out as she does, begging the gods to do something.

To save them.

When I finally reach the town square, my breath catches in my throat. The market is nearly empty, with only a handful of stalls still open for business. So many of them sit abandoned, with the cloth awnings torn or littered with large holes.

What happened here?

Is the curse to blame for all this?

Hopping off Storm's back, I approach a market stall, sparsely stocked with produce that looks as if it's seen much better days. I eye it warily.

"I'll sell it to you for half the value," the farmer says wearily, rubbing his forehead. "Whatever you want."

Guilt tugs at my chest. "No," I assure him. He needs the coin more than I do. "I'll give you what it's worth."

"Thank you." He shoots me a grateful look.

I gesture to the apples. They look decent enough, and both Storm and I can eat those. "A half-dozen, please."

The farmer names his price, and I hand over the coins. The amount is less than I expect him to charge for how many apples I'm buying, but I don't fight him on it. Luckily for me, Storm's saddle is equipped with a leather bag for storage. I take the apples and put them in there.

"What happened here?" I ask.

"The mining sickness came first," the farmer tells me, eyes darkening. "And that was all it was, for a while. Then, more and more, the few miners that remained started coming back empty-handed." He hesitates, pressing a hand to his mouth. "We didn't think it could get much worse."

Dread grips my stomach.

"It spread to our land," the farmer continues. "Our crops... They'd near harvest, and then they'd turn black. Ruined." He pauses, as if the words weigh heavily on his shoulders. I imagine they do. "We couldn't eat them. We couldn't sell them."

"The crops are dying?" Fear rises into my throat.

The farmer nods. "It's a miracle that I have these to sell. They're all I have this season."

Gods above.

If the land itself is sick, then...

It's so much worse than I could have ever imagined.

I clear my throat. "Is there fresh water?"

"Yes, thank the gods," the farmer tells me. "There's a small creek just up the road, at the edge of town."

Thanking him, I nod and tug at Storm's reins. I'd wanted to stop here and rest, but after seeing the town's desolation, I don't want to stay a moment longer than I need to.

I can't. There's no time to spare.

Leading Storm out of the town, we pass through farmland. Running water echoes in the distance, telling me we're close.

But even out here, that awful stench still permeates the air.

My steps slow as I approach. Reaching the edge of a large field, I crouch, touching my fingers to the soil to steady myself.

On the ground before me, are blackened clumps of what used to be some kind of vegetable. It's so dark and rotted, that I can't tell what it once was. Fuzzy, green mold has claimed it, covering whatever it is with a layer of sickly fur. Looking up from the decayed vegetable, I see the plant itself hasn't been spared from the rot. Its once green leaves are now a sickly shade of gray, with vile spots of blackened disease.

Slowly, I rise to my feet.

The rot has consumed the entire field. No crop has been left untouched, devoured by its ravenous hunger.

Panic laces my movements, quickening my speed. I tug Storm away from the field, and cross what area remains between me and the creek.

When I reach the stream, I kneel at its bank.

Anxiety sets me on edge, and I dip my hands into the water. Is it truly safe? Or has the water been infected, like the land?

Cupping some in my hand, I lift the water to my nose. It doesn't smell off, and it's crystal clear, seemingly untainted. I take a small sip, letting it linger on my tongue before swallowing.

Once I've deemed the water to be safe to drink, I swallow several greedy gulps. With some coaxing, Storm laps water into his mouth. I pull out some apples, one for me, and three—actually, make that four—for Storm. After we've both eaten and rested, I wash my hands in the stream and wipe my mouth. Catching a whiff of myself, I grimace. I smell nearly as bad as the rot.

I eye the water, considering whether or not to wade in and clean myself. Though, without any soap, I doubt how much good it will do.

I can bathe when I return to High Keep.

After securing the last two apples in the saddle bag, I mount Storm and urge him forward, into a fast trot.

Anger knits my brows.

Whether Maelyrra Pelleveron wants to admit it or not, the curse has the Gold Court firm in its grasp. It won't be long now before angry, desperate humans reach her doorstep. Maybe then, she'll be forced to listen.

But Maelyrra has never cared for the humans living within her borders. Few noble fae ever do.

Resolve blazes in my chest, roaring like the strongest of fires.

When I am High Queen, things will be different.

With a flick of the reins, Storm breaks into a gallop. Come dawn, the day after tomorrow, I will arrive at High Keep.

And I will do whatever it takes to save my people.

Even if it costs me my life.

CHAPTER
THIRTY-FOUR

NEVER, IN A THOUSAND years, would I have thought that I would be so relieved to see Keuron's tiled roofs looming over the horizon. The rising sun shines in my eyes, peeking through the gaps between the tall buildings.

I ride into the city and weave through the already busy streets, as if an unseeing force is at my back, driving me forward. Urgency powers me, despite the fatigue that's long settled into my bones. I pull on Storm's reins, slowing to a stop when I approach the drawbridge that separates High Keep from the rest of the city.

"You there," the guard calls from atop the tower. "No one is to enter the castle, by order of His Majesty, the High King."

I furrow my brow. Vorr must know how dire things are, if he's barricaded himself in the castle.

My mouth twists. How can he hide in his tower, while his people suffer and die? Viridian must be furious.

"I am Crown Princess, Cryssa Thurdred Pelleveron Avanos." My voice booms, amplified by my haste. "I have grave news, and I must see my husband *immediately*."

The guard falls silent. There are hushed whispers I can't make out and a shuffling of feet. Then, a voice rings out.

"You heard your future queen! Well, what are you waiting for? Open the gate!"

Briefly closing my eyes, I let out a breath in relief.

Lymseia.

The gate rises, lessening my anxiety—but only slightly. Lymseia dips her head to me in greeting when I pass, and I return the gesture to convey my gratitude.

She waves me off, as if to say, "*There's no need to thank me.*"

I snort. Typical Lymseia.

I ride to the main entrance and disembark, leaving Storm there. Without a moment to lose, I push through the double doors and move through the halls.

"Where is His Highness?" I call out, frantic, to any servant that might be nearby. "Where is my *husband*?"

"The library," someone says, pointing to the main staircase.

As if on command, my feet carry me up the stairs and through the halls, not once slowing down.

Until I see him.

In the main library, Viridian sits at a table, bent over a book and some loose parchment that's scattered in front of him. He doesn't notice me at first, engrossed in whatever it is that's captured his attention.

I step inside, the sound of my breathing the only noise I make.

Startled, Viridian lifts his head. His long face brightens when he sees me, as if a heavy weight has been lifted off his shoulders. Instantly, he rises from his chair and closes the gap between us, taking long, purposeful strides.

"You came back," he breathes, a hand reaching out to gently cup my face.

"Of course I did." My eyes meet his, and it's so easy to lose myself in them. "How could I not?"

My words seem to melt his expression. He looks at me with a mix of pure joy and wondrous surprise, as if he never thought it possible that I could want this.

That I could want him.

I raise my hand to cover his, pressing his palm into my cheek.

"I'm sorry." His voice cracks and threatens to break. "I'm so sorry. I shouldn't have—"

"You have nothing to apologize for," I promise. And I mean it. Guilt rises up into my chest. "I should be the one apologizing."

"And I would tell you the same thing you just told me." The tenderness I hear in his words wraps around me, softer than even the gentlest caress. "You have nothing to apologize for. Nothing at all."

I search his features, looking for any hint of anger, any trace of resentment.

But I find none.

He stares back at me for a moment, his face telling me everything words can't. I hope—no, I know—that my expression does the same. His thumb brushes my cheek, fingers grazing my chin. Then his gaze breaks from mine, falling to my arm.

His brows knit together. Roaring fires blaze in his amber eyes, like a spark catching dry grass.

"Who did this to you?"

Arching a brow, I look down at my arm, following his

line of sight. Bruises circle my forearm where Loren's fingers met my skin.

"It's nothing," I tell him, lowering my arm.

"Little Fawn," Viridian grumbles in warning. "Tell me who's responsible."

"We were arguing. Loren, he—"

Viridian growls. "I'll *kill* him."

"No!" I shout. "No, you won't. I'm fine."

But he doesn't seem to hear me.

"Viridian," I demand, turning his face to mine. "Look at me. I'm all right. I'm here, with you. I chose *you*."

He closes his eyes and takes a deep breath. Then he dips his head and touches his forehead to mine, wrapping his arms around me.

"I love you," he breathes. "Gods, I love you."

"And I love you," I tell him. It feels so good to say it out loud. Now, I want to say it a million more times, just to see how it makes his face light up again and again. "More than anything."

Taking my face in his hands, he crushes his lips to mine. The kiss lights a spark inside me, drawing me in.

"More than anything," he repeats.

I wrap my arms around his neck, pulling him closer.

"Viridian," I say, when we pull away. My voice turns deathly serious. "The situation out there—it's so much worse than we could have ever imagined. The horrors I saw..." My lips draw back when I cringe, the image of Hylmfirth fresh in my mind, like a raw wound.

"That's what I feared." His tone is as grave as mine. Heavy. There's something he's not telling me. But before I can ask, his expression shifts and he changes the subject. "Your father is stable?"

"Yes," I say, gathering my thoughts. "Viridian, there's so much we need to talk about."

"I know, and I want to hear about everything—your family, what you've seen. But only after you rest and bathe. You've had a long journey." Placing his hands on both my shoulders, he gives me a light squeeze. "This can wait a night."

"But—" I protest.

"Please, Cryssa," he begs, and it weakens whatever willingness to fight I have left. "Don't neglect your own well-being. I've only just gotten you back."

I sigh. He's right, and I know it. "All right."

Viridian nods, still holding my gaze. "I'll have Tiffy bring a hot meal to your chamber. She's been worried sick about you."

My heart swells.

Tiffy. I've missed her.

Viridian presses a kiss to my forehead before nudging

me forward. "Go. I'll be waiting for you."

SOMEHOW, THE TUB is already filled with hot water when I get to my chamber. Though, the room is empty, save for me. Lymseia must have sent for someone to run my bath when I arrived at the gate.

Peeling my sweat-stained dress from my body, I leave it in a heap on the floor of my washroom. I lower myself into the tub, the hot water already soothing my aching muscles. I scrub my arms with soap until my skin is free of dirt, oil, and sweat. Lifting my fingers to my scalp, I slowly work the soap into my hair next. When I'm done, I sink lower into the tub and lay back, so all but my face is submerged.

I revel in the silence. Closing my eyes, I take long, deep breaths that fill my lungs.

Now that the adrenaline that's been powering me is gone, my limbs feel heavy with exhaustion. As does my mind.

I soak like that until I hear my chamber door open.

"Your Highness?" Tiffy calls.

It takes me a moment to realize that she's calling for me.

"In here," I reply, shifting into a sitting position.

Metal clanks—the dinner cart, most likely—and then Tiffy appears in the doorway. Her scrunched face relaxes when she sees me, lips spreading into a wide smile. She picks up a towel and unfurls it, holding it up for me.

I stand and step over the tub, and then Tiffy wraps the towel around my dripping body. She takes another towel to my hair, wringing it out. Once I'm dry, she drapes my dressing robe around my shoulders and fastens it around my waist.

Ushering me out of the washroom, Tiffy clicks her tongue.

"You look so thin," she tells me, fussing like a mother hen. "Come, eat. The kitchens reopened just for you. Oh! And I made you some tea."

I sit at the end of my bed, and Tiffy rolls the cart with my dinner right up to me. She watches me intently as I pick up my fork and knife, only visibly letting go of the tension in her shoulders when I take my first bite.

"I've missed you, too, Tiffy," I say in between bites.

That seems to melt her expression. She bends down and pulls me into an embrace. "I didn't know where you'd gone, or if you'd ever return."

I frown slightly into her shoulder. "I'm sorry I worried you."

She pulls away. "There's no need." Her voice slows. "I heard about your father. How is he?"

"Stable, for now." Worry creeps into my stomach. *Hopefully, I have enough time to save him.*

To save all of them.

"The gods will watch over him, Your Highness," Tiffy assures me, patting my arm. "He'll recover. You'll see."

I nod and take a sip of tea.

"Well," Tiffy says, brushing off her skirts. "I imagine you've had a long journey and need your rest. I'll leave you to it."

I offer her a small smile. "Thank you, Tiffy. For everything."

She smiles. "Of course."

With that, she slips from my chamber, gently closing the door behind her.

Chewing slowly, savoring every bite, I finish my dinner and drain my tea. Standing, I push the cart away from my bed, leaving it up against the far wall so it's out of the way.

I sit at my vanity table and run my fingers through my tangled hair. Working through the knots, I manage to tame my auburn mane and weave it into a single braid that falls over my shoulder.

417

As I'm finishing my braid, a soft knock sounds at my door.

A sense of calm washes over me.

"Come in," I call, knowing who waits outside.

CHAPTER
THIRTY-FIVE

VIRIDIAN OPENS my chamber door slowly and steps inside. Without turning around, he presses it shut behind him before making his way to me.

I rise to meet him, and his lips find mine. His arms circle me, and the safety I feel while he holds me is unparalleled. I press my palms to his chest, gripping his shirt.

He breaks from the kiss, touching his forehead to mine.

"How is your father?" he asks, voice low.

"He's all right." I sigh. "For now."

But that could change any minute.

Viridian hums in agreement, as if he knows what I've left unsaid.

"And Acantha?"

"She's well," I say. "She's strong."

His hand finds my face, thumb brushing back and forth against my cheek. "That seems to run in the family."

My mouth curves into the hint of a smile.

"How are you?" Concern tightens his mouth. "I know things were..." he pauses. "Not well between us when you left."

Now, finding his eyes, I smile. "I'm perfectly all right, now."

His mouth perks up. "I'm glad." Then his expression turns serious. "Would you like to talk tonight? About what you saw?"

"No," I murmur, my eyes falling to his lips. "That can wait until tomorrow. Right now," I say, my body thrumming with desire, every trace of fatigue stowed away for the moment, "I want to kiss you."

He raises his brows, expression darkening. "Is that so?"

"Yes," I say. Then, placing a hand to the back of his neck, I pull his face down to mine.

We collide. His mouth is no longer gentle, no longer

soft. No, now, he kisses me with such need, it's as if I am the only thing in the universe that will ever quench his undying thirst. I run my hands through his hair, grabbing fistfuls of it while I draw him in, closer. He responds, arms snaking around me and clutching my torso.

"Please," I breathe. Right now, there's only one thing on my mind. One thing I so desperately need. "Let me have you. All of you."

"Are you sure?" Viridian's voice constricts, the way it does when he's anxious or unsure of himself. "You know what this means. Once it's in place, the mate bond cannot be broken."

"Yes," I tell him. And I mean it. Every fiber in my body has waited for this moment. I've never been surer about anything in my life. "I want this. I want *you*, Viridian. Now and forever. Every part of me is yours."

"Gods," he grinds out, eyelids fluttering. "You have no idea how long I've been dying to hear you say that."

Biting my lip, I let out an exhale.

My lack of experience suddenly makes me self-conscious. "You should know that I've only been with one other man." I don't dare let myself think about the others he's been with—how much more experienced they are at pleasuring a male compared to me.

But he only licks his lips, looking at me like a man

starved.

"There hasn't been anyone else for me, Cryssa. No one but you."

"You..." I pause. "You've never...?"

Viridian steps closer to me until I'm backed up against the wall. He grabs my face with one hand and tilts it up to his own.

"I may have never been with a woman, but that doesn't mean I haven't repeatedly dreamed of fucking you senseless until you're screaming my name."

"Oh gods," I gasp. I can already feel the wetness gathering between my legs.

Viridian flashes a wicked smirk at me. As if he knows it, too.

He lets me go and slowly takes a step back. "Get on the bed for me, Little Fawn. I'm going to make both of our fantasies come true."

Biting my lip, I do as he says. I lay on the bed, propping myself up onto my elbows so I can look at him.

Viridian's eyes lock with mine, deep amber smoking like embers. He pulls his shirt over his head and discards it, letting it fall to the floor. My eyes roam across his broad chest, and I ache to touch the toned muscle I see there. He takes something from my vanity table, and then moves to the bed, closing the space between us. Watching me intently, he pulls his hands evenly apart, stretching a hair ribbon until it spans the width of his shoulders. His knees press into the bed, one on each side of my waist.

Still maintaining eye contact, he roughly grabs my wrists while he straddles me, moving my hands above my head.

A breath escapes my lips. All I can do is look at him, at the dark haze falling over his expression, his hungry stare. I'm transfixed.

He takes the hair ribbon, slowly, intently, tying it around my wrists. He pulls the ends of the ribbon, until my wrists are bound. Tight.

My chest rises with my breath, my breasts with them. My nipples brush against his chest, already hardening under my silk dressing robe. My thin, thin dressing robe.

Lightly, he tugs at the tie at my waist—the only thing keeping my dressing robe closed around me. With two fingers, he pushes the silk aside, exposing me. Fully.

His stare leaves mine, only to look down at my nipples. He lowers one hand to my chest, between my breasts, while the other pins my wrists down.

The slight touch has me arching my back and parting my lips.

Viridian's hand on my chest moves upward to the base of my neck, fingers pressing down on each side.

I gasp, tilting my head back to lean my neck into his touch. I need him.

Gods, I need him.

"I'm going to devour you," Viridian says thickly.

Licking my lips, I muster a nod. He kisses me hard. His tongue sweeps into my mouth, claiming mine for his own. I squeeze my hands into fists and tug at the restraints.

Viridian's hand unclasps from my wrists, and he lowers his face from my mouth to my neck. The warmth of his breath sends shivers down my spine. Heat gathers in my core, until it's almost too much.

His lips part, and he leaves a scorching trail down my chest and stomach with his tongue. When his face is between my hips, he looks up at me. The intensity in those amber eyes has me breathing heavier, the embers in his stare enough to drive me more desperate with need.

"Please," I pant.

"Say it, Little Fawn. Tell me what you need."

"You."

"Mmm, I'd imagine you do, don't you?"

"Please. *Viridian*. I need you. So badly."

Viridian's eyes close, and he dips his face to my inner thigh. He breathes in the scent of me, inhaling deeply. Then he opens his mouth, gently sucking at my skin and lightly nipping at it with his teeth.

I whimper.

And it's only the slightest noise, but it seems to extinguish the last ounce of whatever self-control he has left.

Roughly, he hooks both of his hands under my thighs, and in one motion, pulls me closer to his face. When he does, his mouth meets my warmth. I'm so tender there that I moan and arch my back into him.

His tongue flicks me while his lips suck and play. He draws another moan from me, and I writhe on the bed, my hips bucking against his mouth. He removes one hand from the back of my thighs and presses down on my lower abdomen to keep me in place.

I can't stop moaning now. And I don't care who hears.

The only thing I can think about, the only thing I can sense, is Viridian's mouth and the searing pleasure that has me seconds away from coming undone. Without stopping what he's doing, he slips a finger into me, and then two, curling them to caress me from the inside.

Shattering, I cry out, barely able to fight the urge to close my legs around his face.

I breathe heavily, still reeling from the euphoria.

Viridian moves himself on top of me. "I'm not finished with you yet," he growls as his eyes find mine again.

My breath quickens. My body feels like it's on fire. It's blistering, in the best way possible.

He unfastens his pants and lets them fall to the floor. Revealing himself.

My eyes widen at the sight of his massive length.

Oh, gods.

Then, with one hand, he positions himself against me. He rubs his erection into my wetness. Closing my eyes, I throw my head back, barely able to contain how gods-damned good it feels, just rubbing against me.

"Look at me, Little Fawn," he commands, his voice hoarse. "I want to see how good it feels when I stretch you out."

I open my eyes and look at him. He stares back at me, gaze mingled with mine, as if he were hanging onto every breath, every moan, every plea.

I gasp when he enters me. He moves slowly, at first, going deeper and deeper, until he's completely buried in me.

My voice breaks—a mangled, blissful sound.

Viridian keeps his stare locked with mine, even as he pulls himself out, only to thrust back into me again.

And again. And again. And again.

Sweat slicks my skin, the sweet friction between our

bodies driving me wild.

Pressure builds in my core, and I can feel my muscles spasming. Pulsing. Clenching around him while he drives into me over and over and over.

My moans come faster. Each louder than the last.

"Harder. Please—oh gods, *harder.*"

Viridian does, the fire in his expression burning brighter. Need directs his movements, his hips rocking into mine until I'm so close to the edge.

"Viridian," I cry.

"That's it, Little Fawn," he murmurs. *"Scream for me."*

He doesn't stop, keeping an even, steady pace. I can feel myself trembling.

Then I am screaming.

"Viridian, Viridian, Viridian."

And I come undone.

It's not much longer before he comes crashing into me. And when he does, the overwhelming sensation fills every fiber of my body. Because it's not just my own pleasure I feel.

It's his, too.

Even though it's barely been a minute, another all-consuming crescendo has me gliding farther into ecstasy. I cry out, and it's the sound of raw, unadulterated pleasure.

Viridian kisses me softly, lips lingering on mine. He moves to lay beside me, and gently pulls me to his chest, tightly wrapping his arms around me.

I don't know how long we lay there like that.

But I know that I've never felt at home in a man's arms the way I do now. With the mate bond locked into place, I feel whole. As if my entire life, there was a missing piece. A hole that I never knew needed to be filled.

Viridian's happiness meshes with mine. Now, I'm not sure where mine ends and his begins.

Then I hear his voice in my mind.

"I love you, Cryssa Thurdred Avanos."

Smiling at him, I reply.

"And I love you. More than anything."

"More than anything," he repeats.

I rest my head on his chest. And at some point, my droopy eyes close.

CHAPTER THIRTY-SIX

THE WORLD FEELS right again when I wake in Viridian's arms. As if this is right where I'm meant to be.

Then I remember Hylmfirth. And I wonder how long my peace will last.

But then I look at Viridian, still sleeping soundly beside me. With both of us still naked, the night's events replay in my mind. Though, instead of feeling shy in his presence, knowing all the sinful things we did last night, I feel at ease. As if just being near Viridian is enough to relax me. He grounds me. He balances me.

My mate.

I can't help but smile at the thought. Gently, I pull away and rise to a sitting position. Softly, I rest my palm on his cheek and let my thumb wander in small circular motions against his cheekbone.

He turns his face into my touch, and then opens his eyes slowly, adjusting to the light.

"Good morning," he says, his voice a low rumble.

"Good morning." I smile.

Covering my hand with his, he sits up and presses a kiss to my lips. He lingers, and I bring my free hand up to the other side of his face. Viridian's arm slips around me, palm pressed to the small of my back.

We break from the kiss, and I feel Viridian's stare on my face.

"What is it?" he asks. Warmth spreads in my chest, knowing that he knows me so well, he can immediately sense that something's wrong.

"Hylmfirth," I say, narrowing my eyes. "What I saw... They're dying, Viridian. It's not just the mining sickness. It's starvation, too. I saw it with my own eyes. All the crops turned black, as if they're diseased."

"Like the East Tower," Viridian murmurs.

"Yes." I hesitate. "And if whatever dark magic poisoning the East Tower can spread that far—and to the other Courts—then it's not just any dark magic." I pause, meeting his eyes. "It's a curse."

I expect him to go pale, to ask questions. But he doesn't. Instead, I get the sense that somehow, he already knows.

"Some part of me was still holding onto hope that it wasn't," he says softly. "But hearing reports of how much worse the situation has gotten... I knew that hope was misguided."

His reaction tells me there's more to this that he hasn't shared with me yet.

I lean forward. "Tell me what happened while I was away."

"My *father*." He practically spits out the word. "After the wedding, when he'd realized you were gone, he shut himself away in the East Tower. Since then, he's had the castle on lockdown."

"Right," I say. "When I arrived, the guards at the gate told me no one was allowed in or out. Lymseia's the only reason I'm here."

"Exactly." Viridian sighs, pinching the bridge of his nose. "The council is trapped here with the rest of us, but he refuses to see them. I've demanded an audience with him again and again, but he won't even see me." He takes a deep breath. "He's panicking. That, I know."

I reach for his hand, intertwining my fingers with his.

"Why?" I ask. "What is he so afraid of?"

"I'm not sure," Viridian admits. "But I know him. He knows something about this curse. Much more than he wants us, and especially the council, to believe. But he won't tell me anything." Then he tilts his head back, pressing his eyes shut. "You have no idea how many times I've asked. I don't know what to do now. I'm at a loss, Cryssa."

"I know." I give his hand a light squeeze. "How is the council taking all this?"

"They're absolutely furious." His brows knit together. "I can't blame them. *I'm* furious." He shakes his head a little, passion filling his words. "What kind of king hides behind stone walls while his people are suffering? While they're dying?" I see the spark light in his eyes. The fire that now burns. "I will not stand idly by while dark magic destroys this kingdom from the inside out. I can't."

"And you won't," I assure him. "We will get to the bottom of this. We will make things right."

He nods, pressing his mouth into a fine line.

His gaze finds mine again, softening. "I love you."

"And I love you." I lean forward, touching my lips to his.

He kisses me and smiles against my lips before

claiming my mouth again. My hands find the back of his head, my fingers stretching through his hair. He holds my face with both hands, and his sweet kisses lose their softness. My skin feels hot, electricity trickling across my body.

Then his mouth parts from mine. He lowers his head to my neck, touching his lips there. Waiting.

Letting out a breath, I close my eyes and lean my head back.

Viridian licks his lips and then presses more kisses to my neck, moving up and down. My breath quickens. He sucks and lightly nips at the skin just beneath my jawline.

I let out a soft moan.

Viridian's hands cup my breasts, lightly kneading them. The touch stokes the fire burning inside me. I lay back, pulling him down with me. He steadies himself above me, hips pinned to mine.

"Mmm," he hums, voice low. The sound alone is enough to melt my core. "Do you want more, Little Fawn?"

"Yes," I breathe. "Gods, yes."

He grins wickedly. "I was hoping you'd say that."

He rocks his hips, driving his hard length against me. I curse, wrapping my legs around his waist. I'm already wet for him.

And he knows it.

But he doesn't make me wait, this time. Lowering his hand to his erection, he poises himself against me and thrusts. I gasp, my fingernails clawing at his back.

Viridian quickens his pace, pounding into me over and over and over. His grunts fall in time with my moans. My breathing grows heavy, and so does Viridian's.

Sensing how close I am, Viridian's mouth mingles with mine, drowning out my cries when I climax. He works himself through my waves of pleasure, until he groans, and his ecstasy washes over me.

Finding my gaze, Viridian catches his breath. Tenderly, he brushes my hair out of my eyes and presses a kiss to my lips, before nestling his face into the crook of my neck. He lays here, on my chest, and I run my fingers through his hair. Every moment we spend like this, entangled in each other, is pure bliss.

I wish it would last forever.

Because something tells me I might not have many moments like this left.

A hurried knock at the door has both of us lurching upright. I clutch the sheets, holding them up to my chest in an effort to cover myself.

He glances at me before clearing his throat. "Enter."

My chamber door opens, revealing a near-trembling

servant.

"What is it?" Viridian asks, dark brows pinched together.

The servant casts a shy glance at his feet. "The High King demands to see you, Your Highness."

Viridian groans, touching his fingers to his forehead, between his brows. "Very well. Tell my father we'll arrive momentarily."

"Oh, His Majesty was very clear—he only wants to see you, Your Highness." The servant pauses, eyes shifting to me. "Not Miss Thurdred—erm, I mean, Her Highness."

That leaves a sour taste on my tongue.

Why would Vorr single me out?

Viridian seems to share my distaste. "All the same, tell him my wife *and* I will see him in the throne room shortly."

Swallowing hard, the servant nods and disappears.

Rushing from the bed, Viridian and I dress quickly.

"Tell me you weren't expecting this," I say, peering over at him as I attempt to fasten my bodice.

"No," he huffs, pulling up his pants. "I was not."

"All right," I mutter to myself, wondering what's come over the High King. Something's drawn him out of the East Tower.

435

And I don't know if that's a good thing.

VIRIDIAN SCOWLS the whole way to the throne room. I can't blame him. My own brows are furrowed, and tension gathers in my shoulders.

He shoves open the set of double doors and storms inside. Raising the crown of my head, I follow at his heels.

The High King sits before us. Touching a gloved hand to his forehead, a weighted expression wears down his features. His breathing is ragged, sluggish, as if every breath is riddled with struggle and pain.

Vorr slowly lifts his eyes to Viridian. Then, they shift past him and land on me, narrowing.

He directs his attention back to Viridian. "You were told to come alone."

Viridian stays silent, amber eyes simmering.

"If you'd excuse us, Miss Thurdred," the High King says, not once breaking eye contact with Viridian, "I'd like a moment alone with my son."

I hesitate for a moment, and then turn to leave.

"No," Viridian says, a wave of power rippling from him. "My wife—my *mate* stays."

Butterflies flutter in my stomach, pride swelling in my chest.

His mate.

Vorr starts, "Viridian—"

"Anything you wish to say to me, you say to her, too."

Vorr furrows his brow. "So be it." He takes a breath. "Let it be known that I warned you—neither of you will enjoy what I have to tell you."

"Very well." Viridian steps closer to me. Hooking his arm around my waist, he pulls me to him, pressing my back to his torso.

Vorr hangs his head. "The mining sickness you spoke of... I know the cause."

If he hadn't already gotten my attention, then he does now.

"What is it?" Viridian asks, his voice carrying the weight of his—and my—concern.

"Dark magic," Vorr says, his voice low. "A horrible curse—*my* curse."

My abdomen tightens. The image of Hylmfirth is clear in my mind.

"Your curse?" Viridian echoes, as if he doesn't believe him.

"Yes." Vorr lifts his head, burnt-orange eyes swimming with guilt. "When I was young and in love, I—I made a mistake. One I almost regret."

"What did you do, Father?"

"I took something." Vorr's voice weakens. "Something that wasn't mine to take."

"What did you take?" Viridian asks. "Perhaps it can be returned. There may still be a chance we can repair what's been bro—"

"No." Vorr's expression hardens. "It can't. The time for that is long gone."

"Why not?" Viridian asks, shaking his head slightly, as if he can't contain the tidal wave of emotions swirling inside.

Vorr says nothing, pressing his lips into a fine line.

"Father," Viridian presses. "Tell me."

"Another time, son." Vorr's eyes shine with pain. "Please."

"Fine." Viridian grumbles. "But we *will* return to this matter."

"I'd expect nothing less from the future king."

I give them a moment, before interjecting. "What does any of this have to do with the mining sickness? And the ruined metals?"

"A cursed sickness shall poison everything the wrongdoer touches," Vorr recites, as if he heard the words for the first time just yesterday. *"But by the blessing of*

Theelia, the righteous heir and lost golden daughter will unite as one. For from the bonds of love will come the ultimate sacrifice. And only from that sacred gift, shall these wrongs be righted, and this curse be broken."

My head is swimming.

"Viridian..." I start. "There's still something I haven't told you."

In front of us, Vorr closes his eyes, as if to brace himself for a blow.

Viridian slows, and the intensity of his stare tells me that I have his undivided attention. As if his father weren't still here with us. "You can tell me anything."

"I know," I assure him. Placing my palm on his upper arm, I give him a light squeeze. "When I saw my father—" I pause, struggling to find the words. "*I'm* the lost golden daughter, Viridian. Lady Helenia Pelleveron is my birth mother."

His dark brows rise, shock hanging on his features. "How?"

"My mother, Nira, served the Pelleverons. At the time, Lady Helenia had a human lover."

I see Viridian working out the details in his mind. "She took you home."

"Yes."

The color drains from his face when he realizes. "*The*

439

righteous heir and lost golden daughter will unite as one," he recites, putting the pieces together. *"For from the bonds of love will come the ultimate sacrifice. And only from that sacred gift, shall these wrongs be righted, and this curse be broken."*

Turning back to his father, Viridian's handsome face twists with anger. With pain. "This marriage... It was all a scheme to right *your* wrongs."

Vorr doesn't even try to deny it. "Yes."

"The ultimate sacrifice..." My voice trails off. I cover my mouth. "Viridian... One of us has to die."

My nightmare suddenly makes sense now. The God of Death's words fill my mind.

"When the time comes, you must choose. Choose life, without love, in a cursed land. Or choose death in the name of love, and sacred sacrifice."

No.

Not one of us.

Me.

I'm the only one that can break the curse.

"No." Viridian's voice is hard. "No. No one is going to die." He looks down at me now, holding my face between both hands. "You hear me? I *will not* let anything happen to you. Not now, and not ever, Little Fawn."

I nod, though the motion is empty.

Then a terrible realization dawns on me. One so awful, I almost can't bear to speak it aloud.

But I do. "Viridian, your mother..."

What feels like forever ago, Viridian told me that his mother had been with child for a second time, and that both she and the child died. Now, I see that was a lie. A story meant to conceal the true cause of her death.

His amber eyes sharpen. Then he turns those daggers onto his father.

"Mother didn't die in childbirth, did she? There was no second child."

Vorr just stares at him and swallows.

"*Did she*?"

"No," Vorr rasps at last, looking down at his gloved hands. "She didn't."

"That's why you wear the gloves," I say, voicing my realization out loud. "Because anything you touch—"

"Falls ill," Vorr finishes for me, eyes sad. "Yes."

"And all the miners..." Viridian's voice rises. The air surrounding us hums with electricity, goosebumps trickling down my arms. "How many will die before your sins have been atoned for?"

"I don't know." Vorr is near silent. "I know I've been a coward, Viridian. I've been too ashamed to face what I've done." He takes a breath, touching his fingers to his

441

forehead. "You and your mate are the kingdom's only hope, now. My time has... My sins have come for me. I can feel it."

"What?" Viridian's voice loses its edge, and the electricity pulsing around us subsides.

"My time in this realm is nearly gone." Vorr looks at us through clouded eyes. His words sound like a goodbye. "You are a far greater male than I could ever be. And a far better king."

"Father—" Viridian protests, voice wavering.

"It's all right, son." He forces a small smile.

Viridian's lip quivers, but his hard expression doesn't break. I hold him closer and rest my head on his shoulder. He leans into the gesture.

"Go now." Weakly, Vorr waves us away. "I'd like to be alone with my thoughts."

Viridian merely bows his head. Tightly grasping my hand, we leave the throne room.

Double doors close behind us, and it feels like the final nail in Vorr's coffin.

CHAPTER
THIRTY-SEVEN

TIME SEEMS to have frozen still since I've returned to High Keep. Despite his recent withdrawal from the East Tower, the High King hasn't lifted his ban on passage in and out of the castle. Servants speak in hushed tones, and I would have sworn High Keep itself had died if there wasn't any movement through the halls.

At Viridian's command, and with the High King's seal, the most illustrious healers from the Copper Court have been sent to Slyfell to treat my father. As it would turn out, there is so much more to the metals than their ability to be molded and shaped into swords, candelabras, and other items. Metals, as Myrdin explained to me, have magical properties of their own, that can be channeled by their wielder. Copper is used for alchemy—the brewing of potions and tonics for a multitude of purposes. One of which is healing.

It makes sense why I hadn't learned about this before. Humans are rarely gifted with the capacity for magic—it's much more common among the fae, especially noble fae. Besides, the structure of our lives doesn't leave much room for us to cultivate our abilities, even if we are lucky enough to have them. With Pelleveron blood running through my veins, it's quite possible I possess some capacity for magic. Now, I'm eager to learn, to explore my own potential abilities, and how to wield them. But something tells me I won't have enough time.

Heaviness sets into my chest.

I brush away the thought, and in its place, my mind drifts to thoughts of home. We've received word from the healers reporting on my father's health. So far, he seems to be maintaining a stable condition. It's been longer than I'd thought, probably much longer than he would have without the healer's care. I hope, with the healer's tonics, we have more time to save him and to lift the curse sickening the land.

Vorr's curse.

Somehow, I still can't wrap my mind around it. Wondering what he could have done, who he could have wronged that would be powerful enough to cast a curse as strong as the one that plagues us. Whoever the strange woman that Tiffy spoke of was, the servants, and the High King, are right to fear her.

The truth of my own identity only sparks more questions. How did the stranger know about me, the lost golden daughter? How could she have known about my circumstances, nearly a century before my birth? How could she know that I was destined to be Viridian's mate? That her actions on that fateful day would be the very reason I come to High Keep, at all?

"What is it?" Viridian asks, peering over at me as we walk the grounds. It feels good to be out here, instead of drowning in the paranoia that fills the castle walls. "Something troubles you."

I press my lips together.

"The curse?" he asks.

I nod, and I don't have to see myself to know pain swims in my eyes.

"It could be either of us." Viridian takes both my hands and grips them tightly. "It could be me."

But I know it won't be.

In my dream, Death told me *I* would have to make a

choice. And I understand that now.

I'll have to choose to break the curse or to walk away with my life.

I don't have the strength to tell Viridian that he's wrong. To crush the sliver of hope in his eyes, that he might not have to live in a world where I don't exist.

A world without his mate. I can only imagine how painful it will be for him when our bond is severed. I almost wish we'd never bonded at all, so he wouldn't have to endure that.

But I'm selfish. And I'm glad to die having been bonded to him.

So, I don't tell him.

"I don't want it to be you," I say instead.

"I can't go on without you." Viridian's voice trembles, as if the very earth he stands on might fall out from underneath his feet. "I won't."

"You'll do no such thing," I say, my own voice beginning to shake.

"Cryssa." Viridian steps toward me, taking my face in both hands. "Don't ask that of me."

I squeeze my eyes shut and turn my face.

"Look at me," he says, gently turning my head back to him. "Please, look at me."

I do, my eyes welling with fear, sadness, dread, all

mingled together into an ugly concoction of emotions.

"You are stronger than you know, Little Fawn." Viridian's eyes bear into mine. "Stronger than anyone here thought you could ever be. And yet, each time, you've proven every single one of them wrong."

I take a deep breath, unable to tear my gaze away from him.

Viridian lingers for a moment, before taking my hand. "Come."

We resume our stroll, simply enjoying each other's company. The weight of our conversation still bears down on my shoulders. I can tell I'm not alone in that— Viridian's withdrawn, eyes narrowed. I cock my head, turning my attention to the natural beauty that surrounds us. The birds chirp off in the distance, and I can make out the bustling of the city beyond High Keep's walls.

Still, I keep thinking of what he said. I replay his words in my mind, over and over again.

"Why do you call me that?" I ask, wondering why I haven't thought to ask before. With my fate looming over me, I want to ask him everything I can before my time runs out. "Little Fawn?"

Viridian's lips curve into the hint of a smile, his eyes cast down at his feet. "Because at the time, I thought of you as a fawn, finding herself alone in a den of wolves.

Noble fae were so much stronger than you, so much faster, with much sharper senses."

I watch him as I listen.

"But as I quickly came to learn," he continues, "fawns are much more resourceful than I'd given them recognition for. At a glance, they may seem weak, but that is all part of their true strength. Repeatedly, they are underestimated by the wolf, yet each time, they survive."

Viridian looks at me now, with love and admiration written all over his face. With awe and wonder lacing his words.

It's at this moment that I realize this whole time, he's been talking about himself. That *he* is the wolf in the fable he's telling me now.

"Whatever the odds, you do so much more than survive here, Little Fawn." His voice washes over me with new meaning. "You continue to rise above it all. To make all those who ever underestimated you wonder how they were blind to your strength in the first place."

My lips part. Warmth spreads through my chest, rising to my cheeks.

Viridian bends his neck, lowering his lips to mine. He kisses me, and it's soft and tender and tells me everything words can't. I wrap my arms around him, clinging onto him as if my life depends on it.

Now, I know how far I am willing to go.

How much I am willing to give for love.

How much I am prepared to sacrifice.

And when the time comes, I know what choice I will make.

CHAPTER
THIRTY-EIGHT

THE CASTLE WAKES to the sound of screaming.
As do I.

With nothing but the moonlight to guide him through the darkness, Viridian rises, springing to his feet the moment his eyes open. I'm up almost a second after, frantically lighting the candle by my bedside. Candelabra in my grasp, I follow him, darting into the hall.

Voices ring out from across the way, and it takes less than a moment to find the source.

"Come," Viridian urges, moving with a sense of grave purpose.

But I'm already ahead of him, practically flying through the hall past the gold-rimmed windows and into the foyer at the top of the main staircase.

The flicker of candlelight is dim, but it's enough to make out the grisly scene that waits before us.

There, with a sword plunged through his chest, pinning his limp body to the wall several feet above the ground, is the High King.

Viridian pales. His body goes deathly still.

Behind us, someone vomits. There's a shuffling of feet, and the sound of someone being whisked away.

I stare up in horror. Nausea grips my stomach. Closing my mouth, I swallow hard, unable to turn my face away.

Vorr's head lolls to one side, his face gaunt and ashen. His torso slumps forward, flesh digging into sharpened steel. Blood still drips from his body, a mass of dark red staining the stone walls and gathering in a puddle on the floor beneath him. There's a gaping hole where his heart should be. His chest is mangled around the sword wound, as if his killer drove the weapon through him multiple times before piercing his heart.

Below him, sitting in the pool of his blood, is his bronze crown.

My breaths turn shallow.

This was no accident.

Someone killed Vorr and put what's left of him on display, for everyone to see. Even his crown has been purposefully placed, as if symbolic of the murderer's intent.

An end to the Bronze Court's hold over the Inatian throne.

Though, if that truly is their aim, they didn't finish the job. Then, I remember Vorr's last words to Viridian and me.

"My sins have come for me."

He must have known his wrongdoing—whatever mistake he attributes the curse to—would end his life. That even though the curse itself wouldn't take him directly, its icy hold would still direct the sword that ended him.

But now, Vorr isn't my concern.

Viridian just stands there, eyes fixed on his father's lifeless form.

I see everything he doesn't say aloud.

The grief. The shock. The apologies that will forever remain unsaid, forever waiting on his tongue.

I do the only thing I can. I wrap my arms around him, offering support with my body. I send whatever comfort I can give down the bond, hoping it's enough to soothe him, if only a little. In response, he leans into me, unsteady. Though he still doesn't look away.

Maybe he can't look away.

I finally turn my face. When I do, the realization settles over me.

"Viridian," I start. As far as we know, Vorr had yet to lift the command on High Keep preventing anyone from entering or exiting. The gates have remained locked, keeping everyone inside. "The one responsible for this is still—"

"Here, among us." He scans the small crowd gathered around us. They're all servants, mostly, some lesser fae diplomats spread out amongst them.

"I don't think it's any of them," I tell him. I look at each of their faces. At the horror, the shock, and the fear I see there. Most of them are human, whose families have served for years.

"Neither do I." Viridian's voice hardens, quiet rage seeping from his expression. There's that electric pulse again, buzzing in the air around us. "I want to see the High King's council," he announces, demanding the immediate attention of all those who still linger here. "*Now*."

Without another word, Viridian moves to the staircase, amber storms raging in his eyes. Free of any hesitation, I go where he goes, close by his side. Electricity fills the air around him, so palpable, I feel as though I can almost reach out and touch it. Through the bond, I can sense the power roaring inside him, just beneath the surface. Now, I know there's more untapped power dwelling inside him than I ever could have known.

Perhaps even more than Viridian himself knows is there.

With a wave, Viridian slams the door into the council chamber open. The wood slams against stone, so hard I think it may splinter.

"Viridian," I say, with a touch to his back.

My voice seems to snap him out of whatever frenzy had taken control over him. His eyes widen, looking at the open door.

He takes a breath, deeply inhaling. "I'm sorry. I lost control of myself."

"It's all right," I tell him, sending more waves of calm through the bond. I feel his thundering emotions on the other end, wrath and grief and fear swirling around themselves into a lethal tempest. "You have every right to be feeling the way you do."

"But I am the High King now," Viridian finishes for me, taking another long breath. "And I must maintain decorum."

"Yes." I nod. Reaching for him, I press my palm to his

cheek. "You're not alone. Not now, not ever. I am with you, every step of the way."

Viridian touches his forehead to mine. "Thank you."

The chamber door opens, and Viridian and I both straighten our postures. Hopefully, we look every bit the High King and Queen we have to be, in this dark hour. I don't have to see Viridian's face to know he's unsure of himself. I am, too. Neither of us knew we'd be forced to begin our reign like this, in the wake of such tragedy.

And because of that, our appearance before the council is more important than ever.

We must stand united in our strength.

Once everyone is seated around the long table, I nod to Viridian. Placing my hand on his upper arm, I give his shoulder a light squeeze and find his eyes.

He dips his head to me, before facing ahead.

"What is the meaning of this? Surely, you know it is the dead of night?" a noble fae male with dark hair and silvery eyes—who I recognize as Head of House Larmanne—asks. He rubs the sleep from his eyes, the slight movement potent with annoyance. Asheros Larmanne sits beside him, looking equally as tired, but lacks his father's irritation.

"I have summoned you here, Lord Larmanne," Viridian says, looking at him with a shrouded expression, "because my father is dead."

The elder Silver Court lord's face falls. The annoyance coloring his expression vanishes, leaving no trace behind. "His Majesty is..."

"Dead," Viridian repeats. "Yes." He doesn't miss a beat. "He was murdered. And the murderer is still in the castle, somewhere among us."

While he speaks, I search the councilor's faces, looking for any sign that something might be off. If someone here is to blame for the High King's death, they may falter. Even if only for a moment.

Viridian and I stand at the head of the table—me to the left, and Viridian to the right. To Viridian's right, sit Tanyl and Myrdin, representing House Tarrantree, of course. Myrdin's brows are wound tight with pain, and he leans forward toward Viridian, as if to offer him comfort. Tanyl shares his son's expression, only, he hangs his head, muttering a soft prayer.

I doubt that Myrdin or Tanyl are responsible, though, I can't be sure. I can't think of what either would have to gain by killing Vorr—if the murder was a grab for power, why would they spare Viridian? As long as he lives, the Bronze Court's claim to the throne is secure.

Though, with Vorr gone, I fear Viridian may have a target on his back.

Next, I look further down the table, to Tanyl's left. Representing the Silver Court are Lord Eldred and Asheros. The former still looks as if he's seen a ghost, face void of color. Asheros has gone still, brows raised in shock.

I don't know much about the Silver Court's allegiances, but Myrdin's told me they stand on shaky ground with the Bronze Court. Gold and Silver have been allied for decades, but in more recent times, House Larmanne has cooperated with House Avanos. It doesn't clear them of fault, but their ties to the throne are long-distant, making them lack the motivation.

Then, I direct my attention to my side of the table. Directly to my left, sit the Steel Court representatives. Lymseia's mother and sister: Head of House, Lady Kylantha Wynterliff, and heir-apparent, Vestella Wynterliff. Myrdin's told me that the Steel and Bronze Courts have been allied for decades, sharing common goals for peace and stability for the kingdom. Given Lymseia's position as Captain of the High King's guard, it seems that they'd be unlikely to murder the High King and jeopardize her place here. Then again, with Lymseia's proximity to the High King, it's possible that they conspired together.

No.

I trust Lymseia. She wouldn't do this. And if her mother and sister are responsible—which I have no reason to believe they are—then they would have done so without her knowing.

Which only leaves one court left. The one noble House that has always contended the Bronze Court's rule.

Just as my eyes land on her, Head of House, Lady Maelyrra Pelleveron, opens her mouth.

"With our kingdom weak, now more than ever, we need *fae* sitting on the throne," Maelyrra interjects, mouth curled with distaste. To her side, a young fae male hardens his expression. His head of dark red hair, sun-kissed skin tone, and yellow eyes tells me that he's Maelyrra's son, Nisroth Pelleveron. To be here, at her side, he must also be the Gold Court's heir-apparent.

"I'd suggest you tread very lightly, Lady Pelleveron," Viridian warns, blue flickers of electricity twisting up his arms, "before you say another word about my wife."

Most Heads of House and their heir-apparents gasp, all focus trained on the blue ripples circling Viridian's forearms. Taken aback, confusion and fear etches into their faces. The room falls eerily silent. Eyeing Viridian, Nisroth places his palms to the table, poised to stand. Watching. Waiting to see what Viridian will do next.

I let their shock set in for a moment, before clearing my throat.

"I am your High Queen. And I *am* fae." My voice

echoes through the chamber, and I move my eyes to each of the council members. All of whom stare at me. "But I am also human."

"Even worse," Maelyrra retorts, making no effort to hide her disdain. "A *half-breed*."

Nisroth makes a face I can't read.

Viridian curls his fist, gathering his power.

But I don't give him the chance to wield it. "Then I am your half-breed. I am of your blood—Pelleveron blood."

Maelyrra's eyes widen, but Nisroth only furrows his brow. It's clear by the look on her face that she knows that I'm Helenia's daughter. Her niece. She lowers her voice. "I thought I'd had you disposed of."

"Well, I wasn't," I grind out, suppressing my anger. "And you *will* bow before me, or you will make an enemy of the crown." I raise my chin. "So, choose wisely."

Maelyrra clenches her jaw, face red with fury. Making a much wiser decision than I thought her to be capable of, she stays silent. But Nisroth only narrows his eyes, his focus falling to the table.

"Your Majesty," Lady Kylantha says to Viridian. "You believe the late High King's murderer is still in the castle, correct?"

"Yes." Viridian nods, relaxing his shoulders. The blue

electricity fades, until there aren't any sparks left. "As of right now, my father's orders not to open the castle gates are still in effect. "With the drawbridge down and the gates closed, no one should have been able to enter or exit without the guards hearing of it."

"But how exactly can we be sure of this?" Maelyrra crosses her arms, leaning back in her padded chair. "For all we know, the killer was able to sneak in and out, undetected."

Viridian glowers at her. "Why such doubt, Lady Maelyrra? Do you have something to hide from the crown?"

"Not at all, Your Majesty," Maelyrra says, sticking out her chin. She looks like she's about to say something but decides not to.

"With all due respect, Your Majesty," Lord Eldred Larmanne cuts in, without once looking in my direction. "How can we be sure that Her Majesty the queen is free from any doubt? One could think that the…circumstances of your marriage and your father's involvement may serve as a reason for—for the late king's unfortunate end."

I take a deep breath. He's right. I *do* have reason to want the High King dead. To escape this place, this marriage, one could believe that I'd do anything to clear my path—even if it was the High King himself that stood

461

in my way.

But I love Viridian. I want this marriage and to be here with him. To rule by his side.

I have no fear of the council's suspicion. Because I know Viridian knows my heart, my intentions. And with the mate bond in place, I couldn't lie to him, even if I tried. He'd know.

"I understand your reservations, Lord Larmanne," Viridian says. "But my wife was with me all night. And as some of you may know, mates can sense through their bond when their partner is dishonest." Now, he looks at me. "Cryssa, did you murder High King Vorr?"

The look in his eyes tells me that this is all just for show.

So, I play along.

"No," I tell him, shaking my head. My voice is genuine, because I am being genuine. "I was beside you the entire night, until we woke to the screams."

Viridian's gaze voices his thanks. He turns to the council, palms facing upward. "She speaks the truth."

Eldred Larmanne seems to redden and withdraw into himself. The rest of the council tenses, exchanging hushed whispers and nervous glances.

"Following this meeting, I will speak to the Captain of the Guard and immediately begin investigating this."

Viridian promises, his quiet rage seeping from his words, "I will do everything in my power to find my father's killer and make them pay dearly for it."

He waits a moment, looking to me as if for permission before continuing.

I meet his gaze and nod.

Then, Viridian continues. "This council is now adj—"

His head snaps to the door. As does mine.

"Is that?" he asks, voice trailing off.

"Yes," I breathe, panic rising in my chest. The sounds of struggle echo in the hallway, not far from the council chamber. "We're under attack."

CHAPTER
THIRTY-NINE

T HE SUN HAS NOT even risen yet, when more
screaming fills my ears.

Viridian and I surge into the hall. Anger powers each
of my breaths. We haven't even had a moment to breathe,
or lay Vorr to rest, before needing to respond to another
attack.

Only, this one is much more severe. And much more
dangerous.

Humans—crazed, desperate humans—swarm the
halls like an infestation. They're armed with what seems
like the first sharp object they find in one hand, and

torches in the other. To get inside, they must have swum across the moat surrounding High Keep and scaled the castle walls.

It can't be a coincidence that Vorr's death is followed by this. Can it?

Could Vorr's murderer have somehow let the human rioters inside? But why?

Voices cry out.

"Down with the king!"

"The metals are gone, and so were you!"

"If we die, then you'll die with us!"

Even as they tear down our banners, set any furniture or cloth aflame with their torches, and push past fleeing human servants, I can't help but pity them. After seeing Hylmfirth...

These people have lost everything. Their loved ones. Their livelihoods. Even the food that sustains them.

They don't understand why the miners fell ill. Why the mines have nothing left to give. Why their crops died.

They don't know about the curse.

What they do know, is that their High King did nothing while they starved and suffered and died.

Of course they're angry. I would be, too, if I were them.

But I'm not them. Not anymore. Now, my greatest

concern is for my husband and mate. If any of those humans touch a single hair on his head...

I will not hesitate to unleash hell on earth.

"You have to go," I urge Viridian, pushing him away. "They'll see your ears and they'll kill you." It doesn't take much to know these humans are on a warpath. They'll kill any fae they see to feed their craving for vengeance.

"No," Viridian's voice is firm. "I'm not leaving you. And I'm not leaving them," he says, motioning his head to the servants. "We need to get them out of here."

"Fine," I tell him. "But I'm not leaving your side."

"I wouldn't dream of it, Little Fawn."

"Good." I nod, and then we head northeast, toward the kitchens and the servants' quarters.

Luckily, it seems as though the rioters are leaving the human servants alone, though, they don't seem to care who gets caught in the crossfire. Most of the servants seem to have already left, though some have been trapped between burning wood and stone walls.

Viridian scans our surroundings. He lunges for a torn banner that, somehow, managed to escape the flames, and throws it over the fire. Quickly, with the banner between his fingers and the burning debris, he picks it up and throws it out of the way. Viridian draws his hand back and winces, sucking in a breath through clenched teeth. The motion doesn't fully clear the path, but it's enough that the servants are able to pass. They quickly give us their thanks and run off, asking the gods to watch over them.

I almost want to tell them to save their prayers. But something tells me that the gods *are* watching.

Perhaps even a little too closely.

Directing my attention back to Viridian, I outstretch my palms, my hands feeling empty. I close my fingers, as if around a phantom weapon. Looking around, I dart to the nearest suit of armor and wrench its sword from its hand. The blade is dull, since I know it's purely meant for decoration, but it'll do some serious damage if I need it to.

"Good idea," Viridian quips, doing the same. He tosses the sword between his hands, probably to get a feel for its weight.

Now that we're both armed, we continue our sweep of the halls, helping servants escape wherever we can. I don't let my eyes linger long enough to take in the severity of High Keep's ruin.

"Viridian! Cryssa!"

We both turn toward the voice.

"Thank the gods." Lymscia slows from a jog when she approaches us. "Are you two all right?"

Panting, I nod. Viridian does the same.

"Good," Lymseia breathes. "Myrdin and I were

worried when we couldn't find you."

"Where is Myrdin?" Viridian asks, concern lacing his voice. "Is he hurt?"

"He's fine," Lymseia assures him. "He's guiding the council members outside, to the grounds. He told me to meet him in the forest. They're taking cover there."

"Good," Viridian muses approvingly. "That's wise. Noble fae may be powerful, but the humans greatly outnumber us."

Lymseia glances between us. "I came to get you both and escort you there. The others are waiting."

"No," I tell her, my tone firm. "Get everyone out first, and then come back for us."

"But Your Majesties—"

"You heard your High Queen," Viridian says. Unseen, raw power rolls off him in waves. "Do as she commands."

Lymseia presses her mouth into a fine line. I can tell she's not happy about it, but she doesn't fight back. Instead, she only nods. "Very well."

A crash echoes off the walls ahead of us. Lymseia quickly bows. Then she takes off down the corridor, toward the sound, where a group of servants stand huddled together. They shiver with panic, the movement nearly as violent as the rioters storming the castle. They ease when Lymseia approaches, moving where she directs.

Once he's sure they're cared for, Viridian looks to me. "Where to next, my queen?"

"Upstairs." I motion my head in the direction of the main staircase.

He nods, and we move ahead as a unit. Slowly, we ascend the staircase, rising to the second floor. When we do, both Viridian and I turn our heads from Vorr's body, where it still hangs for all to see.

A group of rioters obstruct our path, their faces twisted with the kind of hatred that only grows from despair. They don't bat an eye at Vorr's corpse. Perhaps they don't know that he's the very king they've come to slay.

Only, someone else did the deed before they could.

One of the rioters makes a move for me, but Viridian blocks the blow with his sword. He barely has enough time to react before another strikes. He dodges the first attack but isn't quick enough to avoid the next one. I thrust out my sword, and the rioter's axe clangs when metal meets metal. With all my strength, I push Viridian's attacker back, managing to create some distance between us.

Viridian takes a breath, unscathed.

But it's only for a moment.

Taking the offensive, Viridian slashes with his sword.

Though its edges are blunt, it's still enough to knock a few of the rioters back, howling in pain. Judging by the way they're hugging their upper bodies, I can tell Viridian broke a few ribs.

Raising my own blade, I watch my enemy with a keen eye. It's strange to think of my kind—of humans—as the enemy, but right now, they're the only thing threatening to take everything from me.

I won't let them hurt my mate.

I can't.

So, I step forward, driving my sword forward in the process. I do so with enough force that my sword, though dulled, pierces my adversary's chest. He staggers back weakly, but then forward again, unrelenting.

It's then that I notice how gaunt the man's cheeks are.

Oh gods.

This man has the mining sickness.

Fear constricts my chest and tightens around my throat. This man will fight like hell, doing as much damage as possible before he falls. He has nothing to lose.

Because he's already dead.

I don't have time to wonder how many more of the rioters are sick. My logic tells me that most of them, if not all, are. After all, why else would they take such a risk? Why else would they risk death while raiding the castle, or execution for treason after the fact, if they do survive?

Though, that was Vorr's rule. Not ours.

I don't know what we'll do to the rioters that survive this.

But right now, I can't afford to be distracted.

Beside me, Viridian clashes with two rioters, one on either side. Sweat gleams across his forehead, his loose black hair sticking to his skin. He counters and parries each of their blows, but I can see him tensing his muscles.

He's restraining himself, I realize.

I reach out to him through the bond. I can't take the chance that he won't hear me amidst the chaos surrounding us.

Viridian, I tell him, as I stave off another strike that comes my way. *Don't hold back.*

Across the way, I see Viridian raise his brows. All the while, he doesn't miss a beat, launching a jab back at the rioters circling him.

You must know what that means, Little Fawn, he replies in my mind. Even mentally, his voice is tight. He doesn't want to do this anymore than I do.

I sigh. *I know. Strike to kill.*

Viridian's brows furrow, amber eyes raging like an endless storm. Electricity sparks to life around him, static blue energy circling his arms, from his fingertips all the way up to his shoulders. He thrusts out his palms, sending power buzzing through the floor.

The human rioters before us seize when it reaches them, their bodies going rigid with a jolt.

Then they all fall to the ground.

I raise the crown of my head, staring down at them. I should feel sorrow. Guilt, even.

But I don't.

Instead, I only feel relief. Now, they can't hurt us.

And maybe, since they'd succumbed to the mining sickness, we've spared them from a gruesome death. Though, I'm not sure if I believe that.

"Come," Viridian motions for me to follow.

I do. Quickening our pace, we finish our sweep of the second floor. Doubting there's anyone in the East Tower, all that's left to search is the west wing of the castle. A weight lifts from my shoulders when we find it empty.

"It's clear," Viridian says, exhaling. He starts, as if to move ahead. "Let's go meet the others."

"Wait," I say. Dread lines my stomach, squeezing a tight fist around it. Something in my gut tells me I can't leave the castle. Not yet. "The throne room."

"What about it?" Viridian asks, jaw tight with concern.

"I'm not sure," I murmur, looking up at him. "But I know something's wrong."

His expression turns grim, the corners of his mouth pinched. "Little Fawn..." He sounds as if he's begging me to reconsider. To walk away now, while I still can.

I know where his mind is going.

Mine goes there, too.

And it is for that very reason I must go to the throne room.

He lets out a breath, hanging his head. "Very well."

I nod to him, and then we swiftly descend the main staircase. Taking a sharp turn toward the throne room, I press my palms to the double doors, forcing them open.

"Stay where you are," a voice warns, every syllable laced with a threat. "Or the girl gets it."

My eyes wide, I freeze, my hands still outstretched to hold the doors open around Viridian and me.

Viridian's hand grips my shoulder, as if to hold me back. But my mind doesn't register the movement.

All I can do is stare.

Horror fills me. My eyes find Tiffy. She clutches her attacker's arm with both hands, so tightly that her knuckles have turned white. She breathes deeply, and though her jaw is tense with fear, she maintains a level expression.

I lower my gaze and tilt my head down when I glare.

There's a dagger pressed to Tiffy's throat.

CHAPTER FORTY

"IF YOU HURT her," I snarl, baring my teeth, "you *will* be sorry."

The man restraining Tiffy, who I deem to be the ringleader, only laughs. "There's nothing more you can do to me."

I swallow my retort, instead, flicking my eyes to his companions. On each side of the throne room, are two more rioters: one archer and one swordsman. How they got a hold of these weapons, I don't know.

But I do know that those darkened blades aren't just any metal.

They're pure iron.

Turning my head slightly, I glance over at Viridian. The heavy look in his eyes tells me that he knows, too.

I take a deep breath to keep myself calm. Panic sends jitters skittering across my skin, and pumps adrenaline through my veins. Unlike steel, which is made from iron mixed with enough alloy to nullify its effects, pure iron is harmful to fae. One touch, even the gentlest of taps, is enough to leave blackened burn marks on fae skin.

Being demi-fae, I don't know how it will affect me.

But I have no intention of finding out.

Looking away from Viridian, I study the archers positioned on either side of us. They stand at attention, their arrows drawn. Based on the darker color of the arrowheads, I know they're iron-tipped, too. All it takes is one wrong move, and they'll set them loose.

I raise the crown of my head, straightening my posture. I may be afraid, but I don't want the humans to think I am. I want them to see a formidable opponent.

Someone that won't fall easily.

Mirroring me, Viridian does the same.

The ringleader smirks, motioning to Tiffy. "If you cooperate, then maybe I'll let her go without a scratch."

Tiffy closes her eyes, squeezing them.

I stay silent, my brows drawn together.

"We're looking for the High King," the ringleader says, moving his focus to Viridian. "And you're going to tell us where he is."

Viridian swallows, jaw ripe with tension. "The High King is dead."

"Dead?" one of the swordsmen barks. "What do you mean he's *dead*?"

"You told us he'd be here," an archer says to the ringleader, voice sharp.

"He is here," the ringleader booms, silencing the others. His face red, steely gaze still pointed to Viridian. "They're lying."

"We're not lying," I interject. I brush my hair behind my ears. Hopefully, the sight of my rounded ears will make them trust me. Make them think I'm one of them. "He was murdered. Someone else got to him first."

"No!" the ringleader shouts, applying more pressure to Tiffy's throat with his knife. She cranes her head back, wincing. "You're going to tell me the truth. Or your little friend gets it."

At his sides, Viridian balls his hands into fists. That quiet rage seeps from his expression, and the faint, blue flickering around his arms tells me he's a second away from unleashing his magic.

The ringleader draws his lips back and sucks in a

breath through his teeth. With one hand still pressing the dagger to Tiffy's throat, he yanks a fistful of her hair with the other, jerking her head back.

Tiffy lets out a scream.

"Tiffy!" I call, instinctively.

"I won't ask again." The ringleader's voice drops with lethal intent. "Where. Is. He."

My heart rises to my throat. My lungs constrict, every breath more ragged than the last. I wrack my mind for solutions, for anything that can get all of us out of here alive.

But I'm not fast enough.

"All right." Viridian holds up his hands in surrender, his eyes sad. As if he knows he's about to do something stupid, but he's still choosing to do it anyway. "I'm the High King. *I'm* the one you want."

"No!" I cry. Has he lost his mind?

The ringleader's eyes go dark. The kind of darkness that holds pain. The kind of darkness that thirsts for violence.

For blood.

The ringleader releases Tiffy and shoves her aside. The swordsmen raise their blades and rush forward.

"Tiffy!" I run to her, taking her in my arms. "Run! Find the others!"

Tiffy nods, fleeing from the throne room.

The ringleader draws another iron dagger, now gripping one in each hand. The swordsmen move behind Viridian and me, blocking our exit, while the archers and the ringleader close the circle in front.

We're surrounded. There's five of them.

Against the two of us.

They close in around us.

Turning around to face the swordsmen behind us, I raise my blunt sword.

"Now!"

Like water rushing when a dam breaks, Viridian's power pours out from him. Blue lightning snakes across the floor. The rioters jump back, but the swordsmen aren't quick enough. The lightning wraps around their legs when it reaches them, spiraling up to their chests. They shake violently, Viridian's magic thrumming through them.

They fall in a heap. Glassy eyes stare up into the abyss.

The ringleader howls, fuming.

"I don't want to hurt you." Viridian holds out his hands defensively. "But I'll do what I must."

The whole time, he looks at me, eyes urging me to *run*.

No, I tell him through the bond. *You're mad if you think I'll leave you.*

He smiles weakly, voice soft in my mind.

It was worth a try.

The ringleader only spits at Viridian's feet. "There's only one way out. For either of us."

Viridian's dark brows stitch together. Any trace of softness is gone, replaced by pure rage. He pushes me back, and then sends more electric currents tearing across the floor.

I surge forward, slashing at the closest archer. I stun him and land a strong kick to his chest that knocks him onto his ass. If we weren't fighting for our lives, I'd be proud of that move.

"Enough!" The ringleader yells, voice hoarse. *"Get him!"*

What happens next is all a blur. The God of Death's words sound in my mind.

"Choose life, without love, in a cursed land. Or choose death in the name of love, and sacred sacrifice."

It's time.

This is how far I'll go.

This is how much I'll give for love.

This is how much I'll sacrifice.

The remaining archer draws back his bow.

Before my mind can process what's happening, I throw myself in front of Viridian. Just in time, my body stands between him and those who would do him harm, outstretched like a shield.

Only shields are made of durable metal. And I'm made of blood, skin, and bone.

But that doesn't seem to matter.

Because the arrow pierces my chest.

A blast of energy bursts from my body. It's colorless, invisible to the naked eye. Whatever it is, it's strong enough to topple what little furniture remains and knock the human rioters onto their backs.

Suddenly, the world around me slows. It's as if everything is moving through water or bracing cold winds. Part of me doesn't even want to think any of it is real.

Burning, white-hot pain overtakes my senses. No fiber in my body is spared.

Gods, it burns. It *burns.* It feels like I've been set on fire, from the inside out.

I stagger back, looking down at my chest.

The arrow meant for Viridian...

Raising my hands to my chest, I fall to my knees. Hard.

I can't breathe. My breaths have turned shallow. I'm gasping for air.

I see Viridian screaming. But I don't hear the sound. Agony etches into his face, leaving no corner unscathed. Then his expression shifts, with lethal stillness. Death made flesh. His amber eyes look like liquid fire, a stark contrast to the blue lightning that fills the throne room. I see him stalk forward, while the rioters that are stupid enough to get back on their feet cower before him.

Dazed, I shake my head. My eyes close involuntarily. When I open them again, I see bodies on the floor. More jolts of electricity flash.

Then it all stops.

My eyes nearly roll back, but I force them open. Liquid fills my throat. I choke on it.

The ceiling seems to spin away from me. Then the back of my head slams on stone.

I don't feel it.

Viridian whirls around, face paler than ever. He runs to me, falling to his knees at my side.

"No, no, no," he murmurs, picking up my head and setting it on his lap.

I cough. Something wet spills onto my lips. Raising a trembling hand, I touch my fingers to it. Red stains them.

Viridian takes my hand, my blood smearing all over his skin.

My eyelids flutter.

"Don't you dare," he commands, gripping my face. "Look at me, Little Fawn."

I try.

"Look at me," he repeats, eyes frantically searching mine. His words become more panic-stricken each time he repeats the order. "*Cryssa*. Look at me."

I choke, wheezing. The burning in my chest finally starts to dull.

"Cryssa," he pleads. Tears race down his cheeks, his face twisted in anguish. "Cryssa, don't close those eyes. Those beautiful, beautiful eyes."

I'm crying now, too.

"It should have been me." His voice trembles. He shakes his head, as if he can't contain his raging emotions. "*Damn* it, Cryssa. You should have let them shoot me!"

"No," I say, mustering as much strength as I can. All the strength I have left. "I couldn't. I—I wouldn't."

"And I can't—" He stops, pressing his lips together. "I can't lose you. I can't."

I cough again, blood spurting in my throat.

"No." His voice grows even more desperate. "Please, Cryssa. Oh gods—*please*."

Numbness tugs at my eyes. Darkness clouds my vision.

"I...love..." I choke.

485

Viridian looks at me, amber eyes desperately hanging onto every word.

You, I want to say.

But my throat doesn't obey.

The last thing I see is Viridian's face above mine. His mouth moves, but I don't hear the words. I don't hear anything. I barely feel his hands on my face, holding me tight.

I succumb to the darkness.

CHAPTER FORTY-ONE

VIRIDIAN

I CAN'T FEEL HER.

I can't *feel her*.

I try to reach out again, but there's nothing there. No one to reach out to. There's no bond.

The doors to my mind have closed.

And she's not there.

My wife, my *mate*, isn't there.

"Damn you!" I cry, slamming my palm to the stone floor. Cryssa's body is limp in my lap, but I can't bring myself to let her go. "Damn your curse!"

Damn it all. Damn my father. Damn the gods who sat by and let this happen.

How could I have let this happen? I told her that I wouldn't let anything happen to her.

I failed.

I couldn't—I didn't—protect her.

I lean my head back, my face pointed to the ceiling. Heaviness sets into my chest. The weight of her absence in my mind is unbearable.

She can't be gone.

She can't be.

Touching my forehead to hers, I cradle her head and rock back and forth. Her hand falls from mine, but I snatch it up again. I clutch her hand tightly, weaving my fingers with hers in desperation. As if the moment I let her go, she'll vanish before my eyes.

She's not here.

She's not even in this realm. Not anymore.

My muscles tense. Grief meets rage, the two thrashing violently inside me. Electricity pulses in and around me, surrounding us in a blue shimmer. I want to throw something, anything. If I could kill Cryssa's murderers again, and again, and again, I would. But I can't. So, I open my mouth and scream. I scream the way she did when I locked her chamber door. I scream until my voice runs ragged. Until my throat feels raw.

It's not enough.

Killing the men responsible for her death isn't enough.

None of it will ever be enough to quell the wrath swirling inside me.

I shouldn't have let her come here, I think, sweeping my eyes over the throne room. The grim sight of the carnage I caused is the only thing that meets me, and I turn away. I close my eyes, pressing them shut.

I'd known right from the start how this would end. The moment she insisted we go to the throne room, I'd known right away where this would lead.

How could I have been so foolish?

She would have been so angry with me if I'd stopped her. If I didn't let her come here. If I'd picked her up, carried her over my shoulder, and left this place. She'd have been kicking and screaming, damning me to hell for getting in her way. Maybe she would have even come to hate me again.

But she would have been safe.

She would have been *alive*.

That would have been the only thing that mattered. That she walked away with air in her lungs.

Not iron in her chest.

My shoulders shake. That blast of energy when the arrow sank into her heart instead of mine...

Tears flow down my face, and I do nothing to stop them. I don't need to go beyond High Keep's walls to know she did it. To know she broke the curse poisoning the land.

She did it.

She saved us all.

But at what cost?

"Why?" I shout, though the walls can't hear me. "Why her?"

Why her, and not me?

It was *my* father's curse. It should have been *me* who paid the price. Not her.

None of this was hers to bear.

Gritting my teeth, I pull her to my chest and wrap my arms around her. Closing my eyes again, I touch my chin to the top of her head.

When I do, the air around me goes cold and utterly still.

I don't have it in me to be wary. If there are more humans here to kill me, then I won't stop them. I won't fight.

Taking a breath, I open my eyes.

Silence meets my ears. No sounds of movement in the

halls. Not even the familiar sensation of air moving through the room. It's as if time has frozen still.

A warm glow has me squinting my eyes. Then, a dark shadow.

When the glow subsides, there are two figures standing before me.

Closest to me, is a feminine figure with rich brown skin and coppery hair that hangs in ringlets framing her face. Her eyes seem bottomless—only pools of warmth and light.

Beside her, is a masculine one. Whereas the female's eyes are endless light, the male's are endless shadows. He wears a long, black cloak that seems as if it's made from darkness itself. It moves like sand, the ebony grains shifting over themselves. His hood hangs down, draping his shoulders, shrouding inky black hair and a pale, gray-toned complexion beneath it.

Instantly, I know who they are. Their names linger on my tongue.

"Theelia," I say to the female. Then, I shift my gaze to the male. "Nemos."

The Goddess of Fate. And the God of Death.

I should be angry. After all, it was Theelia who blessed us. Theelia who marked Cryssa for death.

But there is no fury in my heart.

"Because fate willed it," Theelia says. Her voice is smooth and airy. As if her words are spun from the very light shining inside her.

"What?" I cock my head, confused.

"You asked us why it had to be her." Theelia's calm demeanor does not shift. "And the answer is because fate willed it."

I furrow my brow. I want to curse, to demand why fate had to pick her, of all the people in the kingdom. Hell, of all the people in the realm. But I don't.

"Why appear before me?" I ask, dropping my gaze. My time alone with Cryssa is dwindling. My time to grieve. To stay here, with her, before I say my final farewell.

Theelia looks to Nemos, as if for permission. The god dips his head.

"There is a way to save her," Theelia begins slowly, eyes downcast. "Only you can return her to this world."

"But tread carefully," Nemos warns, a knowing edge to his voice. "Doing so will bind your lives. If one of you should fall, so will the other."

"Tell me how," I say, without hesitation. There is nothing I wouldn't do, nothing I wouldn't give, to see Cryssa's eyes open one more time. To hear my name on her lips. To feel her heart beating beneath my palm.

Theelia dips her head and looks to Nemos.

"There is still time to pull her back into this world, before her soul reaches my domain," Nemos tells me. "Using your mate bond, you can reach her."

"How?" I ask. Despair gives my tone a hard edge. "The bond is gone." The cold emptiness that's taken its place is a harsh reminder that the once unwavering connection between Cryssa and I is no longer there.

"No," Theelia cuts in, her expression open. "It is not gone. Not yet."

Furrowing my brow, I can only cock my head.

"You cannot feel the bond because your mate is no longer of this world," Nemos begins. Those dark eyes never once flicker or show any hint of emotion. Neither does his voice. "However, if you were to follow her into the next realm, you would be able to access it."

"I have to die?" My mind struggles to make sense of this. "How am I to save my mate if I, too, am dead?"

"You do not have to die," Nemos corrects me. "Merely, your soul must be separate from your body. That, I can assist you with."

I press my lips into a fine line.

When I don't speak, the God of Death continues.

"I can temporarily withdraw your soul from your body. But you will not have much time, for there is only so long your physical form will last without your soul."

If I don't return to my body before it's too late, I will die. And so will Cryssa, for a second time.

"Why tell me any of this?" I ask, suspicions rising. "What could the gods have to gain?"

Nemos turns to Theelia.

"There is much more for the two of you to do in this realm," Theelia tells me, a calculated look crossing her expression. "It is not her time. Nor is it yours."

I fall silent for a moment.

"All right," I tell them at last. "I'll do it."

Nemos doesn't hesitate. "You must make haste. Once your mate falls into my embrace, there is no returning."

"Then I won't waste another moment." A newfound purpose surges through me, adrenaline coursing through my veins.

I have to save her. I have to bring her back.

Back to this world.

Back to me.

Nemos only bows his head and closes his eyes. To his side, Theelia watches.

A tingling sensation spreads across my skin, not sparing a single part of my body. Dizziness clouds my vision and dulls my senses, but it's only for a moment.

Then, I'm floating.

Looking down, I see myself—now slumped on the

floor, beside Cryssa's body.

Nemos flicks his eyes up, directly at me. "Go now, little king."

I turn away, scanning my surroundings. I'm still in the throne room. Stone walls still surround me, my father's splintered bronze throne still displayed in the room's center. But now, I can see so much more, beyond the throne room.

The stone walls surrounding me are opaque, merely a near-invisible barrier between me and the never-ending darkness. And, just as Nemos promised, I feel the bond again. Relief surges through my chest.

I feel her.

She's here, somewhere. Though, the connection between our souls is faint.

Even now, my time to save her grows short. Our bond becomes even weaker the longer I wait. I raise my hands and kick my feet, attempting to move forward. To my surprise and relief, I do.

I surge forward, this time simply on command—no movements required.

As I do, I see small, glowing orbs sprinkling the darkness. I approach one, my eyes wide.

These are *souls*.

The souls of the dead, moving toward the great

unknown as if they're being drawn there by an unseen force.

Urgency powers my movements, and I become more frantic with each new soul I approach.

I pass many souls.

Yet, none of them are my mate.

None of them are Cryssa.

I feel as though I am losing her all over again, the pain and agony of her absence in my mind like a wound torn anew. This is my one opportunity to bring her back. My one opportunity to save her.

To return her to my arms.

"Cryssa!" I cry out. My throat tightens, making my voice hoarse. "Cryssa! If you can hear me, Little Fawn, say something!" I snap my head back and forth, searching for a sign. Anything that shows she heard me.

But I am only greeted by silence.

It's as if I am shouting in a sea of nothingness, my voice swallowed by the dark.

"Cryssa Thurdred Pelleveron Avanos," I yell, my voice breaking. *"Answer me!"*

"Viridian?"

I briefly close my eyes, tilting my head back. Comfort washes over me in waves, knowing she heard me. Knowing that she hasn't drifted beyond my reach. "Cryssa!"

"Viridian! I'm here!"

"I'm coming, Little Fawn," I promise her, moving toward her voice. I urge myself to go faster, and I do, flying through the nothingness like a falling star.

Then I see her.

And she's as beautiful as the moment I first saw her, that night in Slyfell.

Only now, she shines like the sun, emitting magnificent, golden rays.

Her eyes go wide when she sees me, mouth twisted with happy sobs. Then we're diving toward each other as fast as we can, our arms outstretched, two burning embers set to collide.

We crash into each other, swirling around each other like the eye of a storm. My arms wrap around her the moment she meets my chest, and she grips fistfuls of my shirt, as if she needs my closeness more than she needs anything in the entire universe.

Taking her face between both of my hands, I kiss her. Hard. She kisses me in return, her arms draped around my neck, pulling me closer.

"Viridian, how—"

"There's no time. I'll explain everything once we return."

She scrunches her brows together, as if she can't wrap

her mind around how any of this is possible.

I take her hand, focusing my mind. Grounding myself, I find what I'm searching for: the tether that ties my soul to my body.

Gripping Cryssa tight, tighter than I ever have before, I pull her to my chest and circle my arms around her waist. Then, I dive, praying that we still have time. That out there, my heart still beats.

That I'm not too late.

The throne room comes back into sight as we approach.

Nemos nods to me when we pass through the ceiling, as if to say, *"Well done."* Theelia bows her head, a warm smile taking shape on her face.

Still clinging to Cryssa, I don't stop until I crash into both of our bodies.

CHAPTER
FORTY-TWO

CRYSSA

M Y EYES FLASH open. I'm gasping for breath.
I lurch upright, practically swallowing large
gulps of air until my lungs no longer burn.

Beside me, Viridian does something similar. Wiping
his mouth, disbelief clearly written all over his face, he
places a hand on his chest and breathes in slowly.

I look down at myself, pressing my palm to my
sternum. There's still a tear in my clothes where the iron-
tipped arrow pierced me, but it's gone. And so is the hole
in my chest.

Viridian snaps his head to face me, arms reaching out to me. He's over me in an instant, clearly beside himself as his hands frantically search me for injuries.

"Are you hurt?" he asks, his forehead creasing with worry. He continues to scan my body, eyes wide.

"No," I murmur. My mouth opens in shock, the corners of my lips tugged into the hint of a smile. "I'm...perfectly fine."

All the tension vanishes from his expression. He lowers his shoulders, pulling me to him with one hand to the back of my head. I smile into his shoulder, embracing him. He places a kiss to the top of my head, his nose to my hair as he inhales deeply. As if he were trying to memorize my scent.

"Thank the gods," he murmurs, over and over again. "Thank the gods."

I swallow, replaying the last moments I remember in my mind. The humans, the arrow...

I shouldn't be breathing.

I should be dead.

I *was* dead.

"How...?" I look at Viridian, meeting his gaze.

"The gods," he starts. "Theelia and Nemos. With their help, I was able to pull you back to this world."

Viridian cups my cheek, touching his forehead to mine. "Back to me."

Tears well in my eyes. Pure elation spreads through my chest, making me feel lighter than air.

I pull his face down to mine and kiss him.

There is nothing gentle or sweet about it. No, it's a kiss that's been through loss and fear and anguish. It's a kiss of love, stronger than any force in this realm.

I feel Viridian's relief and joy through the bond. His emotions mix with mine, overwhelming my senses.

We've been given another chance.

"Viridian..." My voice slows. "There must have been a cost." There always is.

He levels his expression, though his mouth doesn't tighten. "Our lives are bound. If one of us dies, so will the other."

My chest constricts.

"What if... What if something happens to one of us?" Human lifespans are much shorter than that of the fae. I can only assume demi-fae fall somewhere in between. "What if it goes off my life expectancy and not yours?"

"Cryssa," he says, brushing both of his thumbs back and forth across my cheeks. "I don't care about any of that. All that matters to me is a life with you. Whether that's fifty years or hundreds. There is no future for me that you're not part of."

I find myself nodding, fighting the moisture that gathers in my eyes.

I fall into his embrace again and rest my head against his chest. Closing my eyes, I take several deep breaths that fill my lungs so much, I can't hold it for long.

I'm breathing.

I'm here.

I'm alive.

As I cling to my husband, my love, my mate, I offer my own silent prayer to the gods.

There is still much to do, but all of it can wait. We'll rebuild the kingdom later. We'll restore stability to the realm. We'll deal with Vorr's death.

Pulling away, I find Viridian's eyes and smile. His amber eyes are the lightest I've ever seen them. Light with joy. With love.

And right now, he's all that matters.

EPILOGUE

CRYSSA

OUR CORONATION is held less than a fortnight later.

In that time, efforts to repair High Keep have begun, though they're still underway. It seems the human rioters caused more damage than we thought. Vorr's body was brought down from the wall and tended to by the finest Copper Court healers in preparation for his burial, and all the blood stains have been removed from the stone. Though, I can never truly forget the sight. Every time he passes the entrance to the East Tower, Viridian flinches and turns his face away.

We've begun to search for Vorr's killer, though, there isn't much to guide our efforts. Whoever murdered the late High King knew how to cover up their tracks. Despite this, I continue to assure Viridian that we will have justice, in due time. Every time I do, he only offers me a small smile with a squeeze of my arm.

Meanwhile, Viridian and I decided to pardon the surviving rioters, though we made it clear that should they act against the crown ever again, we will not be merciful. So far, the kingdom is at peace—though it seems to stand on unstable ground.

Still, we could not wait to act. With the passing of power from Vorr to Viridian and me, while countless humans across all of the five Courts work to rebuild their lives, we knew the crown needed to be present in each of them. After deliberation with the council, Viridian and I decided to send one representative from the council to each of the five Courts' capitals. And where it was possible, we chose people we trust. Which we found to be few.

Myrdin, to Redbourne. And Lymseia, back home to Illnamoor.

Myrdin accepted his assignment without question.

Lymseia, on the other hand... Well, that took some convincing.

"You can't just send me away," she'd protested,

crossing her arms. "I'm the Captain of the High King's Guard."

"We've granted you a higher position, as a diplomat," Viridian had told her.

"Then who will take my place?" Lymseia had asked, pressing her palm to her brow, clearly distressed. "You can't pick just anyone."

"We need someone we can trust. We need you, Lymseia," Viridian had pleaded. "If you accept this assignment, then you will be solely responsible for choosing your successor. And we will appoint them without question. Deal?"

"Fine," Lymseia had grumbled. "But I'm not going anywhere until the position is filled."

"Very well." Viridian—and I—had sighed in relief.

The position had been filled by one of Lymseia's most trusted lieutenants: a demi-fae soldier from the Silver Court, named Sura Vilsdottyr. I didn't know much about the ranks of the High King's Guard, but even I was impressed by her skill and the articulate way in which she speaks.

When the curse broke, the rot disappeared from the East Tower. What once was an isolated cavern of sickness and decay, now looks like any other part of the castle. Despite that, it remains abandoned. Though, Vorr's expanse collection of black leather gloves still lay out on the table in his bed chamber. Viridian can't bring himself to dispose of them. And I don't blame him.

The ill miners all made miraculous recoveries. The people say that at some point, an invisible blast spread through the land, and they suddenly were healed. The harvests show signs of being bountiful again, and the flow of metals between the five Courts is abundant, once more.

All is as it should be.

Though, when I think of the curse, there are still so many unanswered questions.

What did Vorr take?

Who is the stranger, with power strong enough to strike fear at the very mention of her?

And more importantly, where is she now?

I hope to someday find answers to these questions. Though, I don't know if I ever will.

Tiffy knocks at my door and opens it, poking her head in.

"It's time!" she squeals, giddy with excitement.

She enters my—and now, Viridian's—bedchamber, and shoos him out. "I'm sorry Your Majesty, but we need ample room to get her ready."

Viridian only laughs, backing away with his hands held up in surrender. "Of course, I understand." He leans down to press a kiss to my cheek, that wicked smile tugging at his lips. "I will see you in the throne room, my queen."

I return his smile, happy nerves jumbling in my stomach. "You'd better be waiting for me."

"I'd hate to disappoint you." He winks at me, as Tiffy quite literally shoves him out the door.

I chuckle, amused by the scene playing out before me.

"Now," Tiffy says, turning her attention to me. "Let's get you ready."

I bathe, only emerging from the tub once Tiffy is satisfied, and my skin practically shines. Then, she helps me into a beautiful, bronze colored gown. The heavy fabric is woven with bronze metal, with beautiful rose detailing on the outer skirt. Tiffy styles my hair in elegant braids and twists around my head. All of it is up, off my back, and frames my face. She's arranged it in such a way that my crown, when placed on my head, will sit beautifully in a bed of my auburn locks.

"You're ready." Tiffy places her hands on my shoulders, finding my eyes in the mirror. "How do you feel?"

"Wonderful," I breathe. And I mean it.

I'm the happiest I've ever been.

She gives my shoulders a light squeeze. "You should!

You look beautiful, Your *Majesty*." She emphasizes my new title, and her excitement is contagious.

I stand and make my way down to the throne room, where Viridian waits outside, in the hall. Made from the same material, with the same design, his fitted jacket and pants match my dress. His loose black hair has been combed back off his face.

When he sees me, his expression lights up, and he immediately flashes me a smile.

I kiss him and pull out strands of his hair when I lean back. I twist that tendril of ebony hair over my finger, and then let it fall in front of his eyes.

"I like it better this way," I say, meeting his gaze.

Viridian's grin only spreads wider. "Then I'll keep it like this." He gestures to the double doors. "They're ready for us." He pauses, looking at me now. "Are you ready, my queen?"

I take a deep breath. "Yes. Yes, I am."

Viridian nods, holding out his arm for me.

I take it, and we step into the throne room. It's filled with people. All of the Heads of House and heir-apparents are in attendance—with the exception of the diplomats we sent to represent us—and we extended an invitation to any of Keuron's citizens who desired to attend.

Father and Acantha beam at me as we pass them,

moving down the aisle. Both are well cared for by the crown. Acantha spends her time with Slyfell's human communities, helping them to regain their livelihoods. No longer needing to work in the mines, Father now spends his days learning how to whittle. Loren isn't here, but then again, I didn't expect him to be.

I return their smiles, and then look ahead.

Viridian and I approach the bronze thrones, stepping up onto the platform.

A priestess of Ixtia, the Goddess of Wisdom and Leadership, stands before us. She bows her head when we approach, and then holds up her hands.

Very much like we did on our wedding day, Viridian and I exchange several vows and promises.

Viridian goes first. "I, Crown Prince, Viridian Avanos, vow to lead with wisdom, compassion, and integrity. To put the kingdom first, above all."

Then, the priestess looks at me expectantly. "Do you, Crown Princess, Cryssa Thurdred Pelleveron Avanos, vow to lead with wisdom, compassion, and integrity? To put the kingdom first, above all?"

"Yes," I say, with pride rolling off me. "I, Crown Princess, Cryssa Thurdred Pelleveron Avanos, vow to lead with wisdom, compassion, and integrity. To put the kingdom first, above all."

Only, unlike our wedding day, we don't make these vows to each other. No, we make these promises to our subjects. To the people that sit before us. And to those who aren't in attendance here today.

"Then with the blessing of Ixtia, and all of the gods," the priestess says, "it is my honor to bestow upon you, the titles of High King and High Queen of all Inatia."

Then, she places bronze crowns on both of our heads.

It is heavy on my head, but I welcome it and the responsibility it brings.

Taking Viridian's hand and raising it up above our heads, I find my father's face in the crowd, unable to contain my joy.

Turning to Viridian, I meet his gaze. Those amber eyes stare back at me, and I know they hold my future inside them.

"Long live the High King and Queen!" the priestess proclaims.

The crowd echoes her sentiment. "Long live the High King and Queen!"

And so, our reign begins.

LIFE AFTER our coronation is like life at High Keep was before, and yet, it is entirely different, all the same.

Viridian and I have many more responsibilities now. But we take each day, one step at a time, grateful for every moment we have. We still dine together in the evenings, and I spend many free moments in my studio, drawing. Now, we hang some of my drawings in frames around the castle. I wonder how long they'll stay there, even after Viridian and I are nothing more than dust.

Now, we sit together in the great hall. Viridian no longer sits across from me, a table away. He's taken up a new spot, directly to my right, while I sit at the head of the table.

"We have news from Myrdin," Viridian says, taking a bite of meat and potato. "He's arrived at Redbourne and has settled in."

"Good," I muse, relieved. "He'll do well. He's good with people." Out of all those we could have chosen to represent us, while the kingdom recovers from the damage caused by the curse, Myrdin was the first one I thought of.

"He will." Viridian nods. "Someday, he'll make a fine Head of House."

I voice my agreement in between bites.

"And what of Lymseia?" I ask, my brows stitched together.

"I don't know," Viridian admits. His expression morphs to match mine. "She hasn't sent word."

Worry lines my stomach. My movements slow.

"She'll be all right," Viridian says, more to himself than to me. "We'll hear from her any day now."

I nod. Though, I can't shake the feeling that something's wrong.

The sound of the door scraping stone tears me from my thoughts. A servant stands, waiting by the threshold.

"Come in," Viridian beckons.

The servant enters and approaches the table, hands clasped tightly. As if he's nervous, or unsure.

"What is it?" I put my fork and knife down and lean forward.

"There is news of Lady Wynterliff," the servant says.

We exchange glances. Then Viridian waves his hand, as if to prompt the servant to continue. "Please, tell us."

The servant swallows. "There was an ambush at the Steel Court's border."

My heart sinks.

"All who accompanied Lady Wynterliff are dead."

Viridian's face pales. "Is she hurt?"

"I do not know, Your Majesty."

"What?" Viridian asks, furrowing his brows. "How do we not know?"

Worry constricts in my chest.

I don't need the servant to convey the message to us. His expression alone is enough to know what's happened.

And when he does say it, it only confirms my fears.

"She's disappeared, Your Majesties. There's no sign of her."

Clenching my hands into fists, I look at Viridian and meet his eyes. His mouth curls with rage, jaw clenched.

He speaks our suspicions aloud. His words hang heavy between us.

"Lymseia's been taken."

TO BE CONTINUED

(The *Of Metals and Curses* Series will continue in book 2, *A Shattered Kingdom of Steel,* which will feature our favorite badass Captain of the High King's Guard as our FMC.)

AUTHOR'S NOTE

Thank you so much for reading *A Broken Throne of Bronze*! It means the world to me that out of the many books to choose from, you set aside the time to read mine. Thank you!

I had so much fun writing this book. I've always been a fantasy reader, fascinated by complex worlds and lore, but never felt confident enough to create one of my own. While this isn't my first published novel (I write fast-paced urban fantasy under my other pen name, Lauryn Evans) this *is* my first full-fledged fantasy romance.

While this is the end of Cryssa and Viridian's love story, there's still so much in store for the *Of Metals and Curses* series. (But don't worry, we'll see more of Cryssa and Viridian soon!) I plan for there to be five books in total, with an overarching plot that continues to develop with each installment. Each book in the series will focus on one the five Noble Houses and Courts. As you read at the end of the epilogue, the next book, *A Shattered Kingdom of Steel*, will focus on House Wynterliff and the Steel Court.

If you enjoyed reading this book, please consider leaving a review on Amazon, Barnes & Noble, or Goodreads. Reviews do so much to help small authors like me.

If you're dying for updates on book 2, including release dates, cover reveals, and more, I encourage you to sign up for my mailing list on my website, (https://rennaashleyauthor.wixsite.com/renna-ashley---fanta), or find me on social media (@rennaashleyauthor on Instagram, Facebook, and TikTok, and @rennaashauthor on Twitter). I'd love to connect with you!

Until next time,

Renna

GLOSSARY OF TERMS

PEOPLE

- Crown Prince Viridian Avanos: Son of High King Vorr and the late High Queen Azalinah (Tarrantree) Avanos, heir to the high throne and heir-apparent of the Bronze Court.

- High King Vorr Avanos: Current High King, first of his line, and head of the Bronze Court.

- High Queen Azalinah Avanos: Late High Queen, wife of High King Vorr, and Viridian's mother.

- Head of House, Lady Maelyrra Pelleveron: Current head and ruler of the Gold Court.

- Lady Helenia Pelleveron: Younger sister of Head of House Maelyrra Pelleveron.

- Lady Lymseia Wynterliff: Second-born daughter of Head of House Kylantha and Lord Onas Wynterliff.

- Head of House, Lady Kylantha Wynterliff: Current head and ruler of the Steel Court.

- Lord Onas Wynterliff: Husband of Head of House Lady Kylantha Wynterliff, Lymseia's father.

- Lord Myrdin Tarrantree: Son of Head House Lord Tanyl and Lady Phaendarra Tarrantree, heir-apparent of the Copper Court.

- Head of House, Lord Tanyl Tarrantree: Current head and ruler of the Copper Court. Brother of the late High Queen Azalinah.

- Lady Phaendarra Tarrantree: Wife of Head of House Lord Tanyl Tarrantree.

- Lord Asheros Larmanne: Son of Head House Lord Eldred and Lady Avourel Larmanne, heir-apparent of the Silver Court.

- Head of House Lord Eldred Larmanne: Current head and ruler of the Silver Court.

PLACES

- Inatia: The kingdom in which the five courts reside.

- Keuron: Capital City of Inatia, not affiliated with any of the five courts.

- Slyfell: Cryssa's home city, and seat of power in the Gold Court.

- Hylmfirth: A small, human village in the Gold Court that sits between Slyfell and Keuron.

- Illnamoor: Seat of power in the Steel Court, and Lymseia's home city.

- Redbourne: Seat of power in the Copper Court, and

Myrdin's home city.

- Greyhelm: Seat of power in the Silver Court, and Asheros's home city.

- Mhelmouth: Seat of power in the Bronze Court.

TERMS/PHRASES

- Head of House: Title that indicates that the individual is Head of their noble house and ruler of their court. Of course, all the courts bend the knee to the High King.

- Heir-apparent: The next in line to become Head of House.

- Theelia's blessing: A rare divine message from the Goddess of Fate that reveals the identity of one's mate or killer.

- *Gohlrunn*: A kind of weighted gold alloy used in the Gold Court to craft expensive items such as paperweights.

- "May the metals be pure": A wish of good luck or good fortune.

- The Fyrelith: A rite that typically occurs when a High King or Queen dies without an heir, in which Heads of House and heir-apparents compete in a fight to the death for control of the throne.

GODS/GODDESSES

- Theelia: the Goddess of Fate

- Nemos: the God of Death

- Imone: the Goddess of Mercy

- Allora: the Goddess of Peace and Beauty

- Yoldor: the God of Good Fortune

- Ixtia: the Goddess of Wisdom and Leadership

- Ohesis: the God of Marriage and Family

- Oara: the Goddess of Endless Waters

- Valhyr: the God of Honor and Glory

- Phyro: the God of Fire

- Therran: the God of Earth

- Cemius: God of Deception and Veiled Truths

- Ragmos: God of Mischief and Trickery

- Yva: Goddess of Desolate Winters

PRONUNCIATION GUIDE

PEOPLE:

- Cryssa: Chris-suh

- Viridian: Vu-rid-ee-un

- Grorth: Grr-or-th

- Acantha: Uh-can-tha

- Vorr: Vore

- Maelyrra: May-leer-ra

- Nisroth: Niz-roth

- Lymseia: Lim-say-uh

- Asheros: Uh-share-owz

- Myrdin: Mur-dinn

- Nefine: Neh-feen

- Azalinah: Ah-zuh-lee-nuh

- Tanyl: Tan-ell

- Phaendarra: Fae-en-dar-ruh

- Thurdred: Thurr-drid

- Avanos: Uh-vā-nose

- Pelleveron: Pell-uh-vare-on

- Tarrantree: Tare-on-tree

- Larmanne: Lār-mān

- Wynterliff: Win-ter-lif

- Hrudarrk: Huh-roo-dark

PLACES

- Inatia: I-nay-sha

- Keuron: Cure-on

- Slyfell: S-lie-fell

- Illnamoor: Ill-nah-more

- Redbourne: Red-born

- Greyhelm: Grey-helm

- Mhelmouth: Mell-mith

GODS AND GODDESSES

- Theelia: Thee-lee-uh

- Allora: Uh-lore-uh

- Ohesis: Oh-hee-siss

- Nemos: Nee-mose

- Valhyr: Val-here

- Phyro: Fye-roh

ACKNOWLEDGMENTS

It's such a surreal feeling to be sitting here, writing this. When I first got the idea for this book, I had no idea if I would finish my draft, or if anyone would even be interested in reading it. Through all of the excitement, anxiety, and every other feeling I felt while working on this project, the book is here, in your hands. And that's so freaking cool.

This book was a labor of love, and it only came to be with the help of many people.

First, to Maddy and Shannon: I cannot emphasize enough how much your edits, suggestions, and conversations about this book helped to shape it into what it is today. I know that I tend to underwrite, and the biggest part of my editing process is fleshing out what's already there and looking for opportunities to expand. Thank you for pointing me in the right direction, and for helping to bring out some of the best moments in this book.

To my mom: Thank you for reading my draft, and for being just as excited about this story as I was. Thank you for encouraging me to write it, even though I was intimidated to write a fantasy romance novel at first. Between helping me proofread (just *one* more time), and giving me honest feedback from a reader's perspective, you helped so much in getting this book ready to publish. Thank you so, so much for all the love and support!

To Ryan: Thank you for the awesome map of Inatia! You truly brought this world to live with your amazing, amazing talent, and I can't thank you enough. It was a pleasure working with you!

To Kellie Marie McCann (@milwaukeemomma on TikTok), Jennifer Sebring (@jennifersbook on TikTok), Nicole Edwards (@nicolethemom_ on TikTok) and everyone on the ARC team for this book: Thank you for taking a chance on this story and for setting aside the time to read and review. I appreciate everything you've done to help with this release!

To my TikTok community of book besties (you know who you are!): Thank you for the endless love, support, and excitement! Seeing your comments on each of my videos only made me more excited for ABTOB's release, and I hope that you love this book as much as I do.

To you, the reader: Thank you for following Cryssa and Viridian's journey, and for sticking with them as they grew to love each other, warts, and all. I hope you enjoyed it!

And, as always, I save the best for last: To Peter. While this book was the most fun to write, it was the hardest to edit. Thank you for talking me off so many ledges. For helping me see through the lies that my brain wanted me to believe. For leading me back to my roots, to the reasons I love this story so much, when I was so lost in imposter syndrome that I couldn't find my way back on my own. You are my rock, my love, my light. My mate. (Haha, I just *had* to slip that in there.) This book wouldn't be what it is without you. I'm so, so thankful that I get to do this by your side. I love you :)

ABOUT THE AUTHOR

Renna Ashley is a headstrong New Englander who'd rather be at home, wrapped in a fuzzy blanket, while reading a good book. She loves anything chocolate (especially chocolate chip cookies) and has a soft spot for swoon-worthy love interests and women with swords.

If you would jump into a fantasy world the first chance you got, then head over to Renna's website for updates on new releases, freebies, and more!

When she's not out swooning or swashbuckling, you can find her on:

Instagram: @rennaashleyauthor
Facebook: @rennaashleyauthor
Twitter: @rennaashauthor
TikTok: @rennashleyauthor

Made in United States
Troutdale, OR
12/11/2024

26183243R00306